Cities of Refuge

G. P. Wayne

For Jacqueline and Nigel,
whose support and encouragement I will never forget

Contents

Part 1: Burning Barrels

Part 2: A Soldier's Love

Part 3: A Promise Made To Abraham

1

**Burning
Barrels**

Chapter 1:   Trouble With Geometry

Look up a long slope, dark in the night-shadow of the hill it approaches; a black sheet laid across the stark horizon, above which are a mass of stars, and a Hollywood moon so big and brash it comes close to drowning its stellar companions. Along the cold razor of the skyline, shadow-puppet deer bounce carelessly across the moon, fleet silhouettes leaping and cavorting in a riot of backlit panic.

The deer are being chased by a naked man. Not just naked, but huge. Enormous. Improbably fat for a man running at speed – cartoon fat; unreal and unrealistic; grotesque, eerie, nightmare naked, ghostly white.

Now and then, the outline of a hand can be seen, but not the arm to which it is necessarily attached. No visible means of support; progress is akin to a phosphorescent bouncing ball, barely touching the ground, or a sagging, helium-filled balloon pulled along by an invisible string.

Here's the thing: despite all the bulk, all the wobbly rings of moonlit fat bouncing up and down in ghastly synchronisation, the running man is moving really fast. He is gaining on the deer. Movements, far from appearing encumbered, seem easy and fluid, almost graceful, as if the vast bulk is a prosthetic costume worn by a very fit man. As he runs, the excess flesh ripples in the wind like silicone that refuses to set.

Interrupting an arcane debate between two heavily armed philosophers, Harry lifted his head to peer beyond the brush they had chosen as a hide. At eye-level he could see nothing. To his left, cobwebs shimmered when the moonlight touched them, fine lines stretched improbably between frosted rock and tangled scrub – a scene of perversely forbidding beauty. To his right, stunted trees extended fragile silver branches, which twinkled in the swaying wind. Other shapes, lurking, were less fanciful: jet black, hard-sharp, mournful silhouettes in two menacing dimensions. To Harry they seemed lost, abandoned; sentinels forsaken at far-flung posts where they stubbornly remained, shorn of identity or purpose, but not loyalty or their sense of duty. Never duty.

Or is that me?

"Anything?" Alf whispered.

"No – thought I heard something," said Harry, "'though I couldn't be sure, what with the fucking lecture going on in my ear..." Alf had been regaling him with an obscure diatribe on the dangers of geometry. Harry – cold and bored – was not particularly receptive: "...a lecture in which you're saying – basically – that we've all been poisoned by triangles?"

"Sure, that's about the size of it," Alf agreed. "There's more, but you get the gist?"

"Actually, I had it the first time round, back when I still had the will to live; young minds unwittingly constrained by the geometry of the environment? Euclid: public enemy number one?"

"You're not taking this seriously, Harry." With an irritated rustle of undergrowth as he re-settled himself, Alf fell silent. Harry could see nothing of his tiresome companion except a momentary glint of moonlight along the barrel of Alf's rifle.

"I thought they'd have shown up by now" said Alf. "What time is it?"

"About 3.30 I guess, something like that. What's the matter – you cold?"

"I'm fine. My arse hurts."

"Well, give your buttocks a break – try talking less."

"I'm just saying, Harry...our ancestors lived in a world without a single straight line in it. Every feature of their landscape, shaped by nature alone, an *irregular* world as only nature can make it. Look around you now. Compare all this, the natural flow of nature and its shapes; compare this to our urban world – hard, formal, relentless. Concrete and steel and glass in flat planes defining all the unnatural, regular spaces of our world. And if we grow up in boxes, it shouldn't be a surprise to find that most people's ideas are shaped the same way. 'Square', as they used to say. Do you seriously think we could *not* be affected psychologically by this relentless, fascist geometry?"

"Aha! The F word. I don't think I've ever heard you rehearse an argument in which Fascism didn't put in an appearance."

"It's a good word."

"It's a massively overused cliché, actually."

"Can you think of a better description?"

"Don't need to – it's your argument."

"OK...conformity then. It's the architecture of conformity – what about that?"

But Harry could indulge Alf no more. He changed the subject. "You've seen them, right? Really seen them?" Alf sighed. "Many times; many, *many* times. Why don't you believe me? I told you – five of them – a stag and four does. You saw the tracks didn't you? They come through here every night on the way to the lake."

"So, where the fuck are they, then?" Harry demanded. There was no reply. He settled back, shouldering the butt of his rifle to peer along the barrel and check his arc of fire once more, habitually pushing the safety off, then back on. Reassured by the soft click, he closed his eyes and merged with the night; wind-driven leaves rustling under the creaking branches from which they were still falling; barking foxes, some distant but one quite close; hooting owls and other occasional bird calls, the scurry and rustle of their prey in the leaf litter; the persistent drip and trickle of water everywhere; the heavy grunt now and then of badgers rooting in the soft earth; the warm smell of moss, wild garlic, the thick tang of mud and mulch.

A movement caught Harry's eye. At the same moment, Alf jumped to his feet. "What the bloody hell is that?" he shouted excitedly, pointing up the hill.

Harry followed the outstretched arm and saw shadow-puppet deer crossing the skyline. Deer? Why break cover? Why hadn't Alf opened fire – an easy shot, so clear against the moon. But something was wrong with the picture. The last deer wasn't...well, it wasn't a deer – of that, and only that, Harry was certain. Then his mind staged a short rebellion: in a frozen moment that may have lasted nanoseconds or an eternity, his senses seemed to reset one by one like a computer restarting its various sub-systems after a power cut. Cold boot: everything silent...the night sounds returning one by one...mouth dry...now flooded with bitter-tasting saliva...the penetrating musty smell of wet undergrowth...the cold gun barrel in his hand. Finally, his eyes re-focussed on the procession along the skyline.

Harry forced himself to look at Alf, who was still staring open-mouthed at the procession atop the hill. "What is this, Alf – a runaway Sumo wrestler? Another weird local custom, like rolling burning barrels? Or what?"

Alf snapped his mouth shut but followed the spectacle intently. "Jeez...look at him go...holy shit – he's catching the deer...he's running like a Trojan out there. Absolutely fearless..."

"How the hell can he see where he's going?" Harry was standing now.

"I have no idea. I'm amazed he got that far. Oops...oh...too bad." Even as Alf spoke, the figure lurched violently, pitched to one side and disappeared from view. They heard something large crashing through successive layers of undergrowth and a single, choked-off scream; not of pain, but all-consuming rage. Then silence.

He's catching the deer.

The pair scrambled up to the top of the hill and peered down into a semi-circular escarpment lined with trees growing at odd angles towards the centre like teeth, but they could see nothing within the dark hollow.

Listening intently, Harry was surprised to hear sirens and turned back towards the town. "Something's going on down there," he muttered. From his vantage point, he could see emergency vehicles racing through the still-dark streets, lit here and there by flashes of blue or the arc of headlights. "Lots of activity. Very unusual. And I can't figure out where they all came from."

"How do you mean?" asked Alf, coming to stand at Harry's side.

"There aren't that many emergency vehicles in Okehampton. It's a small town. Where did they all come from?"

"And where are they going?" said Alf.

"Away from us, I think." As Harry looked east, he saw a flickering light in the sky. Moments later, he heard the faint but steady drone of a helicopter.

"See it?" Alf asked.

Harry nodded. "Looking for something?" Both men turned simultaneously to peer behind them into the darkness beyond the escarpment. Then they looked at each other.

"Coincidence?"

"Bollocks," said Harry, recognising the inevitable when it fell into his lap.

"Yeah," Alf agreed, wishing he had a stout length of rope instead of his gun, which was now little more than an encumbrance. "We should go get some help."

"No time for that," said Harry irritably. "Let's get on with it."

Okehampton's local garage was as dark as the hills above it. Subject to power cuts, a black market born out of fuel rationing, supply shortages and a profound lack of paying customers who could circumvent the stringent movement restrictions, it now opened for only a few hours a day, and not at all after dark. In the warmth of their patrol car, parked on the forecourt, Mick Collins and his partner Ravinder Mann sipped stewed tea from an ancient thermos flask.

They sat in comfortable silence as they drank. The main road to Exeter was clear; licensed commercial night traffic was a rarity. Trucks and buses crammed with refugees were still being stopped at the end of the M5 motorway, turned back at gunpoint with instructions to head for Bristol and then westward over the Severn River towards the notorious Welsh camps they so desperately wished to avoid. No-one had any sympathy left for the refugees: in two decades, the constant westward flow of the needy and the dispossessed had exhausted all charity.

For the two policemen the night was coming to an uneventful end, or so it appeared, when a procession of emergency vehicles sped past, driving fast along the road that followed the edge of the moor, lights flashing, sirens muted. Mick, the plastic cup now cradled dangerously in his lap, started the engine and put the car in gear. Rav picked up the handset and called in, but there was no answer.

"What the hell is going on?" Mick demanded as they bounced over a speed bump on their way out. "*Oh shit...*"

"I don't know – the radio's dead. Hey, did you turn it down?" Rav leaned forward and restored the volume to a normal setting, at which the radio burst into life with repeated calls for them to respond. As Rav made the usual excuses, Mick – trousers now wet in a predictably incontinent location – turned left out of the forecourt and accelerated hard after the flashing blue lights in the distance, concentrating on driving rather than the wild and largely incomprehensible chatter gushing from the radio. "Are you getting any of this? What is it – what's going on?"

"Fire up at Parkfield – the old hotel. And something about the army..."

"The army?"

"Didn't you notice – they weren't civilian fire engines? They're military, and so were both the ambulances."

Of course. All the vehicles were green. That was what was odd about them. Mick was doing ninety now, screaming along a road more suited for half that speed. As he rounded a blind bend he had to brake hard because the last ambulance in the convoy was astride the road, attempting to turn right into a narrow lane. The patrol car, tyres smoking and brakes shuddering, came to a halt only yards from the vehicle in front, beyond which a procession of rear lights danced up the hill towards the moor before disappearing into the darkness, one by one. The last ambulance finally made the sharp turn and drove up the narrow lane, the patrol car following. Strangely, the radio had gone from a frenzy of chatter to silence, neither officer noticing quite when this transition had occurred. Rav called in repeatedly but now there was no reply at any volume.

At the top of the hill, the road levelled out. Mick slowed, opening his window to jettison the tea he wasn't already wearing. The road ahead, more or less level, wound across the moor in a gentle curve leading away to their right, the surrounding ground flat and stony. All along the road were parked various military vehicles; jeeps, ambulances, fire appliances, an excavator being unloaded from its flatbed transport, several cars with military pennants and markings, three huge dump trucks, and an armoured personnel carrier parked at an angle blocking off half the road leading to the remains of the Parkfield Hotel. Most of the interior of the hotel had collapsed, reduced to a pile of rubble contained by the three remaining exterior walls of the ground floor. Inside the rubble and under it a fierce fire was still burning, glowing white-hot through the debris. Men were running this way and that, following the faint shouted orders drifting towards the two officers in the car.

Handing the plastic cup to his partner, Mick locked the doors and drove up to the APC where several tough-looking professional soldiers manned an impromptu checkpoint. One of them stepped forward to stand directly in front of the car, not bothering to raise a halting hand since the squat machine gun he held in a business-like way conveyed the message clearly enough. A spotlight on top of the APC swung round, the powerful beam shining directly through the windscreen. A second soldier tapped on the driver's window with the barrel of his gun while a third, unseen until now, appeared beside the passenger door and leaned against it. Mick lowered the window, his determination not to be intimidated somewhat undermined when he found himself looking down the business end of the machine gun.

The soldier knew full well where his gun was pointing, a threat reinforced with a tight smile as he lowered his head to the window, allowing the gun to drop out of sight.

"Good evening officers. Can I help you?" he asked, in a tone that brooked no request for help at all.

"What's going on?" asked Mick. "We got a call…"

"Sure. It's a fire – all under control now, thanks. *We* have it under control."

"Good," said Mick evenly. His knuckles were white on the steering wheel. "We'll just have a look then and report in."

The soldier was unmoved. "Can I see your warrant card, officer?"

"What?"

"Your warrant card please." The soldier held out his free hand. "I need to confirm your identity."

With a sigh, Mick unbuttoned his breast pocket and removed his warrant card, handing it to the soldier, who paid it scant attention.

"So…*Mike*," said the soldier with a knowing leer, "here's what I need you to do. I need you to get on the radio for me so they can tell you what I'm telling you now, which is that

9

everything is under control and you should return to base. Can you do that for me *Mike?*"

With some effort, Mick released the wheel, flexing his fingers. "I don't get it mate. I really don't get it. I'm just out here doing my job. It's my job to come up here. All I did was ask you what was going on – not unreasonable considering all these military vehicles, is it? – and all you're doing is trying to wind me up. What happened to professional respect? And my name's Mick, not Mike. See this car, see anything particular about it? It's a police car; I'm a police officer and I'd like my fucking warrant card back." He reached out and grabbed the warrant card from the soldier's unresisting hand and put it back in his breast pocket, from which he also retrieved his notebook. "My turn: I want your name, rank and number, your regiment and the name of your commanding officer."

Rav was momentarily stunned by the sudden change in mood of his partner. Every time Mick lost his temper, Rav found himself holding his breath, waiting for the punch that never came, the shot that was never fired – not so far. He knew that look: profound disappointment and weary resignation beneath a white-hot righteous anger. Despite his bluff manner, Mick was a good man, something of an idealist whose ideals always seemed to fail him. Then Rav remembered the radio.

"You won't need that information," the soldier replied, then exchanged a glace with the guard blocking the car's path, who responded by shifting his weight, and the gun, in a meaningful way. "This area is under military control, officer. Check with your station ops – they will confirm what I'm telling you. I'm under orders not to allow anyone to pass. You are now blocking the road for any emergency vehicles that need access. You cannot proceed beyond this point so right now, you need to turn around and drive back to the main road. *Right now, Sir."*

Rav had got through on the radio. "Mick, they're ordering us back to the station" he urged, tugging on Mick's sleeve to distract him. He decided it was a rather girly way of getting attention and stopped tugging. *"They're calling us back Mick, we have to leave now."*

But Mick continued to glare at the soldier, pen poised over the notebook. "I want this bloke's name, rank and serial number."

"Mick, these guys aren't kidding – look at them. *Look at them, for God's sake!*"

The three soldiers, weapons at the ready, stepped back far enough to bracket the whole car, but not each other. One of them cocked his gun, a sound sufficiently compelling to bring Mick to his senses. He put the car into reverse and backed slowly away. There were no gateways or tracks bordering the roads up here; the last thing he wanted to do now was get the car stuck in front of the watching soldiers. He had no option but to try a variation of the three-point turn; the road was narrow so it took him several shunts to get the car facing the opposite direction. At the apex of each shunt the headlights shone out over the moor; at one point Mick could have sworn he saw a very big man running fast across the broken ground, but he was distracted when a nondescript Ford estate drove up, honked its horn and stopped, waiting ten yards away while the police car thrashed around in the middle of the road like a beached whale in stripy fluorescent pyjamas.

At the ninth shuffle, there was turning room enough to drive safely away. As they accelerated, Mick Collins glanced at the Ford estate. At that very moment the driver bent down to retrieve something from the passenger foot-well, reappearing only when the patrol car had passed. The soldiers never moved from their fire-ready positions. When the spotlight gave up chasing the retreating car and fell away, Rav looked back to see the soldiers stand aside and waive through the nondescript estate car with barely a pause.

Chapter 2:   Caravan Capers

Billy Bliss, the current bass player in The Vikings, was leaning against the side of the tour bus; eyes closed, a watery sun warmed his face a little, but he was too cold to loiter in the damp of the chill November morning. With a baleful glance at the dirty blue caravan across from the campfire, he opened the bus door and climbed back in.

The frenetic exchanges were no less heated than when he left. The warmth was pleasant enough, the atmosphere homely, thick with tobacco smoke, the smell of bacon recently fried, last night's beer and dubious curry, all overlaid with the ambivalent semi-sweet bedroom fug generated by so many people living in a confined space. Jake, the Vikings' founder member and bandleader, and never an early riser, had yet to put in an appearance. Everyone else was crowded around the small table on the part of the lower deck that served as a communal area.

Billy retrieved his bag of grass and some papers and sat further down the bus to roll a joint. He couldn't help but overhear the argument, but he had no desire to participate since they were all arguing – still – about the wrong thing. The real issue wasn't about whether to involve the police – a daft idea since there was no way they could afford involvement with any kind of authority – but what on earth they should do next. The whole idea of bringing the police in was simply a way to divest themselves of the problem by dumping it on someone else. Gutless, really – not that Billy had any notion of an alternative. Joint assembled, he stepped outside again to smoke it and stare at the caravan. It would never tow with all that weight on board, he decided, noting how the flimsy carcass was sitting so low on its suspension it looked like the coachwork was bolted directly to the axles. That would be an instant pull if they were spotted on the road, in which case they'd end up involved with the police anyway. Was it worth the risk? What was the risk? Risk of what?

A few moments later, the door opened behind him. "Gimme a bit of that, you fucking hog," said a gruff voice right in Billy's ear, as Jake confiscated the joint with ninja-like dexterity. "I need a piss."

Joint clamped under his luxurious Mexican-bandit moustache, Jake walked to the end of the bus and, after a prolonged tussle with a zip, relieved himself on the grass. Tall and gangly, his skin, at best pale and unhealthy, Jake looked almost translucent in the wintery morning light, as if he was fading into the landscape. He wore only an unbuttoned cotton shirt of some indeterminate but still-pale colour, and black leather trousers whose shiny patches, frayed stitching and baggy seat, a half-inflated balloon, insisted they, and perhaps the wearer, were long past their retirement date. No-one had ever seen Jake without them and legend had it he never took them off. (Jake, committed to the maintenance of his personal myth, said that evacuation and procreation were the only times a man had an excuse for being caught with his pants down).

"Phew…that's better…I needed that," he muttered as he walked back, trying to coax the zip up without injuring himself. He too examined the caravan intently. "Well Billy Bliss, seems like I missed all the fun last night. What's got everyone so fired up they can't let an old man enjoy a lie-in, huh?"

Billy wasn't fooled by this, but played along. While gathering information, Jake often liked to pretend he didn't know what was going on.

"They found him up on the moor…" said Billy, his eyes shifting meaningfully to the caravan, and back to Jake.

"Who did?"

"Harry. Harry and Alf Jarrott. They reckon they were hunting – deer or something – and then this bloke came running out of nowhere, fell down a hole and knocked himself out."

"He must have come from somewhere," said Jake, glancing again at the caravan.

"You gonna keep that? Can I have the butt as a souvenir?"

Jake handed back the filter, all that remained of the joint. There were plenty more questions on Jake's mind, but none that he thought Billy could answer. "So what do we do with him, Billy? What's the next move?"

"I dunno. We've got a gig to get to. I really don't know."

"Yeah," said Jake, opening the bus door. "Me neither."

Inside the bus, Jake glared briefly at Alf Jarrott, who had been rash enough to sit in Jake's seat. With no way to avoid the withering stare, Alf quickly decided to relocate himself, provoking an unseemly scramble as people got out of the way. Ignoring the un-musical chairs, Jake dumped himself down and accepted a proffered mug of tea with barely a glance at the donor. Everyone seemed nervous – everyone except Harry who, sitting opposite Jake across the table, seemed calm and sufficiently self-possessed to return Jake's look without flinching, the only one to do so. *He's got a tight rein on his horses, does our Harry*, Jake reminded himself. He liked their charismatic and resourceful tour manager but didn't entirely trust him, for reasons he could never quite unravel. Cas, the band's morose guitarist, had put it best: "I don't know what he's doing with us," he observed. "He's just not untogether enough." Jake knew exactly what he meant; whatever Harry was, he wasn't rock and roll.

"So Harry, I hear you made some new friends last night."

"Well one, anyway…" Harry replied. Alf sniffed.

"Who is he?"

"No idea."

"Oh really?"

Alf chipped in. "He was unconscious when we found him, hasn't come round yet."

Jake continued to direct his questions at Harry, not looking at Alf at all. "Why did you bring him here?" Harry didn't answer, but looked away.

"Don't you want to know how we found him?" pleaded Alf, who was in the process of discovering he was no longer a welcome guest. Maybe an opportunity to tell the tale once more would return him to the grace from which he had unwittingly fallen when the band, feeling threatened, had quickly closed ranks.

Jake turned to him with an indifferent expression. "Not really. How you found him isn't the problem. How to get rid of him is the problem Alf, wouldn't you say? What the fuck we do next is the problem." He took a swig of tea. "I mean…dear oh dear…I go to bed and all's right with the world. I sleep for a few hours, the sleep of the fucking innocent…" (someone chuckled) "…then I wake up and hey, guess what? I get out of bed and find I'm standing in a pile of shit. A huge pile of shit dumped right where my slippers are supposed to be. Where are my fucking slippers anyway?" Jake had never owned a pair of slippers in his life.

Alf scanned the faces peering at him in the confined space, seeking support, but their expressions were closed, hard – this new and rather serious turn of events represented a threat to a way of life they loved and treasured, and no-one was taking kindly the notion that their lifestyle might have been jeopardised by Alf and Harry's little adventure last night. If Alf got the impression they thought it was his fault, he wasn't far wrong, and this seemed wholly unfair to him. It wasn't his idea to bring the body back to the camp and he felt a need to make this clear, now wanting far less credit for his part in the affair than he had previously laid claim to.

"I wanted to leave him where he was, but Harry..." Alf glanced accusingly at the tour manager, "...Harry said we should help him, didn't you? Tell them, Harry...," his voice was rising, the pleading pathetic, "...tell them I didn't have anything to do with it. Really, I swear it wasn't my idea, not my idea at all."

"OK already," said Jake, "just calm down. Everybody stay calm, we'll figure this out. He's still unconscious, you say?" Harry nodded, Alf sensibly choosing to remain silent. "Do you know how badly he's injured, how far he fell? If he has internal injuries he could be dying right there in the caravan. Maybe he's brown bread already. Did you think of that, Harry? Think what we'd do with a corpse on our hands, at all? Your DNA – and Alf's here – you two will have left a trail that anyone could follow, so you're both in it up to your necks. And *now*..." pausing for dramatic effect, "...so are we. All of us."

"I know," Harry replied. His face lacked any expression.

Cas, quiet up to now, leaned forward, the shock draining the colour from his cheeks. "A corpse? Fucking hell, what do you mean...*a corpse*? Is he dead then? Do we know if he's still alive? Shouldn't we call a doctor or...or...something?" Even as he faltered, Cas knew this was not really a viable option.

Alf brightened, spotting an opportunity to recover a little credibility. "Hey, I know..." All heads turned towards him. "What about Guido? We could give him a call..."

Alina, their wiry Polish keyboard player, leaned forward, brushing her unruly blonde hair out of her face. "Guido's OK, we call him, yes? He did good for me, real good." One terrible night eighteen months back, camped at the same farm, a pregnant and fearful Alina had tried out of desperation to terminate the foetus single-handedly using an insane combination of eastern-European folk-lore remedies and a deadly back-street technique involving a knitting needle and some ether. Inexplicably terrified of pregnancy, she hadn't considered the wisdom of being attended by a local crone off her head mainly (but not entirely) from inhaling the ether leaking from the old mask she held over the girl's face. Only the hurried intervention of the big pastry-chef from the little Italian-Indian-Chinese fish and chip shop in Okehampton saved her.

"Guido...yes...good idea, girl," said Jake. Turning to Alf, he asked: "He's still around then?"

"Shit yes. He's still there...I can call him if you like." Alf took out a mobile phone and started to open it, but Cas reached forward and snatched it from him.

"Never use mobile phones, you fucking idiot," said Jake, rolling his eyes to emphasise his considerable exasperation. "What on earth is the matter with you, man? Don't you know anything? Harry, go with Alf in his jeep. Bring Guido back here, but don't tell him why. If he asks...tell him Alina needs him."

Harry nodded and stood up. Billy volunteered to go with them; he wanted to keep an eye on Jarrott, now trying to retrieve his phone from Cas, who held it out of reach. "Never use these things," Cas advised, throwing the phone across the table to Phil the drummer, who dropped it deliberately into Jake's mug, splashing cold tea over the table. Jarrott fished the phone out of the mug with two grubby fingers and tried to wipe the liquid off on his jeans.

"Thanks a lot Phil," said Alf, obviously annoyed.

"Why, you're *very* welcome," said Phil, who clearly didn't give a shit, and wanted Alf to know it.

Guido heaved himself out of the jeep and strode purposefully towards the bus, followed by Harry and Billy. A giant of a man with an equally outlandish passion for food and everything to do with it – choosing ingredients, cleaning, preparation, storage, cooking, decorating and eating – he only just managed to get through the door.

Guido was a florid Sicilian who passed himself off as Italian because he couldn't bear all the Mafiosi nonsense that would inevitably accompany any discussion of his native land or its inhabitants. In fact, he was raised largely in Naples, a podgy street kid with little talent for crime and no stomach for violence. Despite his mother's saintly forbearance and the frequently vicious but well-meaning application by his stern, black-shrouded banshee grandmother, of a leather strap to the back of his soft wobbly thighs, inevitably Guido got into trouble anyway, hanging out with the wrong crowd (the only crowd that would have him, and that merely for the sport). The only escape – from the tiny flat, the desiccated dragon in her perpetual widow weeds, the poverty and heat, the city he hated, the gang that no longer wanted him and the police who now did – was to enlist in the army. A few hundred Euros in the right hands saw him sent off for basic training, but he couldn't get his weight down and the mandatory obstacle course, across which all conscripts had to hang, duck, run, jump and drown, remained just that: a huge, insurmountable obstacle. Guido became more and more desperate; if they threw him out, he was sure prison would be his next billet.

It wasn't that Guido didn't try; God had made him to be jolly and plump and nothing Guido or the drill instructors tried could shake God's conviction that Guido was the right size. They would threaten Guido, but God doesn't scare easily and Guido's weight stayed the same while they starved him and made him run and run and run until he passed out, which always happened, because he tried so hard and *would not* give up. When they shouted endlessly at Guido and beat him with sticks, God imbued Guido with a divine but perverse endurance despite Guido wanting only to die and the earth swallow him up. When, as punishment, he cleaned every square inch of the entire training camp with one hundred and nineteen tooth-brushes (the cost of which they deducted from his paltry pay, chiding him for not taking proper care of army equipment), The Lord looked on benevolently while making sure his creation maintained the girth that He, in all his wisdom, found seemly. Every week his fellow trainees would unwillingly push – and sometimes violently pull – Guido through the obstacle course, resentful because Guido's fate had been meanly tied to theirs for the amusement of the instructors (who knew by now that it was God's will Guido would never complete the course on his own, because Guido himself could not possibly have tried any harder to do what they wanted, and it was therefore agreed by all the staff that a higher power *must* be involved). And every night for the first month, Guido prayed to that higher power. After that, he gave up praying for ever, because by then he knew for sure that God wasn't listening, or just didn't care. Guido never stepped foot inside a church again.

Inevitably, during yet one more futile assault on the course (and on a day when all the cadets turned out to enjoy someone else's humiliation) Guido thrilled them by falling badly, breaking his ankle. Laid up in the infirmary, he was tended by a kindly doctor who as a child had also suffered from carrying more weight than his peers thought proper, or girls found attractive. It didn't take long for the doctor to figure out there was more to Guido's ill-concealed concerns than were spoken. Curious, he kept the boy on the ward a bit longer than necessary, and it was while Guido was enjoying his elongated recovery that they both discovered he had a talent for bandaging. After only one demonstration, he could wrap complex dressings with a skill and gentle precision that put most of the nurses to shame. The doctor started talking to Guido about medicine, about medical procedures, about diagnosis and cure. He had no trouble remembering what he was told; the Latin names for bones and tissue, the jargon and the tools, the details of medical procedures he started to read about in the various journals the doctor gave him, the machines and medicines and the names of ailments real and perceived, the treatments for them, the ultimate power of the placebo and it's holy place in military medicine.

One morning – the morning it was no longer possible to keep him on the ward – the doctor took Guido to the adjutant and demanded the boy be transferred to the medical corps. Somehow (and there was never a day that passed without Guido remembering his patron in gratitude), the doctor managed to persuade the exasperated officer to transfer Guido to a training school for orderlies and field medics rather than discharge him. Three days later, Guido found himself at the army medical school, mysteriously excused from the normal demands for physical fitness that applied even to medical trainees.

In the following three years he studied hard, qualified as a medical orderly, served in the field on exercises and at numerous camps and was seriously considering a career as a doctor when fate, and his origins, betrayed him. On a ward in the vast Nato barracks outside Heidelberg to which he had been posted, a delirious Sicilian corporal whose foot had been blown off during a live fire exercise mistook Guido for the long-lost son of his family's most deadly enemy, the worthless rabble from the next village with whom the corporal's clan had waged a vendetta reaching back, it was said, to Roman times. The family of their enemy was led by the foul-mouthed whore of a mother, her scum offspring – thieves and pederasts to a man, it was well known – trailing around behind her like so much vermin, lying and stealing and raping as did all their kind. (The worthless father was long dead, his face blown off at close range with a shotgun some years back. The culprit was never found, not that anyone looked; secretly, the soldier believed his own father to be the assassin, which made him proud).

The corporal probed Guido about where he came from; in the offhand replies he detected deceit. This was no Neapolitan: he knew a Sicilian accent when he heard one, no matter how faint, how well disguised. He asked more questions, but the orderly was constantly evasive. What was this rotund attendant hiding behind the twinkling eyes, what secret cradled within the vast hands? Had Guido recognised the corporal, perhaps known the name if not the man, and so was keeping the knowledge hidden behind smiles and acts of friendship designed to lure his supposedly unsuspecting enemy closer, a classic stratagem for the kind of intimate betrayal, that cold dish so familiar to the inhabitants of the hills around Palermo? It was the blood feud – it had to be – it was the debt that can never be repaid, the wronged honour that merited no less a response than perpetual revenge down the generations, even when the act that triggered the vendetta could no longer be recalled with certainty. What else could it be? History! Honour! *Revenge*! Why else would the fat orderly lie?

On becoming convinced that Guido would certainly assassinate him given the chance – and only the Holy Father himself knew how many ways a medical orderly might know to kill a sleeping patient – the corporal had inadvisably lunged at Guido with a scalpel he had stolen. Forgetting that he couldn't walk, let alone fight, the corporal promptly fell over. Guido, utterly and equally inept in defence or attack, waved his arms around ineffectively as he tried to back away from the murderous soldier waving a scalpel. In doing so, he knocked over a tray of used, empty and uncapped syringes awaiting sharps disposal, several of which improbably speared the corporal in his good leg. Panicking, both Guido and the soldier grabbed at the needles, plungers were depressed by hands unknown, and sufficient bubbles of air were pumped into the corporal's bloodstream to kill the Sicilian on the spot. (The accident subsequently triggered a bloodbath in the Sicilian hills when the warring families found their perpetual vendetta revitalised by the news of this latest outrage in the long and deadly history of outrages. The whore mother actually had the nerve to beg the priest to visit the corporal's family and plead their innocence in this matter, the hot and dusty cleric solemnly attesting to the family's utter bewilderment at the death so far away and their complete lack of involvement in it. This of course was seen simply as a delaying tactic while the whore mother armed her murderous family members. The priest was a known fornicator almost certainly enjoying favours from the whore mother, defiling the holy cross by taking her bent over the altar for all they knew, such was their joint depravity. On their way to kill the whore mother some weeks later, the dead corporal's two strapping brothers went first to the church, made their confessions to the fornicating priest, then promptly threw him head-first down his own well on account of his perfidy).

Guido, acquitted of any wrongdoing at the court martial, was none the less discharged with a small amount of back pay and a seat home on the next plane out of the base. He never turned up for the flight.

Instead, he wangled a seat on a cargo haul of food parcels into RAF Northolt, just outside London, walked off the ancient Hercules with a friendly wave to the crew and disappeared into the night. He soon made contact with the network of Italian immigrants still living in the UK, shamelessly exaggerating either his Neapolitan or Sicilian provenance to suit circumstances and company. Like so many of his itinerant forebears, he found ready employment in the catering trade, working menial jobs for little more than board and lodging in kitchens, slaughterhouses, hotels, roadside stalls and even – rather unnervingly – in the canteen of a navy base in Plymouth (where he slept in a disused freezer). He picked up short-order skills, developed a bonhomie that endeared him to his customers, and mastered the English breakfast, a dish that would stand him in good stead wherever he went next.

The skill he acquired that really changed his fortune was baking bread. Guido had a real talent with flour and water and yeast, and the navy base had excellent ovens, no power restrictions and copious supplies of top-quality ingredients. He was soon turning out a wide variety of loaves, brioche, crispy rolls, ciabatta, pitta, feather-light croissants, sweet crusted bagels and a host of other delicacies that disappeared as fast as he could get them out of the oven, as fast as he could master the latest recipe.

One day, during an exploratory trip on his ancient Vespa scooter across Dartmoor, he took a break in Okehampton, liked the town, saw an advert for a chef in the window of the local restaurant, bluffed his way into the job and settled down, renting a nice little two-bedroom house on the edge of the town which belonged to the restaurant's owner. Like everyone else he needed a second income to survive, which he earned by baking to order for the locals using materials he now obtained in a steady supply from friends he bribed back in Plymouth, getting up at 4am every morning so he could bake the day's orders before he had to start prep for the lunch covers at the restaurant. (The restaurant was now quite popular, and lunchtime the busiest of the day since their energy permit only allowed them to open eight evenings a month.

Word spread quickly about the flour-dusted Italian bear, his wonderful bread and deliciously crumbly pastries. The locals soon came to favour his produce as much for taste as availability – with power restrictions constraining the use of their massive ovens, bread was only available two days out of seven in the supermarkets and bakery-chains, sold out within minutes of appearing on the shelves. Guido cooked his bread at home using bottled gas, and never had any trouble getting replacement cylinders: he only had to mention in passing he was running low and two new bottles would show up outside the door the next morning. He knew who his benefactors were, and made them special treats now and then, but in true English fashion nothing explicit was ever said; no more than a tacit acknowledgement ever made.

He also had a third source of income but this he didn't discuss with the locals at all, except a very select few, and that only after considerable caution had been exercised, time had passed, familiarity gained, questions asked, behaviour noted and checked: Guido operated a black-market medical facility out of his spare bedroom offering a broad range of services for people who, for whatever reason, found the official channels of healthcare unavailable.

Alina was one of those people, and Guido had certainly saved her life. She jumped to her feet with a huge smile, threw her arms as far as they would reach around Guido's broad shoulders and kissed both his cheeks. "Oh Guido, it's so good to see you. How you doing?" She pulled playfully at his beard. "Love the beard, baby…bushy baby. You look like Cossack, all ready to invade…" For a moment, she looked rather fierce, but the sunny smile returned just as fast as it had left.

Guido was oscillating wildly between pleasure at seeing Alina well and happy, and puzzled by the fact that Alina clearly *was* well and happy. "Hey angel, how are you?" he beamed, taking in the others with his toothy smile. "Hi boys, how you all doing huh?" Then looking into Alina's face with a serious expression: "But you don' look sick to me, eh? What's a matter with my li'l angel?"

"Sorry Guido, that's my fault," interrupted Jake, half standing and holding out his hand. "How are you old chap? You look well."

Guido grabbed his hand and shook it enthusiastically, patting his belly with his other hand. "I'm damn good, I tell you Jake. I eat well, drink wine, make love to beautiful woman – they all too thin round here but I feed them up damn quick – I make bread like you get in Heaven – sorry I don' have something for you. You should have called first. But hey, it don' matter, it's good to see you my friend, very good." He paused for breath, and glanced at Alina. "But why you bring me here? If she not sick…?"

Jake looked up into Guido's twinkling eyes, a very direct look. "We need your help, Guido, but this is different. It's not her, it's someone else. I have to tell you too – there could be trouble."

"OK, so nothing new huh?" said Guido. There was nowhere for him to sit and he towered over the table, making everyone slightly uncomfortable. "I tell you what; you tell me what you want, then I decide if I want to get in trouble, eh? If I help, fine – trouble is my problem. If not, nobody feels bad and you all come to my house tonight so I cook for you, make you fat and happy like me."

"Sure," said Jake amenably, "That's fair, although we'll have to take a rain-check on the meal. But let me ask you this – is it true you can't examine a patient without leaving your DNA around, Guido, even if you wear gloves? Is that true?"

Guido nodded. "Sure, it's true. Don' worry – I understand you Jake. I understand you very well. I leave clues, I get in trouble. So…*good!*" He nodded his head. "Anyway, police don' have my DNA. Italian army, sure – but not police. But if they want some DNA, all they have to do is test my bread, eh?" Everyone laughed. "Anyway, don' need no DNA jus' to hear a story Jake. Is OK, you can tell me. I'm a doctor." More laughter. Guido was grinning like a happy bear, teeth very white against the thick black beard.

"Hey, where's Jarrott?" interjected Billy.

"Probably outside," said Jake, rising. "Guido, let's go over to the caravan." Guido nodded, backed down the steps and squeezed himself out of the door. Jake glanced at Harry, who stood and followed. The others were still seated, looking at him expectantly, but Jake shook his head. "You stay here, and keep Alf here too if he comes back in. Start stowing the gear – we have to move off exactly at seven tonight or we won't arrive before the morning toll kicks in."

Outside, Harry and Guido were waiting for him.

"Alf's not here," said Harry. Neither was the jeep. Jake didn't reply, but his expression hardened as he walked towards the caravan, the others following. Guido's medical black bag was perched on the step by the caravan door. Jake picked it up, opened the narrow caravan door, put the bag inside and turned to its owner. "No offence old chap, but can you get through there?" he asked apologetically.

Guido smiled, not in the least bit offended. "Sure, you two give me a push, I get in. Let's go." He heaved himself up the single step, turned sideways and, after a few moments of pushing, squeezing and heaving that in other circumstances would have been hilarious, he popped like a cork through the doorway into the caravan, where he stopped dead in his tracks. "Ai..Madre di Dio" he whispered reverently. Momentarily forgetting his feud with God, he crossed himself several times.

The others couldn't get through the door because Guido was blocking it. Jake poked him with a finger and Guido reluctantly moved further inside. "What do you think," Jake asked as he came through the door, followed by Harry. Guido turned slowly to look at him, then at Harry, his expression unreadable in the gloom.

"I think he likes his food even more than me," Guido quipped lamely, eyes not twinkling any more. They were hard and very dark now. No-one laughed. For a few moments all three stood silent, contemplating the extraordinary sight before them. Then Guido picked up his bag and got to work.

"Now I want to hear the story Harry," said Jake. "And this time, from the beginning."

Chapter 3:   No Vacancy's

Alf parked his jeep by the side of the road and surveyed the burnt-out wreck of the Parkside Hotel. There was virtually nothing left of the great Victorian house, just a derelict shell formed by the three remaining ground floor walls enclosing a big pile of wet rubble, strangely flattened. The front of the building no longer existed at any level, but he noticed there was insufficient rubble around the perimeter of the house to account for the collapsed masonry, and wondered why anyone would have bothered taking it away in the middle of the night. The acrid charcoal smell was everywhere, inescapable. Huge puddles of dirty water littered the surroundings, and much of the ground on either side of the road had been churned into glutinous mud.

Alf first heard about the fire on the radio while driving Guido and Harry back to the camp. He began to pay attention because the hotel was on his watch list and, according to Guido at least, it appeared to have burnt to the ground during the night. Now he understood where the emergency vehicles had been going, although he still couldn't explain where they had come from. He asked Guido a few innocuous questions as he drove; the time the fire started, the number of casualties and fatalities, where the guests had been taken when they were evacuated, but Guido knew nothing more than he had already volunteered. When they arrived at the camp, Alf stayed in the jeep. Waiting until Guido, Harry and Billy had disappeared into the bus, he abandoned the pretence of examining the dashboard wiring, dropped off Guido's black leather bag by the blue caravan and drove quietly away.

Further down the road past the hotel wreckage, a police car was parked at the entrance gate next to a forlorn sign swinging gently in the wind that claimed there were "No Vacancy's." He could see a uniformed officer in the distance walking rather aimlessly towards a nondescript Ford estate parked a long way off, but it drove away before he got there and now the officer was left staring out into the landscape. Another uniform appeared from behind the remnant of the east wall and Alf recognised

Ravinder Mann. The same age as Alf, they had gone to school together.

Alf got out of the jeep and started picking his way through the debris and the sheets of filthy water. "Hey Rav, how you doin'?" he called out. The policeman saw him and veered in Alf's direction.

"Hello Alf. You're a long way from the pub. What brings you up here? This area is closed to the public, you know."

"How are we supposed to be able to tell? There's no signs anywhere, are there?"

"Well, I'm telling you now," said Rav in a stern official tone. His expression softened and he looked a bit sheepish. "Blimey Alf, sorry about that. Take no notice – been a long night, that's all."

"Sure, I understand. Don't worry about it. What happened to the old place? Meant to visit one day but never got round to it. I used to quite like the look of it, even though it was a bit of a shambles."

"Me too...I think the attraction *was* the run-down look of it. It had real history in those walls and woodwork – real wood too, I'll bet. Shame really".

"A fire, evidently? But what was the helicopter looking for – it was flying all over the moor last night."

"No idea. It's all a strange business if you ask me, Alf," and with no further prompting he described the events of the previous night, tactfully omitting only the bit where his partner nearly got them both killed, because Mick meanwhile had joined them, eyeing Alf with a certain distaste, but otherwise ignoring him.

"So they were army vehicles then?" Alf asked carefully. He didn't like the look of Mick, who seemed to be suppressing a powerful rage. Barely.

"All of them. They must have been stationed fairly close, although by the time we got there the fire was under control. But they kept us well away, closed the road, and I can't help wondering what the military were doing putting out a fire in a civilian hotel."

"Or why they took the remains away," added Mick. "Further up the road there are tracks of heavy vehicles turning round.

Trucks, I'd guess. We saw an excavator when we were up here last night, didn't we? And remember on the way back, the stream of dump trucks we passed going in the opposite direction?"

Rav nodded. "What are you getting at?"

"Doesn't it seem odd the way they cleared up all the rubble. Look around you – there is nowhere near as much debris as you normally see after a fire, is there? Not for a building this size."

"I was thinking the same thing," said Alf. Mick scowled at him.

"There's something else you can add to your theory in that case," said Rav, pointing to the strangely flattened pile that remained. They filled in the basement, as far as I can see. See the excavator tracks that run up towards the house, like they gradually pushed all the rubble into the basement and then drove over it, compacting it like that. Why would the army bother to do that? It's almost like they were trying to cover it up."

"If that was true, they were going about it the wrong way, wouldn't you say," said Alf. Both policemen turned towards him for an explanation. "If they were trying to hide something, do you think they could have drawn more attention to themselves?"

"I didn't mean they were trying to cover up the fire, Alf. Just the basement – the hole in the ground," said Rav.

"It would have been dangerous to leave it open like that," said Mick, offering qualified support for his partner. "Animals could fall in, or even trespassers," the last addressed to Alf. "Maybe it was just a safety thing."

"Maybe," said Rav, unconvinced, "and if they needed a cover story that's the one they would use – the safety angle." Alf found this observation rather astute, although it did suggest Rav was now considering the other kind of cover-up.

"But one thing's for sure," said Mick, "we'll never know, never find out what happened here, not now. There is no way the fire service could investigate this, or our boys – no remains, no forensics, no photos. All the fucking evidence has been ruined, completely destroyed."

Exactly, thought Alf.

"It started when Jarrott mentioned he liked to go hunting," Harry Bracey was a disciplined man, and liked to impose order on anything he was involved in. As he and Jake watched Guido's methodical examination, he started his story where methodical men always start.

"I used to hunt when I was a boy and I said as much, said how I missed it. Jarrott suggested we take a trip to the moor one night, go after some deer he'd been tracking. He claimed to know someone who would butcher a carcass for us, and buy the cuts we didn't want." A thought occurred to him. "That wasn't you was it, Guido, by any chance?"

"Mmm…*venison*," said Guido, nodding conspiratorially. "Sure, I do a little surgery sometime. Road kill – you know, some car hits a few sheep, some bullocks get lost and wander into the back of some van completely by accident…"

"Was Alf telling the truth about the deer?" Jake asked Harry.

"Apparently so."

"So you don't think he had any idea of what was to come?"

"Did he have foreknowledge of the events? No, I don't think so. I think he was as amazed as I was, frankly."

"Did you shoot some deer?" Guido asked. Harry shook his head, to the chef's obvious disappointment. "OK – go on," urged Jake.

"We set up a hide and waited, waited a long time. Then, quite suddenly, several deer ran across the top of the hill in front of us, and *he* was running after them." Harry glanced down the caravan.

"But you didn't shoot no deer?" asked Guido, looking up from where he was kneeling. Harry ignored him.

"There was something really surreal about it, Jake, pretty damn strange – this enormously fat man, stark bollock naked and running like the wind. Running for his life, it looked like. And although I wonder about it now, you know – maybe it was a trick of the moonlight or the angle or something – but as far as I could see – Jarrott also saw it, by the way – as far as I could tell he was running at least as fast as the deer. Jarrott reckons he was actually catching them."

Harry paused, expecting questions, but none were forthcoming. Jake mouthed the word "naked" several times, shaking his head. Guido was pining as he probed and pushed and measured. "My mother used to make the venison stew. *Unbelievable.* I tell you for sure, you love it, take it from me. Venison...wonderful, very good for you." He glanced up at them, his eyes twinkling again.

Jake and Harry exchanged amused looks. "Anyway, he was running really fast, and although the moon was full and we could see pretty well, you couldn't possibly see well enough to run across ground like that, not safely anyway."

"And that's when he fell?" said Jake.

"Correct. Down a gully, quite deep too – about thirty feet I'd say, having climbed down it. Jolly hairy it was, too."

"What made you climb down, rather than call for help? Wasn't that the obvious thing to do, call for help?"

"Well, thing is...you see, there was a bit of a debate about that, actually. Alf...er...Jarrott said the same thing you did, but...oh yes, I forgot...in fact, actually it was the chopper that made my mind up. That was it, now I come to think on it. All the ambulances and fire engines when they went through town, lights flashing and sirens going. Jarrott thought it was strange they all appeared out of nowhere, but they were heading away from us, heading towards a helicopter we could see in the distance over the moor. It wasn't static, hovering; they were looking for something."

"For him," said Jake, and it wasn't a question.

"Olive oil flavoured with rosemary to seal the meat," said Guido, removing his stethoscope. "She used to keep this bottle of No.1 virgin with a sprig of rosemary in it, you know, in the bottle."

"That's what it seemed like to me," said Harry. "A search party. Jarrott also thought so; too much of a coincidence. So we climbed down, found him lying there at the bottom of the gully, out cold. There was nothing we could do for him, had nothing to cover him with or anything. I had a look at him, best I could. No sign of injury I could see, nothing obvious. That's when I decided we should bring him here."

There was a pause. Harry looked away, clearly not yet willing to unfold the carefully wrapped climax to his story. Jake watched him for a moment. "I need a smoke," he declared. "You know, this would be a damn sight easier to understand if our man there wasn't out cold, if we could ask him what the fuck is going on. What do you think, Guido – can you wake him up?" Guido shook his head without looking up from his examination. "I don' think so. He's really out, and I don' know why neither. Is a worry."

Jake turned back to Harry. "Thing is, that's all very well, but I don't understand why you didn't get off the moor and make an anonymous call from a phone box for an ambulance. Wouldn't that have been the best thing to do? Why get us mixed up in this? You have no idea who he is, why they were looking for him, what he's done, nothing. You went to a lot of trouble to get him here instead of turning him over. What's the story on *that* one Harry?"

"You better see for yourself," Harry replied, looking toward the other end of the caravan.

Alf Jarrott stood atop a craggy outcrop of rock two-hundred yards behind the burnt-out hotel, and fifty feet above it. The two officers were sitting in their car, bored and fractious for reasons of their own and entirely indifferent to Alf's incursion into the danger zone. After their conversation, he had walked carefully over the ruins, paying particular attention to the filled in area because if that was the bit they covered up, it was also the centre of interest. It was a big basement, he decided, pacing out the walls where he could see them – a few inches of white tile sticking up here, the lintel of a doorway crushed into its frame. He walked away for a better perspective, then climbed the mound in the centre. It was still hot underfoot so he couldn't stand up there long, but looking down he got the idea there might be more to the basement than just this central area. He thought he could see from the studwork and part of a wall the place where a corridor might start, right at the edge of the infill. That would mean the basement extended out beyond the walls, under the garden at the back perhaps, down beneath the car park on the right or the lawns on the left, now obliterated.

After a bit more pacing and studying, Alf decided to climb up to a point where he could see the entire layout of the hotel and grounds. From this vantage point he let his gaze rest on sections of the landscape one at a time, like a pilot scanning discrete arcs of the sky, and several times he couldn't help but notice a small mound behind the house, a tiny tumulus seemingly out of place in the middle of formal gardens. A lot of work had gone in the layout of the gardens, that much was clear even to Alf, despite the devastation. The geometric combinations of beds and borders were well ordered, yet off to one side, and quite jarring in its appearance, a circular mound protruded sporting nothing more than some spotty grass and...and something Alf couldn't quite make out. He jumped down, walked quickly to the spot and climbed the shallow mound, which was only about a foot high and six across. In the centre was a square metal plate, three feet to a side. An access hatch, an inspection cover perhaps, or something else? Alf looked at the house, estimating the distance. He was fifty yards away, so unless this was a sewer access point or something connected with the water supply, its location was a puzzle. Unless...

Alf looked round carefully. Out of sight of the patrol car, there was no-one else around that he could see. He reached down, grabbed the two recessed handles and pulled. The hatch came up easily, revealing a concrete shaft and a ladder that disappeared into the darkness. There was an alarm sensor stuck to the underside of the hatch and its mate on the rim of the shaft, but no bells rang, no sirens wailed: presumably the alarm system had been designed to alert people in a building that no longer existed. Alf dropped a pebble into the shaft, and heard it bounce on a hard surface after only a second or two. Twenty, maybe thirty feet, he reckoned. He took out his phone and turned it on, feeling a trickle of cold tea run across his palm, but the phone came to life. He switched it into torch mode, took it in his teeth and climbed down the ladder, pulling the cover back into place above him.

At the bottom, Alf found himself in the middle of a corridor stretching away into darkness. Orienting himself, he walked towards the house. On the left, a door marked Surgery, which opened on a small room with an examination table in the centre, some items of medical equipment on shelves, a few cupboards on one wall. He made a note to come back, make a thorough search and steal anything worth scavenging. Right now, he had to move fairly quickly because he didn't know how long the phone battery would last. Experimentally, he turned off the torch and was shocked by the density of darkness, so thick it seemed suffocating. Alf felt like he was breathing the stuff in, coal black air filling his lungs, filling them up to bursting because he couldn't breathe the vile stuff back out. His heart started beating rapidly, thundering in his ears. He realised he was scaring himself and turned the torch back on. The panic subsided, leaving him feeling foolish.

Back in the corridor, he found several more rooms; business-like offices and formal meeting rooms, bedrooms with unmade beds and clothes strewn about, signs of recent occupancy and hasty vacation. One large room was obviously a lounge: pictures on the walls, a wide screen TV, some big speakers and several armchairs passed through the torch beam, but everything was waterlogged and something heavy had fallen on the TV, smashing it neatly in two halves. Other corridors led from this central area, and Alf was awed by the sheer size of the place. Moving fast now, he found a door marked Training, but it was either jammed or locked. Another marked Kitchen, with precisely that beyond it. Showers, more bedrooms, a classroom – this place had it all, he told himself as he came to the part of the corridor where the rubble had come through the roof and he could go no further. Was there more beyond the rubble, he wondered. It seemed likely, but what the hell was this place? Who built it, and when? Did anyone in town know about it, because he sure as hell never heard any mention of a place like this, nothing to do with the hotel? In any case, Alf had been furnished with architectural plans of the place at his briefing, and this basement complex was definitely *not* part of the plan.

The light flickered and Alf cursed, but the torch returned to its duty – just a warning. He would have to come back with a bigger torch, more batteries, maybe a few lanterns. This could take a while. He started back, but noticed a heavy metal door, partly open, and decided to investigate: after all, it had No Entry emblazoned across it, and what could be more inviting? He tugged on the half-open door but it wouldn't budge, so he had to squeeze through the gap, entering a short corridor with a door to the left and a room at the far end. The door – stencilled Armoury – was buckled and detached entirely from one hinge. Clearly it had been forcibly opened; there were scorch marks at the hinges, the lock escutcheon had blossomed outward in several torn petal shapes and the whole thing was leaning at an angle, held in place only by the remaining hinge. A long dark smear streaked down part of the wall to one side of the doorway. Alf followed the smear with the torch beam, starting at chest height, from where it gradually progressed down the wall and made a ragged journey along the floor of the corridor leading to the room at the end. Hopeful, he pointed the torch back to the armoury, but the gun racks and storage units inside were all stripped bare. Alf reversed out and followed the dark smear to the end of the hallway, entering a room that was clearly military, neat and orderly except for a sizeable dark stain covering the centre of the linoleum floor. Metal desks, filing cabinets, telephones, local maps on the wall with pins stuck in them, all the accoutrements of the services. Another massive steel door directly ahead was marked Code Room. This door was intact. Alf examined the lock – it was a combination and key pair and the door was very substantial; no easy way past this one.

Back in the corridor, he retraced his route to the shaft and followed the corridor in the opposite direction, away from the house. It terminated in a large store room with several walk-in freezers, shelves full of ration packs, and orderly rows of canned goods, cleaning materials and suchlike – nothing worth stealing unless you knew a fence with a grocery store (which he did). He returned to the bottom of the shaft once more and shook the torch. It seemed to be holding up, so he went back to the door marked No Entry and squeezed through for a second time, unwilling to leave just yet. He ignored the dark streaks deliberately, keeping the beam of light on the room ahead. To his surprise, the door to the code room was ajar. It had been locked, he was certain; then again, he examined the locks but couldn't remember if he actually tried the door handle. Why was he certain it was locked? Hell, of course it wasn't – couldn't have been – it was open now, wasn't it? Still, how did it open on its own? He grasped the side of the door and pulled it wide. It was heavy, silent on its hinges but quite unlikely to open on its own, even if not properly shut.

Shining his torch past the door, Alf was disappointed to discover there was nothing in the code room but a table, two metal chairs, a wall safe – open and bereft of content – and a row of sockets of various kinds mounted along the wall at the back of the table. As he turned away he saw something on the floor; an ID badge. He recognised the photo immediately. "Well well, it's marathon man," he muttered, and stuck the badge in his pocket.

Alf heard a click and looked up, but there was nothing in the beam, which was definitely fading now. With a sense of urgency, he squeezed back past the metal door and made his way back to the shaft. As he put a foot on the first rung, he heard the distinct sound of metal on metal in the direction of the storeroom, but there was nothing he could see from where he stood, at least as far as the beam reached down the corridor. The storeroom would have to wait. The beam flickered and the battery suddenly gave up. Very thankful he was already grasping the ladder, Alf scampered upwards. He could barely contain his excitement at the thought of coming back, at what he might find down here given enough time and batteries. As he pushed the hatch aside and peeked over the top, he ran through a quick inventory in his mind: he would need a shovel and a crowbar, a decent hammer, some chisels, containers for the spoils...but that was later. Right now, he couldn't wait to tell the others, because no matter what had transpired, the story he now had to tell was a certain salve for any irritation over his perceived ill-behaviour, real or imaginary.

Carefully replacing the inspection cover he was reminded of his training: that information was a currency he could use, in this case to buy back their affections and trust. He didn't understand why they blamed him for recent events, why they were being so cold towards him. He knew they really liked him; he was their friend, a fellow kindred spirit. He was certain they didn't suspect him. Nor was he going to let them throw this good thing away, even if he had to bribe them to see sense. They were much too valuable to let slip away like this.

In fact, Alf Jarrott never went back to the basement complex built under the Parkfield Hotel, never discovered its full extent, never uncovered any of its secrets. Nor did he see, as he drove away, the middle-aged man in a grey overcoat walking slowly near the nondescript Ford estate that had returned to its parking spot a few hundred yards past the hotel, the driver gazing out at the landscape one minute, and gone from it the next as if he'd fallen into a hole. However, the next day Alf did hear some chilling news from Officer Ravinder Mann: at approximately two in the morning there had been some kind of explosion. The news was chilling because Alf had intended to return later that night. Had he not been detained by an unexpected visitor, he would certainly have been down there at the time of the explosion. The official explanation, Mann informed him, was leaking gas set off by an underground remnant of the fire.

What Rav could not say, for he knew no more about it than he told Alf, was that the explosion was actually caused by a chain of timed charges, professionally placed and distributed, which thoroughly demolished the entire underground structure. The old hotel remnants, the rubble and plaster scroll work, the scorched beams and joists, the shattered slate and marble facings and ceramic tiles with their little individually hand-painted blue flowers, the diamond shaped pieces of coloured glass fallen from beaded windows set in solid teak doors, the illegal Victorian lead water pipes and the brass taps with white enamel coatings on the outer half of each spoke, capped with the words "hot" or "cold" in tiny letters; ugly escritoires, French polish marred with rings from glasses set down by infuriated guests unable to find the secret compartments that desks like this ought to have; the cast iron baths dulled by too much scouring, heavy oak bed-heads and tight-drawer dressers whose mirror silver had retreated from the edge of the glass as if shrinking from images they were too exhausted to reflect; frayed wiring where rats had chewed away the insulation; creaky formal chairs and faded Axminster carpets, dark stained floorboards and a century of coins that had fallen between them; the sober brick walls with their dusty painted softwood picture rails and the ornate cornices that crowned them; overgrown gardens where a rockery had toppled into careless disorder, flowerbeds and shrubs spindle bare in the November chill; the car park and its bays marked out in faded white lines for cars that would never again stand between them;

35

and all mysteries of the secret underground labyrinth over which the hotel had evidently presided: every trace of Parkfield and its strange, covert history subsided into obscurity with a dull but powerful crump and a single heave of the earth like a thrown sheet settling over a bed, a tiny earthquake that threw down all traces of the building into a series of vast, waterlogged pits.

The only survivor of this cataclysm was the original Victorian greenhouse, a fragile affair of wrought iron perched on its own some distance from the house, all the glass panels intact. A few days later some boys from the town, finding nothing to see or steal despite the racy apocrypha that had lured them up there, expressed their boredom and disappointment by methodically smashing every pane. When heavy rains filled the pits to overflowing in the spring, Harlequin ducks built their nests and no-one ever disturbed them.

Chapter 4:   Behold, A Son!

All three men crouched at the end of the caravan, studying the body on the floor. It was a grotesque sight, reminding Jake of some huge, white larvae straight out of an insectoid horror movie. He was glad it wasn't moving, although it was certainly still breathing, the chest rising and falling every now and then. There was so much flesh it created a blurred perimeter like a gingerbread man whose consistency was too thin to hold the shape of the cutter, spreading outward to form a kind of skirt that touched the floor and melted across it, sliding away from the body everywhere except above the shoulders and below the knees. The face was peaceful, and strangely angelic. It was a young face, and Jake wondered what he would look like without the jowls, the chubby cheeks and the rolls around the neck. The arms were bulky and indistinct unless you lifted one, as Guido did during his examination, to reveal folds of fat hanging off the upper arms, wrists as thick as the hands attached to them. The fingers were podgy and soft, nails neatly trimmed and clean. There were no signs of injury anywhere except the kind of scratches and bruising you might expect a naked man to suffer after a mad midnight dash across the moor, and several vivid red bands around the shoulders and upper chest edged by bloody welts along the side of each strip where something had cut into the flesh. They reminded Guido of the way the back of his legs looked after a dose of the Banshee's leather strap; to his considerable astonishment, his hands began to shake in anger.

Below the weals, the vast bulk of the chest and stomach rose upward, outward, sideways and down; gravity had plenty to work with. Where, during the examination, they were revealed by lifting aside some of the almost liquid rolls of fat that concealed them, the sheer bulk of the man made his genitals look tiny, cradled between thighs so heavy and vast that Guido, seeking signs of fracture, had been unable to feel the bones he knew *had* to be under there somewhere. There were no knees as such, just strange flaps of skin, but the calves seemed much less overweight than the rest of him, in fact looking quite toned, big muscles with clear definition which tapered away to ankles that actually looked quite dainty given the subjective scale of the whole. The feet, now the focus of their combined attention, seemed in most respects quite normal; normal size, regular number of toes, although with quite a lot of cuts and severe bruising in places, but again, these were further testament to last night's misadventure. There was just one thing about the feet, or rather, with the right foot, that wasn't normal. It had a QR code on the sole, and all three men were staring at it when Harry, at long last, rode his tightly reined horses into the final furlong.

"That was what made me decide, Jake," said Harry. "Seeing that...well, after that I couldn't just leave him to the wolves."

"Wolfs?" Guido was astonished. "Really? Sure, I hear 'bout big cats on moor, I go looking now and again 'cos I like big pussies..." They all chuckled as Guido wiggled his eyebrows and licked his lips suggestively. "I go looking for boar also, not that I catch, but I did hear them one time, and I see tracks OK, but not no wolfs. Oh no, I don' hear 'bout no wolfs."

"He means the people in the helicopter, Guido," explained Jake. "The authorities." Guido was disappointed, but tried to hide it by nodding sagely.

"Harry, when you saw the QR code, what did you think it was?" asked Jake.

"No idea, but I didn't like it the second I saw it. Who does that to a person, stamps them like that – it's a tattoo, isn't it Guido?" Guido nodded. "It reminds me of Jews with numbers tattooed on their arms, you know - the death camps and all that. Christ Jake, we don't even do this to criminals. What on earth could he have done to deserve being treated like this?"

"That's what we need to find out. Go on...what happened next?"

Harry continued his story, describing how Alf had been able to reverse the jeep up the gully to where the man was lying. How they found some webbing with which to fashion a harness round the huge shoulders and under the arms, then used the winch on the jeep to haul the body up a ramp made from the detached tailgate, and pull it onto the floor of jeep. Guido nodded, looking at the red weals with a new understanding. "Yeah, sorry about that. Couldn't think what else to do at the time, you know, just the two of us..." said Harry.

"Tell *him* that," said Jake, but Harry was undeterred.

"When we got back, we brought him in here – with a bit of help from the others. We...er...we didn't want to wake you, Jake, thought it best if..."

"Yeah, right," Jake cut in. "Move on."

"How you get him in here?" asked Guido, remembering the tight squeeze. He was nowhere near as bulky as the patient.

"The wall behind you, Guido. It opens up so you can have a little covered veranda on the end of the caravan. We opened it up and hauled him in through there, not the door, obviously." He turned to Jake. "Other than that, there's really not much else to tell, old bean. Really, that's about it I think. Anyway," turning back to Guido, "what's the diagnosis, doc? How is he? What do you think?"

Jake knew what *he* thought – that Harry was hurriedly moving the conversation on, purposefully leading them away from the events of the night. In which case, to what purpose?

"He has concussion, and contusion at base of skull consistent with blow by blunt object," said Guido, unwrapping the cuff of an old but serviceable blood pressure monitor from his patient's arm. "I can't see it 'cos I can't move him that much, but I feel it and there is some blood, but not much and is dry. Bleeding stopped quite a while. No fractures, as far as I tell, but you see what I deal with here, an' is not easy, OK? Very bloody not easy, I tell you. I think some shock for sure – see how lips are a little blue? An' I don' understand why he's still unconscious, too long now, make me worry – maybe the shock, I don' know. Also, temperatures is not right in different places. I think maybe hypothermia, so we treat that and for shock while I do more tests. Right now, we need...we need...Christ, wassaname?" Guido scratched his head. "You know, *dessert inglese*, is the stuff kids love at party with a ice cream, the stuff that wobble...hey, yes! *Wobble*. Just like our man here." He poked a finger into the mound of flesh, which quivered obligingly.

"Jelly?" offered Harry.

"That's it! Si. Jelly, grazi! You got jelly, Jake?"

"On the bus, maybe – I don't know. We can get some in town if not. Why jelly, Guido – you having a party?"

39

"Jelly is sugar, glucose, and is warm melted Jake, warm liquid – we don' put in fridge and wait till it wobble, OK? We get core temperature up, heat body from inside. We careful, melt the jelly and put with a little water, I put a tube in the throat so hot jelly goes down straight to belly, right to middle of body. Best thing for hypothermia: this is what we do now. Let's go..."

The last was more like an order than a suggestion; the army medic in Guido taking control. Harry found some jelly in the bus and melted down the cubes he tore off the squidgy packs while he explained to the others what they had found out, keeping to himself intimations of what they hadn't. Guido meanwhile stayed with his patient. After piling on more blankets he inserted a rubber tube down his patient's throat and cleaned the motor oil out of a small funnel in readiness while Jake watched, disturbed and thoroughly dissatisfied, pondering the things that Harry hadn't seen fit to explain.

By the time Alf Jarrott got back to the camp it was past six. Daylight was fast evaporating. The band had finished packing and were ready to move off, but Alf found them all – Guido included – sitting round the table in the bus, still unable to agree on what to do about Caravan Man, as they were now calling him. As Alf came through the door, the conversation stopped dead and they turned towards him with a commonality of expression that made him feel like an intruder. No-one spoke, but if the atmosphere was less than cordial, Alf didn't care because he would soon fix it, fix everything. He stepped up to the table, slapped the ID badge down, crossed his arms and stood there, looking down on them with an air of weary forgiveness as he waited for his inevitable restitution. For a moment, nobody moved; they all sat staring at the white plastic sheath as if afraid to touch it. Then Jake picked it up, studied the badge briefly and passed it to Harry.

"Where did you get this?" Jake asked. Alf didn't reply; he was watching Harry, who studied the card intently, both sides, before meeting Alf's look and repeating the question. Alf wasn't prepared to show his hand just yet; after the way they had treated him he was going to make them work for it. "Good likeness isn't it? And now we have a name for him."

As the card was passed round the table, each saw that below the photo a name was printed: Reuben. No surname, and no other information except for a QR code at the bottom of the badge.

"Very biblical," said Phil, passing the card to Billy across the table instead of giving it to Alina sitting next to him.

"Behold, a son!," said Harry, to general bewilderment. "That's what it means," he explained. "Reuben was the first son of Jacob, born of his first wife Leah. She called him Reuben – behold, a son – because she was pissed that Jacob was spending too much time with his second wife Rachel, and she hoped she could turn Jacob's head in her direction with the arrival of his first son. Apparently it also sounds like Hebrew for 'He has seen my misery,' so basically the subtext was: 'The Lord has noticed my misery, and now my husband will love me.'"

"Did it work?" asked Phil.

"Nope. The wives and servants were a bit interchangeable, as I recall. I suppose being Genesis, there simply weren't that many people and everyone had to do their bit to get the population going and build up the tribes. Jacob certainly did his duty – twelve sons in all, and a daughter."

"Wow, hidden depths," said Cas. "Check out Harry Bracey, theologian to the stars."

Hidden depths indeed, thought Jake. When the card made its way back to him, he stood up. "Harry, come with me. Alf, stay here."

"In your dreams mate. I go where the card goes," said Alf crossly. Things were not going to plan. The three of them, with Guido following unbidden, trooped over to the caravan and knelt at the feet of the unconscious man. Jake held the QR code on the card next to the tattoo; they were an exact match as far as he could tell, although the code printed on the ID card was smaller, which made the comparison difficult. Harry took a turn, comparing code sections at random to see if they were in the same orientations. Satisfied, he stood up.

"Alf, it seems you know more about this than you've told us...so far," Harry said, with a flat menace that Jake had never heard before. "You better explain yourself right now, because it seems to me that you may be a bigger liability than..." he glanced down at the card, "...Reuben here." It was the first time anyone had named him and they all felt the subtle change in their relationship to the unconscious man, the abstraction now a person. "And while you're at it, where the fuck were you this afternoon? Where did you sneak off to after you dropped us off?"

Alf stood up to counter the threatening way Harry was towering over him. Jake also stood at the same time, flanking him. Guido moved to block the doorway; although he had known Alf for some time, he didn't trust the skinny opportunist with his penchant for gossip, and regretted ever taking him into his confidence. Jarrott looked pleadingly from face to face, clearly frightened.

"Hey, come on guys – what's going on? I'm on your side, you know that...listen, I swear to you, all I know is that there was a fire last night up on the moor – Guido, you told us about it in the jeep, remember, and that was the first I'd heard of it. That's where the fire engines were going last night, Harry, do you see? I went up there – I didn't *sneak away*, as you put it – I just thought I'd go and have a quick look to see what was going on, if it had anything to do with Reuben here...I was just trying to help. Shit, I can't believe you people." His voice had risen gradually, ending on a high note of brittle disillusionment.

"And that's where you found this?" said Harry, holding out the card. Alf nodded sullenly, his arms crossed protectively in front of his body. "Where, exactly?"

"In the debris. I was just looking around, you know – and there it was, just lying there on the ground."

"Where on the ground *exactly*?"

"Er...the car park. It was in the car park."

"A lucky find then?" said Jake to Harry, who repeated: "...*it was just lying there.*"

"Did you see anyone else? Was anyone else up there?" asked Jake, taking the card from Harry to study it afresh. Alf thought for a moment, trying to recall from his training the body language he should suppress when giving evasive answers. "Not that I noticed," he replied.

"What about the staff – where were they? What happened to the guests, assuming there were any? Where did they all go to? What about casualties – was anyone hurt, killed even?"

"No idea," Alf retorted. "Really – there was no-one around when I got there. Place was deserted."

"So there's nothing else you can tell us then, is that right?" said Harry. Alf nodded and stepped towards Guido and the door. Jake made no move to stop him.

"I thought I was helping you, thought it was the least I could do," Alf complained to Guido, who remained unmoved and unmoving. "I thought you'd be pleased."

"We are, Alf, we are," said Jake behind him. "But you've done enough. We don't want you to get in trouble over this – best you should go now, keep your distance until we get this sorted, you know – maintain deniability, isn't that what they say? It's OK Guido, Alf's going home now. Thanks for your help, Alf – we'll see you next time we're down this way."

"What are you going to do about him?" Alf asked, torn between wanting to be involved and getting the hell out of the caravan.

"No idea, but we'll figure something out. Anyway, best you don't know. See you Alf, take care now."

Jake ushered the unresisting Alf to the door, and continued to watch him as he drove away. Only when the jeep had disappeared out of sight did he leave the doorway and join the others, already deep in their discussion about the new information, what it all meant, and what on earth they should do next.

With the clock against them, a hurried conference took place at which Jake laid out the alternatives. "We can dump him somewhere on our way, and forget about him. Of course, he's unconscious so it would be easier to do before he comes round, but then again..." he looked at Guido, "...the doc here is worried about the fact he hasn't come round yet, so if we dump him, we might also kill him.

"We could also turn him over to the police, or maybe the army – who it seems were probably looking for him. Or..."

"Or we could take him with us," said Harry, provoking further debate. There was no real agreement but each made clear that they found all other options unacceptable.

"OK," said Jake. "Since there seems to be no other choice, he stays with us for now. Guido, can you get home from here – I don't want to drive back through town?" Guido nodded, shook hands all round and left, after giving a few last instructions to Harry regarding the patient.

"Alina, you OK to go in the caravan, look after our man there?" Alina nodded and began to gather a few things for the journey. Cas started the bus and reversed it back towards the caravan, which they hooked on. All glanced apprehensively at the caravan from time to time, but the suspension seemed to be holding up.

"We'll be stopping in about three hours," said Billy as he helped Alina into the caravan. "Sure you'll be OK?" Alina looked grave, then laughed. "Of course. What you think, tough Polack girl gets beaten by big slob? Hah! Jelly in my hand, Billy; jelly in my hand."

"Helps when he's unconscious, don't it?" said Billy, closing the caravan door and boarding the bus as it pulled away. Alina sat down on some cushions and began to read, but the caravan was bouncing about too much over the rough ground. She turned round and pulled the curtain aside, catching a panoramic view of the fields and hedges running fluidly across the tidy hills as the caravan turned through the gate. A few moments later, it shook from side to side as the bus swerved around an estate car parked by the side of the road, and she lost her balance, falling backwards onto the prone passenger. As she moved back to the cushions she couldn't help but giggle at the soft landing.

"Hello."

Alina spun round and found herself staring into a pair of large blue eyes. Her charge was watching her. His face was impassive, nothing to read but the curiosity of the stare, which was open, wide-eyed and unblinking.

"Hey, you wake up. How you feeling?" she asked cautiously.

"I...where..." He looked round the caravan, noted it was moving. "Are we going somewhere?" There was a childish innocence to this that Alina found reassuring; she knew she needn't be afraid of this one. It was a strange question though; maybe he was not quite right, something in the head maybe? A rush of questions came to her, and she picked the most obvious.

"Who are you?" she said. Considering this, the man she already knew to be called Reuben seemed increasingly puzzled. After some time, he looked at her with a disarmingly placid expression.

"I'm sorry, but I don't seem to know."

Chapter 5:   Reuben's Red Route Rumble

The first stop was made near Cirencester as they plotted a careful loop around Bristol; at the confluence of several arterial motorways, it was one of the major surveillance hotspots in the South-West and a place best avoided. They kept forty miles eastwards of the city, travelling quiet minor roads and byways that effectively doubled their journey time but kept them away from self-powered cameras, patrols and choke-points. They were following the Red Route, a constantly changing network of rural businesses who sold or bartered red diesel – supplied preferentially to farmers, but that could only be used legally for agricultural purposes. Without the cheap black market fuel, the band probably couldn't have afforded to tour at all.

Cas pulled up at a popular night-time service stop where there were enough trucks and trailers to shield the bus from unwanted attention. As Billy opened the bus door, Alina came running up the side of the bus.

"He woke up," she told them breathlessly. "Come. See." Grabbing Billy's hand, she pulled him towards the caravan, the others following.

"Stay calm everybody, let's not put on a show out here," growled Jake bringing up the rear and relieved when they were all crowded together in the caravan. Alina had lit a storm lamp and in the flickering light the band stared at Reuben, who sat propped against the wall staring back. He was entirely swaddled in blankets and sleeping bags, with just his head and feet poking out.

Jake squatted down in front of him. "Hey man, how you doin'?" Reuben studied Jake carefully but didn't reply.

"He don't know who he is," said Alina. "Isn't that right Reuben?"

"She...Alina?...she asked me...asked me questions. I couldn't answer her."

"She does that to me all the time," said Harry. Then, to Alina: "What did you ask him?"

Alina actually blushed. She couldn't remember the last time her cheeks had burned like this and found her embarrassment baffling because she surely had nothing to be embarrassed about. "I ask him, I ask him normal things Harry, normal things. Not funny stuff...you know, what is name, where from, what he's doing on moor..."

"Did you ask him about the QR code?" Alina nodded.

"Did you tell him about the ID card, the name on it?" She nodded again.

"Did you tell him about us – tell him your name, my name? Did you tell him what happened, how we found him? I'll bet you even told him about Guido?" Alina was glaring at him now.

"Easy folks. It's not her fault Harry," said Jake. "No-one said anything different, did we? I'm just glad he's woken up, that's all, so let's all take a break. We haven't got much time, remember?"

"Whatever you do, don't tell him your name, Phil," warned Billy.

Tension dissipated by the laughter, Jake turned back to Reuben, who had watched the exchange with seeming incomprehension. "So, you know your name is Reuben. Is that right – is that your name? Does it sound familiar to you?" Reuben shook his head. "OK, well...how do you feel?"

Reuben thought for a moment, his body strangely still. "I think I'm all right," he said carefully. "Yes, I am. Where are my clothes?" He looked up past Jake and scanned the other faces. "Hello."

Outside of Shrewsbury they were caught in a routine traffic trap. The policeman took one look through the window and directed Harry into a lay-by where vehicles could be searched at leisure. Everybody woke up, if indeed they'd been sleeping at all: they were all on-edge. Harry parked the bus carefully and jumped down to the door. "Stay here. I'll sort this out," he said, and left the bus, walking quickly to head off the two policemen coming towards him. Jake watched as Harry produced papers, ID, smiled a great deal, pointed vaguely in different directions and then stood chatting amiably with one officer while the other went off to interrogate the computer in the patrol car. After a few minutes, he returned and spoke briefly to his partner, who nodded and dismissed Harry with a bored gesture. Harry returned to the bus, started the engine and pulled away, waved out into the sparse traffic without so much as a glance.

Jake came up beside Harry, leaning against a rail. "What was that all about?"

Harry kept his eyes on the road. "Nothing, usual stuff. Just routine."

"Yeah, but what did you say to them?" said Jake, with evident admiration. "You have some gift there, my boy, some gift I must say. How many times now have you pulled that off?"

Harry just grinned, looking straight ahead. Jake thought it remarkable the way Harry could get on with authority where Jake and the others only riled them. No matter how polite, how courteous, how self-effacing Jake was, policemen just wanted to bang him up the second they laid eyes on him. His lifestyle made him the enemy, not his nature or personality. There was something horridly inevitable about it.

Both men remained quiet for a while, staring out towards the future as it slipped beneath the wheels of the bus, turning it into the past. "Speaking of inevitability," said Jake, still staring ahead, "I had a real sense of that in the past twenty-four hours."

"Speaking of inevitability? Did I miss something?"

"I was talking to myself."

"OK."

"You know, from the moment you and Alf turned up with Reuben, it seems like we've been railroaded," said Jake. "What choices have we had, really? It feels like we had no option but to bring him with us, to get involved in something we don't understand. Did we ever have a choice?"

"We could have dumped him."

"Yeah, and you could have left him up on the moors, but you didn't, did you?"

Harry was silent for a while, reflecting on his own motives. "It's the Greek tragedy syndrome."

"What?"

"You know, the inevitable overtaking us no matter what we do. That's what makes it a tragedy – everyone does exactly what they should, what's logical, what appears to be the best thing, and yet it's clear from the start that every action takes us nearer to a place and time where something terrible will happen, must happen – a disaster with our name on it. And we know it, too. We can feel it, we know it's bad, but we keep on going just the same."

"You think there's a disaster waiting for us?"

"I don't know. How can we know that? Anyway, don't blame me. You started it, talking about inevitability and all that."

"I never said we were in some kind of Greek tragedy. That was your idea."

"I know – the slippery slope. Isn't that it? Maybe we are no more than puppets...in which case, the trick is to know who's pulling the strings."

"No free will then – just destiny or manipulation? I hate that."

"Maybe. Or perhaps it's the appearance of free will that makes the whole thing inevitable, fooling us into thinking we make choices when all we do is pick the best of the worst options. That's hardly free will, is it?"

"Well, it's all too fatalistic for me. I have to believe I can make my own choices, that there's more to it than just pride and punishment, fate and failure. It's all so fucking depressing; if the Greeks hadn't had their heads rammed so far up their own complexes, maybe they would have written a few comedies as well."

"They did, actually, but I'm not sure how funny they are now. Still, it is amazing to think how much of their knowledge, their discovery, remains true to this day. The cradle of civilisation and all that – philosophy, maths, literature, drama – they invented it all."

"And a fat lot of good it did them," said Jake. "Remember, they also invented hubris didn't they? I've been to Greece. I've seen Athens. The cradle of civilisation is just a pile of ruins."

"They didn't invent hubris, they just named it. Anyway, things change; it's what we call progress."

"Oh really? Like what?"

"Well, even in these straightened times, you can still enjoy a great view of the Acropolis over a latte at the Starbucks down the hill."

They made camp near Wilmslow. Everyone slept until midday, when Alina and Billy took a couple of bikes down from the rack and pedalled off towards town on the lookout for food and gossip. While Cas practiced in the bus, Phil, Harry and Jake opened up the rear wall of the caravan. Reuben was awake, still lying on the floor.

"Do you want to get out?" asked Jake.

Reuben nodded and started to lift himself. "Do you want some help?" said Phil, reaching in, but Reuben ignored him and ponderously hauled himself up. Leaning on the wall with one hand as support, he took several cautious steps down the caravan towards the opening, but Jake stopped him.

"Better put something on, my boy. It's chilly out here." Reuben looked thoughtful, then bent down to retrieve some blankets, causing Jake and Phil simultaneously to avert their eyes. A few moments later, he stepped carefully out of the tilting caravan.

"Hey, check out Nero in his fetching toga." Phil called out. Reuben had wrapped a blanket round his vast stomach and thrown a duvet over one shoulder. He stood straight, looking around him, took a few steps towards the bus, stopped and turned back: the effect was strangely regal.

"How are you feeling?" asked Harry, who had been studying the big man thoughtfully. "Do you remember anything about last night?"

Reuben shook his head apologetically. "I tried to remember, but there isn't anything there. I'm sorry."

"Don't be," said Phil. "That must be seriously weird."

"Is it? I don't feel weird."

"Don't you want to remember?" said Harry.

"I don't know. I feel like I ought to, but..." Reuben seemed oddly indifferent about his missing past.

"Maybe something bad happened," suggested Jake. "Maybe you blocked it out of your mind. You were naked up there on the moor when we found you, and people don't usually go running around up there in the dead of night in the middle of winter, not even with clothes on."

"Why have I got a QR code on my foot?" asked Reuben.

"We don't know," Harry replied. "Have you seen it?"

Reuben shook his head. "I can't. I tried last night but I'm so big I can't see my feet. I don't like it."

"Don't like what?"

"Being big like this. Why am I so fat?" For the first time, Reuben appeared animated, not out of anxiety or frustration so much as a powerful and driving curiosity. "Why would someone put a code on my foot? How did I get so big? You don't have codes on your feet, do you?"

Jake shook his head. "No, we don't. But you have no idea why you do?"

"No idea," Reuben repeated blankly. Jake looked to Harry, perched on the open end of the caravan floor. "Thing is Reuben, we have no idea what to do with you," said Harry. "You seem to be OK, but if you can't remember anything about where you live, who you are...well, how can we get you home? How can we help you?"

"I really don't know. Everyone keeps asking me if I remember, and I know it's important, but I just...I'm just sorry. The only thing I remember is waking up in the caravan."

"OK, so you don't remember anything right now," said Harry. "Maybe it'll come back to you in time. Tell me, do you recognise this at all?" He handed the identity card to Reuben, who studied it carefully. "Is that me?" he asked.

"Looks a lot like you, don't you think?" said Jake. Reuben looked doubtful. "This is how you know my name?" Jake nodded.

"And you found it near where I fell?"

"Do you remember falling?" asked Harry.

"No, only what Alina told me when I woke up. Also, I have a lump on the back of my head." He reached back gingerly to confirm it was still there, and winced when his fingers found it.

"All right," said Harry. "Let's see what else you know, but don't *know* you know. You know how to talk, so your mind isn't entirely blank. You must have learned other things too, but right now you don't remember them."

"What kind of things?" demanded Jake suspiciously.

"I don't know, skills maybe? Basic stuff – reading, writing. It's a starting point."

"That's right," Phil chipped in. "If he learned to play the piano or something, he might still remember how to do it if he sat at a piano again." Harry was rummaging around in the caravan, emerging with a sheet of paper and a pencil which he gave to Reuben. "Write your name, Reuben. Here, on this bit of paper."

Reuben took the paper and rested it on the floor of the caravan. He bent over and wrote his name in capital letters, even and well-shaped.

"Right, you're literate then." Harry took the piece of paper from him. "Give me the pencil a second." He wrote a column of numbers, and handed it back to Reuben. "Can you add them up?"

"Christ," said Phil. "You setting him an exam or what?"

"Three hundred and seventy four thousand, two hundred and twenty six," said Reuben. He had barely looked at the figures.

"Give me that," demanded Jake, writing down the number Reuben had given, then laboriously adding the column of numbers himself with the aid of little carry-forward figures at the bottom. "He's right," he announced after a couple of attempts. "You did that in your head?"

Harry thought for a moment. "Can you draw? Try drawing something." Reuben obediently took that sheet back from Jake, turned it over, looked briefly around the camp and then set to work. Moments later, he handed the sheet to Harry, who whistled softly. "Take a look at this Jake."

Phil moved so he could look over Jake's shoulder, but didn't understand the significance of the lines and squiggles Reuben had drawn. "What is it?" he whispered to Jake, but it was Harry who replied. "It's a map. A map of this camp."

"Oh, right," said Phil, unimpressed. *He* could have drawn that.

Harry had a different reaction, and one he kept to himself; he noted the dotted lines representing the fences, how a gap had been left where the fence was down, the shading where a bank had formed along one boundary of the open space they occupied, the course of a barely visible ditch that ran beside a thin hedge, the precise positioning of the bus and the caravan, both oriented correctly relative to the gate and the track beyond. Reuben had evidently taken all this in during the short time he'd been standing there, and drawn it entirely from memory without looking up once.

Jake was amused but otherwise unenlightened. "Maybe he was a map-maker," he joked with Harry, who continued to stare at the map. There was something about it, or the way it had been drawn, that was familiar to him. "It's cold out here. Let's get back in the caravan."

They made their final camp in a clearing surrounded by woodland about ten miles from Penrith, in the shadow of a rusted wind turbine that no longer turned. Once a caravan site, the old bore hole still worked once power was restored to the pump and filters, so the most essential requirement – water – at least was assured. The road crew – who had set off from the Devon camp a day earlier – came over to meet them, and after the usual exchange of gruff and intemperate greetings that were part of their tradition, they were introduced to their visitor and told enough to satisfy their immediate curiosity, specifically about the QR code. Vicky Leathren, long term partner of sound man Nicky Dicky and the nearest thing they had to a mother figure, was quick to point out that the immediate concern was to find some outsize clothing, and disappeared into the truck. While the others caught up with recent events, she found a large sack from which she cut two holes at opposite corners, and this served as a kind of smock which at least covered the top half of the huge man. The lower extremities were more problematic until Phil remembered a picture he'd seen of Fijian men wearing a wraparound skirt rather like a kilt. With a number of large safety pins and considerable ribald comments from all concerned about where they should and should not be stuck, Reuben - who accepted the attention with an air of passive indifference – was eventually wrapped in their biggest blanket, one whose size was sufficient at least to conform to a general notion of decency.

The crew of four was led by Nicky Dicky (real name Nick Richardson), an electrical engineer in his early forties who mixed the front of house sound, maintained their equipment and tried to keep up with Vicky's demands that he pay sufficient attention to the education of their eight year old son Jimi. The other three roadies were called Sam, Sham and Pharaoh: No-one knew their real names, or bothered to remember them. When the band formed, the first crew had been dubbed with these nicknames; in keeping with the traditions by which travelling groups maintain the fabric of their unity, replacement crew members over the years were allocated the same names along with the job title. Their immediate reaction on meeting Reuben was one of glee – they were always short-handed, especially with the grunt work of heaving the many flight cases around, and they quickly realised a big man with a strong back could be pressed into service.

By the time Vicky and Billy had finished covering a decent proportion of his vast bulk, Reuben had been conscripted, pending only a hurriedly arranged intelligence test demonstrating the ability to lift something heavy and put it down where he was told. While the band unpacked the spare generator, connected the bore hole pump and set up a chemical toilet they had recently borrowed from a lay-by, Reuben was heaving massive steel-reinforced cases alongside the grunting crew members as they unpacked and checked the gear and the miles of cable they carried to cater for any contingency.

As the crew worked, Harry studied their visitor; he appeared willing and compliant, doing whatever they asked without comment or complaint, even when the crew indulged their aberrant sense of fun by having him pull down a large container from the truck and immediately making him put it straight back in exactly the same place. Harry was quite struck by the sight of Reuben standing with a speaker cabinet held up to his chest, awaiting instructions as to its destination. No-one else could have lifted the cabinet on his own, but Reuben stood nonchalantly holding the big box as if he was waiting in a supermarket checkout line with a bag of groceries. But the thing that most struck Harry was that Reuben was smiling, something nobody had seen him do up until now. He was clearly enjoying himself.

For the most part, Reuben seemed childlike and innocent. It took everyone a while to realise that while they were consumed with curiosity about their guest, Reuben was not consumed by an equivalent interest in himself. They were sitting in the bus drinking hot mugs of tea in cramped conditions; normally they would clear the whole lower deck once a permanent camp had been drawn up, moving their daytime detritus to the caravan, where Billy and Cas would also sleep.

"I feel bad," said Vicky, picking over the remains of her supper. "We can't just leave him like that, on his own out there. It doesn't seem right."

"He's OK," said Cas, guitar in hand as usual. "He doesn't seem to mind."

"I know, but it just doesn't seem right."

"Thing is Vicky, he can't get through the door, so there's no way he can come in here with us, is there?" said Jake. "We can't all sit in the caravan just to keep him company. We can't all *get* in the caravan, come to that."

"I know that Jake. It's just...well, it's like we're treating him as an outsider."

"He *is* an outsider," called Phil from the back of the bus where he was paradiddling on the back of a seat, waiting to see how long the others would put up with the stealthy but penetrating tap of drumsticks on vinyl.

Vicky glared at Phil. "I don't know what we are going to do with him, where all this is going, but if he's going to stay with us he deserves to be treated like a human being, not a damn pet locked in a caravan."

"We haven't locked him in, Vicky," said Jake patiently. Vicky was not someone you chose to wind up unless you had suicidal tendencies. "He's not a prisoner, is he? We should be careful though, and I don't think it's a good idea to get too fond of him either."

"He seems so...well, innocent."

Phil snorted. "Ah, how sweet. Maybe you should adopt him."

"Mock me Phil, but remember this: you have to sleep sometime..." said Vicky.

"Yeah, not with you though," said Phil, but very quietly.

"I always assumed that if someone lost his memory, he'd spend all his time trying to get it back," Jake told Harry. "Reuben doesn't seem to feel like that."

"I know what you mean," Harry agreed. "I wonder if it's because we remember our past, so we know what we'd be missing if we lost it. It seems to me that Reuben doesn't miss his past because he has no idea what he's lost."

"No *sense* of loss either." A pungent, acrid smell wafted down the bus. As one, they all turned to Nicky and shouted: "Soldering Iron!"

"Bollocks!" swore Nicky, quickly retrieving the soldering iron from the edge of the table on which he was working. Placing the hot tool back in its curly wire stand, he brushed ineffectively at the new burn marks in the plastic as if he could rub them out, evidence of previous failed attempts notwithstanding.

"It does seem strange," continued Vicky. "He doesn't ask any questions. You'd think he would want to find out who he was, where he was from – that kind of thing – but he doesn't seem to care much. Like you say Jake, he doesn't seem to miss his memories, doesn't seem bothered about getting them back either."

"Unless, of course...?" Harry left the question hanging.

Jake shook his head. "I don't think so. I've wondered the same thing – if he's faking it. We haven't been *that* tough on him, no bloody interrogation for Christ's sake, so I guess it shouldn't be too hard to keep up the act if his memory came back – or if he never lost it in the first place. But you know what? I only think like this right up to the minute I see him, and then I *know*, absolutely know for sure, that he doesn't have a clue. He's a blank slate – you only have to look at his face to know there's nothing written there, no life, no guilt, no happiness, no past, no fear or threat or any damn thing at all. Nothing. He hasn't got a fucking clue my friends, not a God-damn clue."

"You forgot love Jake – in your list, said Vicky. "No love. Supposing he's lost someone, loved someone but doesn't remember? That would be terrible – he might have kids, a wife, a home...it just seems so...unnatural."

"Like everything else about him is natural, right?" said Harry. "His weight, the QR code, running around on the moor stark bloody naked. What about the ID card? What's *that* about?"

What's *love* about? wondered Phil.

Chapter 6:   Vikings

The third day in camp was also the day of the first gig, and the well-oiled machinery of their profession soon transformed the agreeably aimless lifestyle that preceded it into something more ordered. Gear was checked for the last time, inventoried and stowed in the reverse order to which it would be required. Mid-morning, Harry, Cas and Sam, their rigger and crew boss, were standing by the bus, watching Reuben lift the last of the cases into the truck on his own. Sham and Pharaoh – lighting and backline respectively – were standing with their hands in their pockets watching Reuben work.

"Is he coming with us?" said Sam hopefully. His workload would be considerably reduced if he could get the big man to do most of the shifting for him, and Reuben was bloody keen – do anything you asked, no hesitation, no questions. It was wonderful.

"Sorry Sam, he can't," Harry replied. "For one thing, I think he's making you guys a bit lazy."

Sam looked over at his crew-mates. "They're just supervising, you know, teaching Rube the ropes."

"Rube, is it?" said Cas, dubious. "Anyway, we couldn't get him in the cab of the truck unless the band stays here, which might make doing gigs a bit tricky. Unless you don't need us anymore – you boys got a new act, been rehearsing on the quiet maybe?"

Sam laughed. It was common in the touring world that a crew would form its own little outfit, taking advantage of the dead time between setup and sound check to bash out something once the gear was set up, an act known colloquially as "testing." The band condoned this modest encroachment on their territory, on condition that the instruments didn't sustain any damage and that the real band was never, *ever* subjected to the result: while The Vikings did indeed have their own shadow band, the crew were universally recognised as the most discordant, inept, rhythm-bereft outfit to ever steal a few moments of their employer's indulgence. In blind panic, one promoter had wanted to cancel a gig after hearing what he mistook to be a sound check by the band he had booked, so knowingly disturbing was the racket the crew made and the aggression with which they made it.

After the crew departed, the band had a few hours to themselves before the sound check. Alina and Reuben were playing with Jimi; that is, Reuben was lying on his side, and Jimi was bouncing himself repeatedly off Reuben's enormous soft tummy. Using the uncomplaining man as a horizontal trampoline, he rebounded each time into Alina's waiting arms and shrieked with pleasure as she pushed him back for another go.

Vicky had been apprehensive about contact between her son and the stranger, but Jimi had taken to Reuben very quickly and was soon following him around when not required elsewhere. For her part, Vicky saw that Reuben was careful and protective of the boy, making sure he could see him whenever heavy equipment was being manhandled. They asked each other no questions and Vicky decided that this was why they were getting on so well – no demands, little conversation, a mutual acceptance of each other without the need for anything more. Children live in a continuous present, the past and the future yet to invade the immediacy of their conscious world, and it seemed to her that Reuben's life must be very similar; no burden of guilt, no thought of a future. She said as much to Cas, who was starting his gig-day warm-up exercises.

"I know what you mean about the past, but I don't agree he has no future," he said, fingers running across the so-familiar scales guided by muscle memory alone.

"I didn't say he had no future, just that he couldn't think about it."

"OK," conceded Cas. "You know, in one way, I actually envy him." Vicky looked surprised. "We – all of us – have baggage. Sure, I've done some good things in the past, even some great things, but they aren't what I remember most, what I think about much. Mainly, I find myself going back over things I did that I'm ashamed of, mistakes I made, things I did badly or wrong, the times I hurt people...you know, the things we regret and would undo if only we could. Nobody wants to undo the good things. It's the memories of the things we'd do differently if we only had the chance – aren't they the things that haunt us, all of us?" He looked over at Reuben and the gleeful bouncing child. "In some people, the past is so powerful it overcomes the present, and they live in some nightmare where everything they do is discoloured by what they have done before, or had done to them.

"Reuben has none of those things, suffers from none of that. It really doesn't matter what he was, who he was, what he did. Sure, he's lost something – some kind of knowledge of how he got here, the course of his life, maybe the authority of his experience – but he's also gained the freedom not to feel bad about it, be driven by it. You can't feel guilty about something you don't remember doing any more than you can apologise for it, know what I mean? You can't miss what you never had, or never knew you had."

Vicky nodded. "What about his future, though? How can he have one without knowing what he wants, or even what he likes. What compass can he use to decide which course to follow?"

"Well, he can't continue on a path he doesn't remember, so you're right on that score. You could also say he has more freedom about his future than we do, because he can't be driven towards a future chosen simply to assuage his guilt, to wash clean some past sins in search of forgiveness or as an act of contrition, driven to succeed with something he's failed at in the past. What he *can* do – maybe the only choice he has – is to take the course that appears in front of him. How spontaneous a life would that be, Vicky? Would that be such a terrible thing – to accept what comes, accept what is given and get on with it?"

"For me it would," said Vicky. "It's too vague, too purposeless, like drifting in a boat never knowing where to steer. I have my son, my daft husband and his bloody soldering iron; I have their future to consider and work for and support. And my own, of course – don't get me wrong: you know I'm not a martyr to my family, but my sense of purpose comes from them, from loving them and caring for them. That's the choice I made, not a burden I accidentally picked up along with my knickers after a hot night in the back of the truck with Nick eight years ago. But what I get out of it is this: I know who I am and why my life is the way it is. I don't have many regrets Cas, and I don't think I've made many sacrifices either. What I have now suits me fine. I like to know there's a continuity, a safety in my future – my family's future – that only fate can interfere with. The world is uncertain, but I have my thread of certainty to follow and I'm glad of it, even if you philosophy types would say it's an illusion. It's my illusion and I'm sticking to it, so there."

She stuck her tongue out at him, and they both laughed. Cas was the accredited philosopher of the band and they all took the piss from time to time, just to make sure he didn't get carried away with the metaphysics and convince himself that he no longer needed to practice his guitar-playing: his constantly shifting beliefs already appeared to entail washing himself less frequently than he used to, and this was taking philosophy as far as the band were prepared to allow.

At the sound check, it seemed to Jake that everyone was a bit subdued. He felt a bit anxious himself, his thoughts darting back to the camp every few minutes. He was about to ask the others if they felt the same when Nick took him aside.

"Reuben's back at the camp then?" he asked. "I thought he'd come with you." The band always cycled to the sound check unless the gig was too far away, in which case they'd travel in with the crew earlier in the day. (The exception was when they could park the bus at the gig itself, but this was infrequent). After the gig they would all travel together back to the campsite, their bikes packed in back with the stage equipment.

"On a fucking bicycle?" said Jake, quietly incredulous. "Of course he's back at the camp. Vicky's looking after him, and Jimi of course. They're staying in the caravan with him until we get back."

"Yes, but who's looking after her? Who's looking after my son? What have you got us mixed up in here, Jake?"

"Christ, you've seen him Nick. He's gentle as a lamb."

"That's right, a ridiculously strong lamb with a fucking QR code on his foot and a head for figures. This is no ordinary bloke,

Jake. His size alone should tell you that. And what about the people looking for him?"

Jake was annoyed. The sound man knew very well where this was leading, where it had to lead, and it seemed pointless to raise the issue right now.

"Let's cut to the chase then, Nick," he said, keeping his voice level with some effort. "He may be a fugitive – from what we have no idea – but right now we have a gig to play and we should get on with the job. If you had concerns you should have raised them back at the camp. I wasn't going to risk bringing him to town because you can hardly miss the bloke, hardly expect him to stay unnoticed and out of the way, can you? So don't fuck around Nick. You've worked all this out already and you know the score as well as I do. You're just giving me a hard time now because you weren't consulted before we brought him along. You weren't there, right? And I don't need your fucking permission either. Anyway, there's nothing we can do right now, so let's do the gig and tomorrow we'll talk about what to do next, where we go from here, OK?"

"You sure she'll be OK...and Jimi...?" said Nick. His concern was clearly genuine, and Jake felt a bit guilty about the way he'd laid in to his friend. "Yeah," he replied kindly. "They'll be fine. Trust me: I know my punter, my boy, and he's a good 'un. Take my word for it."

"Punter? You don't even know if he likes the band. He hasn't seen us play yet." Walking away, Jake roared with laughter.

"How could he not like us? We're the fucking Vikings!" he shouted over his shoulder, raising a clenched fist to the players on stage.

"THE FUCKING VIKINGS!" they shouted back enthusiastically, raising defiant fists high. After that, things went well.

Or well enough. It seemed to Jake that all the songs were played slightly faster than usual. The gear appeared to get packed in record time, to judge by the number of pints he'd managed to drink before Nick announced they were ready to leave. No-one moaned, no-one wanted one more pint, even Cas didn't have yet one more female with whom to conduct a discrete negotiation. Harry had run the show with his usual military precision and had extracted the fee in cash just before the band went on stage, the only method of payment Harry would countenance. ("No point in arguing the toss with a promoter after we've done the gig – if they refuse to pay or come up short, we can't take the music back, can we?") As they drove back to camp, Nick sat at the front of the bus, leaning forward in an anticipatory way that made everyone else feel nervous.

Arriving at the camp, Jake strode quickly to the caravan, followed closely by Nick. He opened the door and pulled himself in. Reuben was reading, sitting propped up against one wall. Both Vicky and Jimi were asleep, lying on the cushions. The abrupt entrance woke Vicky up; she rubbed her eyes and smiled at her husband, wondering why he looked quite so relieved. "How was the gig?" she asked, looking over to Jimi. "Was there trouble? We fell asleep. I'm sorry about that Reuben. We weren't much company for you, were we?"

Reuben smiled. "Yes you were, Vicky. It was nice to watch you and Jimi, so peaceful when you are asleep. It was so quiet, I just sat here and read my book. I enjoyed your company, really."

Vicky returned his shy smile, gathered up the sleeping boy and bade them good night, Nick following close behind. The others had gathered around the caravan door expectantly. Seeing the family all safe and well burst the bubble of their anxiety and they too turned to their respective quarters. All except Harry, who came in to the caravan and sat down beside Jake on the floor opposite Reuben. He wanted to explore other avenues, to see if he could jog Reuben's memory, although right now he didn't know exactly how he might go about it. Before he could open the conversation, Reuben spoke.

"Harry, Jake – there is something I must tell you. I didn't say anything in front of Vicky because...well, I don't know why really. It just didn't seem right." He paused, putting his book down carefully. "I understand a little how you must feel. I can't tell you anything that can help you, and yet I have realised that you are all being very kind to me. I don't know why, really – you don't know me any more than I seem to know myself. But I want you to know that I am grateful. I like being with you, and I'm glad it was you that found me.

"But I feel afraid. I don't know why. I can't think of anything that I should be afraid of – something bad that might happen to me, I don't know...really, this is so hard to explain. I just feel like there's something coming, something..." Reuben was clearly distraught. Neither Jake nor Harry had seen him this animated. At the same time, he looked more vulnerable than ever. To the surprise of both men, he looked up and grinned.

"So I'm afraid! Hey, call the police, alert the media..." he said, and waited. Jake and Harry realised at the same moment that Reuben had made a joke, and all three laughed all the more after the delayed reaction. It was getting hard not to warm to their outlandish visitor.

"But that isn't what I have to tell you," said Reuben, serious once more. "It is this: I know that there are other people out there who know about me, and so do you. I think they must be looking for me, because I have this QR code on my foot. For whatever reason, this makes me special to them. They were looking for me the night you found me, weren't they? I think they are looking for me now, and I also think this could get you in trouble. If I have done something bad, something that brings trouble to me, it will also bring trouble to you. And I think it's already here."

"What?" Jake exclaimed, clearly alarmed, but before he could continue, Harry laid a restraining hand on his shoulder. "Go on, Reuben. What happened?"

"It was still light when Vicky and Jimi came in. They brought some food, and we ate it. It was funny, really; Vicky said how nice it was we could have a chat. A quiet evening in, she called it. Jimi thought so too, wanted to talk about all kinds of things. They both lay down on the cushions and fell asleep. We never talked about anything at all, so it really was a "quiet evening." But you know what was nice? I liked it that they could fall asleep with me sitting there. I felt they were my friends, that they trusted me, and it made me feel, well – it made me feel like I belonged here. It also made me feel sad; it's the first time I wanted to know about my past, really wanted to know because it hurt not to know. I wanted to know if I had friends, other friends, because if I did I would want to remember them. I don't know if I have any friends, if I ever had any."

"You have some now, Reuben," said Jake, laying a comforting hand on the big man's arm.

Harry somehow doubted that Reuben had forgotten any friends. Some part of him knew that this man had never had friends, or a normal life. "You said you think the threat to you, the thing you are afraid of, it's here? You said "...I think it's already here" – isn't that what you said?"

"Yes, I'm sorry – I got distracted trying to explain how I feel. Let me complete my report: after they fell asleep, I sat here for a while as the light faded. Just before I lit the lamp, I looked out of the window and saw a man two-hundred and twenty metres away in some bushes. He just crouched there for a while, so I watched him. After about thirty minutes he backed off, staying crouched until I couldn't see him anymore. I don't know how long he'd already been there before I first saw him, of course."

"Any idea who he was?" asked Harry, clutching at straws. "Could you see what he looked like, describe him to us?"

Reuben shook his head. "Did he come back?" asked Jake.

"No," said Reuben. "I checked several times." Everyone remained quiet for a few minutes, digesting the news. Harry was the first to speak.

"I think we should keep our heads down and not overreact. It could have been a local, some busybody who doesn't like travellers, even a hunter scouting around...there are any number of explanations. I also think we should all keep an eye out for people hanging around out here. It's isolated enough that anyone loitering should be easy enough to spot. I'll mention it quietly to the others, but let's play it down, make it about the local council maybe, rather than about you Reuben. We'll just keep this between us right now. How does that sound?"

"It's a good strategic assessment," said Reuben. They agreed at that point to call it a night, and as Jake and Harry closed the door behind them, the light went out in the caravan. They walked over to the bus in silence. Harry was reflecting on language, the way it reveals background through a turn of phrase like "let me complete my report" and "a good strategic assessment." Harry was familiar with this type of language, but

65

what he really wanted to know was how Reuben came to share that knowledge.

Chapter 7:   Burn Rate

Another two gigs had been played before the transformation was noticed. Vicky was the first to comment, observing that the sack shirt she made for Reuben was hanging loose where before it was stretched tight. (There had been some concern that if he had an appetite equivalent to his frame, Reuben would eat them out of bus and caravan, but his demand for food and drink was normal, although he did seem to require a great deal of water). One night the band returned to camp rather drunk, and in possession of a plastic container holding a quantity of the distillate of unnamed vegetable matter that got them that way. Billy and Phil decided to get Reuben drunk, but the next morning all they had for their efforts were severe headaches, queasy guts, an empty container and a vague recollection that the big man had been quite unaffected by the copious amounts of alcohol they had seen him drink.

Indeed, much to Billy and Phil's irritation, Reuben appeared to be in fine fettle, suffering no ill-effects after their collective indulgence. Crouched at the back of the truck, he was listening attentively to Nick's exposition on the arcane mysteries of sound system design, aided by wiring diagrams and acoustic dispersion patterns drawn on the back of old lyric sheets. Jimi sat beside his father, trying to look interested while secretly hoping that his giant friend would soon lose interest so they could go and play in the woods, but after a while his boredom got the better of him and he went off in search of small animals he could terrify in the undergrowth. He was under strict instructions not to wander out of earshot of the camp, but like all young boys he found the exact dimensions of this prohibition unclear, and therefore somewhat elastic.

The woods were quiet, the soft carpet of leaves muffling his footfall, making him feel like a commando on patrol. He moved silently from tree to tree, using all available cover to shield him from the enemy positions. He was going to sneak up on them, burst into their fort and mow them down with his massive 20mm chain-driven multi-barrel machine gun – a length of hazel with a convenient notch around a stubby knot that fitted his small hand exactly the way he thought a gun should – but just as he made ready for the final assault a pheasant burst out of the bramble a few feet away with an explosive protest which made Jimi jump. He recovered his wits sufficiently to bring up the stick to his shoulder and blow the pheasant away in a hail of hot lead, annoyed with himself for breaking cover and humiliated that he'd been flushed out by a bird. He knew about pheasants, because last year Harry had been his friend and they had walked in the woods together while Harry, who knew a lot about things, told him the name of the birds they saw and which mushrooms were edible and how to recognise a badger toilet and fox droppings. Once, they saw deer tracks, and Jimi had seen them several times since, proud he could recognise the little cloven marks on his own. And on one occasion, Harry had shown the boy how to flush quarry from the undergrowth, where to look in expectation, how to follow the quarry with a gun as they burst from cover, how to lead them with the barrel and not to close one eye but aim with both eyes open, and they would pretend to shoot the birds they flushed with sticks standing in for the shotguns Harry said he owned. Harry was nice enough, but most of the time he was serious and quiet, and didn't like it when Jimi kept talking. He knew a lot of stuff, and Jimi loved to watch him build little traps to catch pheasants and rabbits, or make pretty lures to hook fish from a stream. He was less keen when Harry made him pull the feathers out of game or made him clean out the carcass and Jimi refused outright to eat the game his mother cooked as a treat, although he did like the fish once the head had been cut off; one cold dead eye staring up off the plate was just too weird and scary. Jimi liked Harry fine, but Reuben was the same as Jimi, not something different and grown up, just bigger. They were real friends, where Harry was just another grown-up looking after him. Not that he needed looking after.

Jimi came to a small brook which he negotiated carefully; his mother always went mad if he got wet, so he was careful to keep his feet clear of the water as he stepped from one shallow bank to the other. There were strange, bulbous mushrooms growing in the bank, but he remembered they could be poisonous and was content to beat them into fleshy shards with his stick as he sat atop the bank. The water laughed and played for him, dashing in and out of the weak sunshine, glittering between the shadows of overhanging branches. He picked a stone out of the water. It was smooth but very cold, and he dropped it back in with a splash that covered his shoes despite all his caution. They would dry out before he got back.

He liked being in the woods with his new friend, because Reuben didn't treat him like a child. They talked about stuff, real stuff, and Reuben never laughed at him the way the other adults did when he said something they all thought was funny. Sometimes Reuben would scoop the boy up and settle him across his massive shoulders, which Jimi loved because it was like he was sitting on top of a tank, a fearsome walking bulldozing death-machine that he could guide through all the bushes and bramble that he couldn't traverse on foot. He would pull Reuben's ears to guide him – not too hard of course – left, go here, right a bit, up this path, straight through those bushes, and his willing human Humvee would blunder around while Jimi scanned the horizon from his vantage point seeking out any signs of the enemy. Sometime, an overhanging branch would advance towards him and his tank would become mischievously unresponsive, so Jimi would reach out and grab the overhang, sliding off the big man's shoulders to swing free before dropping to the ground, dash after his runaway steed and remount it, bringing it back under control.

And Reuben never told him off or got angry with him, like when he kicked a stone that hit Reuben in the head and made a cut. Frightened by the blood, Jimi stood petrified but his friend just laughed, wiped a little smear of blood from his face and dabbed it on the middle of Jimi's forehead. "There," said Reuben, "first blood to you, NinjaJim." Jimi loved the nickname and Reuben used it only when no-one else could hear. It was another thing that he liked about Reuben, why he wasn't just another stupid adult – he knew what a secret name was and why it was powerful only so long as you didn't share it with anyone else. What Jimi really wanted was to find a secret name for his friend, but so far he hadn't come up with anything nearly as good as NinjaJim. For his new comrade, Jimi wouldn't settle for anything less.

There were still plenty of berries on the bramble, and Jimi was feeling a little peckish. He started to collect the fruit and eat it as he went along, wandering between close-grown ash and clumps of hazel down a slope into a small clearing. A mighty tree once stood in the centre, but now all that remained was a wide stump cut close to the ground. He jumped up and surveyed the clearing from the stump, from where he noticed a strange looking metal shape half-hidden in the grass a foot or two away. It was curved and had big teeth that reminded him of the enormous log saw in the truck that took two men to work it, one at each end. Curious, he jumped down beside his find, heard a click, and felt a terrible and savage pain in his leg. As his lungs forcibly expelled every ounce of breath from his young body, Jimi screamed once and passed out.

"...so we use balanced cable instead. That way, we can make the microphone leads pretty much as long as we like without picking up interference, although you do get signal loss the longer the cable..."

"Uh huh. More resistance?"

"Yes, exactly. So, anyway – that's what the snake is for, it connects the stage boxes where the mikes are plugged in on stage to the mixing console, which obviously you want down the back of the hall and preferably in the centre. The gigs I hate most are where I'm off to one side. How on earth can you mix the sound for the whole audience when you listen to such a distorted version of it, all one sided like that?"

Nick and Reuben were poring over their drawings, and they had also unpacked several cases so that Nick could demonstrate the way things fitted together, how so many components were wired up in complex and variable schemes night after night.

"I'd like to see how this all works," said Reuben. "Do you think I could come to a gig one day? I'd really like..." He stopped dead and jumped to his feet, standing bolt upright and very still.

"*Jimi!*"

"Hey, what the..." shouted Nick after him, because Reuben was running off, compelling Nick to follow. "What about Jimi?" he shouted at the retreating figure.

Over by the bus, Harry and Sam were examining a fuel pump. When Nick started shouting, they looked up and what he saw made Harry swear.

"Fuck. There he goes again. That's what I saw that night, exactly it, only this time he's got clothes on, thank God."

Reuben was already at the edge of the camp, at the tree-line and accelerating when Harry joined Nick in pursuit. They could barely see the big man, although they could hear him crashing through the undergrowth. Harry couldn't tell if he was having a déjà-vu moment or simply that these events were eerily familiar. The crashing stopped. Harry and Nick jumped across a small brook and were wondering which way to go when Reuben called out off to their left. They sprinted down into the clearing and stopped dead. Reuben was kneeling by the unconscious boy, all three horrified to see Jimi's leg skewered between the rusting jaws of an ancient trap.

"What should we do?" asked Reuben. He appeared near to tears, pleading: "I don't know what to do."

"We need to release the trap," said Harry. We'll need a metal bar or something to get the jaws open. I'll go back...," but before he could complete the sentence, Reuben had grasped the jaws of the trap in each hand and forced them away from the boy's leg so violently he snapped one jaw clean off. Before the stunned Nick could move to help his son, Reuben had cradled Jimi in his arms and was off again, running back to the camp even faster than he left it. Nick and Harry set off in pursuit, stopping only to pick up Reuben's blanket, which they found draped over a low-hanging branch. By the time the others caught up, Reuben had reached the camp, injured boy in his arms and nether regions flapping in the wind, found a shocked Vicky and handed the boy to her. She was cleaning the cuts with a swab as Harry ran up and handed back the blanket. Reuben had no idea he'd lost it.

Jimi was conscious. Tears were streaming down his face as his mother cleaned, dried and applied various disinfectants, all of which stung like hell.

"Oh God," whispered Nick as he knelt by his son. "How bad it is?"

"He's OK," said Vicky. "It's not as bad as it looks, lots of blood but superficial." They told her about the trap. "We'll have to take him to town to get a tetanus shot in that case," she said, her voice unsteady as she dabbed away.

"It was old," said Harry, "and there was a rock in the jaws that stopped it from snapping completely shut. That's why there isn't much damage, I suspect. A trap like that would take your leg off otherwise. Jimi was bloody lucky."

"Lucky?" said Vicky, getting to her feet. "You call this lucky?" Her hands were shaking as she held them out; they were covered in blood, in stark contrast to her chalk-white face.

"Hon, we *were* lucky. Jimi was lucky," Nick reassured his wife, gently taking her hands and wiping some of the blood off carefully with a towel. "If it wasn't for Reuben, we'd never had known, and maybe we wouldn't have found him for hours." He looked over to Reuben. "How did you know?"

Reuben looked puzzled. "I heard him scream. You didn't hear it?"

"Well, I was talking to you, I think. Or were you talking to me – I can't remember? I just know that one minute we were talking, the next you're off like a flash. Boy, you can sure shift when you want to, I mean...you know, for a man your size..." Nick tailed off. He felt profoundly grateful to Reuben and now it seemed he was dangerously close to insulting the man who had saved his son.

Jake had been standing off to one side, listening as the tale gradually came clear to him. "Did anyone else hear the boy scream?" he asked. There was a general shaking of heads: only Reuben, it seemed.

"Well, you have fine hearing my boy, and I wouldn't want to race you to the bar any time soon, that's for sure. You'd get my pint every time. But seriously..." he scanned the faces around him, "...we owe you our thanks – all of us." He offered his hand and Reuben took it, followed quickly by the grateful Nick. One by one, the others shook his hand in turn and quietly thanked him. Phil kept his voice gruff in case his manhood became threatened, muttering "Top man," but keeping his eyes on the clasped hands. Alina reached up and kissed Reuben on the cheek, delighted to see that it made him blush. Sham and Pharaoh simply patted him on the back and went back to the troublesome fuel pump. "Yeah, good effort Rube, good effort," said Sam as he went after the other roadies; the pump was really bugging him. Vicky was last; she threw her arms round Reuben's neck and literally hung there with her feet off the ground. Tears were streaming down her face. "Thank you, Reuben. You are a wonderful friend. I'm so glad you're with us. Thank you so much...thank you..." She tailed off and pulled away, brushing at her wet face with one sleeve as she turned back to her son.

"What about me?" complained Jimi from where he was lying. Everyone was completely ignoring him. *He* was the one who had nearly died in the cunning trap the enemy had set for him, not Reuben.

"Shut up before I kill you myself," his mother retorted, sniffing indignantly as she set to work.

Chapter 8:   Extra Dimensions

By the end of the second week, it was clear that the weight was falling off Reuben at a startling rate. Vicky had taken a renewed interest in his welfare of late and insisted on measuring his waist every couple of days. According to her measurements, he was losing an inch a day, particularly since he'd started exercising.

"It was after he ran to find Jimi," she explained to Harry one morning as they watched Reuben trying to do push-ups; he could manage the weight, but his arms were not long enough to lift his stomach clear of the floor. "He told me he liked running, but it was the first time he'd tried it since...you know. There's been no stopping him since, and it's certainly helping him get the weight down."

"I went jogging with him yesterday," mused Harry. Since the accident, Reuben had taken to jogging five miles around the outer perimeter of the woodlands that surrounded the camp, a run he was now taking three times a day. "It wasn't so much I couldn't keep up, but the pace he set just killed me after a couple of miles. OK, I couldn't keep up then. Shit – he wasn't even breathing heavily, and carrying all that weight too."

"He has a tough time with the callisthenics though," said Vicky.

"Not for much longer if he keeps up this weight loss," said Harry. "You know, I try to take him as he is, try to get to know him, but I can't get over the weird aspects. He makes me wonder, not so much about him – it's not I don't trust him – but he represents the kind of mystery I don't like."

"Rather than the mysteries you do like?"

"Some things are pleasant mysteries, Vicky – women, for example." Vicky nodded graciously, refusing the bait. "There are lots of mysteries I like, but they don't normally involve people with QR codes on their feet, that's what I'm saying. I just don't know what to think about him."

Vicky giggled, holding her hand over her mouth. "Well, if you don't know what to think, ask a different question: how do you *feel* about Reuben?"

Before Harry could answer, Jake ambled over, the first coffee of the day in hand. "Not a pretty sight, is it?" he remarked laconically as he sat down beside them. It was true; wearing only a sack and blanket, the sight of a man that big attempting exercises his body couldn't possibly accommodate was a little grotesque. "Can't we find him some fucking clothes that don't make him look quite so ridiculous?"

Vicky took this personally, and looked a little embarrassed. "I'll see what I can do, Jake. It's not easy, you know."

"Hey, Vicky – I wasn't having a pop," said Jake. It was a bit early for him to be treading on eggshells. "I just meant that...well...he's losing weight fast, so we should be able to find something he can fit into soon, that's all. Really." Vicky was mollified, and after slight pause announced she might take a bike-ride to town later on, to find some cheap sportswear, cheap and very big sportswear, with a lot of elastic bits.

"You know, at this rate he won't be recognisable in a few weeks, he's losing so much weight," Harry remarked.

"I hope that's true," said Jake. "We can't keep him here in camp much longer, surely? I'd feel like I was in some kind of open prison, the way we keep him here."

"He's never complained about it though, has he?" asked Vicky. Jake and Harry both shook their heads.

"No, he's been very good about it," said Harry. "No complaints, not even a hint. He seems to understand the risks and the dangers, and so far he's been good as gold."

Jake nodded. "And we have no idea if anyone is *really* looking for him at all. This could all be one giant bout of paranoia. Other than that one night with the man in the bushes – and only Reuben saw him, not that I'm suggesting he made it up, but he could have been wrong, we have to bear that in mind, don't we? Other than that, we've had no reason to think there's anything going on we need to worry about. I think we could let him out soon, take him to a gig maybe. I know he'd really like that."

All this time they had been talking under the assumption that Reuben, exercising forty yards away, couldn't hear them, so they were discomforted when he strolled over, smiled diffidently at Jake and asked: "When do you think it would be OK then?

You're right, I really would enjoy it, I'm sure I would. No pressure or anything, Jake. Whatever you think is best, that's all."

What struck Jake was not so much that he could hear them at such range, but that Reuben acted as if he'd been sitting right there with them, part of the conversation rather than eavesdropping from a distance. His hearing was certainly very acute, Jake reflected, but how could Reuben know that? What did he have to compare it with?

"I admire your patience, my boy. Really do. How about this: when you can get on – and stay on – a bicycle, you can come to a gig. It's actually a necessary condition, but I also think that if you have a target, and you keep on exercising like you have been, by the time you can ride a bike you'll look a fair bit different, maybe different enough to fool anyone looking for a *very* fat man."

"Because I'll only be an ordinarily fat man?"

"Sure."

"I look forward to it," said Reuben dryly.

Harry was reminded just how much Reuben's personality had developed in such a short time. He'd been like a slate wiped clean, a baby at first, but lately there was something about him that Harry liked despite all his reservations, an uncomplicated affection based not on knowing someone's vague past, but their detailed present. It may be a limited way to look at another person, but it did have the virtue of being a very focussed look. Vicky was right; maybe he did think about some things too much. When you boiled it down, Harry simply liked the big man. He didn't need to think about it; thinking made no difference at all. But he knew there were problems somewhere out there and they were heading this way, but he couldn't blame the big man for that. Problems unseen, over the horizon right now, but sensed none the less; such unformulated threats continued to bear down on him because he knew that not thinking about them would never yield answers, or solutions, or strategies. No-one had ever prepared adequately for war by refusing to think about it, and Harry was certain a war was coming. He just didn't know who with, when it would happen, what they would be fighting for or where they would make their stand. The only thing he knew for sure: when the questions were resolved, Reuben's past would be at the heart of each and every answer.

Ten days passed without incident. The band played three more gigs, one a poorly promoted disaster at which only a handful of people turned up, the others playing to packed and enthusiastic houses. Reuben continued his regime of exercise and study; Nick had given him the entire library of manuals and other documents that came with each piece of equipment, and while Reuben had no idea what most of the gear actually did, he knew every socket, every connector and every control by heart. He read assiduously, fascinated by everything they could find for him.

What he couldn't do, on the day after Jimi's accident, was fit into the XXL track suit that Vicky had found in a charity shop. But ten days later they held an impromptu celebration when, after only a small tussle and no tearing sounds, Reuben emerged from the caravan with his bulk mostly constrained within the confines of the acrylic zip top and elasticised bottoms. A little cheer went up, after which everyone giggled like schoolchildren. A bottle of homebrew wine appeared, and they all took swigs before passing it on.

"You look mighty fine," said Billy, walking slowly round the big man. "Yes sir, mighty fine. How's the bike riding?"

Everyone laughed except Reuben. "I don't want to break any more bikes," he said, looking crestfallen, but he couldn't keep his face straight for long and started grinning. "But soon, Billy. I'll be up there with you, and then we'll see about this bass playing caper. I've heard enough talk, now I want some action, some proof."

"Whoa...check out Action Man," Phil exclaimed. "He's calling you out Billy, watch out now. Who's got the bottle?"

The first attempt to ride a bike had been hilarious, except that the bike got trashed and required welding to restore its ability to carry a more modest load. Reuben was not seriously injured, and he didn't mind being the fodder for the barrage of affectionate jokes that inevitably ensued; most of the time on the road very little actually happened, so any incident no matter how small would be remorselessly drained of its entertainment value until the corpse resembled an Egyptian mummy. While they had the welding gear out, Nick and Sam discussed whether they could reinforce one of the bikes for the purpose, but it remained no more than a plan because only four days later Reuben rode a bike round a complete circuit of the camp without damage to man or machine. It was a strange sight because the bike could barely be seen; Reuben's body flowed round the frame, enveloping it, giving the impression he was miming the motions of cycling while floating across the ground. Each day he got a little thinner, a bit stronger, ran faster and cycled further, until Jake had to remind him to be careful how far he went from the camp. Reuben, looking suitably abashed, promised to restrict his cycling to the circuit around the woodland perimeter he already ran several times each day.

On Christmas eve there was a real sense of occasion about the camp. Not only was there a gig on a festive night – expected to be one of the best of the year in a venue they liked – it was also Reuben's first official night out. His choice of attire for this auspicious event was still limited to the track suit, now looking a little loose on him, but he patently didn't care. He was excited – another first for the observers – and it was contagious. The crew left at midday, taking Vicky and Jimi with them; this was a night of celebration in which everyone would participate.

At the given time, they mounted up and rode out of the wood to the tarmac road, Reuben in the middle so those behind could keep an eye on him. The gig was only eight miles away, nothing strenuous, and they made it in less than an hour at not much less than their customary pace. Reuben had no trouble keeping up and made them all laugh when they freewheeled down a hill and he shot ahead, going "Wheeeee" all the way to the bottom.

He's just a big kid, thought Jake, smiling to himself in the darkness as he savoured the ride. The night air was sharp and bracing under a clear winter sky, where small clouds fled from the half moon like startled birds. They saw no people, heard only the occasional barking of a lonely dog. The roads remained virtually empty; before they reached the outskirts of town they saw only one car, a nondescript Ford estate going in the opposite direction.

The venue was a modern community centre with a fine hall, good acoustics and a stage deep and wide and high. Best of all, it had a decent generator and its own healthy supply of red diesel, which mean the crew could pull out the lighting gantries their own generator could not support and fly them safely. Virtually every bit of equipment they owned had been deployed: it was a curious fact looking back on it that the crew and the band all worked very hard that night, more so than usual. Although no-one said as much, there would probably have been little disagreement with the notion that they were going the extra mile for Reuben. He was one of them now, and they wanted to meet him in all their finery, to show off their skills and revel in professional glory, for Reuben to see and know, for the first time, the very best of them.

Before the show, the band took Reuben to the bar. If anyone was worried about how he might react on his first social occasion – everything was a first for him, they realised – they needn't have. Reuben was quiet, shining, his biggest problem being to stop grinning like an idiot.

"Keep an eye on him Nick," said Jake at the bar. "Stay close."

Nick laughed. "Jake, you could see our boy anywhere in the hall – look at the space around him." This was quite true; the sheer size of him meant you could pick Reuben out just by looking for the one head in a circle of clear space. "Anyway, he can sit with me at the desk and help me keep an eye on Jimi."

The show was everything they had hoped for. The band excelled, the sound and lights were close to perfect, and the audience still wouldn't let them off the stage after four encores. Only the promoter killing the stage generator persuaded the audience that the gig really was at an end, but their leaving was good-natured with many a happy Christmas bestowed by strangers on strangers. An hour later, the band were still at the bar, waiting on the crew to finish packing. They had to virtually restrain Reuben, who apparently felt duty-bound to help pack up, but their arguments eventually prevailed and they set about getting him as drunk as they could afford, all the while keeping their intake abreast of his for the sake of good fellowship.

Billy, who had for some time been standing arm in arm with Alina, remembered he had a small joint in his pocket, and decided to pop out to the car park. Three local men – sullen types drinking steadily all night, never leaving the bar – followed Billy out and there was something about the way they moved, as if a wait was over, the purposeful stride and hard faces, that caught Reuben's attention. All around him were chatting animatedly and no-one paid attention when he followed the men. Outside and to his right, at the back corner of the building, the three men had surrounded Billy.

"What's she doing with you, monkey boy?" he heard one of them say as he walked up to the group. "Is she the sort that likes a nice bit of black cock eh?"

"You OK Billy?" asked Reuben.

"It's nothing really, Reuben..."

"Who the fuck are you, you fat cunt?" demanded one, all three turning towards Reuben.

"I'm Reuben," he replied pleasantly. "Who are you?"

"You taking the piss?" said the nearest man, moving closer as he spoke.

"No. I came to warn you."

"Oh yeah? Warn us of what, porky?"

"They are coming," said Reuben, his expression earnest.

"Who, the police?" said the nearest man, eyes flicking between Reuben and Billy: he couldn't make up his mind who he wanted to hit first.

"No," said Reuben, a frantic note to his voice. "You don't understand. *They* are coming, the ship. They are coming for us. My friend and I must return to our ship. We've been away too long."

"What did you say?"

"We have to return to the ship. We are not from this place. We are from..." Reuben scanned the sky, then raised one arm and pointed. Billy nearly wet himself when the three stooges followed the pointing finger. Their apparent leader, the one who had done all the talking, was the quickest to recover his sense, and turned back. Reuben, looking quite frightened, fixed his gaze on the leader. "We cannot hold these human forms any longer. I assure you Sir, you do not wish to see my comrade and I in our true shapes. Your minds could not withstand the extra dimensions involved. You would go mad in one second." With that, Reuben inflated his stomach, breathing in steadily until he had puffed up his belly like an inflated blimp, bigger and bigger. The track suit bottoms complained mightily and tore down one side. All four men, Billy included, stood with mouths hanging open.

When he later recounted the tale, Billy would swear that, just for a second, even he believed, so utterly convincing was Reuben's delivery. His face was so deadpan and serious, and the puffing up so bizarre, everyone just stood there, frozen by incomprehension. The lead thug broke the deadlock only when he burst into raucous laughter and stepped back, shaking his head in disbelief. "Come on boys," he said to the others, who joined him as he walked towards their car, laughing amongst themselves. "These wankers are fucking nuts."

"What on earth...?" Billy found no suitable question to complete.

"I've been reading some science-fiction," Reuben replied nonchalantly as he let the air out of his lungs. His attention was elsewhere.

"That was so brilliant. They wanted to give someone a good kicking. Me, actually. You really freaked them out there – me too, come to that. Wow. Fucking brilliant."

"Billy, go get Jake and Harry. Get them right now." Reuben was staring into the darkness beyond the car park, unmoving. His tone was so harsh and so authoritative that Billy just turned and ran back into the venue. Moments later, Harry bolted out of the door, followed closely by the rest, spilling out into the night to stop dead in a huddled group, watching anxiously as Harry and Jake approached the still figure staring into the bushes.

"Can you see him?" Reuben asked quietly. "You can't, I know. Listen, there's a man crouching in the bushes over there. He has a gun, a sniper rifle with an infra-red beam sight, the type that doesn't paint a red spot on the target. Thing is, I can see the beam. I can see a thin red line leading all the way back to the man in the bushes. He's aiming at me right now." Harry started to move in the direction Reuben was staring. "Don't Harry," warned Reuben firmly. "You can't rush a man at that distance, and neither can I. You should all stay still and quiet. He doesn't want you. Get the others into the truck."

He turned away and started to walk slowly up the red line shimmering in front of him like a glowing silken thread, one end attached to his chest and the other to his would-be assassin. His only concern was to get clear of the others else they were put in danger – his worst fear come true, Closing the gap between him and the man in the bushes seemed to make sense. If he'd wanted a shot, his assailant could have taken it a hundred times over in the time he'd had Reuben in his sights. It was at least four minutes since Reuben first saw the beam; how long had he been targeted before that? (Since he came out of the door, something unbidden in him answered). The position chosen by the assassin covered the exit and car park well, with a clear shot to the back of the truck and the stage loading bay too. Good position, he thought to himself. (Then: how did I know that?)

He was half way there when the red beam wavered and fell away from his chest. The man in the bushes jumped up and started to run. Reuben immediately set off in pursuit, expecting that his additional speed should be enough to catch up, but it wasn't. The man in front kept well ahead, and then Reuben lost him completely. He stood for a few moments, taking his bearings and listening intently, but heard nothing. (Gone to ground; prepared escape route. He knew this too, somehow). He came to a halt in a lane with high hedges either side broken by entrances to some new houses still being built; (too much cover and dangerous to search). Despite his apprehension, Reuben turned his back on the scene and ran off the way he came, pausing only at the place where the sniper had lain in wait. There was nothing to see in the dark, no clues; he kept moving.

Back in the car park, the band and crew stood close together by the front of the truck, speaking in low voices. Their concern was plain to see.

"I think we should go now," said Reuben.

Chapter 9:   Warming Miss Frosty

During an evening already groaning under the weight of extraordinary events, there was one incident that passed largely un-remarked; when they got back to the campsite, Reuben managed for the first time to get through the bus door.

During the journey, alone in the back of the truck with shifting mounds of equipment piled as high as his confusion, guilt and distress, Reuben endured an unbearable sense of loneliness, and an indeterminate anxiety whose dimensions were bounded by the lack of a past on one edge and no viable approximation of his future on the other. Now, sitting in the bus he studied Jimi, asleep in his mother's lap, and realised that in some ways his own brief childhood was over, the simple certainties shared with the boy during the last few weeks consigned to another life, another era.

Tea and coffee were made and silently passed round, cigarettes lit and joints rolled. Nobody wanted to speak, to start a discussion the outcome of which no-one was keen to reach. Eventually, all eyes turned to Jake.

"What do you want from me?" he asked, knowing full well the answer was leadership. "Look – I've seen some things in my time and been involved in a few capers...but this...this is in a different league altogether..." He tailed off, as uncertain as the rest.

All except Harry, who appeared both glitteringly excited and strangely contained. "Let's start by getting our facts straight," he said, turning to Reuben. "What exactly happened out there? What made you go outside in the first place?"

"I went out to see if Billy was OK..."

"What made you do that?"

"I don't know...it was something about the men who followed him out..."

"Good job too," Billy interjected.

"And when you got outside?" asked Harry.

"I saw them standing round Billy, obviously getting ready to do something unpleasant. I thought I should intervene."

"Boy, some intervention," said Billy. For the benefit of the others, he briefly reprised the events he had witnessed.

"Excellent strategy, I must say," said Jake. "What made you think of it?"

Reuben shook his head. "I don't know...I just...it wasn't worth getting in a fight. That's how it seemed. It was so stupid, so ignorant...it didn't seem worth the effort to fight with people like that. I'd been reading an old sci-fi book about first contact and...well, the idea just came to me as I stood there – if I was so weird, so alien and completely mad they couldn't take me seriously, maybe they also couldn't be bothered to beat me up – or Billy. Something like that."

"And it worked," Billy confirmed unnecessarily. "Boy did it work".

"You should have called me," said Phil from the back of the bus, "I don't mind a bit of ignorant violence now and then."

"For God's sake, Phil!" exclaimed Vicky. Phil stared back at her, unabashed.

"So these thugs were just locals," suggested Harry, "stupid, pissed maybe, a bunch of dickheads just wanting to beat up the black kid. Ignorant, but nothing to do with what happened next?"

Reuben nodded. "Yes, that's how it seems to me."

"So?..." Harry prompted.

"Well...it was while I was trying to convince them I was an alien that I noticed a red line fizzing in the air. I couldn't pay much attention to it, but as they walked away I looked in the direction of the light and saw the beam was hitting my chest..."

"He had you in his sights, in other words."

"I guess so. I was puzzled. First, I couldn't work out what the red line was, and when I realised it was a laser sight I couldn't figure out why he didn't take the shot. He had me in his sights for several minutes, but never took the shot."

"Even so," said Jake, "why didn't you run for cover? Why on earth did you run towards him, towards the danger?"

Reuben contemplated this question for a moment, then lifted his head to meet Jake's stare. "I did it to get away from you...to protect you. It was me they were after."

"How do you know that?" demanded Harry.

Jake leaned forward. "I think it's a reasonable assumption Harry, bearing in mind that although we may piss people off from time to time, I don't remember angry punters ever coming at us with sniper rifles and laser night-sights. Bottles and chairs maybe, fruit – certainly, even the odd knife now and then. No snipers."

"We did have that farmer one time, the one who drove a herd of pigs at us..." Nick offered.

"What about the girl's father who tried to run Cas over with his Land Rover?" said Phil. "It's the only time I've even seen Cas run."

"Fuck off Phil, this is serious," retorted Cas.

"I know where we can get some guns," Phil added hopefully.

"Oh, great," muttered Vicky. "That's all we need."

"Christ Phil, who would you shoot at?" said Harry, his voice brusque.

"We lost sight of you," said Jake, cutting across a foolish argument he could see brewing. "Did you find anything? I assume you didn't catch whoever it was?"

"That's right," Reuben agreed. "I lost him...but..." He looked round the table, uncertain.

"But what?" asked Jake. When he didn't reply, Jake reached out and, with a curiously shy gesture, patted Reuben's hand. "Hey man, it's OK. We're on your side."

"Are we?" demanded Phil.

"Yes we are," said Nick firmly to no-one in particular, looking intently at his sleeping son all the while.

"You'll think I'm crazy," said Reuben.

"Too late to worry about that now Reuben; the mothership has landed," said Billy, deadpan.

"Well – you're not going to believe this, but when I was chasing the man in the bushes...most of the time I could barely see him...we were both running through woods and there wasn't much light. You know I can run pretty fast, but I wasn't getting any closer, couldn't seem to gain any ground...and then, just as I got to a clear patch I saw his outline clearly as he ducked into some half-built houses – that's where I lost him – but the thing is..." he shook his head in disbelief even at what he was about to say, "...he was the same as me. Big. As big as I am. Even at a distance, the silhouette was sharp and clear. He was the same size as me."

If it hadn't been for the profoundly sober delivery, some of the group might have ridiculed this claim. Instead, they looked at each other in confusion, no-one quite sure what to make of this latest development.

"So what you're telling us Reuben is that there's more like you at home, wherever the fuck home is?" said Cas.

"Just a minute," Harry interrupted, "this is getting ridiculous. Are you telling me that another huge sumo guy is hanging around in the bushes with a sniper rifle? That there's an army of gigantic fat blokes running at high-speed round the country, looking for us – or for you?

"And how are they following us? Is the mothership tracking us?" said Billy.

"You're serious?" Jake asked Reuben, who nodded. "Yes, of course you are…sorry." Jake fell back into his chair to ponder this strange turn of events.

"Actually, that's a good question," said Vicky. "How *are* they following us?"

"Is this man you saw from caravan, same man?" Alina asked, her face hard and unreadable.

"Do we think they are connected, you mean?" said Harry. "It's all too coincidental, isn't it? Someone is watching us in the bushes in Devon, then we come up here and a few weeks later, someone is in the bushes again, watching us again, someone who is obviously connected to Reuben here, by weight alone if nothing else."

"Except this time he had a gun, and was trying to kill Reuben," said Cas.

"We don't know that Cas," answered Harry. "And as we've said already, if Reuben was the target, why didn't the shooter take the shot? We don't even know he had a gun – could have been some kind of laser night-vision system or rangefinder, not necessarily a gun-sight."

Reuben shook his head. "No Harry, it was a gun, a rifle. I saw the outline of it when I got my one good look at him."

"Weren't you afraid?" Alina asked softly, as if the question were private.

Reuben looked puzzled. "I don't think so. No...I never gave it a thought. Perhaps I should have been."

"It wouldn't be an unacceptable reaction, given someone was trying to kill you – or appeared to be, anyway," said Vicky. "I know what she means though – you seem remarkably calm for a man who took on a bunch of drunks and an assassin, all in one night."

"Everything happens very quickly in situations like that," said Harry, but Reuben disagreed. "No Harry, it wasn't like that. Actually, everything seemed to slow down. It was the strangest thing; everything in slow motion, stretched out..."

Harry was about to speak when Cas cut across him. "Surely the issue is what to do next, how we can protect ourselves. How do we extricate ourselves from this mess? As Jake said, we're out of our depth in a big way here. Not to exaggerate or anything, but this is some scary shit. How do we get out of it?"

"I know how we can get out of it," said Phil. He held up a bag of grass. "I'll roll a joint."

"You're excluding Reuben from the solution then?" said Billy, "or does your "we" include getting him out of this mess, seeing as how he's the one really in it. No-one's trying to kill *you* Cas, are they? Nor are they following you, or us – they're following *him*." He glanced towards Reuben, who was staring at his hands. "We should think about getting Reuben out of this jam – wouldn't that solve both problems at once?"

"Cas does have a point," said Vicky. "We have to do something, Jake. "I know it's not his fault, but Reuben's being here has put my son's life in danger." She looked apologetically at the big man opposite her. "I'm sorry Reuben, but it's true. I think you were the first to recognise it."

Reuben nodded. "I've known it nearly from the beginning. Whatever is coming for me is also coming for you, if for no other reason than you know me, that you're with me. I'm putting you all in danger simply by being here. It's time I left."

There followed a rapid descent into anarchy, a period of free fall that lasted several minutes. With the exception of Phil, every single member of the entourage simultaneously expressed outrage, disapproval, contempt or shock at the notion that they should abandon Reuben (this aimed at Vicky) or he should abandon them. Confusingly, even Vicky remonstrated with Reuben. "You can't go off on your own. You wouldn't last a second out there," she insisted.

"Hold on Vicky..." Jake started in.

"I know, I know... but I wasn't suggesting he should leave, not for one minute," Vicky retorted, her denial lacking total conviction. She pressed on. "What I was saying was that we have to act, do something. We can't just carry on as if nothing has happened. That's what I'm saying."

"I'm actually not so sure about that," said Harry. "We really need to get a decent perspective on all this. We – all of us – have a tendency to melodrama, let's face it. We blow everything up largely for our own amusement – Cas breaking a guitar string becomes a month-long anecdote of some kind or other, for Christ's sake – that's how bored we get, isn't it?" He stared round the table; no-one disagreed. "So instead of plunging into some massive conspiracy theory where we're the object of a man-hunt conducted by shadowy forces of evil, maybe we should consider reacting only to what has really happened, not what might have."

"What's your assessment, Harry?" asked Reuben.

"Well, basically, when you get right down to it, virtually nothing has happened at all. Nothing. We find a bloke up on the moor and he comes with us on a few gigs. He thinks one-time – and one time only – he might have seen someone in the bushes in Devon, and we have tonight's rather peculiar episode to account for, at which nothing happened again, I remind you. He's got a QR code on his foot and was very fat, although that's changing fast...in fact, can I point out something else here?..." he turned to Reuben. "...it isn't as if you've been trying to lose weight. It's just falling off you at a remarkable rate. Doesn't that suggest that maybe the excess was artificial, like you were part of some obesity study or something like that? Maybe you were made to be fat for a reason, and whatever made you fat isn't happening now, so the weight is coming off again?"

"Jeez Harry, what are you saying - that you think he was part of some kind of top-secret weight-loss program?" suggested Jake.

"Weight-watchers so secret they QR code the participants, hunt them down and shoot them if they escape?".

"See, there you go again," Harry retorted. "Is Reuben being hunted? Are we? I mean – really? Is someone watching us? Are we in danger? Has anyone been shot, or even shot at? Is Reuben dangerous? Are we dangerous? Has anything bad at all happened to us since we found Reuben? Of course not; none of this is real. To me this is turning into a dangerous game where we glamorise and fantasize and scare ourselves silly, a cheap thrill created by convincing ourselves we're out of our depth, like 'Oh my God, we're in trouble now, great forces are gathering to destroy us'. I don't think we're in trouble. I think some of you have been smoking much too much dope. There's no orcs out there; this is not Lord of the Fucking Rings for God's sake."

"What about the QR code?" asked Reuben.

"Fair enough," Harry replied. "That, I have to admit, is a bit strange, but it's hardly life-threatening, is it?"

"No," Jake interjected, "but it was the reason you brought him here. That's what you told me, isn't it?"

"Look at it from the other perspective," continued Harry smoothly. "Let's just say for a moment that Reuben here is wanted by nefarious forces, state agencies, aliens, forces of darkness or whatever. If that's true, how come it took them weeks to find us here? Do any of you really think they couldn't find us, arrest us, even kill us if they wanted to – and in minutes and hours, not days or weeks? We have the most comprehensive public surveillance system in Europe – more cameras than people now, if the stories are to be believed. I know many of them are broken, or don't have power, but we never know which ones, and the coverage is pretty random, but widespread.

"Do we really think we're invisible, just because we move around the country a fair bit and don't use credit cards...well, not our own, anyway? They've got face recognition, vehicle recognition, automatic number plate scanning, satellite tracking, 8G tracking, GPS tracking, phone tracking...not to mention fuel receipts with our registration on, ration coupons...we leave a trail a mile wide wherever we go. Every time we log in we leave our fingerprints all over the local wireless hub. Do you think GCHQ can't tell where we are just by seeing where our email comes from on a particular day? Shit – they could do that back at the turn of the century. If they wanted us – or just Reuben – they'd have come for him weeks ago.

"Right now, we should just carry on as if nothing had happened, like nothing has changed, because basically, nothing has. Anyway, I can't think of anything we can do that changes anything, anywhere we could hide, any action that gives us any kind of advantage or makes us safer – if indeed we are under threat right now, which I doubt. I will say this though: Reuben, you should stay with us. Together, we can help you and you can help us..." Harry tailed off, uncertain for the first time, but the space he vacated was quickly occupied by general agreement with his argument.

"What about it Reuben?" asked Billy. "You gonna stay with us or run off, desert your mates in their time of need?"

Reuben scanned the expectant faces. "If you really want me to...?" he began, but anything else he might have said was drowned out in the cacophony of confirmation. All he could do was proffer a shy smile.

A couple of miles away, the driver of the discretely parked nondescript Ford Escort was also smiling. He leaned back in his seat, removed his headphones and prepared to get some sleep.

Jake slept badly. Around five AM, waking for what seemed like the tenth time in two hours, he misguidedly lit the remains of a joint. Five minutes later, he was wide awake, thoughts running amok like naughty children. He got up, opened the door to his little cabin at the front of the upper deck and crept along between the curtained bunks towards the ladder, the stairs long removed to make space for a shower. He climbed down, opened the door and stepped out onto the grass, leaving the door slightly ajar because the lock was a bit temperamental and several band members had locked themselves out recently.

Now he was outside, all Jake wanted was to get back in bed. The cold was penetrating, damp and unpleasant. He walked to the end of the bus and relieved himself but as he turned back, a movement by the caravan caught his eye. The caravan door slowly opened. He saw Alina framed momentarily against the candlelight inside as she stepped down and shut the door behind

91

her. Apparently oblivious to the cold, she sauntered across the grass with her coat flung over one shoulder, opened the bus door and stepped inside. As she turned to close it behind her, she was smiling to herself. Jake too was amused, until it occurred to him he might now be locked out. He dashed back, hurriedly reached for the handle and pulled. Much to his relief, the door opened. As he stepped inside, he found Alina standing at the bottom of the ladder, one hand placed distractedly as if to climb, the smile still fixed in place. It quickly disappeared as she realised Jake was behind her.

"Oh, it's you..." she said softly. "I...I'm..."

Jake grinned conspiratorially. "You going outside for a pee?" he whispered, standing aside.

"Er...yes...excuse please," Alina replied as she pushed past him. "Don't lock yourself out," he called after her, chuckling to himself as he climbed the ladder. Alina and Reuben – well well. Miss Frosty gets warmed up. And Reuben – his first time, Jake was sure – lost his cherry to the ice maiden. How sweet. A virgin...in this lifetime, for sure, which was how he thought about the "new" Reuben (in light of knowing there was an "old" Reuben).

Old and new lives; an opportunity some would give anything to have. As he got back under the duvet and pulled it over his head, the closet romantic in him was still smiling.

He woke again some hours later, feeling refreshed. Daylight peeked through the curtain edges and there was an unusual quality of silence, peaceful silence, that seemed strange but comfortingly familiar. Pulling the nearest curtain aside, he was greeted by a world of whiteness, the landscape covered in a foot of glistening snow. Jake felt excited and got up, pulling back the curtains to survey a world transformed. He loved the snow and wanted to touch it, to run in it and hear the crunching underfoot, to see the deep imprints of his footsteps alongside the tracks of animals that had passed unseen in the night. Good job it didn't start earlier, he told himself, grinning again; the tracks would have been a bit of a giveaway.

Downstairs, he found Vicky in the galley and Cas, seated in a corner, fondling his guitar as usual. "What's for breakfast?" he called out to Vicky, who frowned.

"Why do you do that Jake? Every bloody day the same – 'what's for breakfast?' – when you know bloody well it's porridge".

"No muesli then? I thought we still had some muesli".

"Oh sure," said Vicky airily. "Muesli coming up". As Jake watched, she scooped some dry porridge oats into a bowl, opened a tin, placed a single sultana atop the cereal and proffered the bowl.

"You know Vicky, I quite fancy a nice bowl of porridge, now I come to think on it," said Jake with a straight face. Vicky turned away, not quickly enough to conceal her amusement as she put some water in a pan, followed by the oats. The sultana was returned to its tin.

"Where is everybody?"

"Alina's off on her own as usual – said the snow reminded her of Poland, so she's off communing with her ancestors, I guess. Nick, of course, is with the crew in the truck – they've gone somewhere to take something apart as usual...or put it back together, I can never tell which. Phil went with them, probably looking for some trouble to get into."

"Boys being boys, basically."

"Yep," said Vicky, stirring the porridge with less than good grace.

"Don't stir all that bad karma into my breakfast please," said Jake, half serious. "The crew keep us on the road, keep us alive, keep us moving...and mainly they keep us safe. We owe them a lot and it's because they get so outraged when a piece of equipment doesn't do what it's supposed to that our shows run so smoothly. They don't allow things to go unattended. They have standards."

"Sure, but you have to admit they are obsessive. Sometimes I swear Nick would rather be playing with his soldering iron than..."

Cas looked up from his guitar with an air of abstraction. "Than what, Vicky?" he asked, face devoid of expression. "Not getting enough, are we?" Vicky glowered at him.

"And the others?" Jake prompted.

"Reuben and Harry are running around somewhere in the woods. I don't know what's with Harry these days – he never used to exercise much and now he's out there all the time." She tasted the porridge but it wasn't ready. "Reuben, I understand; he's trying to lose weight and get fit. Harry though?...sorry, I seem to be a bit grumpy today. Alina, Billy and Jimi are walking over to some hill or other. They think they can do some snowboarding".

"OK." Vicky needed a distraction and Jake had just the thing. "Hey Cas, you'll never guess what I saw last night".

"In which case you better tell me then so I don't waste my time," said Cas, who didn't like to play games except the ones he knew he could win, which were played exclusively with members of the opposite sex.

"I went outside for a piss last night around four and I saw *someone* creeping out of the caravan."

Leaning forward to rest her elbows on the counter, Vicky gasped theatrically. "Not...not the Snow Queen, surely?"

"With Reuben?" said Cas, interested despite himself. Jake nodded smugly. Vicky raised herself upright, pushing her fists in the small of her back like a tired fishwife. "Well, good for her," she pronounced flatly.

"It was probably his first time too," Jake added, leering a little. "Hey, I wonder if his superpowers extend to...you know...?" Cas looked alarmed and found a new scale with which to distract himself. Vicky had a strange look on her face. "What's on your dirty little mind then?" Jake asked her, but she turned away, poured Jake's porridge into the waiting bowl and dumped it on the table with a bang. "There's no sugar, no salt and no honey all right, so don't ask!"

Jake and Cas laughed. "Don't worry Vicky," said Cas reassuringly. "It's normal. His knob. He may be a big guy, but some parts of him are the same as the rest of us. Quite normal."

"Just as well," said Jake without looking up from his porridge. "Just as fucking well. Hey, where's my sultana?"

"I tell you what Jake – better not tell Nicky about this," said Cas. "He might get anxious, you know...possessive...insecure maybe....restless wife, unfulfilled...and super-knobber over in the caravan mere yards away...could be worrying for the poor lad...?"

Someone knocked firmly on the door, three loud taps in a row. Officious taps. Jake glanced out of the window. There was a car parked beside the caravan; the snow must have masked the sound of its arrival.

"Who is it, Jake?" asked Vicky.

"Your marriage councillor?" suggested Cas.

"No-one we know. I'll find out," Jake replied as he moved to the door. Through the window he could see a hatless middle-aged man in a drab grey overcoat carrying a large leather briefcase.

Council. Written all over him, thought Jake as he opened the door. "Can I help you?" he asked, at which – and to Jake's astonishment – the man lifted an admonishing finger to his lips, stepped into the bus and slid past him, pausing to repeat the signal to Vicky and Cas. Both turned to Jake, who shrugged his shoulders. Taking two more careful steps into the bus, the stranger placed his briefcase on the table, opened it and retrieved a black box with some dials and switches on the front and a circular chrome antenna attached to the top. As the others watched, he flicked some switches, made a few adjustments and started to wave it around slowly, alternating vertical and horizontal arcs, all the while keeping his eyes on a small LCD readout. After a few moments of silence, he grunted softly and started to move further down the bus towards the galley, stopping twice to turn around and sweep the antenna purposefully from one side of the bus to the other while moving very slowly back the way he had come. Another grunt, and now he was bending, holding the box over a small inspection hatch that allowed access to the battery compartment under the floor. Apparently satisfied by the readout, he lifted one end of the hatch and smiled as he pointed to a little grey plastic box stuck to the underside of the hatch. Two wires protruded from one end, each clipped to a terminal on one of the batteries in the rack below. Two more wires emerged from the opposite end, but these connected to a circular, coin-sized disk fixed to the front of the box. A red light glowed gently beside the disc, pulsing slightly. Gingerly, their silent visitor unclipped each lead. The red light dimmed; as it faded he pulled the grey box away from the hatch, leaving behind half of the adhesive pad that had secured it in place. Carefully replacing the hatch, he stood up, smiled at the three spectators and placed the box on the table before turning off the device in his hand and returning it to his briefcase.

"May I sit?"

"What is that?" asked Jake, staring at the object on the table. Vicky stood stock still as if poised for flight. Cas, after laying his guitar carefully on the seat, moved closer to stare at the grey box.

"It's a bugging device, Mr. Constable," said the stranger, seating himself anyway. Jake reached out and picked up the box. It was light, the moulded plastic slightly warm in his hand, featureless bar the light and four screws, one in each corner. Jake was pretty sure that the disc on the front was a microphone. "It contains the transmitting components of a phone, with a unique IMEI identity burned in so it can be traced. Probably has a positional accuracy of around two hundred metres, better if there are more than three masts to triangulate against. And of course it transmits any audio it picks up."

For once, Jake was completely beyond words. He stared around him with unseeing eyes, wanting to find Harry or Nick, wanting backup from his trusted lieutenants. In the distance he heard Vicky ask the stranger if he would like a cup of tea, which struck him as remarkably civil.

" You're too kind Mrs. Richardson. Tea would be very nice. My name is Fairfax, by the way."

"Fairfax?" repeated Vicky. "I...I'm sorry Mr. Fairfax, but we don't have any sugar, I'm afraid."

"Who does, these days?" Mr. Fairfax replied wistfully as he lifted the briefcase off the table and put it on the seat beside him. "It's always the little things you miss most, it seems."

"Excuse me," Cas interrupted, "but who are you...I mean...why...?" Before he could finish forming his sentence, the door banged open and Harry came in, followed by Reuben. Both were sweating, brushing snow off each other and laughing. They stopped abruptly as they saw the visitor seated at the table. Before either could speak, Jake passed the grey box to Harry. "You better see this."

"What is it?" Reuben asked, watching Harry turn the box over in his hand.

"It's a bug," said Mr. Fairfax.

"He – Mr. Fairfax here – he found it. He's got some kind of detection thingy, and found it just now," explained Cas.

"Where, exactly?" demanded Harry, passing the box to Reuben.

"Under the hatch," Vicky answered as she placed a mug of tea in front of their visitor. "Here." She stamped on the hatch, which she was standing on. "Connected to one of the batteries."

"How long do you think it's been there?" said Jake, not really expecting an answer.

"Probably since Devon, Mr. Constable. That would be my guess, considering they tracked you down." Fairfax took a sip of his tea, found it too hot and set the mug back down.

"Who tracked us down?" Jake retorted.

"That's right," Harry agreed as he settled into a seat on the far side of the table. "Who put it there, and while we're at it, who exactly are you again...?" Reuben, who could not fit it between the table and the seats along each wall, pulled out a stool and perched with a grave expression at the top of the table, placing the box carefully down in front of him on the table.

"My name is Fairfax."

"Do you have a first name?"

"Not right now." Fairfax tried his tea again and found it to his liking, taking several slow sips.

"What the fuck kind of answer is that?" demanded Cas.

"It means he's not here to be our friend," said Jake, his voice flat. "It means he wants us to call him *Mr.* Fairfax."

"Keeping it formal," Vicky added. "But that's not what Harry wanted to know, is it *Mr.* Fairfax?"

"No, it isn't *Mrs.* Richardson." Fairfax put down his tea, loosened the top button of his overcoat and reached beneath it. Everyone round the table stiffened, but all that came out was a small wallet, which he placed on the table. Harry reached out, his hand hovering over the wallet as he looked across to Fairfax, who nodded. He flipped the wallet open, stared at it expressionless for a few moments and passed it to Reuben, who examined it briefly before passing it on again. Jake, the last to examine it, whistled quietly to himself as he passed it back to Fairfax, who put it back in his pocket and buttoned his coat back over it.

"You...you're..." Vicky couldn't bring herself to say it.

"MI5? Yes, that's right."

"Wow," said Cas. "First time I've met a spy."

"I'm not a spy, Mr. Calinas. You must be thinking of SIS – MI6 you'd call it. They indulge in spying because their business is intelligence, where ours is security – 'community, identity, stability' as we say. Little motto we have, bit of an in-joke really. Your James Bond types on the other hand are after information about other countries, usually with a military perspective. My department looks for intent to do harm inside the UK – rather like the police really. I'm just a humble civil servant trying – sometimes in vain, I must admit – to maintain the internal security of the country, and my work is, by comparison, quite mundane."

"Like GCHQ, Five Eyes...?" said Jake. "How is reading our emails and recording our phone calls not spying, Mr. Fairfax?"

"Well, perhaps it is in a technical sense. Nothing to do with me however, I assure you. Altogether different department, frankly. Of course, that's part of the department's work, but not my game, not my game at all, I'm afraid."

"What is your *game*, Mr. Fairfax? And how have we become part of it? You seem to know all about us." said Harry.

"Well, as I've said, our agency is concerned with internal UK matters, which before the flood was mainly terrorism and economic concerns – trade, industry, that kind of thing – plus organised crime of course, Russian mafia, the Balkan gangs, Chinese Tongs and their ghastly sex-slave trade, South American drugs, illegal arms. Naturally, all that changed. He paused, examined his mug and found it empty. Turning to Vicky, he held it out. "Don't suppose I could impose on you my dear?" he enquired politely with a smooth, self-effacing smile. Vicky grimaced but took the mug and turned away to fill the kettle.

"Too kind. But I digress. As I said, après le deluge the agency remit changed radically, partly to service the incessant new demands of our paranoid masters, largely convinced we were heading for total anarchy, and partly because we realised that the future of the country would depend on keeping the lid on, maintaining some kind of stability in the face of huge social upheaval right across the country..." Fairfax held up his hand, palm forward; Harry was clearly about to chide him, "...please, not long now, just bear with me...thank you...," the last said to Vicky, who had placed a tray on the table with mugs of tea for everyone. He took the nearest and sipped. Too hot again. "We were facing a challenge the size of which no-one had ever contemplated. We needed help, and I regret it is at this juncture in my rather erratic journey that our paths came to cross, through the unfortunate auspices of the late Alfred Jarrott."

Chapter 10: Certain Irregularities

Fairfax bent his head with the air of a man performing a distasteful task, more out of obligation than a duty of care, and took a sip of tea. Partly concealed by the mug, his face was a mask of neutered professional impersonality; the bland, inoffensive expression worn by men who deal frequently with the aftermath of death. As perhaps he anticipated, a stream of questions burst forth.

"Dead? When?" Harry demanded.

"Shorty after you left, as far as we can tell. A matter of days apparently."

"How did he...I mean...how did you know him?" asked Cas, reaching hurriedly for his guitar to clutch it tight to his chest.

"Anyway, who says *we* knew him?" Vicky demanded in a harsh voice, at which Reuben and Harry exchanged raised eyebrows. Jake, scanning faces round the table, noted that no-one was very upset about Jarrott, himself included. He was shocked, certainly, but his thoughts were for himself, for the band. Vicky and Cas were quite pale. Harry and Reuben, on the other hand, looked neither shocked nor upset, both wearing rather a different expression, and Jake was surprised to recognise it: the professional look of people who watch things, a stillness, an impassive demeanour in which only the eyes really moved, and were constantly probing. Jake knew policemen with that look – usually the sharper tools in the box, as he had found to his cost a few times – the look that seemed to press on the object of their fixity, the stare that insisted the eyes saw everything they were looking at, not just the surface. "How did he die Mr. Fairfax?"

"The coroner's report says it was suicide."

"But you don't think so?"

"There were...certain irregularities."

"I'm sorry Mr. Fairfax, but I really don't understand why MI5 should have an interest in Alf Jarrott," Harry insisted. "He was hardly a threat to national security, was he? So I ask you again, what exactly is your interest in this, and us? And how did you connect Jarrott to us in the first place?"

"Well, that's the interesting bit, I suppose. May I speak confidentially – I hope you don't mind? You see, Mr. Jarrott was not a target. He was in fact a local resource – he was what we call a Santa...short for Santa's Little Helpers, you see – our little joke, I'm afraid. As I was trying to explain, when the agency came under such enormous pressure, a decision was taken to recruit outside the normal sphere, more of a grass-roots movement if you like. It was believed that by drawing on well-documented examples – and one example in particular – of a low-level network, we could expand our reach without a lot of screening, vetting, training, and of course cost."

"What example?" said Cas. "The Gestapo?"

Fairfax laughed, a strangled sound that implied a lack of regular use. "Good grief. Certainly not. This isn't a police state you know, despite what you may have heard to the contrary. No, the example I referred to was something else, also German, curiously. Are any of you familiar with the term 'Stasi'?"

"East-German secret police before the Berlin Wall came down and Germany was reunited," Harry responded immediately.

"Correct, although more accurately we could say they were a combination of MI5 and the SIS in one agency, and very good at it they were, too. The Stasi were widely regarded as one of the most efficient intelligence organisations of its time. At its peak, it employed ninety-thousand odd full time staff, but more interesting to us was that they also had a network of around three-hundred thousand so-called volunteers. In other words, about one in fifty East Germans collaborated with the Stasi— one of the most effective penetrations ever of a civilian society by an intelligence agency. Germanic efficiency ain't in it, believe me.

"Of course, with so much power cloaked in the secrecy of a totalitarian state, there were abuses on a vast scale, although some of us think too little attention was given to more worthy exploits – they rescued hundreds of Chilean left-wingers, for example, just after Pinochet grabbed power, got them out of the country before the army could murder them. Perhaps that wasn't enough...to save the Stasi from the judgement of history, that is.

In any case, it's not the losers that write the history, as I'm sure you know.

"When the Berlin Wall fell, much of the Stasi archive remained intact, an absolute goldmine of information about how to build a network in a civilian population. Given the circumstances – Britain being very close to all-out civil war or even total collapse, the anarchy our politicos so feared – the intelligence heads of the day decided to emulate the best of the Stasi models and methods, build an network of our own, but with certain checks and balances in place to prevent the worst excesses of the regime we were modelling ourselves on. We developed a plan, then spread the word through all the usual channels, plus a bit of word of mouth through our regular staff in the regions where net access was down. You'd be surprised how many ordinary people came forward, who wanted to help us for little or no reward. Mr. Jarrott was one of them."

"So Jarrott was a grass?" Jake was agitated, furiously ransacking his memory, trying desperately to recall anything incriminating that might have been overheard during one of Jarrott's visits. "Sounds about right doesn't it, the little shit." He scanned the faces of the others. "Think about it – the photos he was always taking, the information he tried to wheedle out of us. The furtiveness, the leading questions. Makes sense, doesn't it? Fuck!" It was so obvious to Jake in retrospect. How could he have been so stupid not to see it before now? There had been so many visits, so much talk. Now the snitch was dead and it was too late; whatever the damage was, it was done and dusted.

"Guido didn't trust him either," said Cas, completing his own calculations.

"Shut up Cas," ordered Harry, annoyed at the indiscretion, then annoyed at himself for drawing attention to it.

Fairfax appeared to ignore the outburst. "He was not a grass, Mr. Constable. If you want to be wholly accurate, I would use the term 'informer', although this is also rather an emotive term – as is *collaborator*. Pejorative terms; perhaps the lack of precise terminology is why we invented the nickname. But whatever you wish to call it, the fact is that Mr. Jarrott assisted us, along with many other ordinary people, by looking out for certain things, keeping us informed of local events that might be of interest to us, and generally helping us in our work. Considering our work is to protect the UK, perhaps you shouldn't think quite so badly of him."

"Think badly of him? Sounds like you didn't know him very well," said Jake, unable to suppress a note of sarcasm. "But how did you connect him to us? And why are you here? Do you think we had something to do with his death?"

"The fact is, the connection between you and Mr. Jarrott was known to us long before his death, because he mentioned you in his reports from time to time." Fairfax smiled reassuringly. "Nothing bad, to be perfectly honest. Certainly nothing very interesting to us; you're a colourful little band of gypsies, but hardly a threat to national security. He reported only the contact as and when it occurred, and perhaps a mention here and there of certain recreational pleasures, the modest scale of which is of no interest to us at all. Sure, we're interested in the major importers, links between organised crime groups, the money trail, the weapons that come in on the back of many of the drug shipments and vice versa. We have no interest in a kilo of grass or a carton of dodgy Ecstasy. We have no time to pursue end users, no resources. Nobody does. Please believe me, and bear in mind that I wouldn't be telling you this otherwise. Think about it."

Jake didn't think the logic bore too much examination, but suppressed his concerns for the moment. There was an implicit threat in there somewhere, but this wasn't the time to air his suspicions. "Go on please."

"Very well. I should also stress that as far as any connection goes, we do not believe it extends to involvement in the death – however caused – of Mr. Jarrott. If you were suspects, I'd be interrogating you individually and you'd be telling me the story, not the other way round. But we're getting behind ourselves, if I could put it that way, so let's return to the chronology.

"My first involvement in this matter came when the local police noticed our tag on Mr. Jarrott's file – he was known to the police, as they say – and they informed us of the suicide. Now, it is standard procedure to send someone to investigate in matters like this and I was assigned to the job. As I said, my work is clerical. In a case like this, unless foul play is suspected we leave the investigations to the local police, and my job is simply to take statements from anyone involved – officers, witnesses and so on – get copies of the paperwork, police reports, coroner's report, hospital records if the victim was admitted, mortuary and autopsy reports – still a shocking amount of paper considering we live in a digital age, but with so many power cuts it makes sense: you don't need electricity to write with a pencil and paper. It's also my duty to check the deceased's residence, inform relatives, arrange for a cremation if there's no-one else to do it. Housekeeping, we call it.

" After my preliminary investigation, everything seemed fairly straightforward. There were illicit drugs at his house known to cause depression and psychosis, which fitted in with the method – according to the police report he hung himself. There was no apparent intrusion, no signs of a struggle, and I have to tell you that hanging is a most unsuitable way of murdering someone."

"So what makes you think it wasn't suicide?" said Harry.

"I'm coming to that, Mr. Bracey. It's circumstantial – the evidence. On the surface, the preliminary data was pretty clear-cut. I didn't think too much of it at first; regrettably, we have a fairly high suicide rate amongst the Santas. It's the profile y'know; introvert, poor education, bit of a loner, no friends, a predilection for petty crime, a certain falsity in relationships, some paranoia, racist, conspiracy theorist – you knew him; you know what I'm talking about. It was the profile.

"But then I came across a report by a couple of patrolmen who had seen him the day after you left. Following up on that report, several things came to light almost immediately. First, on the night before you left, there was a huge fire that gutted an old hotel up on the moor. Second, from the notebooks and station logs for that night, it appears the military attended the fire, not the civilian emergency services, which is rather odd to say the least. Third, the patrolmen who attended the fire were prevented by the army from entering the site, and the station received a call, purportedly from the MOD, instructing them to keep well clear and ask no questions. That, I have to tell you, is damn odd. Very rare in my experience. Wrong procedure too – the MOD would talk to the Chief Constable's office, never direct to the local station.

"Then – sorry, I've lost count – anyway, according to the two patrolmen, the next day Jarrott is seen roaming around the remains of the burned-out building. Hours later, you vacate the camp and take to the road. Mere hours after that, there is a massive explosion beneath the remains of the hotel which utterly destroys the site, much of it collapsing into previously undiscovered tunnels, quite a little warren of them in fact. An explosion of trapped gas, according to the official report. Whole area more or less flattened, not that there was much to look at after army bulldozers had razed the ground and army trucks had carted off the debris, much to the fury of the police. God, they were livid. It was a blatant cover-up, and by any measure pretty damn inept. There are only two reasons why the military acts like that: either they want the operation to be seen, to be noticed, or they are in such a hurry they just don't give a damn.

"With me so far? Very well. Now, let me tell you what decided the matter. I have to confide in you again – I shouldn't of course – but I don't think it makes a damn bit of difference now. You see, although a Santa like Mr. Jarrott has a general listening and watching brief, sometimes we give them something specific to do. In this case, it was the hotel; Jarrott had been instructed to keep an eye on it for us. Now there's a coincidence, don't you think? And the strangest thing: in his last report – only a day later – he never mentions either the fire or his subsequent visit. Not a trace – his bloody target burns to the ground, there's a massive cover-up involving the military, the police are warned off, yet Mr. Jarrott doesn't give it so much as a single sentence in the whole report. Page after page of local gossip, much of it about you, your drugs, your gigs, something about going hunting, the usual vitriol about poor old Guido...," heads came up, "who we've known about for ages, and good luck to him." Heads went back down.

Jake was feeling increasingly nervous the more Fairfax spoke. Since he sat down, Fairfax had not once looked at Reuben, nor spoken to him, nor had he mentioned his name. Was it because Reuben didn't have a surname, thus spoiling Mr. Fairfax's social management scheme? The realisation that he could still be

105

frivolous at a time like this surprised Jake and made him feel a little better. Fairfax was still talking.

"...and I've eaten at his restaurant. Fine meal, damn fine chef. Good wine list, considering the whole lot was smuggled in. And that's the full extent of my – our – interest in your Sicilian friend, of that I can assure you.

"So, to sum up – Mr. Jarrott deliberately conceals important information from us, and then, apparently, kills himself. Of course, much of this is circumstantial, but I assume you understand now why I'm here."

Jake was squirming in his seat again, unable to keep still. He knew something had escaped him, a question he needed answering urgently, if only he could figure out what it was. He glanced at Harry, who caught his eye and shook his head almost imperceptibly: don't ask. So Harry knew, or suspected. But what was the question?

"Actually no, Mr. Fairfax," said Vicky as she stood and gathered up the mugs from the table. "Anyone want more tea?" Everyone did. "First you say we're not in any trouble over our...um...lifestyle...and you don't suspect us of being involved in poor Alf's death. You seem to know all about Alf, about Guido, about us presumably. So why are you here, how did you find us, and what's that bug all about?" She glanced pointedly at the grey box, now sitting conspicuously alone in the middle of the table. Jake was startled; he'd forgotten about it, so engrossed was he in Fairfax's story.

"Very good questions, Mrs. Richardson. Well done. Right to the point. That..." he pointed at the box, "...is the reason I'm here – and finding you was hardly an exercise in spycraft: I looked at your Facebook page to see where you were playing next, and asked around a bit when I got here. OK?" Vicky nodded, looking vaguely discomfited.

"I don't wish to alarm any of you, but I believe you are in danger from whoever planted that device. I do not know who planted it yet, but I strongly suspect the various events I have described are connected to this box in some way, and therefore to you, although it's not entirely clear how you came to be involved. For people who, on the face of it, have only the most tenuous connection, the most peripheral involvements in these events, you do seem to be drawing attention to yourselves. Why is that? Do you have any thoughts on the subject at all – any of you?"

And for the first time, Mr. Fairfax addressed Reuben directly.

Struck by the proverbial thunderbolt, Jake woke up. At least, that's what it felt like – a burst of electricity that extended outward from his brain, triggered by the question that formed itself, unbidden, amongst synapses still miraculously functioning after a lifetime of relentless abuse. It was followed immediately by an insight regarding the bland man sitting opposite him, the reason the question remained unspoken, and why Harry had tried to warn him off. The question was right there in front of them, buried under the rubble of the burning hotel, hidden amongst all the debris of the story that surrounded it.

Now he saw it: *why did MI5 want Alf to watch the hotel?* Then the look exchanged between Fairfax and Reuben, and Jake's realisation: Fairfax knew about Reuben. *He knew!* There was no question about it. They were being led somewhere by this supercilious jerk, taken for a ride while he insinuated himself into their world. It was only a matter of time before someone mentioned something that would start Fairfax off, a train of thought that would lead inexorably to Reuben by one route or another. This was why Jake couldn't ask the question. Harry had got there ahead of him. Fairfax wanted them to ask about it, was dangling the question in front of them, knowing very well where it would lead. It was a trap.

"What do you want from me, Mr. Fairfax?" Reuben spoke for the first time. To the surprise of both Jake and Harry, he had not so much sprung the trap as jumped clear over it. Vicky and Cas were frozen in place, holding their breath, Vicky caught as she bent forward, the tray of steaming drinks suspended in mid-air over the table. Jake reached forward and took the tray from her, placing it on the table as she sunk into her seat, never taking her eyes from Reuben.

" Well Reuben – may I call you Reuben? – I'm glad we can finally get to the point," said Fairfax, quite unruffled. "I was beginning to wonder for a moment there if you'd lost your voice, you were so quiet. What I want is this: I want you to go into hiding, to disappear while we find out who's after you. I want to protect you – and your new friends – while we find out who your old friends are. Or were." He reached into his briefcase and pulled out a sheet of paper, which he placed on the table by the tray. The other five stared at it, not needing to pick it up: it was a photocopy, enlarged and quite clear in detail, of Reuben's ID card. "And I want to know all about the hotel, at which I assume you were once a guest? *All about it.*"

"So that's the deal then, is it?" said Harry. "So far, you've not really told us anything much at all – we could have got most of this from the news sites, if any of us were bothered, that is. But now I understand. It's a trade: you'll tell us about the bug and the hotel if Reuben here tells you what he knows about what was going on there. Is that right?"

"Admirably perceptive, Mr. Bracey."

Could Fairfax possibly be more patronising? Jake wondered. "Hey Reuben," he said with a straight face. "If Mr. Fairfax here comes clean with us, will you tell him everything you remember about the hotel. *Everything you can remember?*"

"Yes," replied Reuben, unhesitatingly compliant. "I'll tell him everything I can remember." Everybody looked happy. "Good then," said Mr. Fairfax, smiling uneasily as he glanced from face to face, then down at the photocopy. "I found this at Mr. Jarrott's house, by the way. I assume you have the original?" Reuben nodded. "Terrible likeness. Mine's just the same. He found it at the hotel the day after the fire, presumably? I thought so. In which case, let me explain our interest in that establishment:

"From time to time, certain arrangements are made between the UK and other countries – nominally our friends – to host certain facilities – examples made public include facilities like Menworth Hill for example, where all the UK/USA listening devices are installed. Those installations cannot be concealed from the public, and generate too much speculation. So there are other facilities too. Smaller, private, out of the way, and quite secret. Very secret actually. Deniable too, and that's really the point. If you want to do some *questionable* research, experiments that may be prohibited in your own country, you go elsewhere to do it. So long as you know the right people, all kinds of blind eyes will be turned in your direction, yet see nothing, nothing at all, at least so long as you are discrete.

"In general, my agency is kept in the dark about these arrangements, but every now and then we pick up odd little signals that suggest there's something going on, and when we do it's of considerable interest to us, because if any of these cosy arrangements go wrong – the wheels come off as it were – it's always MI5 that takes the blame. Most of these ops are illegal in any case, or very dubious, and frankly, we have enough on our plate without one half of the intelligence community importing mad scientists and their dangerous technologies while the other half goes chasing round after them, trying to stop them blowing themselves, and us, to kingdom come. Or poisoning us, gassing us or worse. Destroying half the telecommunications infrastructure with a virus: that nearly happened once, when the CIA sprang some of the most gifted hackers they had in jail, offered them amnesty, flew them here from the US and locked them in a semi in Croydon with half a million quid's worth of computers, a gigabyte pipe and an endless supply of pizza. Cyber warfare? Cyber revenge, more like it. The programmers had targeted the UK and US infrastructure instead of Iran or Russia or whoever, and what's more they nearly pulled it off. We interceded just in time. Never could prove the collusion, though. It's always like that: very frustrating, I can tell you. Very. Still, we live in hope."

"So you picked up signs that brought the hotel to your attention?" said Harry.

"That's right. We have programs that sift through the PNC – the Police National Computer – and other sources, looking for patterns of events. Clusters of unusual crime, reports of unusual events, environmental disasters, strange behaviour in the populace, all kinds of things."

"And there was a cluster of these events surrounding the hotel?" asked Reuben.

"That's right. At first, it was just the general area we were interested in – Dartmoor, basically – but then we targeted some rather more powerful, and specialised software to the problem and we soon narrowed our focus down to half a dozen establishments that had certain...how can I put it...*odd* characteristics."

"Such as?"

"I'm sorry, but this is leading into territory I really can't discuss. Operational issues. Actually, for the purposes of my explanation it doesn't really matter – the detail, that is – but I can tell you, for example, that the number of guests the hotel entertained could not account for the amount of power they were using, the amount of water, the bottled gas and fuel oil they were getting through. Also, they were bringing in food from quite a large number of places instead of just local suppliers, which seems odd unless they were trying to hide how much they were eating..." he glanced at Reuben speculatively, "...or – more likely – how many people they were feeding – people who were not legitimate guests according to the central registration database at the Department of Justice. And I have to tell you this: they were buying surprising quantities of medical supplies. Specialised gear, powerful chemicals. What were they doing with materiel like that? It's the kind of thing that makes us nervous. Very. And if that wasn't enough, we got really interested when we discovered we couldn't get into their pipe – we just wanted a quick look at the hotel computers – but their system was impenetrable. *Highly secure.* In other words, they had military-grade computer security, the best you can get. You need friends in very high places and a lot of money to get your hands on that kind of kit, *and they had it.*

"After that, we hit a bit of a dead end. We ran some static observation for a while but we got the impression they picked that up almost immediately, so we backed off fast – you never want to alert a target to the surveillance they are under, needless to say. Without additional resources, which we didn't have, and priority authorisation, which we couldn't seem to get, the best we could do was put a Santa on the job, stick the whole thing on the back burner while we dealt with more pressing concerns. Next thing we know, the hotel has burnt to the ground, there's a huge cover-up op with military involvement, Mr. Jarrott appears to have killed himself, and Mr. Reuben here pops up out of the undergrowth and joins a band."

"OK," said Harry, "that's the back story. What about this?" He reached forward and picked up the grey box. "If what you are telling us is true, there appears to be another actor on this stage."

"The man in the bushes," said Cas.

"Sweet Jesus!" Jake slapped his hand to his forehead and groaned. Vicky, disgusted, muttered something under her breath, while Cas wilted under the aggrieved and disbelieving stares from Harry and Reuben. They all turned to Fairfax, who said nothing but offered a modest, knowing smile to suggest he shared their embarrassment. To Jake, Fairfax appeared relaxed, but with something of a feline poise about him, as if waiting for the routine appearance of a mouse. A *predictable* mouse.

"You may as well tell him, then," Harry said to Cas in a gruff voice, but fearing more indiscretions, Jake seized the baton and told Fairfax about the events of the previous night, although he omitted Reuben's observation regarding the size of the would-be assassin; it seemed prudent to do so, although he couldn't say why. Fairfax listened in silence; his only reaction was to pull a small notebook from his pocket and make entries from time to time using a tiny pencil drawn from the spine of the book. Each time he made an note he habitually licked the point of the pencil. Ex-policeman's habit? Jake wondered.

Now Fairfax looked serious. "You're sure the three drunks were unconnected to the man in the bushes," he asked for a second time, pencil poised. Reuben shook his head. "We have less time than I thought. Look here: Mr. Bracey asked, in a roundabout sort of way, who else is involved in this – the other actor, as he put it, who planted the bug, and seems now from what you've told me to be lurking in the undergrowth..."

"And the answer is..." Reuben interrupted "...the people who were running the hotel. Isn't that right, Mr. Fairfax? They're trying to cover up what they were doing there. Maybe they started the fire, called in the army? Maybe they also killed Alf Jarrott – after he found the ID card. If not for that, what else did he find up there?"

"They covered up poor old Alf then – permanently?" Cas wondered aloud.

"That's right," Fairfax agreed. "My suspicions exactly. More worrying is that they only have one more thing to cover up before they disappear for good, and Mr. Reuben is it. That's why they planted the bug, I would think. It's how they found you, of course, and they could have overheard anything you said in here since you left Devon. I must admit I'm puzzled though, because if their man had you targeted then why didn't he take the shot? That would have been the end of it."

"The end of Reuben, you mean. Maybe there's something else they want," said Vicky. "Maybe they want Reuben back, which is why they didn't kill him."

Fairfax leaned back expectantly, rotating the empty mug in his hands. "Perhaps. We could speculate about this all day Mrs. Richardson, but I have to go soon. Anyway, now you know everything I know. That's all I have. Your turn, I believe." He looked pointedly at his watch.

The others exchanged barely concealed signs of amusement. "What?" asked Fairfax, puzzled. "Something amusing? No? Well then - come on then Reuben old chap; I'm running out of time. Fair's fair, don't you think? I've told you what I know, shown you my hand. A deal's a deal eh? Tell me about the hotel. What was going on in that basement? And what were you doing there? Anything you can recollect could be useful, so don't hold back."

Reuben, playing to the gallery in their brief moment of ascendancy, gladly leaned forward to deliver the bad news.

It took Mr. Fairfax rather less time to accept the truth of the situation than Jake expected. In fact, he took the deception with reasonably good grace, asking only a few questions before accepting Reuben's memory loss as fact. "Perhaps I deserved that," he said as he stood up, retrieving his briefcase and placing it on the table between the empty mugs. "Time to go, I'm afraid. Let me leave you with this: we need to get you somewhere safe. I can help you, but you have to abandon the bus and the truck because they are too easy to track, far too easy."

Jake was already shaking his head. "We can't do that, Mr. Fairfax. We have commitments."

"Indeed you do. I've seen your site. Always useful for an assassin to know in advance the exact time and date his victim will be at a certain location, don't you think?" He tugged at his coat, which had ridden up, but knocked over his briefcase. "Sorry, damn..." he muttered as he righted the briefcase, at the same time picking up the photocopy of the ID badge and putting it inside. He snapped the case shut and picked it up. "This is not – really not – a *game*. The apt expression 'deadly serious' comes to mind, and it would be very foolish to believe you have the option to carry on playing your dates instead of taking steps to minimise the risk."

"According to you, it's Reuben they want," said Vicky. "We discussed whether Reuben would be better off away from us. Actually..." she looked at Reuben "...that's not true. It's whether we'd be better off. Quite selfish. Sorry Reuben."

"That's OK Vicky, you know it is. We discussed this didn't we? What do you think, Mr. Fairfax? Should I come with you, leave here right now. I'm prepared to do it, if it's the best thing. Wouldn't the band be safer with me gone?"

Fairfax shook his head. "I don't think so. As soon as they figure out you've gone, the first thing they will do is try to find out where. Who do you think they are going to ask? I daresay they won't limit themselves to polite questions either, bearing in mind the fate of Mr. Jarrott." He moved towards the door, turning as he reached it. "You all need protection, and I can't help you while you roam around the countryside. I need to get you all in one place, somewhere safe and out of the way, hidden from view. Can't hide the bus or the truck, so you would need to figure out somewhere to put them, I expect."

"Christ!" muttered Cas. "I've figured it out." Too angry to restrain himself despite numerous warning glances, he expounded his theory. "We're bait, aren't we? You want to use us to catch the bad guys." In the pin-dropping silence that followed, nobody groaned.

From the doorway, Fairfax laughed, a genuine, full-throated, head thrown back affair. "I think you just redeemed yourself there, Mr. Calinas. Well done." His face resumed its customary sobriety. "I'll be back soon. Think about what I've told you." He stepped out of the door, chuckling again, then poked his head back through. "And tell the crew when they get back – best split them up; send them home for a break."

With that, he was gone, his receding footsteps crunching through the snow. While the others watched Fairfax get into his car, Reuben started passing the empty mugs to Vicky, then stiffened. "Hey – where's the grey box?"

Jake ran to the door, but it was too late. All he could see were the receding tail-lights of the nondescript Ford estate as it faded away behind a thick curtain of falling snow.

Two miles down the road, the car turned off, drove a short way into the woods and stopped. Fairfax reached into the glove compartment and retrieved a pair of headphones. Putting them on, he switched between settings on the receiver into which the headphones were plugged, checking one by one the functionality of the six microphones concealed around the bus. Once he had confirmed they were all operational and the recorder was running, he took a battered sandwich from his briefcase and consumed it in contented silence, watching the falling snow gradually cover the windscreen until he could see nothing at all of the world outside.

Chapter 11: Snowblind

Immediately after Fairfax left, Vicky was overwhelmed with an urge to find her son and decided to look for him. Cas, feeling rather self-conscious, opted to go with her, glad to escape Jake, Harry, Reuben and the unreadable miasma that surrounded them.

"What an amateur," said Harry as the others closed the door behind them.

Jake looked at him, curious. "Why do you say that?"

"He disconnected the bug. Now they know we're onto them."

"Oh shit. You're right. If he'd left it behind we could have put it back, reconnected it. Maybe they wouldn't have noticed. Anyway, I wanted Nick to take a look at it."

"Perhaps that's why he took it," said Reuben. "You know, perhaps we should step outside for a bit of air…it's very stuffy in here." Harry and Jake looked at Reuben; the suggestion was accompanied by a warning look; Reuben said no more, left the bus, the others following him out into the dazzling snow, sharp and bright after the gloom.

"Hey, are you OK?" Jake asked. Reuben didn't look quite right.

"I'm fine. My eyes hurt a bit, that's all. A bit sensitive. Been like it for a week now. Sorry about pulling you out here, but it occurred to me that we shouldn't talk in the bus any more – not about this. Anyway, what did you make of our visitor?"

Harry was the first to speak. "I didn't believe any of it, not really. We should get in touch with Guido, see what he knows. I suspect, unfortunately, that Alf Jarrott must be dead, because that's one claim that's too easy to check. Other than that, I just had the feeling we were only getting half the story. He knows more than he's telling us, of that I'm certain. It's habitual in people like him; information is currency to them and they always expect to get something in return for their outlay. He didn't volunteer anything but conjecture and hypothesis. Most troubling to me is that he's here at all. I can't figure out what he really wants, unless Cas was right and he's using us as bait."

"I think it's a turf war," said Jake. "MI5 versus MI6 or maybe the CIA. Remember how he told us it was impossible to prove anything, to catch these people? A minor official like him – I'm sure that was why he gave us the foreign policy lecture, to impress us with his importance – a minor clerk getting in on a big bust by accident, a chance to be part of the team that takes down a competing agency, to embarrass the shit out of them. Sudden glamour in the midst of all that paperwork? I think he's jamming. Gone all jazz in the workplace."

Harry laughed. "He was a pompous twit, wasn't he? You could be right too, but you know what? It doesn't matter what the politics are, Jake. That's back at GCHQ or Vauxhall. We're on the frontline, and so is Fairfax. Whatever his motives or ambitions, we're part of his scheme. Can we possibly trust him? Personally, I don't think we can – especially if he wants us as bait for his trap."

"Being part of *his* scheme is the best option we have right now," commented Reuben, "since we don't have a scheme of our own. He has access to resources; we have none. And if he knows things we don't, we need to keep him close so we can find out what he knows. Otherwise, if we reject his help, what do you think he would do next?"

"I don't know," said Harry. "Hard to tell, really. He has no proof whatever for any of his claims. He said it himself: it's all circumstantial, even if he's right. He needs something tangible to impress his superiors, get the authorisation he needs. Without us, he has no leads at all. He needs us more than we need him by the sound of it."

"We should not underestimate him, or what information he already has," said Reuben. "Bad tactics."

"Inside the tent pissing out," said Jake as he lit a cigarette.

Harry turned to Reuben. "Hey -you were running slowly today – slower than you usually do. Was that because of the snow?" Reuben looked surprised. "I wasn't aware of that, Harry. What makes you think I was going slowly?"

"Only the fact I kept up with you. Think about it – I've never run the whole course without us taking three breaks for my benefit. Keeping up with you is normally near impossible and even then I know you're jogging while I'm sprinting, more or less. Not today, though."

Reuben, squinting uncomfortably, shrugged and changed the subject. "If he could hide us somewhere safe, would that not be a good thing, Jake? We really are highly visible right now."

Jake was irritated. "Look Reuben, I don't expect you to understand this, but we're more than just a band. We're part of a show business tradition, a tradition that says the show must go on. It's a ridiculous cliché, I know, *but it's what I believe in.* It's important to me and makes me proud to play a modest part in that tradition, keeping it alive in an age of cheapness and exploitation. Values are traded like commodities; as soon as one is unfashionable, it's dropped in favour of some new – inevitably lower – standard. Always the path of least public resistance, the easy option, and the customers are always the victims, the losers. I can't live like that. Standards matter, and should be a constant in our lives, the constant that gives us our self-respect. That's why we have to do the gigs. I've been on the road for a long time now, and one thing I know for sure is that punters count on us to turn up, more so now than ever. We bring a tiny amount of sunshine into lives that might otherwise be filled with nothing but gloom. I'm proud of that, and I'm proud they rely on us. I will not – *will not* – let them down. Or myself. Or the good name of this band and the standards that define it, musical or professional."

Harry gave a derisory laugh. "Well said that man. Break a fucking leg, why don't you? Or better still, have someone do it for you with a sledge-hammer while Vicky watches them stub their cigarettes out on little Jimi, just for the fun of it. *Jarrott's dead, Jake!* It's quite possible they tortured him. Did it occur to you that he may have given us away? I don't know how they found him, but they did, so it's likely that they made him tell them about us before they killed him. Can you imagine a little shit like Jarrott holding out under pressure, or spilling the beans in a pathetic bout of verbal diarrhoea at the slightest provocation?

I think the bug came later, after they tracked us down – the timeline doesn't seem right to me otherwise. There was no time to install it between us finding Reuben and leaving the next evening, no opportunity. In which case, how else could they have connected us to Reuben, except if Jarrott told them? He was on the moor with me when we found Reuben, and he was the one who found the ID card. They wanted to know what he knew, and they killed him once they found out, murdered him to protect their filthy secrets." His voice had risen steadily in both volume and intensity all through the tirade. Now he was only a few decibels short of shouting. "Really Jake, I ask you: *do you have any fucking idea just how heavy this could get?*"

"I do, Harry, really I do." Jake whispered, his face chalk-white. "I'm sorry if I disappoint you. I don't know this world, this place where people can do such terrible things, and do them so casually. I've been close to a few things in my time, and my imagination is sufficiently lurid to fill in the details I didn't get close enough to see for myself, thanks all the same. But I can't operate in this world. I have no skills that apply here. No understanding, no experience; I can't navigate here and I'm easy prey for anyone who comes along. I'm completely vulnerable, and it scares the shit out of me. I hate violence; I simply can't do it even when punches are being thrown at me. I just curl up in a ball and hope to hell I get through it. I run if I can, and I'm not in the least bit ashamed that I do. Fuck that. What is it they say about live cowards and dead heroes? So don't ask me to abandon my world, Harry. Don't ask me to leave my territory, the place where I can defend myself, and the band, where I have friends and allies and I know what the rules are, and how to bend them. I'm good at bending rules, but in Fairfax's world, there aren't any. I'm terrible at violence, and I suspect that Fairfax's world is full of it. So don't ask me to abandon the standards I live by, or the world in which I live by them. And I meant what I said about our commitments, so shove your cynicism." He looked away, clearly distressed.

Harry draped one arm around Jake's shoulder. "Hey man, I'm really sorry. I really didn't mean to imply...you know...Christ Jake, I respect your professionalism and I've learned a lot from you on that score. You're a good guy and a good friend. I know you're on the side of the angels, and I'm sorry if I hurt you. You know I didn't mean to."

Jake turned back and his anger sank as fast as it surfaced. Harry evidently meant every word, his face full of remorse and concern. "Yeah, well...OK...thanks, man. Good of you to say so." He sniffed. "But no more talk about pulling gigs? Next one is tomorrow, right?" He thought for a moment. "Mind you, I can stop taking bookings right now if you like. Then, as soon as we play the final gig in the diary, we can go and hide for as long as you like."

"Really? How soon will that be?" asked Reuben. Jake and Harry both grinned. "About a year from now, son," answered Jake dryly.

Harry nodded. "Assuming any of us are still alive by then."

Vicky was lost. She had started off across the fields following tracks in the snow, two adults walking steadily, circled anxiously by smaller feet at a perpetual run. Then the snow started falling again and the tracks began to fade. In front of her, a likely hill loomed in the distance. Between her and the hill was a small tract of woodland; as far as she could see the tracks led to it, so she wasn't too disturbed at the change in weather, or the fact that Cas had deserted her after only a mile or so pleading incipient hypothermia, having failed to heed her advice and get a coat before setting off.

The woods were quiet, her footfall muffled. Tree limbs bowed towards the ground under the weight of the snow, which the wind would dislodge releasing a curtain of white crystals falling to the ground with a long slithering sigh as the branches, released from their burden, sprang back in a kinetically joyful release. Vicky could no longer see the hill she was heading for and when she turned around she couldn't see the way back either. Her pulse started racing as the snowfall increased but she pressed on dutifully, her thoughts relentlessly focused on finding Jimi. After five minutes of steady progress she could see the trees start to thin out a hundred yards ahead and she could also see the lower slopes of the hill climbing up to merge with the whiteness of snow and sky.

A gust cleared the snow in front of her and she saw someone at the edge of the woods. She stepped forward, calling out and was surprised to see it was Reuben, wrapped up in a massive coat, his big frame unmistakable. He was staring at her, unmoving.

Pleased and a little relieved he had come to help her, she waved again and started running towards him, but in her haste she slipped, fell forward and slithered several feet before picking herself up again, camouflaged from head to foot in powdery snow. By the time she had brushed herself off, Reuben was gone. She walked to the edge of the trees but there was no sign of him. He had definitely seen her, she was sure. What an idiot, not even waiting for her. He must have run off at his customary high speed. Why didn't he wait? She looked around, but she could see no tracks indicating which way he might have gone.

It was snowing hard now; she knew the best course of action would be to get back. The others would probably be back before her. She would feel foolish; they would be annoyed with her. Morons. She shrugged, set off down the opposite side of the hill to the lane that snaked around it and climbed over a gate. Confident she knew where she was, Vicky set off down the lane.

An hour later, her navigational confidence somewhat dented, she staggered into the bus, where she wasn't in the least surprised to find she was the last one back – all the others had returned an hour ago or more. In fact, Nick was about to launch a search party and several people were donning coats, hats and gloves. After a few moments of the anticipated badinage, which she endured with bad grace, everyone sat back down and the discussion returned to their visitor and his story. Vicky leaned over and whispered in Reuben's ear. "How did you get back so fast? Why didn't you wait for me?" Reuben looked startled. "What do you mean?"

"I saw you in the woods. You were looking straight at me, don't deny it." All conversation stopped.

"What are you talking about, Vicky?" asked Harry.

"I just wanted to know why Reuben didn't wait for me, that's all. I spent fifteen minutes looking for him, as well as Jimi."

"Vicky," said Jake carefully, "Reuben never left the campsite; he's been here with us ever since you left."

Anticipating delays on the icy roads, the crew and band left early the following morning, Vicky and Jimi were with them; Nick again was adamant that no-one should remain at the camp on their own, and there was no argument. Vicky's strange encounter had unnerved them, as had the reported death of Alf Jarrott, but the consensus was to continue the gigs, the crew loyally upholding the band's decision to carry on.

While the roadies set up the equipment, Jake called Guido at his restaurant on his phone, reasoning that even if he used a different phone, Guido's would certainly be recorded anyway.

None the less, it was a quick, guarded exchange: Guido confirmed that Jarrott was indeed dead, in circumstances superficially consistent with the events Fairfax had described. Jake in turn sketched Fairfax's visit, relaying the alleged lack of interest in Guido's nocturnal activities but leaving out much else.

When he got back to the venue, the crew were raising the overhead gantry on which they had hung various lights. Sam was sitting in mid-air astride the gantry, aligning the lights with various areas of the stage and checking the safety chains on each unit as he worked his way along the length of the truss. He stopped near the centre, noticing that one light didn't seem to be fixed as securely as he required, but as he manipulated the mounting to see if the bolts were sufficiently tight, the whole lamp housing sheared off from its bracket and fell away. Sam, gripping only the safety chain, shouted a warning to those below as the chain slid link by link though his sweaty hand, but he couldn't hold it and the lamp dropped. Below him, the crew scattered, all except Reuben who stood absolutely still, watching intently as the light began to fall. He took a couple of steps to reposition himself, then reached upward. As the descending lamp dropped past him, he grasped the side rail of the mounting with a sure, swift movement and swung the lamp through an arc at arm's length, slowing the redirected momentum before placing the lamp on the floor. The crew and band burst into applause.

"Wow, great save," said Nick. "These lights are damned expensive." He looked up at the gantry, abruptly frightened when it occurred to him the lamp could have fallen during the show, and the serious or fatal injuries that might have resulted should it have done so. "Sam – get your arse down here and explain to me how the fucking hell this could have happened," he shouted, fists clenched in fury, "and get the goddam gantry back down here so I can check it myself."

While the embarrassed Sam climbed down to make his excuses, Jake studied Reuben, who had returned to the task of unpacking and placing the stage amplifiers as if nothing had happened. Before they had set out, Reuben complained privately to Jake about his eyes, the sensitivity of which had worsened overnight. On waking, the daylight was so painfully bright he couldn't open the curtains. There was nothing to be done – they could hardly take him to hospital given his status – so Jake had donated a pair of dark sunglasses, which reduced the glare sufficiently for Reuben to leave the caravan. Since then, he had not taken them off.

Harry walked from the back of the hall and stood next to Jake, who asked; "Did you see that?"

Harry nodded. "Fast, wasn't he?"

"Cool as a cucumber too," said Jake. "Jeez...when was the last time you saw a cucumber?"

"What's happening to him, Jake?"

"The eye thing?"

"That, and the running. After you got him the sunglasses we went out for a run...well, he ran...I took a bike so I wouldn't slow him down. I asked him to go as fast as he could and I timed him round the course."

"He's getting slower?"

"And he gets winded now like a normal person – well, like a very bloody fit normal person. Bit red in the face when we got back; never seen him like that before."

"I feel so sorry for him," Jake said after a pause. "Which is odd, because he's the most contented person I think I've ever met. He's so untroubled, except about the weird shit that's going on, and I believe him when he says his concerns are for the rest of us, not himself. That's what I mean – he seems to want nothing, accept everything, and gets on with whatever the day presents. He's quietly cheerful nearly all the time. Why do I feel sorry for him?"

"Because his peace is fake. It's a product of losing his memory, not conquering it. He hasn't earned his peace, and it could be taken away from him at any moment. It isn't a product of learning and discipline, like he's mastered some form of meditation or a martial art, is it? It's an accident. He could wake up tomorrow morning with his memory restored, and with it could come the knowledge that he's a mass murderer, a child molester or a mad terrorist, and be overwhelmed by all the hatred, the confusion and self-loathing people like that endure. Wouldn't be so calm then, would he?"

"He could also wake up to find he's very rich, got a fabulous girlfriend, a mansion somewhere and staff to cater for his every whim," retorted Jake, finding Harry's picture quite repellent.

"Sounds more like your dream than his."

Jake giggled. "Oops. Gave the game away. Damn!"

"I don't know which I find more worrying – the man in the bushes or Fairfax."

"You're convinced the man Vicky saw yesterday was the man in the bushes?"

"Aren't you?"

"Don't have time to think about it right now, old bean. Got a gig to do. Frankly, I'm more worried that when we get on stage we won't remember the songs. So much distraction. We haven't rehearsed for ten days. I just hope we haven't forgotten how to play our bleedin' instruments."

Jake's fears were largely unfounded. Although there were a few more rough spots than usual, they were more than adequately compensated by the enthusiasm that infected everyone equally. Crossing the threshold between the dark secret wings and the bright candid footlights, they cast off the travails and uncertainties of a strange and unfamiliar world, exchanging it for the environment in which they belonged, where they prospered and their excitement was not moderated by fear (although they all glanced warily overhead from time to time). They played with childish, exuberant joy, relishing the simple pleasure of playing and playing well, and while the audience was small they were certainly appreciative. By the end of the second encore, the band felt renewed and refreshed, rediscovering themselves and liking what they found.

The bar was already closed, so everyone pitched in to help with the crack – the stripping down and packing. There was an atmosphere of general good cheer between band and crew that lasted nearly all the way back to the camp. As they turned into the lane leading to the site, Nick brought the truck to an abrupt halt. In the headlights they could see an estate car parked in the middle of the lane. Fairfax was standing next to it.

"I was wondering when he'd turn up again, but I didn't think it would be so soon," grumbled Jake. "Everybody, stay in the bus," ordered Harry, as he and Jake climbed down from the truck.

"What are you doing here?" Jake called out.

"Thank God I found you. Someone's been at the camp. I forgot you had a date tonight and went there to see you, but as I got there I saw someone running away down the lane. A big chap – thought it was your man Reuben there for a moment. I had a quick look round the camp but I couldn't see anything, so I thought I'd try to catch you before you got there, just in case."

"In case of what?" said Harry.

"They could be trying to bug the bus again," said Fairfax, putting his hands in the pockets of his coat. "We can't sit in there discussing what we know if..."

The landscape around them lit up with a vivid red light. A moment later, they heard the dull crump of an explosion. In horror, they looked in the direction of the camp where a fireball of smoke, lurid orange underneath and jet black on top, rose fast into the sky above the tree-tops.

"NOOOOO," screamed Jake, and took off down the lane. The truck emptied, the others chasing him. When they reached the clearing, all that remained of the bus was the burning chassis. The caravan, never the most substantial of vehicles, had entirely disappeared; only the single axle remained, bent in the centre as if a weight had fallen on it. The rest of the bus and every small thing they held sufficiently dear to keep in the limited space afforded for personal belongings; all were burned or shattered, the remnants a profusion of tiny fires and smoking, unrecognisable fragments strewn for fifty feet across the grass in every direction.

"Nothing we can do here," said Fairfax, his voice urgent and commanding. "Get back to the truck, all of you, and follow me. We've got to get out of here." Not waiting for agreement, he turned on his heels and started back to the car. Vicky stood by the gate holding Jimi protectively, the child too sleepy to comprehend what had happened. Harry, Nick and the crew were sifting through the wreckage looking for anything they could salvage. Over by the hedge, Cas was kneeling on the ground, sobbing uncontrollably as he clutched the remains of his favourite guitar, now reduced to little more than firewood. Billy and Alina walked over to flank Jake, Billy touching him on the shoulder cautiously. "Are you OK, man? Jake...are you OK?" Jake didn't answer. His face was entirely blank, his expression uncomprehending.

Seeing Jake's distress, Harry walked over. "Nothing much left, I'm afraid. I think Fairfax is right – we better get out of here." He looked round; Vicky was trying to comfort the distraught Cas, who was rocking back and forth holding the tangle of charred wood and broken strings, tears streaming down his face in a flood. Jimi, kneeling next to him, was crying in sympathy. Meanwhile the crew, reaching the same conclusion as Harry, abandoned their search and trudged wearily towards the gate.

"Where's Reuben?" cried Alina, alarmed when she suddenly realised he wasn't there.

"Christ, now what?" Harry too was startled. "Anyone seen Reuben?" he shouted out. The crew stopped by the gate and Sam turned back. "Holy shit! He's still locked in the back of the truck. We forgot to let him out!"

Harry realised the pounding in his ears that he had attributed to the heat of the moment was in fact the sound of Reuben thumping furiously on the side of the truck to get their attention. The crew ran to let him out while the others gradually congregated round the car. Fairfax strode to the back of the truck and quickly briefed Reuben, then persuaded the crew to lock him back inside. With a mixture of bullying and cajoling, he herded the others into the cab of the truck. Only Jake remained, standing like a statue in the middle of the road, staring at the smoke still billowing up between the snow-bound trees. Fairfax didn't approach him, but glanced at Harry, who nodded, walked over to Jake, gently took his arm and led the unresisting bandleader to the truck.

Chapter 12: Small Turd, Big Toilet

Subdued by the shock, in silence they crammed themselves into the truck and followed Fairfax into Penrith, then headed south-east on the A66 down to Scotch Corner, turning south on the A1 just below Darlington. They passed cameras, checkpoints at which they were comprehensively ignored, and numerous disinterested patrol cars. Harry drove steadily, no longer caring who saw them, who monitored their progress. He just kept Fairfax in view, his face closed and his thoughts to himself.

Jake was in a bad way. He sat in the back of the crowded cab, silent and morose, unable to construct in his mind a strategy that would ensure the survival of the band. How could they continue? Where would they live, now their home had been destroyed. He wondered if they'd been fending off the inevitable all this time – keeping the band together for so long seemed somewhat miraculous to him – but now their fate had overtaken them. In a flash and a bang, they were reduced to the anonymity of refugees, just like all the other unfortunates. If they were no longer a band, they were nothing; human detritus, flushed away. A small turd in a big toilet. When Nick turned to ask if he was OK, Jake said as much.

Nick was having none of it. "Jake, we've been together for many years and this is the first time I've seen you defeated like this. It's not like you, and I have to tell you I think you're being indulgent. This is no time to feel sorry for yourself. You're the leader of the band and if you don't lead, how on earth can we follow?"

"Where could I lead you without a bus to take us there?"

"Look – the bus is dead, so long live the bus!"

"Oh really? How do you suppose we could ever get another one?"

"I have no idea, but there's never been a problem we didn't solve one way or another. In any case, it's a test. We've always fancied ourselves as rebels, outsiders; self-sufficient, capable of overcoming any obstacle. It would be sad to discover that was all hot air the first time we were really pressed. How easy is it to boast about our strength when it's never really tested, only to find we fold up and cry like babies when things get tough. Is that who we are, who you are? And I remind you that right now, the bus is *still* the least of our problems."

"That's right," said Phil, "Surely if we could find the bastards who are after Reuben, the people who did this to us, we could make them pay for a new one."

"Hey...didn't we have insurance?" asked Billy.

"Third party only, just the legal minimum for being on the road," said Vicky, wriggling in her seat, "all we could afford." Jimi was asleep on her lap and her leg had gone numb, but there was nowhere to move with the cab so crowded.

Jake showed no signs of interest, made no comment, just stared out of the window into the darkness. "Leave him alone Nick," said Harry. "We should talk about this later."

"I don't think we can," Nick retorted. "I don't know where Fairfax is leading us, but when we get there we'll have to decide what we're going to do next. We may not have much time either, and if we split up that will probably be the end of the band. If we stick together, at least we have some chance of sorting this out."

"You're out of your fucking mind," said Phil. If Jake looked stunned, Phil by contrast, had a murderous look about him. "We've lost everything. I just want to meet the bastards that did this to us. That's all I want."

"We lost everything? Then where's your drum kit?" asked Nick.

"What?"

"Where are your drums?"

"In the back of the truck, you fuckwit. Where did you think they were?"

Nick turned to Billy, sitting in the front with Harry and Alina. "Billy, where's your bass, your amp? Alina, where are your keyboards?"

"What's your point?" asked Jake wearily.

"My point is that everything we need to be a band, we have in this truck – and we *have* this truck. We have our instruments, the amps, the PA, the lights, and us – everything we need to be a band. Everything: we could do a gig right now. We're all alive, none of us is hurt. We *are* a band, we're *still* a band – sure we've lost our travelling hotel, but no-one can take away our music. *No-one.* This band exists right up till we give up on it, go our separate ways. When we give up on each other, that's when the band will die."

"And us too, maybe" said Alina. "We stick together and we fight. Maybe we win, maybe we lose, but we fight together. Same back in Poland when I was girl. Gangs were tough because we stick together. If we break up, they pick us off, one by one. Easy meat. Nick is right. Remember – we're the Vikings."

"We're the Vikings?" said Jake, his voice unsteady.

"Yes we are. Say it again, Jake, but this time mean it," Nick demanded.

"We're the Vikings!"

"Again."

"WE ARE THE VIKINGS!"

"Who are we?"

This time, everyone joined in the roar, all except Cas, whose face was again wet with tears. Jake, sitting next to him, put his arm consolingly round the guitarist's hunched shoulders. "Come on dude. If I can get over it, so can you." Cas turned his puffy face towards Jake. "They blew up my guitar. My beautiful guitar."

"So, only two to go then?" said Jake, his face brightening. The others chuckled quietly and even Cas managed to muster a faint smile; he had three more guitars in the back of the truck. The band had teased Cas relentlessly over the years, insisting that he only really needed one because he never played the others. They were just for show and should be dispensed with, an argument Cas rejected with vigorous inconsistency.

Harry listened to the exchange as he drove, marvelling once again at the resilience of his companions. Only an hour after the bus blew up in their faces, they were already perking up. "I've got to get some diesel soon," he called out. "I'm going to flash Fairfax and tell him." He winked his headlights a few times and Fairfax pulled over. Harry explained his dilemma; Fairfax looked thoughtful for a moment, then nodded. "OK, keep behind me and we'll stop soon. It's about seventy miles – can you make that?" Harry thought he could and they resumed their journey.

Far from taking them to some out of the way garage, Fairfax turned off at the motorway services, Harry not far behind. For years the band had avoided such places with their extensive camera coverage, police activity, the inevitable throng of rowdy soldiers taking a break from their patrols and the hordes of local youth who had remained past curfew and were effectively trapped there until morning. Harry parked in the area reserved for trucks, where they climbed out of the cab in silence. As they let Reuben out of the back, Fairfax came jogging over.

"Reuben better stay here in the truck," he told them even as they were dropping the tailgate. They opened one door and told Reuben the same thing. Reuben agreed, his usual amenable self. "I understand. Can someone bring me some water when you come back?"

Jimi tugged on his mother's hand. "Can I stay with Reuben?"

Vicky looked at her husband, who nodded. "Sure, you keep Reuben company," she told the boy as she helped him up into the back of the truck. "Thanks Vicky," said Reuben. "Come and sit with me," he said, holding out his arms, and Jimi obediently collapsed against him, leaning his head on Reuben's chest and closing his eyes. "Keep him safe," called Nick as they closed the door, locking it at Harry's suggestion. As they trooped across the car park towards the main building, Jake wondered who Nick was talking to – Reuben or Jimi?

If Jake had wondered why the motorway had been so quiet, here was one answer: all the missing traffic was probably parked here. The place was heaving, incredibly noisy and very bright, the services being one of the few public places allowed to consume electricity round the clock. Through the centre of the building ran a long atrium festooned with huge plastic plants. At either side were shops selling confectionary, lingerie and phones; a dentist (closed), a police station, a cafe and a burger bar (also closed); toilets, a first aid station, a Japanese-style capsule hotel (full), three competing coffee stands and a game arcade. All the remaining spaces were filled with slot machines. The cacophony of sirens, beeps, bells and burps they spewed relentlessly over the entire building was inescapable. Not a single machine stood unoccupied.

The dearth of available food meant the cafe was the quietest place in the building. They collected drinks from the counter and occupied two tables in the corner. Fairfax seated himself conspicuously a few tables away, produced a phone and, hunched over with his hand cupped around the mouthpiece, proceeded to talk for fifteen minutes. When his calls were completed he came over and joined the others.

"I made a few calls," he told them unnecessarily. "I think I've found somewhere you can hide for a while, somewhere safe and out of the way."

"Where?" asked Nick, stirring his tea idly. He'd been stirring it continuously since he sat down and had yet to take a sip.

"Nottingham," Fairfax replied.

"Nottingham?" said Harry, immediately alarmed.

Fairfax smiled his thin, unreliable smile. "Yes. A place called Thieves' Wood, amusingly enough."

"No way," said Harry. "No fucking way."

"They *will* be safe there." Fairfax was unmoved by Harry's protests. "Anyway, I just spoke to the Colonel and he agreed to help. Arrangements have been made."

"Shove your arrangements. We're not going there, so come up with something else, OK?"

"What's the problem, Harry? Something you haven't been entirely candid about, is it? Something you haven't told the others?"

"Fuck you, Fairfax."

"I'm already spoken for, I'm afraid."

The others watched the confrontation with varying degrees of astonishment. No-one had ever seen Harry looking so angry and defensive. In contrast, Fairfax appeared calm and self-possessed.

"Would someone please explain what the fuck is going on here?" Jake demanded. There were far too many unanswered questions about Harry Bracey filed in the recesses of his mind, and he suspected an imminent revelation. Harry remained silent, staring at Fairfax with such unbridled hostility Jake was sure a fight would break out if he didn't intervene. He turned to Fairfax.

"Explain to me what's happening here or it's the last we'll have to do with you, I swear to God. I don't care how much danger we're in. I want an explanation. Now. What's all this about Thieves' Wood and who the fuck is The Colonel?"

"Well well. Feisty now, aren't we? You've certainly recovered well Jake, I must say; only a couple of hours ago you were sobbing like a little girl."

"That was Cas, actually," said Phil dangerously, ready to assist with the beating.

Harry stood, no longer capable of restraining his anger. "You don't have to try so hard to be a shit Fairfax, it comes easy to people like you. Go ahead, tell them if you must. I think you want to, that you enjoy it – divide and conquer? *Isn't that it, you manipulative bastard?*"

Fairfax looked up at Harry, his expression mild. "Can I remind you we're all on camera and you're starting to draw attention to us – which is the last thing we need right now? Sit down Harry, sit down and tell them about The Colonel." He leaned forward as he spoke, allowing his coat and jacket to fall open, revealing the shoulder holster. Harry didn't appear to notice it, but Alina did. She immediately stood, walked round the table to Harry and kissed him on the cheek, which surprised everyone. She rarely displayed her affections, even with those she cared for. "Sit down, wild man," she said, pulling gently on Harry's arm. "You get us in trouble, Harry. Wipe red mist from your eyes or I make Phil kiss you too."

"No she fucking won't," said Phil adamantly.

Alina smiled. "Tell us – who is this Colonel?"

"My father," said Harry. With a resigned sigh he dropped back into his seat like a deflated balloon.

"We've all had fathers at some point," said Jake. "What's the problem?"

"They don't get on very well, do you Harry? Bit of a rift, as I understand it," said Fairfax.

"You father is Colonel? In army?" said Alina. She sounded impressed.

"No, we just call him that. He's a chicken farmer."

"He was a full colonel, highly decorated too, as I recall," said Fairfax. "Harry can tell you all about his family history after I've gone. Right now, we have a few things to sort out. First of all, I want you to leave the truck here. It's well protected – there isn't an inch of the truck park that isn't under permanent surveillance, so it will be safe for a while. I also think your...um...roadies...should stay here until daylight and hitch lifts away from here." He turned to Sam, Sham and Pharaoh, seated together at the far end of their table. "You boys can go visit your families, wives, girlfriends or whatever. There isn't enough room where we're going, and you'll be safe if you travel separately. No-one will follow you; they'll be too interested in the truck and with a bit of luck they might stick with it for a day or two before they realise we've gone."

"He's right, boys," called Nick across the table. "If we're coming off the road for a while, there is nothing for you to do except get in trouble. We can't pay you – you realise that, don't you? But don't worry; as soon as we get this sorted out we'll be back on the road, and my first call will be to you. We know how to find you, so long as you keep in touch with each other. Sam, you'll be liaison – when we're ready, you can collect the truck. I'll call you as soon as I have any information. I know where you'll be, don't I?"

Sam grinned. "Sure. Back on my brother's boat. All this extra tidal water has brought fish with it, loads of lovely fish. He's doing so well he's thinking of buying another boat. Sells everything he catches, top money. Not many people who can say their life improved because of the rising seas."

"Well, they earn their money, that's for sure," agreed Nick carefully, mindful of all the fishermen whose nets were perpetually empty because the shoals they had depended on for centuries had migrated north as the ocean temperature gradients shifted, or died as the sea turned to acid. Not that he begrudged the British trawlers their catches or their profits: he'd been out once with Sam and his brother on a working trip, the demands and terrors of which had appalled him. "Vicky will pay you off, and if we don't have enough cash tonight she'll send your money on, OK?" The glum crew reluctantly agreed.

"Shouldn't *we* go too?" said Vicky, meaning her family. Fairfax answered her. "No Mrs. Richardson. I don't think it's a good idea. Three of you travelling will be easier to track. You will go home, I expect, or to your mother's in Manchester, and if I know that, so do they. And your son is vulnerable; in situations like this, children are often used as pawns, quite ruthlessly I'm afraid. I'm sorry, but I think you should know. You need to be realistic." If his intention was to frighten Vicky he had succeeded; she nervously scanned the room for her son until she remembered where he was. "I expect you are right," she admitted, downcast.

"If we're leaving the truck here, how do we get to this Robber's Wood, to Harry's father?" Jake asked Fairfax.

"Thieves' Wood," Fairfax corrected him. "That's the next phase. Over the next two hours, I want all of you – including Reuben – to leave, singly and in pairs, at fifteen minute intervals. Harry and I are going to find some alternative transport, and we'll get Reuben and Jimi out of the truck before we leave. The rest of you should walk slowly, casually, through the car park – not the truck area, the car park – and at the back you'll find a service road. Follow it, going away from the motorway, and when you get to the road at the end, turn left and walk for two miles until you come to a covered shelter. All of you should wait there for Harry and I. Try not to draw attention to yourselves; don't light a fire or start busking, in other words. If any cars come past, which is pretty unlikely, just duck behind the shelter until it's gone."

Hearing he was now enmeshed in Fairfax's plan, Harry began to object, but stopped himself. Getting Fairfax on his own might have some advantages. "You've got this all worked out, don't you?"

Fairfax nodded. "It's my job."

"And where are you and Harry going to be while we're trekking through the snow in the middle of nowhere on a freezing cold night?" Jake asked.

"Harry and I are going to borrow some transport."

With a surly Harry slouched in the passenger seat of the decrepit old Ford estate, Fairfax drove in silence for twenty minutes, heading towards Harrogate.

"I saw the gun," Harry muttered.

"I meant you to see it."

"Does it make you feel big?"

Fairfax shot him a strange glance. "Not big, so much; prepared for certain eventualities, perhaps – although I don't much care for it. How about you?"

"I didn't have a fetish about them, if that's what you mean. Some of my squad loved their weapons more than their wives and girlfriends. I assume you've seen my record?"

Fairfax nodded. "Of course. You never told the others?"

"About my service? Would you?"

"Probably not. How long since you spoke to him?"

"The Colonel? Not since..."

"...you were cashiered?"

"Why there? Why Thieves' Wood? You must have lots of safe houses, other places to take them."

"I can't be there all the time, holding your hand, y'know. I have no backup – this is unofficial. I explained this already. I can't use one of our normal places, and with no minders, I need some help and your father's an old hand, knows the form. He'll look after you."

Harry laughed humourlessly. "You think so? You really think so?"

"Don't you?"

"No, frankly I don't. He's not the man he used to be, not someone you can depend on, not any more. He's just a sad shadow now, useless more or less."

"Really?" said Fairfax, misunderstanding. He was slowing down as they entered the outskirts of the town. "I'm not so sure. I read his record too – one tough bastard, your father. I know he's getting on a bit, but once a soldier..." He turned off into a side street, a row of suburban semis each with its own driveway. There were few cars parked on the street itself, which suited Fairfax's purpose. He pulled over to the kerb, turned off his lights and reached behind him to retrieve his smartphone. The light from its screen illuminated his face as he concentrated, setting various options on the touch-screen the old fashioned way, using a small stylus.

"What are you doing?" Harry asked despite himself.

"It's a key code scanner app. We usually use it to pick up the code when someone locks or unlocks their car, but it can be used to transmit a manufacturer's library of codes in rotation until you find the right one. Takes more time, that's all. The one I'm after is that Toyota people carrier over there. Seats seven I think, should do nicely if I can crack it. Here we go." He started the transmit sequence and waited. After a minute or so, the Toyota's lights blinked once as it unlocked. Fairfax extracted a blank smart card from his pocket swiped the phone, then handed it to Harry. "Here you go, that should get you running. I suggest you let off the handbrake and roll out of the driveway before you engage the E-drive – they do whine a bit, I find. I'll wait for you there; follow me and we'll pick up the others. We've only got a few hours before it's reported stolen and you must get to your father's by then."

"What about the curfew?"

Fairfax nodded, still fiddling with his phone. "I've added the Toyota's number to our 'leave alone' list; that should keep you out of trouble for tonight at least".

Mollified, Harry got out and Fairfax immediately drove off. He stepped into a gateway to conceal himself, and studied the houses on either side of the Toyota. There were no lights in any window he could see. A dog barked once, somewhere off in the distance.

No point in standing here, he told himself. He looked up and down the street checking potential escape routes. Which way to run if something went wrong? He could see the tail-lights of Fairfax's car, which had stopped about three hundred metres away. Harry had half expected Fairfax to abandon him just as soon as he got out of the car. He continued to assess his options if anything went wrong: he was in good shape and could cover the distance to Fairfax in less than a minute. Trouble was, running down the street he'd be in plain view and anyone could take a pot-shot at him. Better to run through the gardens on one side, jumping from one to the next; there were bushes, fences and small trees to provide cover, and he could always duck down the side of a house if things got too hot. If Fairfax didn't abandon him.

He crossed the road. A sweet smell wafted past him; the remains of last night's curry from a nearby bin. His stomach grumbled. Reaching the driveway he walked up the slope and lifted the handle on the driver's door. It opened silently and he climbed in, pulling the door nearly closed but leaving it unlatched. He familiarised himself with the controls, then let off the handbrake. The car rolled backwards out of the drive and he guided it through a quarter-turn so it was facing the waiting Fairfax. Inserting the smart card, he turned on the ignition, selected the electric drive and the car moved forward. Thankfully, it was near silent. There was no movement in his mirrors, no lights, no shouts from an enraged owner chasing him down the street with a sawn-off shotgun, now the suburban weapon of choice in the defence of the vegetable plots on which everyone was learning to depend, or steal from. When he reached the end of the street, Fairfax pulled away in front. Harry turned on his lights and followed, pulling the driver's door fully closed as he turned onto the main road.

The drive back was uneventful, but when they got to the shelter no-one was there. Fairfax drove past, but Harry swung round in the road and parked where the buses used to stop. He got out and walked over to the shelter. "You can come out now. It's only me," he called out. There was a rustle of undergrowth behind the shelter as the band members emerged in single file. Cas and Billy were both carrying guitar cases they had retrieved from the truck. Alina was sullen, having lost the argument that one of them had a duty to help her carry her keyboard through the snow, although she did concede that it would be difficult to remain inconspicuous while carrying a piano like a dead body through a motorway services car park.

"Nice wagon," said Phil. "Where'd you get it?"

"Ow...shit...hey – there's a car coming," Jake called out as he retreated from a losing battle with some bramble. He was trying to free himself with one hand while holding his sax case high up, out of harm's way, in the other.

"It's Fairfax," said Harry. "Let's get going." They piled into the Toyota, Reuben climbing in through the back. Jimi broke free of his father and jumped in behind him. Nick scowled but said nothing; like his wife, he had unvoiced concerns over the bond between his son and the big man.

Fairfax had pulled up behind them. "How much charge does it have?" he asked Harry.

"Three-quarters full."

"Good, that should get you there. Here's the thing though: you have to get rid of it once you arrive, but you can't just dump it close by. Someone is going to have to drive it away, at least a hundred miles, *and* be able to make their way back afterwards. Since you don't appear to relish the role of prodigal son, the logical thing is for you to do it. Will you?"

Harry nodded without hesitation. "Yes, I'll do it."

"It's got a tracker, although they won't start running a trace until it's reported missing. Do you know how to disable it?"

"I don't," said Harry, "but Nick does. We'll sort it out before I set off from Thieves' Wood. You're not coming with us?"

"No," said Fairfax. "I have other work to do – official work. I'll help you all I can, but I'm not losing my job over this. I'm going to take some leave soon and then I'll join you. In the meantime, stay sharp. Get a weapon if you can – the Colonel will know where, assuming he hasn't built himself a little armoury already."

"That's very unlikely..." Harry began, but Fairfax was already at the door of the car. "Stay sharp, Lieutenant," he said as he climbed in, started the car and drove off.

"Why did he call you lieutenant?" said Reuben through the open back door. Harry closed the door without answering. Here we go, he thought to himself; this was going to be a trying journey.

But he was wrong. As soon as they set off, Billy plugged in his pod to the car's stereo, scanned the playlist and made a selection. The big car was quiet and comfortable. No-one wanted to talk, each retreating to a city of refuge within; retreating from the shock of the explosion, the trauma of losing their home and their livelihoods, Alf's death, from the anxiety they all felt. They were curious too about Harry's past and the mysterious Colonel, but the cumulative distress made them reluctant to pry and too tired to bother. As the music played and Harry drove, constantly checking the rear-view mirror, the passengers nodded off one by one, bathed in the soothing melancholy tenor of Stan Getz and his cooling jazz.

Chapter 13: Wise Old Bastard

They arrived at the edge of Thieves' Wood a little after dawn. Harry had driven at a steady speed, occasionally turning off and driving a short way along various motorway approach roads while he watched for any traffic that followed him off the motorway, but none did. When he left the motorway for the last time, he drove for a few minutes watching his rear-view mirror once more. Satisfied, he stopped and woke the others. "We're nearly there. You can walk the rest of the way," he pointed down the road ahead of them, "while I dump the car. I have to take it somewhere...y'know, a good distance away, so I may be a few days."

Jake gave him a curious look. "You going to be OK?"

Harry nodded. "I'll manage."

Everyone got out, Billy and Cas removing their guitars and Jake's sax. Jake held out his hand, and Harry shook it. "It's the big house on the left, four miles on. White pillars, black gates. Clare House, it's called. You'll be fine; just stay put, don't go out. Don't talk to anyone, call anyone. Keep your heads down and I'll be back as soon as I can." He climbed into the driver's seat. "When you run into a grumpy old yokel, just tell him...say...nah..." Harry, changing his mind, merely shook his head, closed the door and drove off. The others stood huddled together in the snow, indistinguishable from any other group of displaced people who'd lost everything.

"Hey, we never disabled the tracker," Nick reminded Jake, who shrugged. Too late now. The wind picked up, setting flurries of snow chasing across the road. As they walked, hunched against the wind, the snow gusting around them, Phil started laughing.

"What the hell is funny?" Vicky demanded.

"Us," said Phil. "Look at us, trudging through the snow like refugees. We could be in Siberia." He chuckled again. "It's like that film my mother used to love, that musical about the Jews getting chucked out of Russia. She used to watch it over and over. That's what made me think of it. What was it...?"

"Fiddler on the Roof," Jake called out. He started whistling.

"Dah da de de, diddy diddy dum dum," went Nick.

"Oy vey!" Jake exclaimed and joined in.

Alina laughed. "Hey, we have this song in Poland. We all sing it: *If I wassa rich man...*" Being a band, they could hardly resist and soon they were all singing along. Reuben didn't know the song but bounced Jimi cheerfully on his shoulders in time with the music as they walked. They were still singing when they reached the gates to Clare House.

"Go away," shouted a querulous voice from beyond the closed gates. "It's not Christmas and that ain't no carol. There's no money here, see, and I've got a gun! Go away!"

Jake looked through wrought-iron gate. He couldn't see the house, just a frail old man standing on the driveway, both hands resting on a rake handle, a small pile of leaves at his feet. He was stooped, making his dirty smock billow out in front of him, and he seemed to have difficulty looking straight at Jake, unable to lift his head sufficiently to do so. Peering out suspiciously from under his eyebrows and looking every inch the irascible rustic, he shook the rake handle at Jake by way of feeble threat. The exertion induced a racking cough which shook him from head to toe, the spasm ending only when he contemptuously spat out whatever poisons his lungs had ejected. The spittle barely travelled far enough to miss his boots.

"We're looking for the Colonel," Jake called out, his voice loud. "He's expecting us." At this, the old man walked slowly to the gates and unlocked them, never once looking up.

"Should have said so, giving me a fright like that. Singing! You lot on drugs, are you? Yeah, I'll bet you are. Degenerates. Hurry up, come in if you're coming." As the last person passed through he relocked the gates with infinite care, checking it three times just to make sure as if he was afraid he might not remember later whether he'd done it or not.

"Where's Master Harry?" he said, looking suspiciously from face to face.

"He's...er..." Jake wasn't inclined to tell the old man about the stolen vehicle.

"Couldn't face the music, eh? Sound about right; no guts." He sniffed loudly and wiped his nose with the back of his woollen glove. "Never would have thought it myself, mind you.

Lost his nerve? Not our Harry. Not a Bracey." Without another word, he started to walk slowly up the drive using the upturned rake as a walking stick. There was little else they could do but follow.

Jake was half expecting the house to be as decrepit as the old man, so he was pleasantly surprised when it came into view. The frontage was Georgian, but there were extensions on both sides that were of a later period. The paintwork was immaculate, the windows intact and sparkling in the white light reflected back off the snow. It wasn't grand, but the kind of house where a large, well-off Victorian family might have lived. Upper class but not aristocracy, money from the professions rather than inherited. Jake started to walk towards the front door but the old man hissed at them. "Oi! You don't go that way. Round the back for your sort."

"Hey," Phil called out to the old man as they set off in slow-motion pursuit. "What's your fucking problem?" The old man stopped, turned and scanned Phil from head to toe with evident contempt. "*I* don't have a problem, son. *I* have a place to live. *No-one* is trying to blow me up. *I'm* not sponging off someone like a bleedin' parasite, someone I've never even met. So shut up, do as you're told and mind your language; there's women and children present." He nodded to Vicky. "Sorry M'am. Ignorant pig, ain't he?"

Vicky grinned. "My thoughts entirely, Sir." Phil snorted, then laughed at himself. The old man turned and continued round the side of the house, through an orderly kitchen garden – "don't you dare tread on my plants, y'hear" – until they reached the kitchen door. Under strict instructions, they all dutifully wiped their feet as they entered the vast country kitchen. With a suitably massive sanded table in the centre and a double-oven range at one end, the many and various gleaming implements and utensils that hung from beams, walls and racks looked well used and cared for. Between them, every nook and cranny was filled with a profusion of dried fruits, herbs and vegetables of every hue and colour, which Jake correctly assumed were grown in the garden they had just walked through. A pair of rabbits hung from a hook, waiting to be skinned.

"Where's the Colonel?" asked Jake. The old man was pumping some water into a large kettle. When it was full, he carried it with some difficulty over to the range and put it on a hob. "Away."

"When will he be back?"

"He'll be back when he's ready, I expect. When it suits him and not before. This way. You can make yersels a cuppa after I've shown you your rooms. There's a little milk in the pantry. Bet none of you have the first idea how to milk a cow, do you? There's no coffee so don't bother looking, ain't had none for six years. Don't miss it neither." He led them into the hall.

Here the atmosphere was altogether different. Although the floor and walls were spotless, the rectangles of bright wallpaper attested to many years of slow attrition. The paintings were not the only sacrifices made: there was no furniture, the places where various items once stood were poignant with lost purpose. As they passed the opposing double doors of the lounge and dining room, both rooms at a glance appeared austere, bereft of the adornments such high, well-proportioned rooms should possess. There, the inverted wall shadow of a missing cabinet; here, a patch of carpet more vivid than the rest for having been shielded from the light by a sofa. This house had seen better times, yet it didn't seem seedy or dilapidated. To Jake, the house appeared to be cloaked in an expectant hush into which their echoing footsteps were absorbed as if, after being sent off for renovation, the life and atmosphere of the place would one day be returned in the same van as the fixtures and fittings.

They didn't have time to explore. The old man had heaved himself up the wide staircase step by step, gripping the thick oak banister as if his life depended on it. He waited on the landing until the others arrived, breathing heavily. "House rules then. Listen and listen good, y'hear? First, keep the place clean. Make it dirty, then *you* clean up. Second – no free rides. You'll all work, round the house, in the yard, in the garden. Do you good, get some fresh air in you. Earn your keep, or you're out on your ear. I'll be giving you assignments in the morning. Got that? Breakfast is when you make it, evening meal is always seven-thirty on the dot. Dress is informal, and just as bleedin' well. Three people on dinner duty each day, I'll put the rota on the kitchen door. Come late and you don't eat, get me? Don't use electric lights unless you have to. Leave a light on *anywhere* and I'll take the bulb out. Never leave a candle burning when you leave a room or it'll be the last one you get. Other than that, don't bother me, don't get in my way, don't do anything I don't like and stay out of my garden."

He showed them several empty rooms, all containing beds – "sort out between you who goes where," – pointed out various bathrooms – "no baths, two showers a week, cold water only" – the Colonel's bedroom and study – "you lot don't go in there under pain of instant chucking out on yer ear *and* my boot up yer arse, clear?" – and finally a storeroom full of boxes. "Clothes in there. Moth-eaten old rubbish, I expect. Suit you lot down to the ground. Help yerself, y'hear." With that, he walked off, cackling away to himself as he descended the staircase one careful step at a time.

Jake and Cas took one room, Phil and Billy a second. At Jake's suggestion, Nick's family took the largest room. Less by connivance than tacit consent, Alina and Reuben ended up with two adjacent box rooms, each containing a single bed. Without a word, Reuben stepped into his room and closed the door. Alina didn't even bother to close the door to her room, but laid down on her bed and instantly fell asleep. Cas was already sitting on his bed, guitar in hand. Phil and Billy felt restless and decided to explore the house and gardens.

"I'm going to look for a mattress for Jimi," said Nick, standing in the doorway to his room. Vicky and Jimi had followed Alina's example and were already asleep on the double bed, the only one in the room. "I'll help you," said Jake. They started to search the other rooms. Most were empty and smelt of disuse; stale air and damp wallpaper.

"I'm a bit worried about Reuben," said Jake, trying another door. "He's barely said a word since the bus blew up."

"Not surprising, is it? My guess is that he feels guilty. Everything that's happening is because of him in some way or other. He blames himself; I'd feel terrible if I was in his place."

"I guess you're right." The room was empty. They tried another one. "That old boy – bit of a tyrant. Who is he – the gardener? Grumpy old git, that's for sure."

"Maybe he's the Colonel's batman or something. Y'know, been with the Colonel ever since blah blah, served him man and boy, all that guff."

"And they call him Batman? Excellent! 'Holy hell Batman, press my trousers'."

"Knows about us apparently, so the Colonel must have told him before he left. I wonder how much though, how much he's been told. We should be careful about what we say."

"I know what you mean. The Colonel may trust him implicitly, or not at all. We'll just have to wait until he gets back. Or Harry."

"He does look like he's been in this house from the day it was built. Daft old codger."

"Good job he wasn't armed. A shotgun in the hands of an old man like that could be disastrous. Don't you think this is all rather odd? Harry's dad, this place, Harry himself? Did you hear Fairfax call him lieutenant?"

Nick nodded. "Odd too, the Colonel – Harry's father – buggering off instead of waiting for us, don't you think? What's that about?"

"Christ, who knows? I don't, that's for sure. All we have is questions, lots of them, and the only people who have answers I don't trust further than I can spit. Hey – here's another mattress." They picked it up between them and carried it back down the hall.

"Where's Harry going to sleep when he comes back," said Nick. "The old git didn't say any of these rooms were his, did he? Didn't show us where his room is either."

"No idea," said Jake. "Maybe he sleeps in one of the outbuildings, worker cottage in the grounds somewhere? Who cares? As for Harry, I guess we'll sort that out if and when he gets here..."

"*If* and when, huh? I've been wondering about that," said Nick quietly as they lowered the mattress to the floor at the foot of the double bed. He straightened up. "Fancy a cuppa?"

At the bottom of the stairs, they met Billy with a steaming mug in each hand. "Hey, come and see what we found," he called

145

over his shoulder as he walked into the dining room. Running full length from the front of the house to the back, the room was enormous, the effect heightened by the absence of furniture. Half way down the room on the wall opposite was another door, leading into one extended wing. Phil was waiting for them, a huge grin on his face and a cue in his hand, standing at the far end of a full-sized snooker table on which the gleaming balls were set up for the break.

"Wow," said Nick as they looked in. "How cool is this?"

"Gonna play?" Phil called out, chalking his cue.

"Nick and I are going to get some tea," Jake replied. "We'll check it out later, give you a thrashing." Billy laughed, waving his cue like a rapier. "Not while I've got this in my hand you won't."

Dinner was served at seven-thirty on the dot. Everyone was seated except Phil, who hadn't reappeared after retiring from his snooker game for a nap. To general surprise, the old man had prepared a meal on his own and laid the table, each place set with a soup spoon. A large pot was bubbling slowly on the hob, the smell making everyone salivate. They hadn't eaten since the gig last night, an event that now seemed for most to have occurred a decade ago, so distant did it all seem.

"Can I help you?" Vicky asked the old man, who shook his head. "Nice of you to ask, miss. Too bad none of the men thought of asking, ain't it?"

"What can we call you, Mr..." asked Reuben politely.

"You can call me Len if you like. It's what they call me – Len O' Loch. Get the pot off the stove will you, miss. Use the cloth hanging on the rail."

"Len of the Loch?" said Vicky, picking up the cast iron pot carefully. "Are you Scottish? Where do you want this?"

"No. Over here please, miss." said Len, closing the subject as quick as Vicky had opened it. He placed a number of rough-glazed bowls on the table next to the steaming pot and began to ladle out portions of a rich brown stew. "You not eating, Len?" asked Jake. The old man hadn't laid a place for himself.

"Already eaten. You'll all be hungry, so finish the pot. Make sure the boy eats his fill. Back to standard rations tomorrow, better make the most of it." The door flew open and Phil stumbled in. "Oh no..." he muttered, preparing himself for rebuke, but Len merely sniffed and ladled out another portion.

"This is delicious," said Vicky, taking a second spoonful. Several people grunted in agreement. "What is it?" she asked. "I don't recognise the flavour."

Len pulled on a tatty coat taken from a rack by the back door. "Rabbit," he said, and slammed the door behind him with a sound like a gunshot.

Chapter 14: Housework

The next day was uneventful. When they came down in the morning, they found a few items laid out on the table – porridge for breakfast, half a jug of milk, some lentils, a few potatoes and an onion, along with a chicken egg in a saucer with a note underneath. "For the boy," it said in spindly writing. Len had left the provisions for them, drawn from a cold store adjacent to the kitchen which he kept under lock and key. A duty roster for preparation of the meals was pinned as promised to the back of the door, although with so little else to do, when it came time to cook most of the band pitched in willingly as they congregated in the only warm room of the house.

During the day and by various routes they all explored the house and grounds, finding two things of particular interest. First was the cellar, a proper vaulted affair that reeked of mould, centuries past and far better times. The extensive wine racks stood empty, home now only to spiders and their gently oscillating dust-brown webs. Old softwood boxes stacked against the walls attested to the fine tastes and bottomless wallets of previous occupants, classic names like Margaux, Petrus, Latour, Gevrey Chambertin, Haut-Brion and d'Yquem stencilled on the sides. All were disappointingly bereft of content. Two massive black-strapped oak doors leading to further vaults aroused much curiosity, both secured with huge iron locks the antiquity of which seemed to pre-date the house itself. Nobody volunteered to ask the gruff old man about the locked doors or what lay beyond them, so their attentions soon turned elsewhere.

Which is when Alina found the piano. It was in the opposite wing to the billiard room and the only room on the ground floor that contained furniture. Like the other items around the room, the piano was covered with a shapeless canvas tarpaulin that disguised what it covered. She only noticed it when she spied its three brass pedals sticking out beneath one edge. As she pulled back the tarpaulin, to her great joy she uncovered a gleaming black Steinway concert grand, still sufficiently in tune to enjoy playing it. Moments later, the house was suffused with music as she gathered confidence and began to run through half-remembered classical pieces, scales, pop songs and bits of jazz – anything and everything that came to her fingers. The others appeared one by one, drawn to the unexpectedly familiar sound. Alina actually considered moving her bed under the piano, so taken was she by playing it, so comforted by its presence. That evening, they gathered round the piano and sang songs hour after hour, Jake blowing softly into his sax, until one by one they slipped away to their beds.

The third day commenced in darkness with the doors of their rooms being thrown open with consecutive crashes, through which poured a stream of invective regarding the terminal laziness that deserved no breakfast. It was Len of course, candle in hand, reproaching them in caustic terms as he went from room to room to rouse their 'goddam lazy arses'. Half an hour later, dawn still breaking over the snowy landscape, everyone was seated round the kitchen table drinking tea. A single egg in a saucer, complete with handwritten note, drew several covetous glances. Len stood at one end of the table with a clipboard in his hand, a mug of tea in the other. "Leave that alone. Boy needs it, not you lot. Here's your work assignments and no shirking. I'll be coming round to inspect what you're up to, and if I don't think you're earning your keep, then no dinner, y'hear?" He glared around the table, then started to tick off items on the clipboard. "Jake and Nick," he announced without looking up, "ditch digging. I'll show you where after."

"We're musicians," said Billy, grumpy and rubbing his eyes, "not bloody labourers."

"Is that right?" said Len. "What, all of you?"

"No...not Nick and Vicky...or the boy," Jake added unnecessarily. "Basically, the band is the five of us – four musicians and a drummer." For all its antiquity, the old joke still drew smiles, plus the customary scowl from Phil that made it worth repeating.

"You the drummer then?" said Len, divining from Phil's sour expression that he was the target of the joke. Phil nodded. "He likes to hit things, don't you Phil?" Vicky explained.

"Oh, do yer? Fair enough," said Len, scribbling something on his clipboard. "You can chop the firewood. Ever used a chainsaw?" Phil shook his head.

"Good," said Len. "With a bit of luck you'll kill yerself. One less mouth to feed. Just don't bleed on my wood, makes a funny smell when it burns. The rest of us can enjoy a nice bit of long pork for supper." He stared from face to face, but no-one understood the reference. "You there – yes, you – the soppy one." He meant Cas. "You can help basher 'ere. I'd stand well back when he's got the chainsaw or the axe in 'is hand. Seen his type before, I have. Stack the wood neat, like. Same as the pile that's there – the air has to circulate to dry the wood – not just chucked in a heap like you see on telly. Bloody acters."

He turned to Vicky. "Miss, you and the boy can work in my garden if you like. Plenty to do out there, and the boy can learn a bit about growing food. Most useful education he could get right now if you ask me. I'll show you what needs doing in a minute." Jimi was staring wistfully at his egg. The old man reached out and picked it up, much to the boy's alarm. "Fading right away there, are you son?" he said, sounding almost affectionate. "Why don't I boil this for you? I've got a few biscuits you can have with it – they didn't come out right – no good without sugar, not like real ones, but OK to dip in the yolk. How about it – soft or hard?"

Jimi smiled uncertainly. "Yes please. Soft please."

"Good man," said Len, as he poured some water from the range kettle into a small pan, followed by the egg, put the pan on the hob and turned over an hourglass timer standing in a recess behind the range. "Keep an eye on that Miss, will you?" he said as he resumed his place and picked up the clipboard.

"Now then, you sir. Can I ask you – no offence or anything – but why the bloody hell are you wearing those sunglasses? You're indoors, in case you hadn't noticed. You afraid of going snow-blind, afraid of the white-out? You're not a pop star now, y'know; can't go skiing later if that's what you're thinking."

"My eyes hurt. The sunglasses make it easier to bear."

Reuben's answer was simple and direct, giving Len pause for thought. "Fair enough. You'll come with me today while I find some work for you, see what you're good fer. And you," turning to Billy, "you get the cushy job, staying in the house. First, wash every floor upstairs and down. Then brush every carpet and sweep up the dust. Then clean the baths, the showers and the toilets. That'll take you all day if you do it properly, less if not, in which case I'll make you do it all again tomorrow." He ticked off the last item on his list and dropped the clipboard on the table.

"OK, that's it. You two..." he nodded towards Jake and Nick, "...come with me and I'll show you what needs digging, and where to put the spoil. Basher - the woodshed is across the yard. Miss, I'll be back shortly. The boy'll be finished by then and we can have a look at the garden, see what needs doing. Let's go, gentlemen."

"We haven't had any breakfast," Cas complained.

"Should have got up when I called you. Too late now," said Len.

"Shall I come with you?" asked Reuben.

"No son, wait for me here," the old man replied, putting on his coat.

"Wait a minute," said Phil. "What about her?" Alina was still waiting for her assignment, looking left out.

"Oh yes," said the old man. "Nearly forgot. Your job is to play the piano. Practice, mind you, not just fooling around. This house is empty of so many things it used to have, but when I heard the music yesterday..." he looked away momentarily, then turned back. "So, that's your work, Miss. I expect to hear that piano all day, right? Non-stop, hard work, practice makes perfect, and Christ knows you're a long way from that. Slack off and you'll be digging the ditch tomorrow with the others, tits or no tits and pardon my French. No sexist nonsense here girl, believe me...oh yes, one other thing. Look in the big cabinet behind the piano. I unlocked it for you. There's loads of sheet music in there – classical stuff, can't even say the names of the composers, me. Beat-oven. Choppin. Bark. Some nice stuff in there, I dare say. Jazz too – more my style. The Colonel will like hearing you play some of that stuff. Remind him of his missus it will, when she used to play, God rest her soul." For a moment he looked sad, his eyes focussed somewhere in the far distance. Then he pulled open the back door with a brusque motion. "Right, let's get on with it."

All day they toiled in the weak but welcome sunshine, to the distant strains of Alina's piano accompaniment. Jake and Nick were shown a blocked ditch and spend the day clearing it. By the time they had finished, a healthy stream of water flowed through it, which they agreed was a most satisfactory conclusion. Phil meanwhile had steadily hacked, chopped and sawn his way through a vast pile of logs, Cas setting each piece carefully in a scheme that mimicked the existing pile precisely. As they worked, the two men talked more, about a wider range of subjects, than they had in the whole of the previous year. While Billy discovered the therapeutic joys of washing floors – he found the gleaming wet surfaces strangely rewarding – Alina was embarking on a thrilling voyage of discovery as she pulled sheet after sheet of music, mostly unknown to her, from the piles in the cabinet, trying each in turn. As she played, through the rear window she could see Vicky and Jimi in the snow-lined kitchen garden, Jimi's face a study in concentration as his mother taught him to identify and carefully remove the weeds and their roots with a small trowel, showed him the various legitimate plants that grew between them and named those she knew, which Jimi repeated aloud as he pointed to each in turn. Reuben and Len had disappeared soon after the jobs had been allocated. No-one saw them for the rest of the day or had any idea what they were doing.

As darkness fell, they trooped in to the kitchen one by one. Alina was still playing, and Billy went to fetch her while the others drank tea and massaged sore bits. Reuben and Len were last to come in, Len heading straight for the pantry from where he produced a sack of rice, a small section of cured ham and some dried peas that had been soaking overnight. He portioned out the rice into a steamer, put the peas on the hob, returned the sack to the store, locked it and left the room. As Alina and Billy entered he came back in behind them, an earthenware bottle in his hand.

"You did OK," he said begrudgingly, setting out some shot glasses. "You'll need a bit of fortification I reckon. I know I do." He poured small shot of colourless liquid into each glass and passed them round. Jake smelled the liquid. "Applejack?" Len nodded, picked up his glass, tossed off the contents in one gulp and slammed the glass down on the table. The others followed suit and the room was filled momentarily with chokes and gasps as the rough liquor burned its way down their throats. "One more for the road," said Len, pouring again, but before he raised his glass he looked over at Jimi. "Not drinking lad? Can't have that," he said, then rummaged through a cupboard to produce a bottle of orange squash, a small amount of which he poured into another shot glass before topping it up with water from a jug by the sink and handing it to Jimi. "Your health young man," he said with mock formality as he toasted the boy with his glass. Jimi lifted his and made a fair job of saluting the old man before taking a sip. The juice was evidently to his taste, for he downed the rest in one gulp and slammed his glass down on the table just like the adults.

After dinner, Len suggested they build a fire in the drawing room – the room that housed the piano – and while wood was being fetched and Jimi put to bed, they pulled the dust covers from several armchairs and two settees arranged around the wide fireplace. Alina sat at the piano and started to play. Before she had finished the first piece, a crackling fire filled the room with warmth and light. Len snuffed out the single candle standing on the mantelpiece and put the stub in his pocket. The applejack made another appearance. He was refilling his own glass more liberally than the others, Jake observed. It appeared the old man was getting steadily drunk, saying nothing but tapping his fingers silently in time with the music on the padded arm of his chair as he stared morosely into the fire.

"So Len, do you think Harry will be back tomorrow?" Jake asked when Alina stopped playing and joined the others by the fire.

"How would I know?" Len muttered.

"Do you know Fairfax?" asked Nick.

"Do you?"

"Er...well, he's just someone we met a while ago. He was the one who suggested we come here."

"Was he now? Should mind his own fucking business...oh, sorry ladies, don't mind me. That's the applejack talking. I'll bet Master Harry loved that idea then?"

"He wasn't exactly foaming at the mouth," said Jake. He thought carefully about what to say next, wanting to probe the old man but afraid he might transgress Len's notions of propriety. "They don't get on, so I understand," he said carefully. Len showed no reaction. "The colonel and the lieutenant. Father and son. Did they serve together?" That was as far as he dared go.

The room was silent. Len looked up from the fire and found an audience waiting on him, willing him to tell them the story they so desperately wanted to hear. He poured another drink and sat studying the liquid as he rolled it around the glass, light and shadow from the fire playing off his bent, huddled shape, wrapping him in musty old mysteries. "No, they never served together," he said slowly. He downed the drink in one gulp. "The Colonel would have liked it, but I don't reckon Harry would have. Wanted to make his own way – used to pull such a sour face when people asked him 'are you Tom Bracey's son' or 'is the Colonel your father, by any chance?' Hated it, hated the thought of favouritism. That's why he joined a different regiment. Don't think he liked living in the shadow of his father much, bloody big shoes to fill. I told him often enough: should have thought of that before he signed up. Took no notice. I told him – in civvy street nobody would know the difference, would they? Even in the other branches of the service, not that he'd do something like that of course. Infantry through and through, like his father and grandfather before him. In the blood, you could say. No, he wanted to follow the Colonel all right, just make his own name, do it on his own merit, which is fair enough, after all said and done. It's not like they weren't close before – so much mutual respect back then. Did everything together, went everywhere together. His father taught him everything he could think of that might be useful, but not as a duty – never forced the boy – the Colonel was too experienced a leader to make mistakes like that. No, he'd show the boy something, catch his interest if he could, and if Harry took the bait, he'd break it down, go deeper into it." He chuckled, or coughed; hard to tell which.

"Harry always took the bait. He was always game. Never disappointed his father, always made him proud. Soldiering, hunting, living off the land, map reading, camping, fishing, shooting, trapping, how to hide, how to fight, how to plan a strategy – he listened and learned like a good 'un. All rather military, you say? But hey - what do you expect? That's who the Colonel was, so he taught the boy what he knew, the skills he had. How could he do otherwise, I ask you? But with love, always, all of it. A soldier's love. And kindness. Loved that boy, apple of his eye, and Harry felt the same way back then I daresay; nothing but respect for his old man. Looked up to him, always did. Well...used to, anyway."

"So what happened?" Jake asked, risking the interruption.

"Saudi Arabia happened, that's what. He was doing so well, too. Graduated top of his class at Sandhurst, made first lieutenant in record time. Would have made captain in another year, the rate he was going. Immaculate record, smart as a whip. Men followed him because he didn't assume command, they gave it him. Deference, that's what it was; he earned their respect like a good officer should, by example. Natural authority. Where's that bottle, dammit?" He poured a large slug of applejack and passed the bottle on.

"Help yourself. Yes, Saudi bleedin' Arabia. They were the first company on the ground after the Arabs chopped the heads off their royal family, which they likely deserved according to all accounts. Should never have happened of course, sending in our boys. None of our bloody business if you ask me, except the Saudis needed help defending that bloody great refinery of theirs and we couldn't say no as usual, since all our oil was coming from there after we fell out with Iran, defaulted on our Russian debts...and alienated pretty much everyone else.

Anyway, things got really bad, just like everywhere else in the Middle East. Factions everywhere all fighting each other, everyone armed to the teeth. Then one day his company was deployed to guard some oil installation, huge place on the gulf coast, vital to everyone. It was an important mission and they gave it to our Harry. Saudi was his first tour y'know, his first posting on active duty. He was more than ready for it, did very well the first year. Decorated for bravery twice. Brave little tyke...that's what was so bloody odd about it."

For the first time, he looked up from the fire and scanned the faces around him. "It's not for me to tell you what happened out there. That's up to him, if he ever wants to discuss it. He never has, not with the Colonel, not with anyone as far as I know. All I can tell you is this: one day he turned up here dressed in civvies looking pale and bedraggled and rather sorry for himself. Told us he'd been cashiered. There was a court martial, apparently, and they stripped him of his rank. Cowardice under fire was the charge. Lost his nerve and half his men, so they say. Disgraced himself, his regiment and his country; dishonourable discharge. He was only here a night or two. Then he was gone. That was the last time him we spoke." Len shook his head in wonder or disbelief, the gesture ambiguous in the flickering firelight.

"And his father of course?" suggested Jake. "Disgraced. Shamed by the son who ruined the family name? Disowned him?"

"Is that what Harry told you?" asked Len.

"He never told us anything. Not about being in the army, his father – none of it."

"Then I've said too much – drunk old fool that I am." He got up unsteadily. "I'm for bed. I'll put that bottle away before any of you get into trouble. Give it here..." Nick passed him the bottle and he put it under one arm, muttering to himself as he tottered out of the door. Moments later there was a thud, a curse, and the unmistakeable sound of an earthenware bottle rolling across a bare wood floor. It was still there in the hallway when they came down the next morning, stopper in place, empty.

Chapter 15: My Boat Is So Small

Reuben lay, hands behind his head, staring at nothing. He couldn't sleep. Odd fragments of Len's story came to him at random, like overlapping echoes, blurred and jumbled so they made no sense, merely a summary of noise. His thoughts chased themselves round and round like crazy dogs.

There are two kinds of people. Those who say the same thing as they mean and those who don't. Those you trust because they have no agenda other than the one they reveal. Those you can never trust because their agenda is always hidden no matter how candid they claim to be. It struck him that his scheme was flawed. *Mind you, while it's true I don't trust Fairfax and I don't trust the Colonel, I do trust Harry despite the fact his agenda is equally mysterious. Not covert, however, like Fairfax. Mysterious. Perhaps it's the personal connection; I've never felt that Harry had a motive towards me other than curiosity and some compassion. He's never given me any reason to doubt him or distrust him and I don't think his agenda is connected to me except by accident. It's not personal, then. On the other hand, whatever Fairfax is up to, it concerns me, affects me directly. I'm his target – I just don't know what he's shooting at. Or is that a pretence? It's what's in my head, isn't it? That's what he's shooting for. He knows what's in there, the nature of it, even if I don't, and he wants it. I've got a secret and he wants to share it. Information he can use for his own reasons, for his own purposes. Nothing to do with me at all. I'm just a means to an end. Everyone wants me to get my memory back. Except me. The old man was right.*

After leaving the others to the chores assigned them, Reuben and Len had walked in silence for an hour or more, Len leading the way. Only when he realised they were nearing the point where they had begun did Reuben understand the old man had taken him right round the perimeter of the grounds, a complete circuit. It was like a reconnoitre – defensive positions, hides, advantageous ground, exposed places to avoid because incoming forces would have the advantage. Where vehicles would come bursting in. Where you could defend without being flanked. Where you could expect a force to infiltrate, to mount a second attack or a diversion, where you could pin a group down in crossfire with the minimum of defenders. Fall backs and regrouping points, places where you would be trapped, or better still trap others. It was all implicit, nothing said; just a nod in this direction, the walking stick pointed at a feature, a wave of a hand or a jutting jaw. How did the old man know Reuben would understand what he was being shown? What prompted that assumption?

Everyone knows more about me than I do. No...that's ridiculous...no it isn't – of course they do, you've lost your mind, idiot! Even so, the old man is one of them. I can't trust him because there's more to him than meets the eye. Why the deceit? Christ! Everyone has secrets except me. Or perhaps me most of all; something so secret I'm keeping it even from myself.

"So you're what all the fuss is about?" Len finally asked him without preamble as they completed their tour.

"I never wanted any fuss. I didn't ask for this dubious distinction."

"We rarely choose the burdens we shoulder, but they fall to us anyway. How are your eyes?"

"When I lower the sunglasses it's like a million needles pricking my eyeballs. Blunt needles."

"Nice."

"Hardly."

"I was being ironic. They say you can run faster...hear things others can't. Is that true?"

"It was. I seem to be slowing down. Falling apart, actually."

"Any other pain – joints, guts, anything?"

"Not really."

"What else can you do?"

"What do you mean?"

"Leap over tall buildings? X-ray vision?...OK, forget it."

"I thought you were going to find me some work?"

"Are my questions bothering you?"

"No, not really."

"Keen to work then. Need to justify your existence?"

"I need something. I know I exist. I have the Cartesian proof at least, but in reverse. I have an existence right now, a physical entity. It's my mind that seems to be missing."

"I eat, therefore I am?"

"All I have is the reflection of myself in the eyes of others. The knowledge of others, but none I can call my own."

"It's true then – you really don't remember anything prior to meeting this lot?" Reuben shook his head. "So you can paraphrase Descartes but you don't remember going to school, your parents...?"

"It is rather strange. I feel like a blank sheet, a tabula rasa. I'm blank on top, but there's other information buried underneath."

"Palimpsest more like. Scraped off, but the impression remains. Under the surface?"

"Correct. I'll give you an example. I know what a television is, but I don't remember ever watching before...before now. Another: I was reading Gibbon's Rise and Fall – you know it? – right; well, reading it was like one long déjà vu experience. Most of my reading is like that, as if there's a thin membrane between me and everything I know, and reading a book presses me up against that membrane, dissolves a little patch of it so I can see my own knowledge, access it again. Nearly."

"Does that include knowledge about yourself?"

"No, not about things I've done in the past, none of it. Just things I might have learned, books I might have already read. Mind you, I haven't found any books about me yet, so maybe there's hope. Maybe I'm the hero of a novel and when I read it I'll remember how great I was."

"And what makes you think you'd be the hero? Supposing you were the villain – would you still want to re-read that book?" Len stopped by a low wall and sat on it, indicating that Reuben should join him. He took a small, wrinkled apple from his pocket, cut it in half and gave him one segment.

"It's odd you should mention *tabula rasa*. I mean to say, curious. On the one hand, you are the literal Latin edition, the clean slate; only the shadow of you remains, nothing of the original – nothing that can be seen with the naked eye, especially not wearing sunglasses. Just smears of chalk dust where your past has been wiped away. On the other hand, you also have a chance to test Locke's proposition – which he lifted from Aristotle and Aquinas by the way – that you are the blank sheet on which your personality will be recorded, or in your case, re-recorded.

Wouldn't it be a waste, given such an opportunity, to write – or attempt to write – the same thing all over again, like a novelist whose second book tells exactly the same story as the first? Curiously, you seem to have a remarkable opportunity. You have sufficient maturity to decide what you write this time around, what life story you choose to tell for yourself, what history you record on that blank parchment. Most of us don't have that choice because by the time we take responsibility for ourselves and what we do – the end of childhood, in other words – the most significant parts of that record have already been laid down, certainly the parts that affect us most profoundly during the course of our lives.

"History isn't always written by the victors. Sure, they write the official version, the state version, the one that historians will read, but those are the epic histories, about cultures and civilisations, armies and wars and Gods. Our personal histories, which no-one else ever gets to read, the record of events which dies with us because the only version is in our heads; these histories are written irrespective of victory and defeat, though they *are* highly coloured by them. We write – and attempt to re-write – our own personal versions of history continuously right up until the moment we die. Out of our experience, some of us will construct personal myths; others, horror stories. Some will be self-aggrandising and their stories wholly inaccurate; most will be self-hating and their stories equally inaccurate. Some spend their lives gloating over small victories, burnishing the tarnished armour of their petty exploits, expanding it in size and significance until they perfect the self-regarding image of themselves as a colossus amongst lesser mortals, albeit largely misunderstood: conveniently, the plebs will always be afraid of the Gods that walk among them, even the lesser ones.

"But for most of us, it's the other way round; the truly victorious are few, their deeds infrequent. The vast majority wallow by degree in their failure, their victimhood, absolved of the responsibility for the outcome of being who they are because everything that happens is done *to* them, not *by* them, inevitably at the hands of conspirators. The loser, the slave, the lot of the common man: one long paean to failure, ignorance, humiliation, thwarted desires, friendships betrayed, potential ignored, our expectations never met, nor those of others; endless mistakes and injustices repeated ad infinitum straight out of Dante, just with the odd good day once every five years to stop you from topping yourself. Bit like going on an extremely long holiday, only to realise it's gonna rain the whole damn time, know what I mean?"

"I've never had a holiday."

"Tough luck. Stop feeling sorry for yourself and use your imagination, will you?"

"I didn't choose to erase what was already written. I don't know what I've lost."

"You don't get any flashes, intuition – I don't know – stuff popping into your head from time to time?"

"Not really."

"But you want it back?"

"I'm not sure."

"I don't think you do, son, I don't think you do. I think there's something telling you deep inside to run like hell from whatever's in your past. I think you're afraid, not of who you are now or what the future holds, but afraid that one day, of its own volition, your memories will return. You don't want that, in fact you're scared of it, but you don't know why."

"Everyone else wants me to get my memory back. They expect me to want that too."

"Sure. That's the thing about other people's expectations. Most times when we disappoint someone else, it's their expectations we fail. Dangerous game, expectations. People maintain an idealised version of each other which we rarely live up to, but they never realise the ideal is made in their own image, not in ours. In other words, it's a shock when it turns out we are not like them, that we're different. People fix you down in their thoughts, like they always want you to be the same as you were the last time they saw you, to defy change. Very un-natural. Nothing stays as it is, including us. Especially us. Some change for the better, some for the worse. But change is inevitable and there is no point whatever in trying to prevent it in others. Take Harry; he's got a real problem with that right now."

Reuben was intrigued. "How do you mean?" he asked, but the old man would not be drawn. He got up and started walking towards the house. Reuben followed him. "I don't think I could fail anyone's expectations," he said, trying to keep the conversation alive.

"That's true. No-one knows what to expect of you."

"Is that why you lied about who you are?"

Len glanced at Reuben, clearly amused. "You're the smart one and no mistake. When did you figure it out?"

"I wrote it down – lenoloc – and saw it straight away. Why the pretence?"

"Two reasons. Easier to assess the situation when people think you're merely the hired help. I also wish to avoid certain questions just now, at least until Harry is back. Right now, I'm free to be a humourless and quite unimportant old git whose only merit is that I hold the key to the pantry. I have a certain freedom in that, just like you have a certain freedom in not having a past."

"What kind of freedom is it, though?"

"You said it yourself. Tabula Rasa: the clean slate. I know people who would kill to get a second chance like that, to wipe away the past they can no longer live with. The freedom to be reborn as exactly what you want, who you want. You have no past to haunt you, and no expectations to pervert your present. That just leaves the future, which is entirely in your hands."

"Is it? I seem to be a passenger in my own life."

"Is it a good life?"

"Not bad, actually. Lucky to fall in with Jake and the gang."

"Yes, they're all right. A bit Peter Pan, living like children, but musicians have to be like that so as not to pollute what they play with cynicism and despair. Still, if you are enjoying your life, what's the problem?"

"I'm not choosing it. Everything is just happening to me."

"That's another way of saying life is coming to you instead of you having to go to it. It's hardly quiet desperation, is it? Sure, it's fortuitous, but so what? Does it have to be hard to live a good life, a rewarding life? If you travel on a river and the current takes you in the direction you are going, why complain that you weren't obliged to row? The Protestant work-ethic; you have to earn your happiness or else it isn't valid? Unearned reward is immoral, is that it? To which I say: bollocks. Life doesn't have to be an effort, an endless struggle – that's for people who define

162

themselves by the struggle, not what it achieves. That's what the fighting soldier is like – it's not the reason for the war, but the fight that attracts them, any fight. That's why some become mercenaries; to find another fight.

Nor does success in life *need* to be hard work, unless you want more out of it than comes your way of itself. Respect, ambition, influence, greed, admiration, power...it's the quest for these things we have to work so hard to achieve, sacrifice so much, and they are rarely satisfactory even if we achieve them. To reach the mountain top may be a glorious moment, but if the challenge of conquering the mountain was all you had, where does that leave the climber once you've reached the pinnacle of the mountain, and your desire? The need for such things is forged in the past, in our memories. Old wounds, old guilt, old hurts and betrayals; most of us spend our lives trying to heal ourselves, but we go about it in some damn odd ways. You don't carry any such burden and I urge you to count your blessings."

"I'm not on a river. I'm drifting in a vast ocean with nothing in sight on any horizon."

"There's a plaque that John F. Kennedy had on his desk in the Oval Office; it's an old Breton fisherman's prayer that reflects on powerlessness and insignificance: 'Oh Lord, your sea is so great and my boat is so small'. Is that it, that how you feel?" Reuben nodded. "Well, the universe is unimaginably vast, for sure. That should make us humble certainly, but it's not an excuse for feeling sorry for ourselves, or a reason to be scared. We are not insignificant, not to ourselves, only to others. Wanting to be significant to others is where the trouble starts. I tell you what; let's go down to the river. I'll show you a nice place to fish. Do you fish at all, 'cos you should? You'd like it. Very peaceful – we'll get a couple of rods out when I have time and I'll teach you the way of the wily fly. Meanwhile, don't concern yourself with the expectations of others. Make your own way in this life and don't pine for something you might regret getting. Remember this: if the Gods want to punish us, they answer our prayers."

I have no prayers, nothing to pray for. Just dreams, as vague as the strange shapes that swirl through my sleep. Who would answer my prayers? Who could? I want to know who I am – no, that's not it – I want to know what I am. Why am I different? My abilities seem to be fading away, but I can't tell if I care or not. Do I want to be different? Is being ordinary something to desire? Is that my prayer? Or was the Colonel right – rather than be what I am, I seek to belong, to be part of something. Would I sacrifice my unusual abilities to find a place in which I am not noticed, not hunted, not separated by my strangeness? Do I even have a choice?

Reuben suspected that, given the opportunity, he might indeed make the sacrifice if it brought him peace. Even the temporary respite of sleep would be good right now, but at that moment a floorboard creaked in the hallway. Half sitting up, he stiffened. The door opened. In the dim light he saw a mattress standing in the doorway. From behind it, a small, muffled voice spoke.

"Think I move in. I was going to move in with piano, but I change my mind. Maybe I like you even more than Steinway, but don't count on it. Creeping about in the night, why bother? Stupid – who cares? Put your bed on floor next to mine." The mattress staggered forward and fell to the floor, revealing Alina, shivering in the doorway. As she closed the door, Reuben lifted the bed-frame to stand it out of the way against the wall, his mattress already snuggled up on the floor next to hers.

Oh well. My boat may be small but at least it's big enough for two. Alina, you may not know it, but we're in the same boat.

2

**A
Soldier's
Love**

Chapter 16: Lost And Found

"We thought we'd lost you there for a moment."

Harry shifted in his chair. "Oh?" he muttered without elaboration, maintaining the truculence that was proving so productive. The bright young thing sitting opposite him wore a superior, knowing smile, but her composure was somewhat undermined by tapping fingers and eyes that wandered compulsively. Where Harry was unforthcoming, this *girl* couldn't stop herself from filling the oppressive silences with chatter. Each time, another piece of the jigsaw fell into place.

"Sure. We got the report about the bus a day or so after it happened, but it was a week before we had confirmation there were no fatalities. No bodies of any sort, actually – live or otherwise – which rather mystified the local boys. We assumed you were hiding out somewhere, correct?"

"It caught fire. We went to a hotel."

The girl rolled her eyes mockingly, reaching into a folder she had made a show of laying out on the table between them when they first sat down. "That isn't what the forensics say, Harry. They say there was an explosion, using a remote detonator triggered by a cellular device."

Harry shrugged. "How could I know that? And why should I believe you?"

"Oh Harry," said the young woman, feigning hurt. "Why would I lie to you? We're on the same side, aren't we?" The loaded question was so clumsy, as were the fluttering eyelashes, that Harry nearly laughed. How could they let kids loose like this, barely trained, rash, and so self-important? A presumptuous office girl with notions far beyond her station. The idea of having a clerk on his side made him grin involuntarily.

"Does that amuse you Harry? We *are* on the same side, you know. The same team."

"And yet, all you've done is ask me questions" Harry asserted rather disingenuously, allowing a petulant note to creep in. "You haven't told me a damn thing about what's going on. All the while, you've been sitting there with your bloody folder and your little tablet with all the answers, knowing full well I'm in the dark." Harry leaned forward, his voice rising. The woman, to her credit, did not shrink back as Harry completed his carefully timed rant with his face only inches from hers. "You know what's going on, don't you? You're just using me, like all the rest of them. You lot are all game players. It's me who should be asking the questions."

Now the girl looked genuinely aggrieved. "You have no reason to be like that. I know this is our first debrief, but really...?" She tailed off, uncertain, eyes fixed on the folder that Harry was fishing for. Then the hook found suitable purchase. "I tell you what Harry, why don't we run through the intel together." She slid the folder across the table. "That way, you'll know I'm not using you, but simply trying to help. To do my job, actually. How about it?"

There was an openness, a naivety about the offer that Harry found both endearing and, given the nature of the girl's work, either very inappropriate or really clever. He rewarded the credulous young woman with a brief but gracious smile as he opened the folder and started to read the top sheet. It was Jarrott's report, which he scanned quickly. There was nothing in it of much interest, except for a highlighted section containing a reference to the hotel. Before he could reach for the next report, the young woman interrupted him. "You know about Parkfield, I assume?"

Harry nodded, bluffing again. "I was briefed. But I haven't had any updates since we left Devon. What's the latest analysis?"

The foolish girl actually leaned back in her chair and folded her hands behind her head. "Oh, well...as you know..." she said airily, "...the project was attracting attention. They briefed you on the background, right?"

Harry nodded again, hardly changing his bored expression. "Cut to the chase," he prodded, keeping her off balance.

"Sorry. Anyway, something bad happened – we can't tell for certain but it appears there were fatalities – and we were getting close to a result. We'd asked Jarrott to keep an eye on the place, and we'd got a lot of inferential data from different sources..."

"Like the mil spec security, too much power going in, food supplies, that kind of thing?" Harry suggested reassuringly, testing the information Fairfax had volunteered. The girl nodded.

"But we have nothing on the fatalities?" he suggested. *We.*

"Only that there was some sort of exercise. Training apparently. Went horribly wrong, but expertly covered up. We have flight plans for medevacs, but they never returned to base according to the logs, even though the helicopters are sitting in the bloody hangers right now, I expect." The girl was getting loquacious, so Harry let her run. "But that was well before the fire and the explosion. The whole complex is buried now, with no chance of finding out what they were up to. We know the project team were whisked away sharpish, and since we can't find out who did the whisking we are rather puzzled. Only the opposition have the resources to pull that off on our turf."

"MI6? Why would they be involved?"

"If the project was imported, they would know wouldn't they?" The girl looked smug. Harry waited her out, idly thumbing through the other reports in the file on his lap. "In fact...it *was* imported, and we know where from," she finished triumphantly, her attention fixed on Harry's face, waiting for a reaction.

"Don't tell me," said Harry without looking up, "it was the cousins, right?"

"Was that a guess?" asked the girl, obviously irritated. "It could be anyone."

"Yes, but this has their fingerprints all over it. Mad science, lots of money, secret overseas research. Typical CIA overreach." The girl laughed. "Well, yes...you have a point there. They do love their technology, don't they?"

"Do you have proof, or is this just the usual *office* speculation?"

The taunt found its mark. "Despite what you field ops think, we do have our moments you know. This wasn't speculation but good intel. You know we tapped into their comms, right?"

"Sure, but it was wrapped up so tight you couldn't get anything from it. You said so yourself."

"Not entirely." The girl just couldn't help herself. "Of course, we routinely monitored the public line but all we got from that was the usual porn, shopping, TV and so on…right up until an hour before the fire started."

"The public line. The unsecured pipe?"

"Yes. Just before the fire, there was a huge burst of outgoing data on the wideband."

"And where was it going. How were the packets addressed?"

"Well, that's the thing Harry. It appeared to be directed at a CIA Langley proxy – multiple hops through blind addresses to disguise the destination, but we identified some of the proxy addresses a while back, and one of them was used in the routing of this transmission."

"Did you capture the data stream?" Harry asked, his interest piqued.

"Only a bit of it." The girl was clearly embarrassed. "The…er…look – the line was dull, routine, and the monitors were not paying that much attention. God knows there's enough to keep us occupied, stretched as thin as we are these days. You know what it's like Harry – so many threats, so few people we can rely on…" Harry nodded but said nothing. "Anyway, they only picked up the last few gigs of data."

"And…?"

"And we have no idea what on earth it is. Some of us aren't even sure it's data at all. I'll be honest with you Harry – it's got us all very puzzled. It's not like anything we've ever seen, and needless to say we can't ask the cousins for help, can we?"

"So there are no conclusions at all about what this is? If it's even relevant, come to that. From what you're telling me it could just be noise. That's not intel, it's wild guesswork."

"Not entirely. We do have some notion of how much computing power they had down there, based on power consumption, some suppliers invoices we tracked down, that kind of thing. And the stream was very concise, organised. No noise has such a clearly defined transmission structure. We estimate that the data was roughly the equivalent in size to the capacity of their systems."

"So it was a data dump. Exactly what you might expect if they were packing up and archiving their records off-site before covering their tracks?"

"Yes. That was also our first conclusion." The girl was concealing something and not making a very good job of it. "And yet...?" Harry let the question hang in the air.

"It never arrived at Langley. Never crossed the Atlantic as far as we can tell. The trace jumps around all over the place, but it ends up back in the UK. After that..."

"After that...?"

"Well...fact is, we lost it."

"Oh, great. You lost it."

"No need to be snotty. It was cleverly done. Better than anything we've ever seen the cousins pull off. That's what puzzles us most – the data itself uses no type of encryption we've ever seen, or even heard of. Assuming that is that it's even encryption in the first place. Then there is the way it was distributed through various streams and routes – so fast we can't work out how it was done."

"So what do they make of this upstairs then? If this is such a puzzle, how come I'm talking to you and not the committee?" The committee was the feared and powerful interrogation branch, members of the inner sanctum, and nobody – friend or foe – who attracted their interest escaped unscathed. In whispered conversations, the more cynical referred to them as the inner scrotum.

For the first time, the girl looked cautious and somewhat apprehensive. "No idea. You'd have to ask them," she replied after a pause, during which she scribbled something on a scrap of paper and slid it across the table. The short message surprised Harry for a variety of reasons; the girl had confided a dangerous truth *and* written it down, a cardinal sin. He read it: *They don't seem to be even vaguely interested. It's a cover up for their friends across the pond. They are sitting on it.*

Harry glanced up into the corner of the room, where a small camera poked a coin-sized lens through the cornice. "Did you hear by the way," offered the young woman with a broad smile, "we've been having terrible trouble with our CCTV recently. Keeps cutting out, apparently."

Wheels within wheels. Without speaking, and for the first time feeling kindly disposed towards the girl, Harry winked. They exchanged silent grins across the table as, with mock relish, he ate the note in the time-honoured if apocryphal fashion of their trade.

It was still raining when he came out of the shabby Pimlico terraced house. Walking slowly, Harry took in the strange atmosphere that hung like a blanket over London, as if ready to dampen any excitement, any movement or colour. The city was grey, silent and pensive below the weighty clouds, which were breaking up to reveal patches of ice blue winter sky. He reached Dolphin Square, once an exclusive complex of residences. Now it was a barracks, and the gardens were churned to mud by the half-tracks, trucks and tents, all entrances blocked and manned. Harry skirted the camp and kept walking until he reached the embankment. Here, steady traffic moved quickly east and west, the strange electric-engined whine a mere undercurrent compared to the bad old days, and the overwhelming noise of petrol and diesel engines. These days, only goods vehicles and buses were licensed to use the dirty, noisy engines.

Along the riverbank, the enormous water-wall towered above him, stretching away to his left as far as Woolwich, and right as far as Barnes (not that the Hammersmith – Barnes sections were ever likely to be completed). Typical of rushed government work, it leaked constantly. While the wrangle between various departments, architects, contractors and suppliers over responsibility had become something of a national joke, the leaky wall had become one of those strange symbols the British take pride in. The Channel Wall, they called it, maintaining it kept Europe isolated, like the old joke 'Fog in Channel. Europe cut off'.

Harry found the dark, sombre wall oppressive. He'd served in Israel, seen pictures from the US-Mexico border, experienced first-hand the misery walls like this always seemed to perpetuate, and either the memory or the damp made him shudder. He picked up his pace, heading east towards Kings Cross where he could catch the first of several trains, buses and lifts he would use to criss-cross the country before finally heading back to Nottingham. Several times he saw foxes dodging cars, bold in the daylight but bedraggled and unhealthy. Little rubbish to scavenge these days, thought Harry.

A bird flew by him, nearly brushing against his arm. He watched it perch on a window-sill where it sang a staccato refrain of dizzying pitch, which Harry suddenly realised was being repeated all around him. Songbirds were everywhere and the racket they were making surprised him, mainly because he hadn't noticed it until now. He knew the pigeons had disappeared (and nobody missed them, except for dinner) while songbirds, tropical escapees, deer, wading birds, foxes, badgers, moles, owls, many corvids, most of the vermin and all the insects (or so it seemed) – all nature had sought refuge in the cities as the floods and the heat took its toll on the agricultural land, the fresh water ran out and, to the east, the sea ran in. Londoners, with their usual eccentricity, viewed the wild life incursions as a blessing and put fluorescent road-work barriers round badger setts, fed their moles, groomed their foxes and pampered the visiting ducks, at least until they could procure an orange.

The birds sounded happy. It must have been infectious, because as Harry walked, hands in pockets, he started to whistle softly to himself. He wouldn't have described himself as happy at this moment, but he was certainly pleased. It wasn't what the girl had told him, it was what she never mentioned. Fairfax was one name that never came up. Even if it was a work name, the girl would have mentioned they had a man in place, and the file should have contained the case assignment, equipment dockets, travel permits and vouchers, but it didn't. Harry found this satisfying, although he couldn't figure out why, not yet anyway. He recognised a familiar sensation, one he had experienced whenever he was travelling towards the front line: the tension waiting for its chaotic release, the combination of fear mixed with eagerness for the fray.

And there was a second omission that pleased him all the more. They didn't seem to know about Reuben.

Back at the safe house, the young woman and her supervisor watched the CCTV footage of Harry eating the note. "Oh dear..." said the man between chuckles "he swallowed that

173

whole, didn't he?...ah...sorry, couldn't resist." He patted the young woman approvingly on the shoulder, where his hand remained. "You played it very well indeed. He's a bit of a bully, isn't he?"

"Thank you Sir. I rather enjoyed it. Do you think Fairfax will take the bait?"

"I do hope so. Do you think Harry will tell him?"

"Can't say for sure, but I suspect there will now be a confrontation of some sort, and it's likely to come out. Harry doesn't hold that many cards, does he? Did you notice that he never asked if we knew who blew up the bus?"

The older man withdrew his hand. "Don't be impertinent. What about the data?"

"Well, it's a calculated risk of course, like anything we do. But if it can be found, Fairfax is the one to find it."

"You're sure it's physical?"

"Quite. The transmission only went as far as the exchange, no further. The night of the fire, a window in the exchange was broken. No signs of incursion, no vandalism, nothing stolen, no damage done. Just a broken window."

"But if they had installed a storage device on the exchange switch, all they had to do was trigger it, dump the data, then pick up the box before it was discovered."

"Yes Sir, that's our thinking too."

The older man pulled on his gloves and walked to the door. "Find it before Fairfax does, will you," he ordered.

"Yes Sir."

"I don't care how," he added casually, without turning, and closed the door softly behind him.

Chapter 17: A Soldier's Love

By the time Harry got back to Clare House, Reuben was officially ill and excused all work. Harry found him sitting by the fireplace while Alina practiced. His face was pale, but more shocking was that he looked gaunt, so extreme a contrast with Harry's most recent memory of him that he was at a loss. But Reuben smiled and motioned him over. "Harry, you're back! And isn't it odd how we sometimes say the most obvious things?"

Harry forced a grin and sat down opposite him. Alina had been running through a most uncharacteristic series of complex, angular jazz chords, thick with resonant harmony and dissonant tensions, each creating a strange relationship with the preceding chord while linking to the one that followed forming a series of unexpected bridges, a melodic architecture that was both pleasing and surprising. When Harry appeared in the doorway she stopped abruptly, followed him across the room and as he settled, planted a kiss on the top of his head. She immediately turned away and sat down next to Reuben, taking his hand in hers.

"Reuben is sick," she said, her face impassive. "Can we get Guido?" Before Harry could answer, Reuben turned to her and shook his head. "You know we can't. We talked about this. It's a long way. We can't get anyone else involved...and he may be under surveillance for all we know."

The last observation was directed at Harry, who agreed. "He's right Alina, and I know you too well to think you believe anything different." He glanced at the clasped hands and smiled broadly, nodding as if giving consent. "There may be someone else though – I'll...I'll ask my father. Where is he?"

"Len the gardener? Your father is tricky bastard, no mistake," Alina burst out. "All right though. I guess. A bit." She suddenly looked rather self-conscious, aware that this was still Harry's father she was talking about, and despite Harry rolling his eyes at the mention of his father's oft-used pseudonym. "Anyway, he is upstairs in study, or downstairs in basement", she continued. "Has been for days now. Harry, what is basement, in locked rooms with steel doors?"

"We haven't seen him much at all," Reuben added. "He seems worried."

"I have no idea what's in the cellars," replied Harry truthfully, "but whatever it is I doubt it's any use to us. But first, Reuben – what's wrong? Tell me how you feel."

Reuben stirred and resettled himself. "You know my eyes were sore before you left? In the week since you've been gone, I've started to have balance problems, and dizzy spells. My joints ache quite a bit, and my muscles are sore all the time, as if I'd just finished some punishing exercise and severely overdone it."

"Are you running a temperature? Any fever?"

"No, if anything I'm rather cold. Didn't used to feel the cold hardly at all. Now I can't stop shivering. My pulse, apparently, is normal and my appetite doesn't seem to be affected much. I'm as permanently peckish as everyone else."

"What is *peckish*?" Alina asked, fluttering her eyelashes at Reuben, who grinned.

Harry ignored their exchange. "Has Fairfax shown up since I left, or been in contact?"

"Not as far as I'm aware," said Reuben carefully. "He certainly hasn't been here, and your father hasn't mentioned any contact. I think he would have told us."

Harry was less sure but didn't speculate. "And what about the man in the bushes? Any sign of him at all? Any unusual events, threats, problems, whatever...?"

Alina and Reuben both shook their heads. "It is quiet, Harry. Nice." Alina glanced at Reuben. "I play piano every day. Reuben listens, sometimes he sits with me and I teach him little things, don't I Reuben? He play good for idiot man. I feel safe here, first time in long time. If it wasn't for illness..." She broke off, looking downcast. Reuben squeezed her hand gently.

"Sorry you two, but I have to go. Just as well by the look of it?" Harry stood, a cheerful expression failing to mask an effort to find some resolve, to bring himself to do something distasteful.

"I have to talk to my father." Leaving the couple to their own devices, he reached the stairs just as the piano began another tune, but this time it was a simple child-like four-hander duet.

176

Reaching the door to his father's study, Harry hesitated. For the briefest moment he was again the small child, apprehensive and reluctant, knocking timidly in the hope his father wouldn't hear. When a strong voice from within the room demanded that he come in, Harry was jolted: his hand was hovering, knuckles clenched, still poised to rap on the door panel.

His father was standing in front of the ornamental fireplace, but Harry looked elsewhere. The room seemed exactly as he remembered it, which surprised him unreasonably. Officer's quarters: plush but functional, tasteful but a little heavy, old fashioned, like a poorly stocked antique shop, rich in detail but neither fussy nor messy. A reflective hush enveloped him, sounds muffled by a thick Axminster carpet and velvet curtains with braided ropes to pull them closed, each terminated by a golden tassel. A heavy leather chair, red and studded, with big wings either side that shrouded the sitter in secrecy. No plants. A vast desk made of real wood that must have seen the demise of half a forest to afford its solidarity. Several small incidental lights on tables, placed low, each lampshade plain, unadorned. Maps on one wall, regimental pictures on another. No family pictures at all except one: second lieutenant Thomas Bracey and wife Marion, Harry a babe in arms, at some remote base in Ghana. The couple leaned to the left slightly as a result of the picture sliding within the frame. They had leaned like that, perched on the mantle, as far back as Harry could remember.

When he could no longer avoid it, Harry nodded to his father who stood, hands behind back, bolt upright and hawkish. Cold eyes flickered with interrogational intensity, demanding answers to questions yet to be asked, his face impassive and unyielding. The perfect interlocutor; professional, patient and certain.

"So...you're glad to see me then?" Harry took one more step into the room and stopped, astonished. His father had burst into raucous laughter so unlike him as to be wholly unnerving. Harry didn't know if he was shocked, abused or just angry. "What...?"

"It's a front. A bluff. All these years and you still haven't figured it out."

"What is...what...I mean...?" was all Harry could manage.

"The look. It's a professional trick."

"The look...?"

"Come on son, collect your wits for God's sake. Is this how you were under fire – a blithering idiot with a blank expression and a loaded rifle?" Still, the Colonel stood by the fireplace, but the broad grin contained no hint of mockery. "The look is a professional device. I used to stand in front of a mirror practicing it, getting the withering quotient spot on. Your mother would indulge in gales of hysterical laughter, in part because she found it hilariously self-important, and in part to see if she could make me laugh despite myself. Good test, intelligent and witty. Your mother in a nutshell."

"You practiced it?" Harry was dumbfounded. His father was never candid like this, rarely self-depreciating. Ever since he left the band to their own devices and drove off in the stolen car, Harry in his imagination had been endlessly rehearsing this meeting, which he knew was inevitable, and which he dreaded all the more because of it. It was evident he'd been rehearsing the wrong script and he was literally speechless as a result.

"Sure. How many times have I told you that we must practice everything we do – cooking, cleaning, shooting, driving, fishing, making love...and taking command. Every person who ever made an important decision knows that certainty is a rare luxury. But the men and women who follow you cannot know this, and you cannot show it. Arguments may trouble you, but leadership requires you conceal this. The impassive face, the hawkish stare – these are the bluffs of a good commander, the hide from which he gathers information about the body language, expressions and speech of his troops, while giving back nothing except cold, hard and impassive logic, a lofty indifference almost. Never a hint of panic, worry, concern or uncertainty. Show these feelings and they are transmitted instantly to the ranks. It's poison son, and if you lead you must be prepared to adopt some method that insulates you, keeps your feelings and fears to yourself. This is my way of doing it. It was all the rage at the academy – Christ, we even had competitions to see who could look the most fierce.

"And I've been using this cheap little trick all my life – force of habit – waiting for you to see through it. Waiting and waiting..."

It was at this exact moment that Harry realised with shocking clarity how much his father loved him. Even more shocking was the flood of love he felt for his father, pursued by a dizzying parade of powerful feelings, old and new, that culminated when, without either man realising, the distance between them had closed and they were hugging each other, slapping each other on the back and generally behaving in a comradely manner befitting both their profession and their affection. An outside observer would have been amused to note how both also made fruitless efforts to conceal from the other a certain misty look, a dampness around the eyes, that was altogether inconsistent with the very British formal reserve they normally maintained. Like father, like son.

"I need a drink," said the Colonel, pouring two shots of his rare malt whisky into heavy cut-glass tumblers, one of which he handed to Harry with a knowing leer. He never shared his prized whisky, not ever. As if this wasn't enough, he still had one more unnerving trick to play, because as Harry went to sit where he had always sat, on the chair facing the vast leather cave, his father shook his head. "You sit in my chair," he ordered, waving towards it, and seated himself behind the desk. "Time to break some old habits, Harry."

The armchair engulfed Harry protectively, its wings like blinkers on a horse, restricting his view to all but that which was directly in front of him: his father. Perhaps the secrecy trade is like this, he reflected as he sipped his drink. People can see little of you, but you also have a limited view of them. His father was waiting again, patient but with an expression of kindness that warmed Harry greatly and gave him a sense that some new respect, this time mutual, had emerged out of old enmities. "Why now, Dad? I'm so glad you've forgiven me, don't get me wrong. But why now? Why is it time for me to sit in the big chair?"

"Well, one answer is that you're in command of this theatre of operations, not me. Another is that when we assume roles habitually – like father and son – those habits can be counter-productive. But the main thing is to examine the premise of your question...and therein lies a different issue altogether."

"What issue? What premise? That you've forgiven me?"

"Tell me this Harry. What should I have forgiven you for, exactly?"

Harry was puzzled. "For my disgrace. What else?"

"How about for being culpably fucking stupid? You are going to feel really humiliated when I've finished pointing out how dumb you've been, and how much suffering we've both endured as a result."

"I am? How have I been so dumb, exactly?" Harry was cautious. His father wasn't given to calling people stupid, but when he did he had an unassailable track record of accurate assessments to back him up, and this made the younger man pay unresisting attention. The Colonel nodded and refilled their glasses moderately "I think so. Here's what I think happened, how you suffered, and made me suffer too, from a wholly self-inflicted wound.

"On active duty, something goes off. Something bad maybe, or something heroic." He cast an odd glance at Harry, one that contained no doubt that his son was capable of both. "But let's stick with the official story – it's something bad. You're put on a charge, tribunal held quietly out of the way somewhere, dishonourable discharge maybe, or forced resignation? Keep the lid on it because the battle is still raging. Out you come, back into civvies, to live your life amongst a load of hippies, taking drugs to suppress the shame, the dishonour, the guilt, hiding from all who knew you before you disgraced yourself, your father, your regiment and your country. That's how it goes, more or less, isn't it?" Harry nodded, suddenly and inexplicably very anxious. "And as a result, your father disowns you, thinks you a worthless shit and not fit to lead a fucking cart. Probably cut from the will..." the Colonel was grinning now "...banned from the house, never to darken my door again. How very dramatic, very Grecian, but you do love all that stuff, don't you son? Harry the protagonist in a tragedy of proportions that puts Euripides in the shade. And you know what Harry? The entire thing, every assumption, every judgement and feeling you believed I held towards you...you invented them Harry. *I never, ever, felt that way about what happened.*"

"You told me to stay away. You were gruff, short to the point of rudeness. The night I rang you when I got back, from the airport. What is it you are telling me?"

"That I told you to stay away for your own good, and mine as it happens. Just as an aside, really, did it ever occur to you that others might be listening? You see, there is a great deal you don't understand my boy, but that's because I never told you so don't feel too bad about it. But in this instance, your foolishness has yet to be revealed in its full ignominy, because I tell you now: *you could have worked all this out for yourself.* The only shame I feel about you is that my son could be such a fucking dickhead, such an emotional puppet instead of doing what your mother and I hammered into you year after wasted year. Use your mind, think things through. Then – and only then – act with total commitment, with the best understanding of your situation that's available to you. In this, you failed miserably, and that's why I'm enjoying our chat, enjoying my right as a father and an officer to humiliate you as I show you what a fool you've been. It's my revenge."

He leaned forward in his chair, his face friendly but serious now. "Look. You know very well how well connected I am. Military, political, intelligence, ministry – how many of the brass used to dine here? We had ministers poncing around year after year, snotty civil servants patronising me about my wine, quiet gentlemen who couldn't hide the fact they spent all their time watching other people – you've met them all, son. All of them. So – *and think on this* – what did you think I would do when the news first filtered through? How long did you think it would take me to hear from one of my many sources that my boy was in trouble? I'll tell you – it took six hours from when the tribunal papers were lodged at the regimental HQ. And let me ask you this: once I heard, been told this most unlikely of stories – my son turned coward for God's sake – what did you think I'd do next? What I would make of it? Did you really know so little about your own father that you thought I'd believe it? Think to myself: 'There, knew it all along. Proved under fire as the worthless wretch I always suspected? Is that what you thought, Harry?"

"Oh...no...you mean...," Harry muttered. The Colonel waited, for he could see the penny was dropping, fast and heavy. Finally, his son was thinking it through. "Exactly. If you hadn't been so keen to make me the villain, the hard-hearted bastard, you would have realised *the first thing I would do is check*. Make calls, see people, call in old debts – anything to find out what was really happening to my son, to my comrade at arms come to that." At this, Harry smiled, for it was a great compliment, but it was clear the sheer size of his error was now dawning on him. "What did you find out?" he whispered.

"Come on. Stop being lazy. You tell me."

"You found nothing. Not a damn thing, anywhere."

"Now, that's my son talking. Correct...well, almost."

"Almost?"

His father leaned back, resting his empty glass on the desk. "It is never possible to completely hide one's tracks through the crooked corridors of power, especially those controlled by accountants. Shabby little bastards forever demanding vouchers, expense receipts, contracts, requisitions. Paper warriors, self-importance in triplicate, and largely myopic. But thorough. Scrupulously detailed. If you have time and infinite patience, you can use these people.

"I was suspicious right from the start. Several people who should have been able to find out exactly what happened said the opposite, that they couldn't find anything out. This was one of those double-bluff situations, since *they* knew very well that *I* knew they could find out any damn thing they wanted. And because they were friends, they made sure I understood how sorry they were – not for whatever it was that had happened to you, but for being obliged to lie to me. But that was a message in itself of course, which they also knew full well. Something was up."

Harry giggled like a little boy, not the least bit embarrassed in doing so. He felt relaxed and that he'd finally come home. "OK – I see it coming now and I feel really, astonishingly stupid. You were dead right, like you nearly always are, you swine."

"What else could I think? There's only one way I could make the circumstances fit the events: you were in bed with the spooks, and they were creating a legend for you, cover built round – and likely depending on – the cowardice story." He raised his hand to stop Harry responding. "Tell me when I'm done. I do want to know, but first, let me tell you how I confirmed my suspicions, because I rather like the sheer banality of the evidence. I called in a favour from an old boy who worked in the MOD accounting centre, a chap nearly ready for the pasture but still lowly and rather unnoticed. I asked him – well, insisted due to the damning nature of the debt, which we won't go into – to look for anything slightly odd about the paperwork coming from the forward command, transport and legal...you'll enjoy this...it turns out that there is a bit of a squabble going on between Vauxhall Bridge spooks and the MOD over who pays for meals in certain situations. Spooks keep eating army grub, apparently, and MI5 won't pay for the missing meals. So when..." the Colonel couldn't stop himself chuckling, "...when they saw that you had eaten several MOD meals on the way back, they billed it to Vauxhall *because you were theirs now*. Petty spite, and a cover blown if anyone with an interest in the matter – like me – cared to look at some scraps of paper or a few records in a database."

"And people like this are running the military and security services?" reflected Harry bitterly.

"They're clerks; powerless, they know only small things, capable of only small acts, admiring nothing but regulation and redress. Not running, Harry. Ruining, more like". Both men sat in silence for a while as they considered the appalling implications.

After a while, Harry stirred, refilled their glasses, (amusingly, it seemed to Harry, like quite a brave, *adult*, thing to do with his father's whiskey) and sat back down. "Shall I tell you then?"

The implications of this offer were not lost on his father. "Matter of conscience son. Up to you. No man can make that call for another."

"Security too, Dad."

His father shook his head. "No, I have clearance. No security issues, believe me."

"How can you have clearance? You've been in civvies for years? You're out of all that, old man. Out to pasture...aren't you?" His father laughed, raising his eyebrows in mock dramatic fashion. "Oh am I now?" he said in a stagey, mysterious manner, but said no more. Harry decided to ignore him, because the need to tell his father the truth was pressing, hard and immediate. He wanted the release, the relief; he could almost taste the freedom. He felt excited and prepared. A few more steps...then his face became sombre and pale as he recalled the circumstances that dictated where his story must start.

"They approached me right after...after the firefight. I lost them all, Dad. Every one of them." His voice choked as sudden tears ran down his cheeks. His father had resumed his hawkish, impassive expression. Now Harry understood why, was grateful, and wiped his eyes. "It was brutal. They flanked us both ways with heavy machine gun fire, but I thought we could break through if we concentrated on one emplacement while...hell, it doesn't matter. Point is, I lost my men. They died and I couldn't stop it, couldn't help them. I watched them die, one by one, and I couldn't stop it happening. I've thought about it over and over and I can't see how I could have done anything different, but..."

"Then stop going over it," his father interrupted, voice peremptory and full of hard-earned authority. "You review your conduct, and when you have learned what you need to learn, you move on. Every commander will lose battles and men under us. We also win them, but in both cases people will die, because that's what we do: we kill each other because we are soldiers. Anyway, you were taught all this, prepared, and you were better prepared than most, so why the fuss?"

Harry flushed with anger. "Don't make light of it Sir. Sure they train you, but tell me this: you've lost men, I know you have. Did the training prepare you for their deaths? Make it easier to bear?"

His father shook his head, but no change of expression touched his face. "I apologise. You are right – there's nothing that can prepare you, not really. But the horror and the loss must be born with strength and stoicism, because there are other men to lead, other battles to be fought. It is your duty to lead. You cannot become afraid of your next command, second-guessing yourself, and you know that too. Anyway, carry on..."

"I was shattered when I got back to camp. The only man who made it. I got some strange looks, but I was too tired and angry to care. The next morning, a spook took me to one side and gave me the line about how I could do something for them that meant my men didn't die in vain. I was about to punch his head off his shoulders, but managed to restrain myself because he was actually quite fit and had been on a number of dodgy ops, so chances were I'd take a kicking. (I trained with him later and I was right, too). Anyway, the gist of it was this: they would set up the allegations and proceedings, I'd take the blame for the losses by admitting some failure, some breach of my duty, one that wouldn't be so bad as to get me incarcerated, but enough to get me disgraced and discharged. Then they would bring me back, train me, and put me in the field."

"In with people who might be comforted to know you'd been discharged a coward? A man with a grudge? People who check up on that kind of thing ? What kind of target is this – what kind of people? This sounds like counter-terrorism. Reminds me of infiltrating the IRA back in the seventies, not that I ever served there. Heard some bloody hairy stories though, I can tell you. Made me sweat just hearing them."

"Sure, I've heard those stories too. They never got that specific, Dad. They worked me, I know that. I was feeling so bad – it was all very immediate and they were all over me like a bad rash before I had a chance even to work out what had happened. They worked me good, piled on the pressure and then offered me a way to escape, dressed up as James fucking Bond. I *am* a coward, Dad. I ran away, took the easy way out, and my thin excuse is that I did it for King and Country."

"So you came back, did the training...then what?"

"I'll tell you what. A stupid waste of time and money, that's what. They got me this job with a band, travellers they called them. Dangerous types they said, running guns and drugs all over the country, linking up with terrorist cells and anarchists, laundering money and so on. Dangerous my arse: I met the band, rather liked them truth be told, and they were desperate to get anyone prepared to travel around in a clapped out bus, living on bugger all and having a laugh. It didn't seem so bad, actually, so I went.

"Dad, it turns out that it wasn't just OK, it was really nice, and never a bloody terrorist in sight. Honestly, what kind of intelligence were they getting back in town? I don't think I've enjoyed myself more than I have in the last eighteen months, not since I got back. The way they live...I don't know. You couldn't understand it, but these people have something vital, something important. They are hopeless, idiotic, foolhardy and quite irresponsible, but they do have a lot of fun, and they are as close and committed as any squad I ever led."

"I think your assessment of my understanding will prove about as accurate as my alleged retirement. That's quite enough, son. Thank you for telling me. You've been a fool, a brave one but that's all the past. I only have one other thing to tell you." The Colonel paused, gathering his son's full attention. "*Never in this life would I believe you a coward, and nothing you have told me today changes that opinion.*"

After a short pause while Harry collected his thoughts, he remembered something he wanted to ask, one last suspicion to extinguish. "Dad...earlier, you said you told me to stay away for my own good. What did you mean?"

"It wasn't you I wanted to keep away. Rejecting you like that – it hurt, because I knew you needed your father, but I couldn't help you, couldn't take the chance. It wasn't you, Harry; it was your new-found friends. I couldn't afford to have them sniffing anywhere near this place, and before you ask why, it's time you had a look in the cellar. Come with me."

Chapter 18: Etheria

Day 24? I've lost count. I don't know why I'm keeping this record any more, except that it is what I'm trained to do. Still watching the house. Harry came back this morning, from where I do not know. Other than that, not much has happened. They all stay within the grounds, which is sensible and takes some pressure off me. No sign at all of the target – I don't even know if he's here or somewhere else. Do they have any idea how dangerous he is, what a cold-bloodied killer like that can do? I was sure he'd blown up the bus but that didn't make sense from any strategic viewpoint so I'm still baffled. Starting to get cold again – do people really like living in the rough like this, hard ground, little sleep? I hate this furtive existence. Dare not light a fire or even move around much to keep the circulation going. Nearly got caught stealing some energy two nights ago to recharge the batteries. Stupid mistake. I cannot get careless now, or people will die.

"It couldn't have been easy, being my son. Having my shade follow you around the service. Did they give you a hard time?"

They had reached the bottom of the stairs leading to the cellars, the Colonel leading. Harry answered the back of his father's head, staring at hair much thinner than he remembered. "Oh, sure...the usual I expect, but laid on thick. Didn't bother me much Dad. You trained me well as a kid, so when the shit was coming from above, I kept my mouth shut and took whatever they dished up. When the shit travelled sideways, I'd deal with it round the back of the mess hall or in the gym if officers were about. Lost some, won a few too, but afterwards it always seemed to be a bit better between me and the man I duked it out with. God, we are just a bunch of primitive apes sometimes, aren't we?"

They both laughed. "What do you expect from people who choose to fight for a living?" his father asked rhetorically as he opened the door to the cellar and switched on the lights. Beyond them stretched a square, vaulted room, twenty metres on a side, with heavy pairs of iron-studded and bound doors facing each other to the right and left. A single door in front of them, standing ajar, led to the deserted wine racks.

"Is what you want to show me connected in any way to Fairfax, Dad?" He followed his father towards the left-hand cellar. Reaching the door, the Colonel cast an approving look over his shoulder, then returned to his search through a well-stocked key ring that had appeared from nowhere. Selecting one that was considerably larger than the rest, he inserting it into the huge padlock. "See, you *can* think for yourself after all; I'm sure it does, actually, but I have no idea how at this time. I am quite certain that he knows a good deal more about our man upstairs than he's let on, to you or to me. I know him too well."

"You know him?" The surprise in Harry's voice was palpable, and only bettered when his father, having released the padlock, slid a well-disguised, head-height panel in the door to one side, revealing an eye scanner. A single green light illuminated as the panel went home. *What the hell is in this cellar?*

The Colonel leaned forward until his eye was level with the scanner. "He served under me. First lieutenant to my captain, then captain to my major. After that, he stayed in the field while I was posted back here and we lost contact." A heavy mechanism began to labour quietly in response to the Colonel's retina being scanned and authenticated, along with body temperature and a host of other biometric details gathered unobtrusively as they entered the cellar.

The right hand door opened. Beyond it was darkness, which swallowed them both when they stepped in. "Stay where you are," his father ordered. The door swung shut behind him. "Do not move; your life may depend on it." Harry stood stock still. The darkness was complete but he felt nothing except expectation. "What are we waiting for?" he asked the nothingness.

"More detailed biometric scans. If either of us are not in the database, we get fried. But don't worry," a chuckle interrupted the disembodied voice, "I put you in using your service data a while back."

"You anticipated this?"

"Not this, exactly. But something like it."

"Preparation being everything?"

"Exactly. Now, cover your eyes." As the Colonel finished speaking, the room was flooded with a light so bright Harry

188

could see the bones in his hands, placed over his eyes barely in time. When the light went off it left the room illuminated in a dim red glow. It was small, cramped and bare. Only one door, the one through which they had entered, which was now open again. On each side were a series of mains switches, each connected to a sizeable distribution box and a power cable as thick as his wrist. Above both rows of switches were long slits through which a weapon could be fired, and Harry immediately realised the disabling property of the intense light was designed to halt an intruder so they could be shot. The idea that his own father was party to such an installation in his own home he found quite chilling.

"He was a good soldier," said the Colonel, engaging each switch in turn. For a moment, Harry didn't know who his father was talking about. "Quiet and thorough. Tough enough, but didn't make a thing of it. Used to exercise with big weights but never showed it, no bulging pecs, no six-pack. Smooth, he was, and bland – the sort you don't notice until he's long gone, long after he's blown up your house and gone down the pub for a pint, quiet as a mouse. Reliable, but so self-contained he was hard to trust." The last switch was turned. "Ready?" Harry nodded, watching his father, who pressed a small button on the blank wall, prompting a great slab of it to slide effortlessly to one side.

I could have killed him several times. Why did I hesitate? What is he trying to achieve? Does he have some plan that has not yet been revealed? Why on earth did they come here anyway? Did he suggest it, in which case how did he know about Harry's father, the house, the isolation?

They stood, side by side, at the top of a short flight of stairs down to the main floor of a vast cavern, bright with harsh light. It stretched away to a distance Harry found inconceivable, since the last time he had been here – many years past – it was only a cellar equal in size to the others. When had this been excavated? By whom, and in what extraordinary secrecy. The sheer scale of the accomplishment stunned him, but not as much as the contents of the room, for every wall was packed with gleaming equipment, much of which whose function was unknown to him. Computer screens were stacked in banks, mounted on panels, freestanding on desks between racks whose purpose was of sufficient importance to merit masses of cable, fibre-optic bundles that snaked improbably through vents, down channels, every which way. Yet there was order here, a military precision which could not be disguised, not that any attempt had been made to do so. Harry recognised some satellite uplink equipment familiar to him from his training. There were several comms stations, sealed encryption boxes replete with hectoring security warnings. A weapons rack, locked but well stocked. Everything was silent, expectant, without power but radiating great promise, stand-by lights twinkling. What they promised, Harry had no idea.

In the centre of the hall stood a command console, a series of screens built in a curve around a control surface of complex panels, switches and keyboards. For some reason, Harry found himself locked in a consideration of how much money all this equipment must have cost, but his irreverent contemplation was interrupted by his father's grip on his arm, urging him down the steps. They walked to the console, where the Colonel turned to his son. "Well, how do you like it?"

Harry had gathered his wits sufficiently on the walk across the hall to answer promptly. He really didn't want to give his father any more opportunities to mock him, albeit deservedly. "Where's the power coming from? This lot must draw huge amounts. There is no way you could run this off a domestic supply, and since I assume this is a secret installation, there is no way you could run it off the grid without the drain being noticed and tracked down?"

"Nice cover-up. You always were good at bluffing, even when you look pole-axed like you did just now. The generators are in the cellar opposite. The fuel is in a series of interlinked tanks under the grounds. Remember when we had the tennis court built, when the workmen shrouded the excavation, saying they had to bring in the digger and remove a load of earth to make the court immune to subsidence? That was when we put in the tanks. Did you never wonder why it took seven months and a hundred truck-loads of spoil to build a tennis court?"

"I wasn't here much. When I was, I took it for granted you knew what you were doing." Harry sounded less than convincing.

"You thought no such thing. But that's another conversation, where you explain to me how on earth you came to think I'd turned into a glorified hippy. Not now, and not here." He swept his arm around in an expansive manner. "Welcome to Etheria".

I miss home. Never thought I'd say that about such a dump. Perpetual gloom, no sunlight. I hated it while I was there, miss it terribly now I can't go back. What kind of logic is that? The same twisted rationale by which I end up in the brambles, scratched from head to foot, shuffling about like an old man? I feel quite lost, even though I know to a few centimetres exactly where my body is. Where is my heart? Is it dying along with my future, now I'm cast adrift like this? No mission parameters. No rules of engagement. No objective and no strategy to accomplish it. This isn't what I trained for; the chaos of warfare. This is the warfare of chaos: no pattern, no plant, and no exit in sight. Why didn't I kill him when I had the chance?

"The installation was one of many built by the military in preparedness for what became known as the OEW – the 'other end of the world'. As far back as the turn of the century, the government knew that climate change would never be stopped, and that the resultant civil disorder would be of a magnitude almost unimaginable. The major political parties held talks so secret the attendees, travelling in windowless buses, never knew where they were taken, or subsequently where they had been, driven by men following pre-programmed satnav instructions with no indication of where they were going. It was agreed that while each administration would make all the right noises, go to all the right conferences and make every commitment prudent PR required, they would pay scant attention to anything that required more than a few million to fund, putting all their considerable resources into measures to ensure the government could keep the lid on when things inevitably turned violent.

"Secret plans were drawn up by grim-faced men and women, their official roles in government and civil service both innocuous and unexciting, especially to the media. Quietly, unofficially, they began the process of establishing a totalitarian state. They planned and executed massive extensions to surveillance systems, most of it done covertly. While the government denied all knowledge, they built systems to intercept, record and store permanently every type of communication the public used. They recruited a pervasive network of shopkeepers, clerks, firemen, programmers, waiters and everything in between as spies, all in the name of national security. Their programmers created software to scan everything they recorded for keywords, phrases, patterns of speech, accent, country of origin, to cross reference names with addresses, credit cards, phones, computers, social media, vehicle registration, DNA, social security, Interpol and terrorism unit files and the various police databases. They built resilient networks that tapped every CCTV camera across the nation while, through their friends in the press and the extreme right, to demonise Jews, Muslims and Chinese immigrants in order to justify their intrusion, quietly smug when the frequently murderous interventions of fundamentalists made the task so much easier. While successive governments passed ever more draconian laws in the ceaseless acquisition of the authoritarian powers they knew they would need sooner or later, installations like this one were built in as many locations as could be reasonably secured. When things got bad, the planners reasoned, command centres may fall or be cut off, so they created a cloud of distributed bases, each a scaled down version of the five major centres, each as capable as the next, all interconnected nationally, and to similar centres across the globe.

"And little good it did any of us in the end. Everything was so ragged, because of course there was nobody really in command, particularly after America descended into civil war. Politicians had become utterly weak and vacillating, slaves to public opinion, the venal media and the focus groups. Pathetic. One minute, they order everybody to man the entire coastline so we can fend off the refugees flocking across the water like so many lemmings who had changed their minds. We get there, catch thousands of the poor wretches that just fell off the edge of Europe because it couldn't hold any more, and what do they tell us? Let them go, because we can't send them back and we'd rather not build any more concentration camps in Dorset.

"There was no leadership, so there were no commands. Some in my place took responsibility, took matters into their own hands, but several were arrested soon after, by order of the ministry. In truth, it didn't really matter. The whole descent into barbarity was one long, slow-motion nightmare, a horror film in which you watch a civilisation slide backwards in time, imperceptible as the advance of the tides and just as certain, becoming a crude parody of itself and a harsh reflection on how little we've learned. Five hundred years of progress largely destroyed, if not forgotten. All that free energy, there just for the effort of getting it out of the ground, and everything we built with it we have largely destroyed through our complacency, greed and immaturity."

"And yet we are stabilising," offered Harry carefully, moved by his father's gravity.

"Well, that's open to question, given the circumstances," his father retorted. "Some see this as an opportunity, and are making plans. Plans I oppose. And I think your mystery man upstairs is mixed up in one. Fairfax too, although he may have different plans for all I know. I somehow doubt it, mind you. Never believed in coincidences. No good commander I know does."

"Who does Fairfax work for?" Harry asked.

"I thought you knew. He's a spook like you, but from the other firm. He's SIS."

Does my reluctance indicate some superior trait? The moral question then; when is the killing of another person defensible? In the service of some greater good. What is my greater good? This time there is no authority from above, no rationale based on my country, my king. If this is honourable, it is a furtive kind, a disreputable kind of honour. Isn't killing someone an act more despicable than any other? Why is that? Why do I not care? There are more terrible things than being dead, like being alive to suffer the worst of them. To kill in order to protect and serve, as the yanks would have it. The ultimate edict of power over each other; the preparedness of one man to kill another. For the greater good, supposedly. I'm trying to protect, certainly, but who do I serve, except myself? And isn't that the danger, where self-serving motives are used to justify any acts. Means and ends, but with a body count. Always the long zipper bags. And yet, I have no choice. No choice at all. Battles come to this, all other options now forfeit, no more decisions to be made. Then the killing begins.

"Does all this stuff work?" Harry asked as he perched himself on the edge of the console. "What could it do now? Surely it's defunct, given the way things are these days. And what was it you called it...Etheria, was it...what is that?"

The Colonel smiled. "My little secret Harry, that's what Etheria is. Our little secret now. When I said 'destroyed but not forgotten', I wasn't being hyperbolic." He glanced around the room with the studious air of a man about to divulge a great secret, and chuckled. "You're quite right, in that the original purpose of these systems is defunct. I realised that a long time ago. So did some other people I knew. Between us, we worked out that we had considerable resources at our disposal that, effectively, nobody knew about. The military as a trained, professional body was all but gone, replaced by thugs in army uniforms rampaging through city streets, shooting civilians in the back and looting their homes, beating the crap out of anyone who dissented with anything they or the government said. Mob rule, a deformed child of chaos. Systems like this were beyond their comprehension. But not ours, and we thought of something really useful we could do with them."

Harry knew better than to interrupt, so he merely nodded as his father drew a breath. "Destroyed but not forgotten, right. But who remembers? Who archives all that knowledge, that learning, that skill and experience we paid so dearly for? We realised two things: while we know there are several good databases around the world, still intact and functioning, which contain huge repositories of information, it would be better still if there were more of them. Safer, less vulnerable to unwitting or unthinking

194

destruction. And the greater the geographic diversity, the faster knowledge could spread back out.

The second thing we realised – and perhaps on reflection this came first –whichever way round it was, we realised that here in this facility we have enough storage capacity to keep safe every bit of scientific data man has ever created, along with the records of how they did it, and why. That, Harry, is Etheria."

Harry threw back his head and laughed with abandon. "Fuck me Dad. You've pinched a vast array of hideously expensive warmongering equipment off the government, and turned it into a library, a gentleman's library to end all libraries. Wow. That is particularly cool on so many levels."

"Isn't it just," replied his grinning father who, in displaying his obvious pride, was breaking yet another personal taboo.

Does he have the data? Without it, we are nothing, no existence, no explanation, no recourse and no proof. And no deal. What are they doing with it? If they destroy it, there is no chance we'll ever discover the truth, if indeed such a slippery thing even exists. I put so much faith in those records, yet I have no idea what they contain. Suppose they unlock no doors, reveal no mysteries? It is unrealistic, so very unrealistic, to place so much hope in something that may be no more than a collection of petty cash receipts, old menus and decorator's invoices. No matter how many times they repainted, it was always the same gloom, the atmosphere of distrust and suspicion, of cover-up and obfuscation. Never a straight answer, just more questions. I am so entirely fed up with questions – boy, they found that out soon enough. I wish I could stop asking them of myself – is this habitual, or a displacement activity to avoid reaching answers, conclusions? We used to say we were better off not knowing, but I never believed that for one second. Ignorance is bliss, but to maintain it you also have to maintain your ignorance.

While the Colonel swept the floor, Harry watched the spirals of dust pirouette through the air. "Is this the only one then. Etheria?"

"No. There are eight UK stations in all, so far. We paired them up so that no single data store was vulnerable. Effectively we have four repositories then, each with specific focus. This one is science, another pair hold the entire contents of the world patent office. The third has technology plans for dummies – how to make phones, computers, generators, medical equipment – and the last pair hold copies of all the critical software that makes nearly everything else work, and as much culture as we could cram into it."

"How on earth did you collect all this data?"

"Well, it was actually quite simple. We had satellite up and down-links so contact with global academic bodies was fairly straightforward, if rather tedious. We had to move very carefully so as not to attract any attention, but when the entire world is in a state of chaos that isn't as hard as it might otherwise have been. Working with other like-minded people we came up with a plan to segment the data, which was then compressed at source into packets ready for transmission. Gradually, we sneaked it through the ether, bit by bit, until each store was full. We also work as a relay station, because other countries have joined our network with similar schemes of their own. That's when the trouble started of course, because for every person you add to a conspiracy, the risk of discovery or betrayal increases by an order of magnitude."

"Betrayal? Who to? Why would anyone want to oppose such a scheme?"

"Because information is power, you dope." Harry looked abashed. "Remember, we are effectively stealing this information from those who are keeping it to themselves for all the usual scurrilous reasons. If my country has this data and yours does not, my country has power over yours. Nothing remotely new about that, is there?"

Harry shook his head. "I've spent too long with the hippies. Right out of practice, I am. Give me time Dad, I'll soon wake up."

"I don't doubt it," said the Colonel, housing his broom. "What's that...?"

Both men turned towards the doorway as one. Harry could hear a soft scratching sound. "Is that a mouse?"

But his father smiled and shook his head. "A very large mouse, I think. Reuben, why don't you stop skulking around out there?" A moment later, Reuben emerged from out of the dim red glow of the lobby and walked to the top of the stairs, showing no trace of embarrassment at being discovered. "Nice place you have here," he remarked casually as he descended the stairs and walked over to join them.

"How long...I mean..." stammered Harry.

"Excuse my son. He's a blithering idiot but I love him dearly for reasons that remain entirely incomprehensible." All three laughed, Harry the loudest.

"I followed you down. My hearing isn't what it was, but I did hear you two come down and I also heard you going down the stairs to the cellar. Alina was asleep, so I thought I'd investigate. I do have some small interest in all this, I think you'll admit."

"Certainly. And I assume you heard my little tale, or most of it?"

"All of it. Etheria – what a noble gesture – but a subversive one as you say. Is this what Fairfax is after, do you think?"

"I don't think so. He's after you, in my view, although I'm sure he'd love to know about this little conspiracy of understanding. But that's only because he's an opportunist, like all spooks. Information is currency and one collects it irrespective of whether one knows where such currency can be redeemed. Force of habit. Anyway, let's lock up here and go upstairs. I'm hungry, and we've covered everything we need to right now."

The Colonel started towards the stairs, but Reuben called out after him. "Actually Tom, I don't think we have. There seems to be something nobody is paying much attention to. Something that may be the most important factor of all."

Harry and his father turned to Reuben. Neither spoke.

"I've seen him twice, the second time when I thought he was about to kill me. Vicky saw him in the snowstorm, and thought it was me. *Who is the man in the woods?*"

The Colonel shook his head. "Let's talk about it upstairs. We'll keep this between us three right now, shall we?" The others agreed, and they followed Tom Bracey towards the door. Harry, behind his father, was curious. "How did you know it was Reuben. The scratching, I mean?"

"It's an old trick," answered his father. "You scratch on the door very quietly. Persistent, but small, like a mouse. The person inside hears the sound, which is faint but close, unthreatening but curious. Of all the people in the house, only Reuben had the wit to use this little trick to give away his position. A witty little joke, isn't that right?"

"Sure Tom," replied Reuben. "I knew it would make you laugh. You'd be amazed at how many people fall for it, Harry. Of course, it only works if the target is alone, and you have to crouch to one side of the door because if the target knows anything about anything, he'll just riddle the door panel with an automatic rifle, or whatever he has to hand. But if the target is dumb enough, they always do the same thing - come to the door, open it gingerly and poke their heads out to see if they can catch a glimpse of the mouse. An undefended head shot from three feet. Anyone who misses that is fucking useless."

This was the first time Harry had heard Reuben swear. About to express his surprise, he was knocked to the ground by something heavy hitting him in the back. As his father helped him stand, they both looked down at Reuben with concern, lying unconscious on the spot where he had fallen.

Chapter 19: Conjunction of A Sharp Stick And Sun Tzu's Behind

Despite all the kilos lost, there was no chance that father and son could manoeuvre a prostrate, dead-weight Reuben up the stairs. Harry went for help, disappearing in a small cloud of dust, leaving his father to ponder the wisdom of allowing any of his guests to share the secret of Etheria, an event which now seemed unavoidable. He smiled grimly as he felt Reuben's pulse – strong and steady – because events were now beginning to gain a momentum of their own and he knew better than to make any foolish attempt to hold back the tide. *There are times you can make plans. There are times before engagement when you can shape events consistent with those plans. But the fact remains that when battle is joined all plans go straight out of the window. What was it von Moltke said? 'No battle plan survives contact with the enemy.' The decision has been taken from me and now I must adapt to survive, or perish if I fail to do so.*

Moments later a clatter from beyond the door announced the arrival of Jake, Cas, Alina and Phil, followed by Harry and Nick moments later. As they alternated between concern for Reuben and shock at the sight of such a bewildering array of equipment, Reuben groaned and tried to sit up, much to everyone's relief. "Steady son," said the Colonel, assisting him. "You went AWOL on us there. Do you remember what happened?"

Reuben stared at the group huddled round him, his blank expression gradually replaced by one of concern. "Er...no...I...where am I? Who are you people? And who am I?" The group exchanged worried looks, all except Alina, who swore violently. "Fuck off idiot. Stop messing around." Reuben grinned weakly, clearly a bit embarrassed. "Sorry, didn't know what else to say. Evidently I passed out then?"

"You did indeed," said the Colonel as they helped him to his feet. "Steady now, no rush." The attention of the group moved from Reuben to his surroundings. "Where is the boy and his mother – and Billy, where's he?"

"They're in the kitchen getting some food ready," said Jake. He looked angry. "I thought we had come to a place where we could be safe for a while. Now I'm not so sure we haven't jumped straight from the exploding pan into the funeral fire. What is this stuff?"

"Good line," muttered Cas as he produced a tiny notebook and proceeded to write with the stubby pencil concealed in its spine. "'From exploding pan to the funeral pyre. That's better. I'll use that."

"Leave that alone please," ordered the Colonel, addressing Nick, who had sidled up to the nearest rack with all the nervous excitement of a geeky kid about to take apart his first watch.

Nick span round, a furtive look on his face. "I didn't touch anything..." He trailed off weakly, then chuckled at the wretched nature of the denial. "Well, not yet, but give me a few more minutes..."

"You may get your chance Nick," the Colonel replied, his tone mild. "In fact, there are a few things that need some attention and from what I understand, you have some skills in this area. But we'll talk about that later. Right now, we need to get Reuben here upstairs and lying down. He's still shaky, we all need feeding, and I have some explaining to do by the looks of it." And with that, they trooped out of the hall, Harry and Jake supporting the pale, unsteady Reuben. The Colonel came last, reset the switches in the lobby and sealed the outer door with a wave of his hand, the blink of an eye, and an enormous iron key.

They all helped to bring food into the sitting room where Reuben was stretched out on the sofa. On hearing the news, Vicky and Billy had rushed in, only to find everyone else calm and sufficiently relieved to be swapping the customary jibes and good-natured insults.

The Colonel stood, hands behind back, in front of the empty fireplace, trying hard not to adopt his usual defensive glare; as a result he looked rather like a benevolent grandfather overseeing a large, unruly family (and felt a little like it too, which he didn't mind in the least). "Play something Alina," he asked the girl, who was still looking crossly at Reuben even as she tightly held his hand. Reluctantly, she let go, crossed over to the

200

piano and began to play, softly and with restraint, improvising a gentle swaying rhythm to support a delicate, sparse melody picked out of spaces between skeletal chords. Vicky had returned to the kitchen with her husband, where she informed Billy, acting briefly as child-minder, that Jimi could be allowed to join the others. As she brought in the plates and cutlery, she smiled inwardly at the sight of her son, sitting cross-legged on the floor below the prostrate Reuben, looking fiercely protective of his friend and strangely adult in doing so. *He's growing up fast. I hope not too fast, but he has to live in this world just like the rest of us.*

When the food was consumed, the debris cleared and left to its own devices on the kitchen table for want of interest, an expectant hush descended on the group as they all turned towards the Colonel, now sitting on the couch next to Reuben, who had sat up to eat a little food. He ran through the same story he had told his son, largely without omission. The general reaction was one of relief, with some looking a little proud to be in on such a worthy secret. Jake was the first to speak. "Well, I do like the fact you've turned this military gear into something useful," he said, echoing Harry's earlier remark. "But your point about knowledge being power means that we've swapped one dodgy situation for another, doesn't it?"

"You could also say that while I had one secret to keep, now I have two," replied the Colonel. "Double jeopardy."

"Can I see the cellar," asked Jimi. "I didn't see it." Reuben reached down and tousled the boy's hair. "I'll show you later Jimi – that'll be OK won't it Tom?"

"Sure Jimi," the Colonel replied fondly. "Reuben and I will give you the tour. But perhaps your mother should tuck you up in bed now, isn't that right Vicky?"

Catching the significant look, Vicky shook her head. "No. His best chance of understanding how serious this is, is to be part of it". Nick leaned over and kissed her tenderly. "That's why I love you. Thanks for reminding me."

"I am nothing if not dutiful," said Vicky with a grin.

"Is there something I can vomit in?" asked Phil, who was studiously ignored. Cas, who had been silent for some time, reached a conclusion. "Fairfax is the key to all this..." he hesitated, uncertain. "He's the only one who knows more about this than we do – at least, the only one we know about...that we've met, I mean."

"Where is he anyway?" asked Jake. "I thought he'd show his face before now. I can't help thinking he's manoeuvred us here because of something to do with Etheria, but I can't work out what his interest in all this really is. It just all seems too...too coincidental." At this, Harry and his father exchanged a quick glance. "I like the way you think son," said the Colonel. "All we can do now is wait for him to turn up and ask him."

Cas looked up from his notebook, in which he had immortalised some new thoughts. "We need a strategy."

"To form a strategy, we need an objective first," said Harry. Cas shook his head. "I've been writing down a few ideas about that, actually. This is what I have so far: we want people to leave us alone and get back on the road. Reuben wants to know who the fuck he is and why he has a QR code on his foot. Tom here..." he glanced apologetically at the Colonel, conscious of the informality.

The Colonel merely smiled. "Go on Cas, I didn't know you had it in you. Spot on so far." Reassured, Cas returned to his notes.

"OK – Tom wants to keep Etheria secret. Vick and Nick want Jimi to be safe. Harry wants to make up his mind, and Phil wants to hit something." Cas closed his notebook, watching the Colonel's reaction.

"Fucking hell, you got that last bit right," grumbled Phil, punching his fist into his palm. The band laughed, because it was a matter of history that for all his talk, Phil was a hopeless softy, an easy touch for every waif and stray with a sad story, a kind-hearted man forever finding liberated domestic pets which he brought back to the bus, despite being refused accommodation for them every single time on purely practical grounds. Phil's anti-social attributes were always catalysed by alcohol; without the booze, he was just a big, gruff pussy cat.

"That's a complex but accurate set of objectives, Cas," said the Colonel. "Now what we need is a strategy that can satisfy as many of those objectives as is practical, given the resources at our disposal." Cas was gratified at this, pleased not to be patronised. "Well, Sun Tzu said..."

"For fuck's sake Cas," shouted Phil. "Every bastard on earth goes on and on about bleeding Sun Tzu, and not a single one of them ever read the fucking book, just picked up a few quotes off the net. Any more of that crap and you'll be learning what it is like to be at the conjunction of a sharp stick and Sun Tzu's behind."

"Leaving Phil and I out of this," interrupted Harry animatedly, "those objectives can be simplified because several of them amount to the same thing. Jimi's safety, getting back on the road – which I want too, in case you were wondering..." he swept a defiant look around him, "...and keeping Etheria secret are connected. The secret is best kept by us leaving here, but we can't do that until we know where we are going, because we can't go back on tour the way things are right now. Agreed so far?" Everyone did. "So that leaves only Reuben needing to know whatever he needs to know, and that's the same information we need to get these bastards off our backs."

"That's about right," said the Colonel. "In order then, we need more information – about Reuben and what these people want – and using that information we need a way to neutralise them, which in turn frees you to return to your music and returns me to my quiet life storing all the knowledge we've nearly thrown away."

"You saving the world, Dad?" asked Harry, curious.

"Yes son, I'm just an old hippy, but with a power complex. I've got the launch codes, y'know. I can rule the world from that cellar, right? All on my own."

"He's kidding about the launch codes", Harry insisted to the rest. "But let's humour the old man; before you can assume your throne, you'll need a way to get Fairfax to tell us what he knows. In practical terms, this must be the first objective – get more information."

Reuben sat forward, his eyes glittering. "If he will not tell us willingly what we need to know, we better think about what we are prepared to do in order to force his hand. And since force is an appropriate word, we should think about who is prepared to make him an offer he can't refuse, if I could put it that way." He glanced down at Jimi, who had turned to face him.

"Are you going to torture him, Reuben?" Jimi asked, his face intent. He turned to his mother. "You're going to make me go to bed so I can't watch, aren't you?"

No-one laughed. In the shocked silence that followed, they digested the unsettling implications of Reuben's remark. Billy stirred, coughed and spoke. "Can I just bring all of you back to reality here," he said quietly, his voice edgy. "We are The Vikings, a band. We do not torture people. We do not kill people. We play music, and make the world slightly nicer when we do...except during the drum solo, obviously."

The moment of tension evaporated as they all burst out laughing, Phil included. Billy turned to Reuben. "I don't know who you are, but I do know that the person I have come to like and respect would not do anything like that. Perhaps that is your old self speaking. I prefer who you are now."

"Perhaps it was my old self in the cellar too," mused Reuben. "I didn't much like what I was saying just before I passed out. It was like I was a ventriloquist's dummy having an identity crisis. Like I was being torn in two, a bit of paper ripped apart. You're right Billy, and thanks." Billy leaned forward, his hand outstretched. Reuben shook it firmly. "Right on," said Jake with grim satisfaction. "We will just have to ask Fairfax politely, and if that doesn't work we'll have to get some drums and make Phil do his long solo. That would break anyone."

"Who is he working for, Tom?" asked Vicky. "Do you know? Is he really MI5?" This was one piece of the puzzle the Colonel had retained. He felt reluctant to lie, mainly through his affection both for her and her engaging son, but a natural caution gave him pause. His dilemma was abruptly resolved when Harry answered. "He's SIS Vicky – that is, MI6. He lied to us about that, but we shouldn't hold it against him. It's his job."

"That wasn't wise Harry," his father stated flatly.

"I don't agree. We are all in this up to our necks - all of us. If whoever is behind this decides the secrets should all be buried, and buried deep, everyone in this room – even Jimi here – will get buried with it. You know how they work as well as I do. This isn't a thriller, where good people don't get hurt, the hero gets the girl and it all works out in the end. That stuff is strictly Hollywood. This isn't a movie."

Alina, irritated that the Colonel had displaced her, now perched on the arm of the sofa by Reuben's side. She looked down at him and winked, then bent her head close to his. "Sure it's like a movie, and you got the girl," she whispered in his ear. "You must be hero, 'cos hero is the one gets the girl."

A buzzer sounded from somewhere in the house, a soft burr with an occasional rasp of impatience. The Colonel walked over to the long sash window that looked out towards the gate.

"I agree," said Jake, his eyes on the Colonel. "We deserve to know what's going on. That's why I'd like to ask that bugger Fairfax what game he's playing."

"Well, here's your chance," said the Colonel as he turned from the window. Beyond him, Jake could see the closed gates illuminated by the headlights of a nondescript estate car. The lights flashed twice.

"This ain't no movie, but he's right on cue, just the same," observed Billy. "Is someone going to let him in then? Jake?"

Jake stood up. "Sure. The show must go on. Tom, where's the key to the gate?"

Fairfax entered the room with the reluctant air of an estate agent surveying a property he had no desire to sell. "The gang's all here I see. Hello Tom, how are you?" He walked over to the Colonel, standing in front of the fire once more, and they shook hands.

"Hello John. We've been waiting for you."

Draping his overcoat over the remaining chair like a shroud, John Fairfax seated himself without invitation, all the while studying Jimi. "Hello, my name is John. Who might you be young man?"

"You have to tell us everything you know," said Jimi. His face was set, eyes hostile. "We are going to torture you if you don't. You won't like it. It will hurt." No-one spoke.

"I believe you," said Fairfax. "I better tell you anything you want to know, since I don't want to be hurt, especially not by you." He lifted his gaze to stare at Reuben, who asked: "But will you though?"

"Desperate times call for desperate measures," Fairfax replied evenly, settling back on his chair. "I only have a partial picture, but I'll do my best. This is what I have so far: beneath the Parkfield hotel, an experiment was being conducted – by whom I do not know with any certainty yet – and you are the subject of that experiment.

"This was a military project. We've had this notion for years about super-soldiers, but always with implants of some sort. Technology like that is susceptible to failure and needs power. But genetic capabilities exhibit no such limitations. The holy grail has always been to make specific enhancements through genetic modification, but no government who could afford to do the work could also sanction experimenting on unborn children, on an embryo, or even the zygote. To judge by early spending patterns, certain orders we have been able to trace concerning laboratory equipment and so on, there is clear evidence that some high-tech biological work was done in that hotel basement, and because some of the orders related to standard equipment used in DNA manipulation, my assumption is that your surprising speed and other enhancements – if I can call them that – are genetic."

"That's really possible, is it?" asked Vicky.

"Certainly," Fairfax replied. "We have many databases of sequences specific to certain characteristics."

"My God!" exclaimed Cas. "What monstrous experiments have you people been doing?" Fairfax laughed. "The monstrous experiment of taking saliva samples from athletes and others with exceptional gifts of one sort or another. Does that appal you, the thought of all those people we forced at gunpoint to spit into a little paper cup?" Cas stared back, unabashed. "We've been collecting this kind of data for 60 years or more, unravelling the mysteries of the chromosome. If it hadn't been for the civil war, the septics would have been churning out no end of little monsters by now."

"Septics?" queried Jake.

"Sorry, septic tanks – Yanks. You know what Churchill said? 'Americans always do the right thing, but only after they've tried everything else'.

"What kind of enhancements?" asked Harry.

"The standard definition, that has been around a while, includes increased movement speed through improvements to muscle chemical exchange processes, enhanced endurance and stamina, higher oxygen uptake and conversion, bigger lungs and heart, better co-ordination, fast blood clotting, improved senses – mainly sight and hearing - and better spatial awareness, reasoning and planning. The last two are intellectual issues, which is why education is also key to this process. What I think you have forgotten Reuben is that you have lived in that basement for all your life. My guess is that you rarely, if ever, came out. You had no friends, no life as any normal child would live, but a strange twilight childhood surrounded by people who just wanted you to do things, learn things. If I'm right, I am most profoundly sorry for you. I truly am." For a man as bland as Fairfax normally appeared, he was now quite flushed with emotion. "In the circumstances, your memory loss seems fortuitous."

Reuben considered this impassively. Jimi had risen to sit beside him, inserting himself between his friend and the Colonel, and was now tucked protectively under one big arm, watching the adults with wide eyes and silent consideration, although his wide eyes kept attempting to close themselves.

"Why was I so fat at first?" Reuben demanded.

"That I do not understand. Why would they let your diet get so out of control, when they were seeking improved physical characteristics?" Fairfax looked as puzzled as everyone else. "But there is something else, Reuben, something more important and rather disturbing. And I think this is where things get a little unpleasant." He glanced at Vicky, who nodded. "Come on you," she said cheerfully as she scooped her son up. "Say goodnight to everyone."

"Goodnight," Jimi echoed dutifully, but he said it to Reuben.

Fairfax started to speak as Vicky left the room, but Jake held up his hand. "Wait until Vicky comes back please," he said firmly, so they sat in strained silence until she regained her place, signalling to Nick with a short hand gesture that all was well. Jake nodded to Fairfax.

" I thought a lot about the location they had chosen, up there on the moor. Thing is, at night it is one place you can reckon it very unlikely to meet anyone else. My guess is that if they let you out at all, it was at night, up there. It's where you were found too, isn't it? Running across the moor – were you really naked?" Fairfax waited for a reply, a disconcertingly childish curiosity crossing his features momentarily. "I was indeed," Reuben replied. "Not a pretty sight, back then."

"Not much one now, you ask me," sniffed Alina, who had contrived to regain her rightful position during Vicky's departure and was now snuggled in Jimi's place under the big protective arm. Reuben patted her head fondly as Fairfax resumed his normal expression. "The other thing that a moor is good for is military exercises." He paused, looking at the Colonel. "If the product of this experiment was someone trained, intensively and exclusively trained in everything a soldier has to know to be excellent at his job, you would need to use methods of metrication to test and evaluate the progress of the experiment. Which, unfortunately, leads me to the tricky part.

"About six months ago, a party of three men were killed in very strange circumstances. On Dartmoor. At night. It was covered up, no investigation was allowed, people involved accidentally – ambulance drivers and the like – were transferred to other parts of the county, *and there was a deliberate effort to keep the security services in the dark.* That is how I became involved."

"How did they die, John?" the Colonel asked quietly. Fairfax answered, but addressed Reuben. "It was precision stuff. Two by hand, one with his own weapon. I've seen the original report, a copy of which was cunningly retained by the local police in case there was some comeback later. Smart, these country boys."

"And you think I did it, but I can't remember it now, is that it?" Reuben had asked the question they were all afraid to voice.

208

The silence was palpable, a texture hanging in the air undisturbed by anyone daring to breathe.

"No," said Fairfax. A collective sigh escaped several lips. "You have, I'm sure, wondered about the QR code on your foot, right? Why mark you like that? You are obvious enough, surely – clear physical characteristics even without the fat. So why the QR code? Got any thoughts?" Reuben shook his head. "I figured it must be for identification, obviously. To be honest, what with the man in the bushes, it seemed silly to think I was the only one like this. As soon as I became aware I was different, I figured that something in my past had made me this way, so what you suggest makes sense. I think I'd nearly figured that out for myself, but hearing you say it brings the idea into focus. And if the people who did this went to so much trouble, why only do it to one person..." he paused, a haunted expression on his face, "to *one child?*"

"I think you are right," said Fairfax. In fact, I'm quite certain. The QR code on your foot is one of two. The other one is situated on the foot of the man who has been following you as long as I have. The man in the bushes. I believe he is your brother. Not only that, but your twin – almost impossible to tell you apart, perhaps. This would make sense – more experimental uncertainties, but a well matched pair of subjects. As identical as you can get, in fact. In which case, one might require a QR code to make sure which experiment was which. Pretty vile, isn't it?"

"Oh man...Reuben...I'm so sorry man..." Billy trailed off, to murmurs of agreement round the room. Jake reached across to pat Reuben's knee. "It isn't you mate – don't worry, I know what I'm talking about. There's no way you killed anyone, isn't that right Fairfax?"

"I agree, for several reasons. First, if you have two subjects you might as well test different programs on each. Waste otherwise – sorry Reuben, I know how that sounds but there isn't any other way to talk about it. Being military, the most sensible option would be to design complementary skills – a two-man team. Isn't that what you'd do, Tom?" The question was pointed, challenging. The Colonel nodded, ignoring the jibe. "Standard pairing for covert infiltration. One forward with combat and demo skills, the other on a perimeter with comms, surveillance, retreat options covered, and as backup. Highly mobile, small enough not to need much transport or draw much attention. But this is just surmise on your part, John. That isn't like you. When Reuben asked you if he was the one responsible for the deaths, you said no. What is your reason?"

"The public wideband again..." he stopped, realising he had said more than he intended. "I was able to track public site requests. They had a very secure system down there, but if you want to go to a site you have to bridge into the public network, and I was able to find the surfing history at the local ISP, which they have to keep by law. There were two clear strands of search, of interest. One was the kind of thing a forward op would be interested in, the other stuff was tactical and strategic – hacking, interception, trace and bugging, exotic equipment and techniques for all the above."

"Could all be from the same person," said Harry, but Reuben responded. "If there are two of me, we'd both use web sites. It isn't an unreasonable conclusion, but it is far from certain." He looked down at Alina, who stared at him with an unreadable but intense expression, as if trying to read his mind, and succeeding. Thus satisfied, she addressed the room. "This man never kill anybody. Believe me, I know this." She patted Reuben's big arm, while with her eyes she defied anyone to contradict her.

Fairfax agreed. "I know this is not good form Tom, but I have to agree with the intuition of our young lady here. My evidence is circumstantial, but frankly I don't care what memory loss he has suffered, his whole demeanour has, from the beginning, been anything but that of a hard man, a trained killer. You tell me Tom – you've known a few, and you too Harry. Is this what the special ops boys are like?" Neither responded, but both looked speculatively at Reuben, whose attention was focused on Fairfax. "You said '*again*'. What did you mean? When you talked about the wideband? What else is it you know?"

Fairfax could not hide his irritation, mostly at his own mistake. "You are sharp, I must say. There is, it seems, a paradox in my theory if you think about it. I assert that if the two of you were trained in different skills, it is your brother who is the killer, the field man, not you. Another reason I believe this by the way is because I think he's quite close by, and I've been looking for him. Tom will tell you that I'm no slouch when it comes to such matters, and if I can't find him he's either very good, or not there at all. I am quite certain he is here, because he has been extremely persistent and very skilled. And yet, if he's the killer I say he is, and he's had you in his sights outside the club you played in – and that's only the time we know about – then why hasn't he killed you?"

"Because Reuben has something he wants," said Harry immediately. "He's had the chance on at least one occasion and there was nothing to stop him. Maybe he is torn between destroying the only person who could identify him, and getting whatever it is he wants."

Vicky was outraged. "God, you men. Did it occur to you that maybe the poor chap might be having a bit of trouble killing his brother...," she had run out of breath, so indignant was her interruption, "...who by the sound of it is the only person he's ever had a relationship with, certainly of any depth. Brought up like that, they were bound to be incredibly close, because all they had was each other. It's his brother, for God's sake. Does everything have to be a plot? And what about Alf? Have you all forgotten that he may have been killed too? Not one of you has brought that up. He died, and nobody has asked Mr. Fairfax about that!"

"Ah...well..." Fairfax coughed apologetically. "Actually...he isn't dead. Strictly speaking, I made that up."

"But I spoke to Guido," Jake insisted, "and he confirmed it."

"Sure Jake, but do consider for a moment what I do for a living. How hard do you think it was to persuade Mr. Jarrott that his life was in danger? That he should accept a generous compensation fee and take to the Welsh hills? For me to arrange to have the story fed to Guido in readiness? Did you know our little informer found another entrance to the complex under the hotel, and spent some time down there after he dropped Guido off at your bus? He found nothing down there, mind you, except the ID badge."

With an unrecognisable fury stamped across his features, Jake jumped to his feet, his hands clenched and shaking with rage. "What is it?" Harry asked, actually frightened.

Jake ignored Harry, taking two short steps toward Fairfax, who stood up.

"You blew up my bus, my lovely fucking bus. You blew it up and were right there to herd us like cattle, to frighten us into coming here. It was your fucking plan all along, wasn't it. Tell me, it was you, wasn't it?"

Without flinching, Fairfax nodded. Jake pulled his right arm far back and delivered a crushing punch straight into the other man's face, then immediately doubled over in pain, clutching his hand in agony. Fairfax fell back onto his chair, covering his face with his hands and groaning, blood dripping between his fingers. And in his new found clarity, Harry admired Fairfax at that moment, because he knew that Fairfax had fallen on his sword. He had rolled very cleverly with the punch, which was delivered so very slowly by fighting standards that it should never have landed on a man like Fairfax. But he had allowed part of the force to find its mark, giving Jake his deserved satisfaction. It was, Harry thought, rather honourable; not a quality he had associated with the man until now. He glanced at his father and in that instant knew that his father had seen, and was thinking, exactly the same thing. A sly grin passed between them.

Reuben hadn't moved, and held Alina where she was, not that she struggled all that much. Billy, Phil and Cas gathered round Jake, while the ever-practical Vicky pried the hands away from Fairfax's face. "Come with me to the kitchen," she ordered in a voice not even an MI6 agent could refuse, and led him tamely out of the room.

"Let me see," said Billy as he grasped Jake's wrist and lifted the damaged hand in order to inspect it. "Can you flex your fingers?" Jake obliged, wincing as he did so. "Nothing broken then," Billy reported as the fingers bent by moderate amounts, but of their own volition.

"That could have ruined my playing," Jake said ruefully. "Worth it though."

"That certainly was a first, Jake," said Cas. "First time I've ever seen you violent."

"Yeah," Phil agreed. "Mind you, considering the racket you make with that sax, I doubt anyone could tell the difference even if you'd broken every bone in your hand." They all laughed dutifully, even the Colonel. A few minutes later, Vicky and a cleaned-up Fairfax appeared in the doorway, carrying trays crowded with mugs of hot tea which were passed round with relish. When everyone was seated, they sipped their drinks in silence while they all considered what had been revealed so far.

For a moment, it appeared to Harry that nobody knew what to ask next, or even if there was a next. Reuben shared no such view; he had unfinished business with Fairfax and his instinct was telling him that the last, telling detail was perhaps the most important. Not important to them all, but to him.

"Mr. Fairfax – John – what is the connection between what my...my brother thinks I may have, the thing he wants that is preventing him from killing me, and the wideband comment. 'It's the wideband again', wasn't that it? What happened *again*? The usage you gave it was that it provided clues, evidence, intelligence. If it had happened again, what did you learn the first time?"

Fairfax glanced over to the Colonel, who shook his head. "John, if he's what you say he is, then he's smarter than anything you've ever come up against. Me too for that matter. I've not known Reuben long but I have learned that underestimating him is virtually impossible to avoid. Just get on with it man, so we can get some sleep. I can't take any more tonight, but Reuben here can't be left hanging, since this is clearly important to him."

Fairfax turned back to Reuben. "It's the data. Just before the fire, a huge stream of data went out over the public line – probably every record they held in the place. Every answer, every vile thing that took place, every name and enough incriminating evidence to bring down a government in all likelihood. I think your brother wants this information...as do I. And I think you are the only person who knows where it went, which is why your brother is keeping his finger off the trigger. Trouble is..."

Reuben cut him off. "Trouble is, if he thinks anyone – you for example – is getting closer to finding the data than he is, he might kill me in order to prevent me from giving it away. I'd be giving him away in the process, as well as what he's done." Fairfax stared hard at him. "That's right Reuben. We're there, aren't we? Time has run out."

"You ran out the clock by coming here," Reuben replied sharply.

Tom Bracey pulled himself upright and did what he did best: take command. "John is right. There is always a moment when the balance shifts, and today's events stack up in a way that has certainly shifted that balance. Up until now, we have – all of us – been passive; without understanding the situation we could not react appropriately to it. That is changing, although there is one more issue to resolve. We either have to neutralise Reuben's brother, or we have to bring him inside. He is the most immediate threat, but also the most promising ally we could acquire. We're all tired I'm sure – I certainly am – so let's all get some sleep and in the morning we'll continue where we left off, with a discussion about how we could achieve either objective. John, you can sleep on the couch here – the fire will keep you warm enough."

Obedient and relieved, they rose as one and trooped out, weary and confused. Harry followed his father up the stair and along the corridor, where the Colonel paused at his bedroom door and peered up and down the corridor before speaking in a low voice. "Fairfax was very candid, don't you think?"

"Was he Dad?" asked Harry. "You know him well. Do you think he told us everything?"

"No. In his job, nobody reveals everything. But he did seem very forthcoming, and that bothers me greatly."

"Why? Do you think he was lying?"

"No son, I don't. I think he was telling the truth, and this is so unlike him it makes me think he must be very desperate. *That's* what bothers me." He turned and opened the door. "Goodnight son."

Harry, given over to a last impulse in a day replete with novel fancies, leaned forward and kissed his father's cheek. Tom patted his son's arm, smiled reassuringly and carefully closed his bedroom door, leaving Harry standing alone in the hall with a smile on his face, a new-found pride and a brand new father who loved him.

Chapter 20: The Butler Did It

Mick Collins surveyed the wreckage as his partner kicked bits of debris from underfoot, then bent to pick up something he had revealed. "I mean, come on Rav – who on earth would vandalise a place like this?" He looked up at the conduits, covers ripped off, the wall panels with their doors wrenched from the hinges, junction boxes levered open with brutal force. The racks were largely untouched, but bundles of wire hung like spaghetti all around them, ripped from the supports but not detached from the equipment they connected. The office was similarly trashed, but all the damage had been done in a way that struck both the officers as methodical, if very rushed. There had been no attempt whatever to conceal the intrusion, which had happened during the night.

Rav straightened up, holding a hacksaw. "First time I've ever heard of something like this, I must say. Look at this..." he brandished the hacksaw. "They came prepared, by the look of it. What could they possibly expect to find in the Okehampton telephone exchange that would be worth all this trouble?"

Jimi woke early. His parents were still huddled in a mound of blankets, and he considered jumping on them but decided that it might be more prudent to leave them alone. He slid from his bed, still dressed because his mother had been in too much of a hurry to make him put on his pyjamas last night, picked up his shoes and tiptoed to the door, which opened quietly enough for him to leave without waking them. He decided to get a drink of water and, after donning the shoes, descended the stairs and made his way to the kitchen. To his surprise, Reuben was already up, sitting at the table. "Hello," he said to the boy, who had stopped in the doorway, suddenly cautious. He studied the man solemnly before reaching a decision.

"You are not Reuben. You are his brother." Jimi waited, poised for flight.

"Yes, I am," said the man at the table. "And you are Jimi. Are you afraid, Jimi?"

The boy considered this, his eyes locked with the stranger, who showed no sign of emotion at all. "They say you are a bad man who kills people. Are you going to kill me?"

"Well, I could certainly murder a cup of tea, but I'm too tired to do much killing today. Maybe tomorrow. In the meantime, how about you put the kettle on?"

"And make sure there's enough water for three," said Jimi's mother from the doorway.

The seated man nodded by way of greeting. "Good morning. I like to get in a few drives myself before breakfast, keep my eye in." He glanced meaningfully at the golf club Vicky was holding by her side. "What's your handicap?"

"That I have no fucking sense of humour whatever," said Vicky, "especially where my son's safety is concerned." But her anger lacked conviction. Her mother's inbuilt alarm system had woken her as Jimi closed the bedroom door behind him. In the circumstances, she didn't want him wandering around outside so she followed him downstairs. The fragment of conversation she had overheard outside the door caused her to grab the nearest object – an old Calloway No.1 graphite driver standing forlornly in an otherwise empty umbrella stand. But even as she entered the room she knew he had heard her coming; he was watching the doorway. His relaxed posture, hands open on the table, and his frank stare were in stark contrast to the fear she was trying to engage out of duty to her child. She couldn't do it. *I don't think I could be more alert than this – my son threatened – but he just doesn't fit the bill somehow. God, I hope I'm right. Anyway, if he's anything like Fairfax described, what would I do with this club? End up wearing it internally, probably.* She lowered the golf club and stepped forward, placing it on the table.

Jimi, both hands holding the blackened kettle in front of him, had frozen on the spot during the exchange, eyes darting from one to the other as if watching a tennis match. Seeing his mother relax, he completed his journey to the sink, but couldn't lift the kettle above the rim in order to fill it. Vicky suppressed her momentary alarm as the familiar stranger stood, took the kettle from the boy and held it under the tap. He returned it to Jimi, who grasped it again with both hands and struggled across the room to the range, barely managing to lift it onto the hob.

The stranger sat back down, an easy confidence about him. He gave Vicky a quizzical look. "Isn't there someone you should be calling?"

Reuben woke with the satisfaction of knowing he had slept well. He opened his eyes to find Alina staring at him, her face only inches from his. Her eyes at this distance were like two lights even in the darkened room, and indeed there was something interrogatory about the steady, unblinking gaze. "Good morning."

Alina smiled and narrowed her eyes, adding to the impression of feline calculation. "Ask me then."

Reuben reached out to touch her, but she pushed his hand away. "Ask you what?" he said, staring at his offending hand.

"Ask me how I feel now," Alina demanded. "After last night. I know you will do this. Do it now, please." Her matter of fact tone told Reuben all was not as it seemed.

"I could be a..." but Alina interrupted him, punching his arm hard.

"See! I know what I talk about. You think maybe I change my mind, like the Steinway better now, go sleep with piano? I don't get killed by piano, do I?"

"It's not as stupid as it sounds, you know."

"Yes it is. Very damn stupid. What you think, you wake up in middle of night and think – 'I know, I kill my girlfriend now'. How many fucking girls you got, big man? How you replace me? With Cas, maybe? Phil – he like that for sure. Bit hairy though."

"Now you're just being silly," Reuben said gently, his concern unabated. "Anything could happen...we just don't know..."

"I know what will happen," Alina announced with a note of triumph. "I will win. See, big man, I know where you keep secret weapon..." she giggled as her hand wandered under the blankets. Reuben started to smile too. "...and I know just how to defuse it!" With that and a dirty laugh, she ducked under the blankets, squirming altogether more than was necessary. "You seem to know how to load it too," said Reuben to the various bulges moving below the blankets. There was a persistent but light knocking on the door. "What do you want," he called out, unable to keep the exasperation from his voice.

"Come quick Reuben, Alina. It's your brother. He's here." Alina sat bolt upright, taking the blankets with her. "We come straight away, Jimi." They heard the boy running off to find others to wake with his important message. Alina jumped up and pulled back the curtains; Reuben groped for his tinted glasses to shield his eyes from the sudden daylight assault. "Hey, wait for me" he called out, but Alina was long gone.

As the first adult to discover their visitor, Vicky was in the unique position to observe each reaction in turn as the others tumbled downstairs. Fairfax, who didn't have as far to travel from his bivouac in the next room, arrived first. He entered the room sideways, an automatic pistol at the ready, but the sight of Vicky and the stranger seated at the table quietly sipping tea gave him pause. He glanced down at the pistol in his hand. "You don't need that," Vicky confirmed, and was relieved to see him tuck the pistol between his belt and his back. Next to arrive were the Colonel and Harry, who Vicky had instructed her son to wake first. While Harry stood well back with an air of professional readiness, Tom Bracey walked over to the seated man to study him at close range, his appraisal frank and thorough. "Good morning Colonel," said the man, rising from his seat. He held out his hand. "My name is Levi, and it would be stating the blindingly obvious to say that I'm Reuben's brother."

The Colonel didn't pause, but accepted Levi's hand and shook it. "Well, you certainly saved us some trouble, I must say. But next time, use the front door will you?" He walked behind Levi, who sat back down, and came to rest leaning against the back door, from where he could see everyone. Harry came and stood beside him.

Billy, Cas and Vicky's husband arrived at the same time, the two musicians standing shyly at one end of the table, gazing at their visitor while Nick flanked his son and wife protectively. Phil stumbled in moments later, stopping only to take in the remarkable similarity between Reuben and his brother. "Wow" was all he managed to say, before joining the others, who were now seated. Levi nodded to each in turn as they entered, his passive demeanour unchanging. Alina was next, and she too was stunned into silence.

"Where's Reuben?" Harry asked her, but before she could answer, Jake walked in. "I'll be damned," he exclaimed at once. "Remarkable!" But Vicky's attention was on the door, because she could hear Reuben approaching. Her sense of apprehension mounted with each footfall. Others picked up on the intensity of her stare and when Reuben appeared in the doorway, the room fell silent.

Levi rose once more. The brothers stared at each other for a suspended moment, then each advanced to the centre of the room in order to better examine the other. Standing together, the spectators could compare them physically: same height, breadth, hair colour and skin tone, although Levi's hair was cut short while Reuben's was unkempt, but other than that you could easily confuse the two at a casual glance. Eye colour was impossible to compare because of Reuben's glasses, but Levi's eyes had a different look about them.

It was, Vicky realised, in the detail like this the men could be told apart. Both were big, well built, but where Reuben looked leaden and tired, Levi looked sleek and well-conditioned. Reuben stood awkwardly – his knee joints were painful and his muscles were sore – but Levi exuded relaxation, and a formidable capacity. What *kind* of capacity, she wondered? Returning her attention to Levi's face, it seemed more lined, more marked. With surprise, she realised that Levi had the history of his life written around his eyes, where Reuben had a child-like smoothness in his facial features, a lack of detail. In Levi's face, Vicky could see sadness and experience; considering what his childhood may have been like, she felt a wave of sympathy for him, which caused her to wonder why she didn't feel such sympathy for his brother. Reuben had endured the same childhood, but he didn't remember it. And the evidence that should have been clearly written in his features had been erased. Something about this fact caught her attention, demanding further consideration, but she put the thought to one side.

The brothers were circling each other warily. Reuben seemed curious and somewhat moved by the meeting, but Levi looked calculating and reserved. "Your eyes hurting you?" he ventured. Reuben stopped moving. "All of me. I'm running down."

"Yes, you are," confirmed Levi.

"How much do you know?" asked Reuben, almost in a whisper. His brother smiled grimly. "How much do you want to find out?"

"You know then? Know what's happened to me. To us?"

"Sure," said Levi, who turned to the Colonel. "It will speed things up a great deal if I tell you now that I overheard everything you discussed last night. We don't need to cover any of that material again."

Tom and Harry exchanged a worried look. "Don't tell me I have to sweep the house again," the Colonel complained. "It takes forever and I never find anything."

Levi chuckled. "No Colonel. I used a rather more low-tech method to eavesdrop on you. I employed the simple expedient of crouching all night in the bushes under the window – the one you looked out of when Fairfax arrived. Crouched with my ear pressed up against a freezing window pane for five hours. My back is killing me this morning."

"Your hearing is like Reuben's?" asked Fairfax. Levi nodded. "So you heard everything?"

Ever the practical man, Tom interrupted them. "It seems to me that since we're in the kitchen we may as well get some breakfast while we're at it?"

"Can I have an egg?" Jimi piped up. Everyone laughed. Jimi didn't think there was anything funny about asking for an egg, but he laughed along to demonstrate his goodwill now that Levi wasn't such a bad man after all.

Breakfast was a hurried affair consumed largely in silence. At Harry's suggestion, they decamped to the lounge and once settled - everyone in the same place they were the night before – all eyes turned expectantly to Levi. "Do you remember any of it?" he asked his brother.

Reuben shook his head. "Not really – I remember things like books I've read, but only when I start reading them again. I have no recollection of anything before that night..."

Levi looked thoughtful, his expression eerily familiar. He turned to Fairfax. "What about you? How much do you really know, I wonder – no, don't bother." Levi raised a peremptory hand. "You won't reveal anything now that you didn't last night, so let's move on. What is your interest in all this? I understand the aims of everyone except you, Mr. Fairfax. Why should I reveal my secrets..." he glanced at Reuben, "...our secrets, to you?" He scanned the room and found no dissent.

"My word, I don't seem to be terribly popular around here. All I did was blow up a bus. Surely you can't hold that against me?" The attempted humour fell flat, but Fairfax wasn't disconcerted in the least. "Very well. My interest – my firm's interest now – is in the people behind this."

"So you're not a loner, not unofficial at all then?" Jake stated with barely concealed disgust.

"Not any more. Strangely enough, that was true at the time I first met you, but the gathering storm has attracted attention upwind, as it were, so now I'm on the job."

The Colonel, standing as usual before the fireplace, bent slightly at the waist as he directed a question at Fairfax. "What is the job, John? Whose side are you on this time?"

"My firm. This is delicate stuff, Tom and it's hard for me. Put it like this: if this isn't imported, then it's necessarily an inside job. Only two firms are capable of that right now, and it isn't us."

Harry caught a brief glance from his father, with whom he had shared the information given to him during his visit to London. Had his father shared the information with Fairfax about the CIA connection and the distinct lack of interest in the matter at the higher reaches of MI5? Harry was nonplussed, wondering if Fairfax was about to reveal to the band his furtive role, since they were hardly likely to forgive him and, he realised, their friendship and trust was valuable to him, which filled him with a certain shame. Thankfully, his father intervened. "They fed that to you, did they, John" he remarked with tactful disingenuousness. "Trying to point you at the brass back at HQ? What's really going on here?"

"It's a cabal, preparing for a military coup, we believe. They were behind the experiments and they are in league with a number of senior military figures. It's not madness or lust for power, either. Quite logical really, giving the ineptitude of the shambles that calls itself our government. Their power is fragmented and relies wholly on the military now to keep order and assert control, and the military are fed up with fighting the population. Brother against brother. Never a good thing, is it?" He leaned towards Levi, an intense expression making his normally bland face angular and aggressive. "They are in trouble now, because they know we oppose their plans – my firm, that is. Call us old fashioned, but to see Britain become a military dictatorship after all we've been though, all we've survived...well, I would say that, wouldn't I. But it's true and there's nothing you can do except believe me or not."

Levi stirred, and looked at his brother. "It's the data, isn't it?" Reuben agreed, turning back to Fairfax, who explained his theory. "They are panicking because if my firm gets the data, they'll hang for it. Or be shot more like. They tried to trick me into thinking it was the chaps upstairs in MI5 behind this, but that was misdirection. It's going on at a lower level – middle bloody management in revolt."

Reuben tapped his brother on the shoulder. "Levi, what is this data. Do you know?"

"I ought to, and so would you if you remembered that we were the ones that stole it, you and I. What's in it? Everything, Reuben. We took the lot; I programmed the routines, you installed them. That was when..." Levi suddenly looked apprehensive, and stopped.

"When what?" said the Colonel gently. "Was this when you escaped, Levi?"

"A few hours before."

"And there was trouble? Like up on the moor that night?" The Colonel's face was entirely devoid of expression. Levi nodded, glancing again at Reuben, who blanched. "It's me, isn't it? Not you at all. Did I...did I kill someone?"

Levi was clearly ashamed. "You couldn't help it. You were trained and you reacted. We had to get out of there or go mad, Reuben. It was terrible, truly terrible in that place. A prison. We were so fat and useless and no matter how little we ate..." he turned to address the others, "...we used to hide our food, pretend we'd eaten it and later throw it down the toilet. They monitored us and how much energy we required, how much food we could consume and so on. But we starved ourselves and still couldn't lose any weight. They were injecting us with something, and what they were up to is in that file." Levi paused for breath, but could not escape Reuben's haunted look, his need to know the truth. "Yes, Reuben. It is you, not me. I'm sorry, so very sorry."

"Hold on," said Billy, his voice cracking from disuse. "That's what you'd say anyway, isn't it? Why should we believe you? We don't know you at all."

"That's true," Levi replied, taking no offence. But last night you came to the conclusion that I was keeping my brother alive because he had something I want. If you connect up the dots, it should be obvious that the data would be the likely candidate – in other words, either Reuben has the data and doesn't know it, or knew where it was hidden but doesn't remember." He turned to the Colonel. "Isn't that how it goes?"

The Colonel glanced at Harry and Fairfax. "That is a logical premise, I believe," he told the man sitting at his feet.

Levi ventured a faint smile. "The only trouble with it is this: I already know where the data is. I just can't get it right now."

"The telephone exchange," said Fairfax, but Levi shook his head. "No, that was a ruse. I smashed the window hoping it might be picked up, and the stuff that went out on the wideband was garbage, just any old crap but designed to look something like an encrypted stream. The reason it went no further than the exchange is because it wasn't addressed to anyone. I just targeted the exchange switch itself and let it dump the garbage."

Harry's mind was racing. *So they lied to me in London. If what Levi says is true, there can't be any CIA connection.* "But Levi, if you didn't get the data out, how can you get it now?" he asked, "the whole place is gone, apparently. Blown up." His father chuckled. "That's got your fingerprints all over it too, John. You do love a good explosion, don't you?"

Fairfax actually grinned, a wolfish expression that revealed something of the man behind the bland exterior. "God yes. The earth moves for me every time." He smiled at Alina, who frowned in return. "Had to, actually – couldn't risk any questions being asked. I had no idea what else was down there – part of it was blocked off – but I did check very thoroughly and the only way to get in, and possibly get past the blockage with enough effort, was via the section I destroyed."

"I don't understand," said Vicky. "Wouldn't you have rather got the police down there, helping you track down these people in London?"

Fairfax shook his head. "No ma'am, I would not. The police are monitored just like we all are, and if the people behind this got wind it was in the public sphere, they'd be gone. Surprised they haven't run already, but I think that's because they are holding tight, and there are too many of them to bolt all at once without drawing attention to their escape."

"Sounds like they still think they can put out the fire," said the Colonel. "They need the data. Levi – if you didn't get the data out that way, how did you do it and where is it now?"

"Oh!" Cas exclaimed. "I've guessed it. "The last place anyone would look, right?" He looked pleased with himself and was rewarded with a curt nod from Levi. "Right...er..."

"Cas."

"Sorry...Cas, that's quite right. It's still there, but cut off as if it were destroyed along with everything else. It was a very skilled job by my partner in crime, the fire upstairs and the explosion below. Delicate." He turned to Fairfax. "The blocked part, that was deliberate. Beyond the blockage is the computer room, and if we got it right, the data is just sitting there waiting for us to collect it."

Fairfax was clearly unconvinced. "If you knew where the data was all this time, why the hell didn't you just retrieve it and do whatever you were going to do next? This doesn't make sense." Several people murmured in agreement. Levi scratched his head. "It's very simple. It is a massive amount of data and I can't get access to a computer system powerful enough to download it, or handle it afterwards. It isn't as if I can just sneak into some data centre and do the lot in 3 minutes. It will take hours to set up, hours to decode, then it's got to be recompiled...how the hell I am going to find anywhere with enough computer power to do that?"

Several people guffawed but stopped hurriedly at the scowl on the Colonel's face. Harry glanced at Fairfax, who seemed to be in two minds about something, but appeared to reach a decision. "Well Levi, it seems you've come to the right place, hasn't he Tom?" The Colonel too seemed indecisive. "Don't worry, your secret is safe with me," Fairfax assured him.

"What secret?" the Colonel asked with ill-concealed apprehension.

"Etheria," said Fairfax.

"Etheria? What's that?" said Levi.

The Colonel was stunned. "How long have you known?"

"Since very early on, Tom. In fact, we've been protecting you for some time. Some of us thought what you were doing was worth protecting. Don't look so surprised. Did you think we'd just forget about the bases, or that we wouldn't notice the odd satellite transmission going abroad, each time to academic institutions or the like. Do you realise that at today's prices you're sitting on a million pounds worth of fuel? But we never thought you a security threat. We did think you might incur the wrath of those who would rather keep the data for their own purposes though. In the land of the blind and all that. But rest assured, my friend. We don't think the opposition knows, because the military aspect is outside of their purview. At least as far as we can tell."

The Colonel appeared reassured, which told Harry a great deal about the relationship between the two men. He trusted his father, and as much as he disliked Fairfax, he had never known his father to misjudge a man in such serious circumstances. The fact he had chosen to reveal Harry's secret, while irritating, suggested his father trusted Fairfax even as Harry could not bring himself to do the same. "It's a network of computers, Levi," said the Colonel. "Powerful computers. Some of them are in my cellar."

Levi was astonished, but not witless. "Can I see them?"

"Later," the Colonel replied. "And don't get your hopes up – I have no idea how most of it works, although I suspect you may get some help from certain willing hands." Nick beamed, pleased to be acknowledged, but more so at the thought of being let loose on all that gear.

"Suppose we can't get the data," Reuben wondered aloud. "Where would that leave us?" Levi turned to Reuben. "This was always the flaw in our plan – how we would access it – but we decided it was better to have the data and work out what to do with it later, than destroy it, and any chance with it of finding out who we really are. But we were taught not to speculate unnecessarily. We have enough variables to deal with already without inventing some more."

Vicky had stood up as Levi was speaking, with the intention of putting the kettle on. "What did you say?" she demanded. "What did you mean, finding out who you really are? Surely you must know, even if Reuben doesn't"

Levi answered, but addressed Reuben. "They lied to us from the start. You don't remember the fake parents – first a couple who looked after us when we were little – they were teachers in fact, but they were quite nice as far as I can remember. Then they went a bit stir crazy when we were six, and suddenly we had some 'new' parents, with explanations that didn't fool either of us even at that age. Nothing they ever told us was true, just what suited their purposes. We can find out who we are, Reuben – at least, who our parents are, where we came from. Don't you want to know? You used to rage about it all the time, the most important thing you said, nothing more important that finding our parents. I used to tease you, say we were born in test tubes, but you beat me up so bad I stopped saying it, even as a joke."

"Do you think that's possible?" asked Phil in a subdued voice. Both brothers stared at him at once, like two watchful animals poised for flight – or fight.

"Given what we can do, what they've done to us, it's hardly unlikely, is it?" said Reuben. He sounded sad. Alina, sitting next to him, kissed his cheek and took a reassuringly firm grasp on his hand, although it wasn't quite clear who was reassuring who. Vicky left the room, Nick and Cas following. Billy announced he needed to excuse himself, at which Jake and Phil glanced at each other knowingly. A few moments later, the not so faint smell of sweet smoke drifted across the hall from the billiards room. "Excuse me just a moment," said Jake, "I need a piss," but unless he intended to relieve himself on the green baize, his footsteps gave lie to the claim. Fairfax shot a glance at the

Colonel, who rolled his eyes. "Bloody musicians," he muttered, although he clearly wasn't much bothered.

Reuben hadn't moved. He didn't look at all well, and he was sweating and shivering simultaneously. Alina draped a blanket over his legs and felt his forehead. "You burn, baby. Poor baby." But he ignored her.

"Tell me about the moor. What happened?" he demanded of his brother.

"They attacked me – a bunch of scavengers looking for something to poach. We were on exercise, hide and seek – they pitted us against each other in turn. One time, you'd hide and I would try to find you, next time the reverse. We looked a sight, Reuben. Two fat bastards slithering around in the mud like giant worms, trying to be inconspicuous. Have you any idea how big bushes need to be for you or I to hide behind in that bloated state? Anyway, it was self-defence, except that you had no control over your actions. I was hiding, and they stumbled on my hide by accident. You heard the shouting and when you found me they were about to kill me, or at least beat the crap out of me. You called out to them, demanding they let me go and one of them shot at you. This triggered everything you'd ever learned about combat: in a matter of moments they were all dead. It was so fast I couldn't do anything to stop you, not that I'm sure I would have anyway. That was the night we decided to escape."

"And the night of the escape. What happened, Levi? I want it all, please – if this is who I am, I have to face it now. Tell me."

"I...I returned the favour, you could say. You were caught in the computer room without authorisation and when they grabbed you to get you off the computer, you killed one and immobilised the other. The hall guard heard the noise and was about to shoot you – they had orders to kill us at any time if we got out of control you know - we found that in the standing orders we took from the safe – anyway...Christ...I..." Levi, distressed and now equally pale, was at a loss.

"You killed him," said the Colonel, completing the sentence for him. "You did what you had to do, son. Both of you have blood on your hands, it seems, but neither of you could possibly be condemned for what you did, not when your actions were so obviously justified by circumstance. Can I ask you something

Levi – it seems rather frivolous but I can't help wondering how old you two are, something that Reuben doesn't know."

Levi smiled affectionately at his brother. "We're seventeen next birthday," he announced.

"Fucking hell!" exclaimed Harry. "I took you for considerably older than that, Reuben. You're just a kid – both of you." The Colonel and Fairfax too were shocked. "This is appalling," said Fairfax, the Colonel clearly in agreement. "These people must be stopped."

Jake, Billy and Cas appeared with refreshments – water from the well, or weak tea, no milk or sugar – and some dubious circular objects that Jimi had ventured on under Tom's supervision a few days back. They were rock hard but, with sufficient chewing, occupied a small but welcome space in their permanently unsatisfied stomachs. Jimi, who had fallen asleep at Reuben's feet, awoke to take one and gnaw on it enthusiastically as the brothers' age was divulged to the returning band members. No-one had cared to recap the earlier revelations, which somehow seemed curiously private.

"I guess it's because you're so big – even after losing all that weight – that we thought you were older," said Vicky to Reuben as she seated herself. Billy, who now had the blissful look on his face that earned him his nickname, started to giggle inappropriately. "Knock it off Billy," said Vicky tersely, but he only grinned at her. "You know what's this is like," he said, trying not to spill his tea. "It's 'the butler did it'. Here we all are in the drawing room and all we need now is for the inspector to come in and reveal who stole the diamond." It wasn't much of a joke but the levity was surprisingly welcome to all except Alina, who had been staring at Levi for several minutes past. "Reuben is sick," she stated, addressing his brother directly. "Why aren't you sick too?" Reuben shot her a surprised glance, and they all turned to Levi, Jake picking up the inference straight away. "That's right. The night of the gig – that was you, right? – Reuben said you were fat as him. Now you're not...just like him. But you aren't ill and he is. What about your...abilities? Are you losing them like he is? Why are you not affected like him?"

"And why did you try to kill him, anyway?" Phil sounded angry. "Your own brother, for fuck's sake. What's that about?"

Levi didn't respond, but turned instead to the Colonel with a pleading expression. It fell on stony ground. "Answer the question please."

Levi shrugged. "As you wish." He looked pointedly at Reuben. "I know what's wrong with him. I know how to make him better. I also know it could be extremely dangerous if I do, but if I don't...I think he may die."

Chapter 21: Black Orchestra

Alina was furious. "You turn up here. You are brother. You can help him but you don't? What they do to you in that place, make you so...not human. Yes, not fucking human. He dies, I swear I kill you." She was straining against Reuben's arm. He could barely restrain her. "Wait Alina," Reuben muttered, eyes on his brother. "Let him speak."

" What's wrong with him is that his batteries are run down," said Levi in a matter of fact way. Cas immediately voiced the question on several lips. "I thought you were both...well...er...genetically engineered. Isn't that right?"

"Sure," said Levi. "They did stuff to us before we were born, modified our DNA, but they also gave us other enhancements as well. They just used us. None of it tested before on humans is my guess. We have implants all over the place. Trouble is, they are interlinked with biological processes – they convert sugar and carbohydrates for example. We also have little pumps in our feet that are powered simply by walking or running that aid blood flow in the lower body when we move quickly, but they don't depend on a power source. But for the rest, there is a catch; they do require power – and when the batteries we both have are not recharged, the implants start drawing power from our bodies. The energy we get from our food is stolen by the implants, and that's what's happening now to Reuben. They give us all kinds of advantages, but they also have something of the Shirt of Nessus about them, if you are familiar with the reference."

Fairfax laughed dryly. "Well, it killed Hercules, so it seems apt."

"In what way?" asked Harry. "I mean, how did it kill him?"

"It was a present from his wife – can't remember her name; he had a few as I recall – but it was poisoned with the blood of a centaur he killed called Nessus. When he put it on, it killed him."

"It was Deianeira," said Levi, "his wife's name."

"Bloody hell, those Greeks were a murderous bunch," said Phil admiringly. "What a way to kill your husband. Better watch out Nick, if Vicky gives you any clothes for Christmas." Nick grinned while Vicky tried to keep a straight face but Fairfax, rather less amused, turned to Phil. "No, that wasn't it. She was tricked. Knowing he was dying, Nessus gave her his blood-stained shirt and told her that if Hercules wore it, it would inflame his passion for her."

"I could do with a shirt like that," said Vicky, avoiding Nick's rueful glance. Her mournful tone made everyone smile. "I don't need one," Alina informed Vicky, which made Reuben blush furiously, delighting everyone much more.

"There's another association, a metaphor that I found in an old dictionary of quotes and fables," added Levi. "*A source of misfortune from which there is no escape, or a fatal present.* That's what they gave us, Reuben and I. A fatal present."

"We *live* in a fatal present," Reuben observed. "Fatal for me at this rate. You say my batteries are run down? I'm sick of being sick. How can they be charged?" Levi glanced at the Colonel, then Harry and Fairfax in turn. "With the charger. Which I have...hidden away."

"Here it comes," said Jake. "Why hide it? What are you afraid of?"

The Colonel knew, and Fairfax wasn't far behind. "He's afraid that fully charged, Reuben will be very dangerous."

Levi was grateful to the Colonel. "It's been my fear from the beginning. It is why I have carried a weapon and been ready to use it. When I thought Reuben was going to get into a fight that night outside the venue, I was ready...I was ready to stop him...*if I had to.*" As he stared at Reuben, an understanding passed between them, Reuben's modest smile an acknowledgement of Levi's unspoken but heartfelt apology.

"Jeez, Reuben. Good job you were an alien that night." The Colonel, Levi and Fairfax seemed puzzled, so Billy told his favourite story one more time. "Interesting strategy," the Colonel commented. "Levi, you have a dilemma but I don't think you can refuse Reuben the help he needs. Have you had time to consider that the recharge might bring back his memory?"

"Yes Sir, I have," said Levi. "Trouble is, even if it did, I'm not certain whether that would be a good thing or not."

Reuben chucked mirthlessly. "I'm hardly dangerous right now, am I? Maybe it's better to leave me this way."

"But you'll die," said Alina plaintively.

"We're talking about two different things here," Harry told Levi firmly. "You cannot let him die, so we must take the risk. If Reuben remembers his past, then he will have to take responsibility for it like everyone else."

"I agree," said the Colonel, to general murmurs of approval round the room. "Where is the charger?"

Levi stood. "It's buried in the woods. I'll go and get it." Harry and Jake both stood with him. "I need some air," said Jake mischievously, "but I think Harry wants to keep an eye on you." He grinned, then led them out of the room. Others took the departure as signalling a break. Vicky took the well-behaved Jimi into the kitchen to find some small reward and make more tea. While Billy and Phil disappeared into the billiards room, Fairfax stretched his legs and the Colonel sat down. Alina checked Reuben's pulse and felt his forehead. She looked worried.

Cas hadn't moved. He was sitting very still, his furrowed brow indicating a pronouncement that was brewing. He caught the Colonel's eye. "We need a new name, Tom – for our little group, this conspiracy of ours. How about The Black Orchestra?" The Colonel looked blank.

Fairfax stopped pacing and turned to Cas. "Schwarze Kapelle? You know about that?" Cas did indeed. The band's resident Nazi expert, he had something of an obsession with Hitler and a war that occurred a century past. "Sure. The plot to kill Hitler, that ended up with thousands being shot, and Rommel committing suicide. It was the shirt that made me think of it."

"What's that?" asked the Colonel, suddenly animated.

"The Shirt of Nessus. One of the conspirators in the Black Orchestra mentioned it. They were losing their nerve about assassinating Hitler and in fear of their own lives. This general, whoever he was – he said that none of them could complain because by joining the conspiracy they had willingly donned the Shirt of Nessus. He thought that willingness important, because he believed that a man's worth could only be measured against his willingness to die for his convictions."

"They didn't kill Hitler though," said Alina. "What happened?"

"They failed," Cas answered. "Several times. Got caught – even poor old von Moltke, who was against it in the first place."

The Colonel was startled. "Von Moltke – you must be mistaken. He was a Prussian general in the previous century. I was thinking about him only yesterday." But Cas was not mistaken. "No Tom. His great-grandson I think – some relation anyway. A pacifist who opposed the Nazis very honourably, bravely, from the beginning. A good bloke as far as I can remember. Died anyway – Gestapo hanged him I think."

"And he was a member of the Black Orchestra? Along with the man who made the reference to the Shirt of Nessus?" asked Fairfax, disturbed that The Colonel looked so agitated. He turned to the Colonel. "Oh God, Tom. Not another one of your coincidences that aren't coincidental. I really hate it when you do that synchronicity stuff."

Tom Bracey straightened, glaring at Fairfax. "It saved your life twice, something you've never been able to argue with. You call it luck, I call it intuition. They were clues, which you ignored and I didn't." He turned apologetically to the others. "Sorry – bit of personal history we're revisiting. It's just strange to me that I should think of someone quite obscure under pressure at a critical moment yesterday, then Levi brings up the shirt today and this connects with the descendant of the man I was thinking about. I must do some reading when we're finished here, see if this is more than *mere* coincidence."

Jimi came running into the room. "Mum told me to tell you that there's some lunch. She says she doesn't care if she gets told off because she's hungry, and so am I." He looked defiantly at the Colonel, then broke into a sunny smile. "She says come now because she's not waiting on her hands and feet, or something...come on..." And with that he was gone, footfalls scampering down the hall, mingled with the crack of snooker balls cannoning like so many thoughts in an empty head.

The charger consisted of eight pads, each the size of a mobile phone, that Levi placed pressed onto specific parts of Reuben's body as he stood, naked except for his underpants in the middle of the equipment hall, shivering less from illness than cold.

"The trouble with these damn things is that the adhesive only sticks to the skin, so you have to be largely naked to get them in place," Levi warned his brother. "They also rip the hairs out when you take them off." A single wire threaded its way from pad to pad, and to a small controller unit with its mains lead plugged in.

Levi, Reuben, Nick, Harry, his father and Fairfax had descended to the cellar to avail themselves of the generator installed there. The others, while keen to observe the process, had been instructed to remain upstairs, the Colonel tersely observing that Reuben was not a circus performer; in any case, he suggested, it was better to restrict the number of people in the room should anything untoward occur. The only objections were from Alina – on principle, and because she felt she had a right to be with Reuben - and from Jimi, who was disappointed that the promise of a guided tour was not being honoured, a point he had the sense not to labour when his mother silenced him with an unusually stern look. Her husband, much to her annoyance, had managed to invite himself by suggesting, not unreasonably, that they might need some technical assistance. Nick was always reasonable, Vicky reminded herself once more: while his very reasonableness was one of the qualities for which she loved him, sometimes it vexed her *unreasonably*.

"This will feel a bit weird," Levi informed Reuben. "The pads work by induction so you'll feel a vibration, a tingling where each pad is placed, but it's nothing to worry about."

"That's a shame," said Reuben, his droll tone failing to support the assertion. "I could do with something to worry about, seeing as how I'm just one big worry free zone right now."

"Right, are we ready?" Levi asked Nick, who had insisted on supervising the technically fraught process of inserting the plug into a socket. Nick nodded, and Levi flicked a recessed switch on the controller box. Reuben jumped as if he'd been electrocuted, which in essence he was. "The initial charge is going to be rather strong, because your batteries are completely flat," Levi observed in a casual aside. "It will ramp down after a few minutes."

Through gritted teeth, Reuben suggested the cure might be worse than the disease but didn't move again. After two minutes he visibly relaxed, after which the observers stood uneasily in silence, the only sound a faint pulsing from the controller. To Harry it appeared that Reuben was getting better by the minute, but there was something about the process that he found disturbing since it reminded him of watching a heroin addict who, as the freshly injected drug passed into the blood stream, slowly and gratefully returns to a normality that was anything but normal. "How do you feel?" he asked cautiously, unable to forget the concerns Levi had expressed.

Reuben was experiencing something of a miracle. The initial charge was shocking in every sense, each pad feeling like it contained a million tiny creatures busily chewing into his skin with molecular bites. Quite quickly, this sensation reduced in intensity to a point where the pads induced only a tingling at each location. The first beneficial effect he noticed was almost immediate: his muscles stopped aching as if a switch had been flicked. Waves of energy began to course through him, each successive surge coming faster than the last until they were no longer separate but formed a continuous low level sensation that was both pleasant and exciting.

Around the fifteen minute mark there was a bleep from the controller and the unit switched itself off. Once it became clear Reuben was not about to turn into a psychotic madman, the Colonel and Fairfax had retired to one corner to converse in lowered voices while Nick, now oblivious to the proceedings, had taken the opportunity to start peering behind racks, opening cases and discretely pressing the odd button here and there, so far with no result. Only Harry and Levi remained beside Reuben, one on either side. Harry was sure he could detect Reuben vibrating slightly in the way he imagined atoms did, since they too contained powerful electrical forces beneath their elemental surfaces.

"How do you feel?" Levi asked. The Colonel and Fairfax stopped talking and joined them.

"Good...ow! I see what you mean." Levi was pulling off the pads. As the last was removed, Reuben flexed his arms, lifted each leg in turn, flexed his wrists, stood on tiptoe for a moment and then removed his sunglasses. "Yes. Oh...that's amazing. Cured instantly, from sick as a dog to fit as a fiddle in ten minutes. Remarkable." With an impish expression he reached out to an

235

alarmed Levi, grabbed his brother under the armpits and lifted him straight up with very little obvious exertion.

"Put me down and stop mucking about," said Levi, his mock asperity combined with palpable relief. Reuben complied and turned to the Colonel, who was watching him closely. "Anything?" Tom enquired, his eyes penetrating. But Reuben shook his head, understanding immediately what he was being asked. "No, it's all physical. No change otherwise." He turned back to his brother.

"My hearing is certainly much more acute – you heard her too, I expect?"

Levi grinned. "Women!. Can't live with 'em..."

"...can't live without them," completed Reuben as he dressed. "You can come in now," he called out in the direction of the door. "I haven't eaten anyone...yet."

Alina appeared reluctantly in the doorway, her eyes on the Colonel, who grimaced. "Fucking insubordinate, the lot of you. And you Nick, for God's sake leave that alone – it's the self-destruct mechanism." Nick jumped back in alarm, but the Colonel and Harry burst out laughing.

"Don't suppose you have a cell down here, or some manacles we could lock these miscreants up in, keep 'em out of trouble?" Fairfax enquired. The Colonel shook his head ruefully. "No, but it's never too late. As it happens, I do know a good blacksmith."

Alina, Billy, Jake and Phil stood between the columns lining the porch, smoking a joint and watching 'the twins' – Billy's quickly adopted term for them - capering on the grass like two overgrown children, while Jimi ran back and forth between them with an abandon more appropriate to his age. The occasional twanging of unamplified guitar strings confirmed that Cas was practicing. Vicky had watched for a few minutes then returned to the house, reassured her son was in no immediate danger. Harry and Nick were now peering together at equipment in the cellar, supervised by a curious Fairfax and the Colonel, who explained the functions of various devices and showed Nick the units needing attention.

The twins ran back and forth at eye-watering speed, stopping to throw small objects that were out of sight before they landed. They took turns at pointing out distant features, demanding accurate identification or descriptions to test of the other's visual acuity in whispered remarks that only the other could hear. Throughout, Reuben sported a broad grin whose fixity threatened to permanently crease his otherwise smooth face. Levi seemed bemused but tolerant, although Jake thought there was still some reservation about him, a tension born out of disagreeable expectations that he believed might still come to pass.

Jake tilted his head to one side, listening to Cas. "Remember back when we were musicians?" he remarked absently. "Nothing more weird than a tab of acid and an out of tune sax. What are we doing here?"

"We're the Black Orchestra now," said Billy. "That's pretty cool, isn't it?"

"You would say that, wouldn't you?" mocked Phil, "given your excessive suntan".

"Well, at least I don't hit things for a living," Billy replied, fondly punching his rhythm section partner in the arm.

"When did we stop being The Vikings?" complained Jake. Alina, who had been watching Reuben intently, turned to face him. "We still are, Jake. Still are. You always say we must be flexible. We can be different things, Jake. We *are* flexible."

Phil agreed. "She's right – and Christ knows that doesn't happen very often. This is the hand we've been dealt. Now we have to play the cards as best we can. Actually, I'm quite enjoying myself. Makes a change from running around like bloody gypsies."

"I miss playing," said Billy. "I need to do some practice." Cas had caught his attention too.

"Fuck that," said Phil emphatically. "Cas just does that to show us up. Never gets any better, mind you. Twang fucking twang all day long."

"That's bollocks," said Jake. "He's improved massively in the time I've known him. So have you, Phil. Tap tap tap tap all the time, on any bloody surface you can find. What – do you think we hadn't noticed?"

Phil grinned. "Well, he doesn't have to be so self-righteous about it, does he?"

"That's Cas for you," Billy observed. "Anyway, there's a perfectly good snooker table begging for us to treat it right. C'mon Phil, time for another thrashing." He turned away, Phil following.

Jake studied Alina, who had returned to watching the twins and Jimi frolicking, apparently without a care in the world. "Don't hurt yourself, Alina." She turned to stare at him. "Too late, Jake. Too damn late. What can I do?"

"You know where this is heading, don't you?"

"You do?"

Jake shook his head. "Only towards trouble. That's my guess, anyway. I'm glad to see Reuben better, but even if they can get the data they talked about, so what? What good does that do us? And I don't want to see you hurt."

"It gives us the advantage," Levi called out from fifty yards away. He walked over to the porch, where Reuben and a reluctant Jimi joined him. "Sorry, I know it's a bit like eavesdropping on you, but I can't help it, and neither can my brother."

"What advantage?" Jake demanded. "It helps you and Reuben here, but what does it do for us?"

"We don't know yet," said Levi. "We don't know the extent of the data, what it will reveal. There will be information that Reuben and I need – that we want to know because it tells us who we are, where we came from. It may also tell us why we were locked up all those years, and what they did to us. But those things are personal. From your point of view – all the band's, and the Colonel and Fairfax too – the files may give us evidence against the people who did this. What we have to figure out then is how to use it."

"You get these people locked up, eh?" asked Alina. "Then we are free again, right?"

"That's certainly possible," Reuben answered as he put his arm around her waist, half expecting her to pull away. Instead, she leaned against him and looked up into his face. "Good. I worry too much on you, not enough on piano. I go play now, OK?" She detached herself carefully from Reuben's embrace and a few moments later the sound of a minor altercation arose when Cas, forced to relocate, refused to acknowledge that unlike his guitar, Alina could hardly take the piano elsewhere.

"Nice girl," said Levi.

"You think I may hurt her?" Reuben asked Jake.

"I don't know. Not directly, old chap. Much too nice for that. But events...who knows?" Reuben looked pensive, but Levi interrupted his thoughts. "There are some things we need to talk about, I think. Let's go for a walk and leave these musos to their music, shall we?"

"What about the data," Jake reminded them. "Shouldn't you be downstairs getting it, assuming you can?"

Levi shook his head. "Not yet, Jake. I have to disguise the origin and the destination, or else we'll have spooks and special forces here within hours. I'm thinking about how to do it, and so is Fairfax because I asked him about this earlier. We have some ideas, mainly to do with making it appear the CIA have retrieved the data, but haven't quite figured it out yet. When we do, that's when we'll retrieve it. Or try to." With that, he put his arm around Reuben's shoulder. "Come with me, brother. I need to fill you in on what you've been doing for the last sixteen years." Jake entered the house, leaving Jimi sitting alone on the porch steps. As the twins walked away they were followed across the unkempt lawns by a strange piano and sax rendition of 'Come Fly With Me,' Alina's piano flying the course set by the music while the sax, like a troubled bird, just flew.

That evening, the war council of the Black Orchestra sat comfortably in the Colonel's study, discussing their options. Harry had disagreed with his father's suggestion that Fairfax should be included along with the twins, to which his father retorted with the well-worn aphorism about having people inside the tent pissing out rather than the other way round. "In any case," Tom told his son, " he has resources at our disposal we may need, and has me at something of a disadvantage since he knows about Etheria. I don't think he'd gain much by betraying it, but I'm not inclined to believe he's been overcome by a philanthropic bent this late in life, for all his claims they've been

239

protecting us. Knowing him, he will use anything at his disposal to get what he wants."

Now Levi was explaining the plan he had devised with Fairfax. "We think that sowing seeds of doubt will slow them down. Right now, they are just trying to cover their tracks in case the data ends up somewhere inconvenient. They will have to assume we have it and will probably move against us. We have only a little time."

Fairfax brushed something from his knee. "I logged in today and it appears that someone broke into the telephone exchange in Okehampton, tore the place to bits. We can assume they believe someone has collected the device they thought was planted there, or they wouldn't have bothered with the exchange. At least we know that story is still holding, but it does mean they will want the twins even more now, since it's logical to assume one of them has it."

"You think they know about the twins – that they're out in the wild? Or just Reuben perhaps? I didn't get that impression..." He stopped suddenly with the words 'when I was in London' still on his lips, realising it would reveal to the twins something he would prefer to keep between himself, his father and Fairfax.

"No way of knowing, although you may be right because if they knew, I think they might have moved sooner to capture Reuben, or simply kill him. But assumptions are dangerous at the best of times, and this is hardly the best, is it?"

"If they believed we died in the explosion – that was our intention – who else might they suspect had picked up the data from the exchange?" asked Levi.

"Me, I'm afraid," said Fairfax. "Most obvious conclusion, given the way they tried to misdirect me through Harry here."

"So your idea is to try and convince them that the CIA has the data instead, is that it?" Harry asked, but Reuben shook his head.

"Not entirely, because even if we succeed, they may assume some physical device still exists, but now they have two problems and the device becomes less important because the data exists elsewhere. We have to slow them down, buy time so we can study the information and figure out how to use it against them. We need to confuse them, make them hesitate."

240

"What if there's nothing in it we can use?" the Colonel suggested. Fairfax had evidently considered this. "Then we manufacture some. We have a little understanding of the project, and it might be possible to bluff them into making a mistake, to make them think we have more than we really do."

"In any case," Levi continued, "we don't know if we can even get connected yet. Too many unknowns I think. What we do know is that the clock is running, time is against us and sooner or later they will find us."

Harry was puzzled. "How? We don't go out – nobody knows we're here. Surely we're safe right now, even though that isn't a reason for complacency."

"The most likely clues may have been left by me, I'm afraid," said Fairfax. The night you drove here, you were left alone by the patrols because I cleared your route. They will have found the truck by now, and maybe connected it with the stolen car. If they also link that to my route clearance – they have access to the police systems – they might put it all together and that would put them fairly close. They may also pick up Harry's DNA from the car, which would lead them straight here, of course."

"If they knew, why haven't they come already?" said Harry, instantly regretting the remark. He held up his hand to forestall any remarks. "I know...I know. They'll be watching first, won't they? Figure out who's here, what we're doing, if we're armed. Cameras in bushes, no static surveillance posts we might stumble across." He glanced at the window as if expecting to see a face peering in.

"If they find Etheria..." the Colonel mused. "They'll destroy it, for sure. All that work."

"They were always going to find it sooner or later, Tom," said Fairfax. "I think we should expect them sooner given the circumstances. I do have some ideas about how we can buy some time, though." He glanced meaningfully at Harry but said no more.

"In which case, I must get to work," said Levi. "I also think it's time Reuben earned his keep." He turned to his brother. "You may not remember your training, but you could keep watch while I try to retrieve the data. You up to that?" Reuben nodded, but looked wary. "What if I...that is..."

241

Levi understood immediately. "Don't make contact. Stay away from anyone you see. The important thing is to alert us, not get in a fight, OK? Come with me now and we'll work out a patrol route. I'll also show you the hides I constructed so you can get out of sight if you're in danger of being spotted."

Everyone stood. "Is there any help we can give you?" the Colonel asked Levi, who was heading for the door. He stopped and turned back. "No Sir, this phase is up to me now. Only John here can assist me, right John?"

Fairfax joined him by the door. "That's right, Tom. Between Levi and I, if the data can be retrieved we'll get it. Whether we succeed in disguising where it's going is another matter, and I would advise you to consider that we will fail, in which case we'll need a way to get out of here rather fast – in fact, we are likely to need a line of retreat either way. Perhaps you could attend to that while we get the data?"

Harry, feeling at a loss after his father had rejected his offer to help in preparing an escape route, stood peering over Levi's shoulder in the equipment hall. Nick was still tinkering with various units, looking happier than Harry had ever seen him, but whatever it was he was doing, it didn't impinge on Levi's ferocious concentration, applied for the ninth hour now without a break. Fairfax, seated across the hall, was studying a system that Nick has brought back to life, tapping keys and sighing frequently at each new page of data that appeared.

It was only by watching Levi that Harry realised just how skilled he was. His hands caressed the keyboard as if coaxing it to do his bidding, fingers moving in a gentle blur. Data passed across the screen so fast that Harry could barely focus on it before new information paraded across the monitor in a cascade of obscurity. "How's it going now?" he whispered. Levi just grunted without any interruption to his rhythm, clearly not wishing to be disturbed, so Harry left him to it and joined Fairfax. "Anything yet?"

Fairfax looked up from the console. "We set up the routing, but Levi hasn't been able to connect yet. We know the connection is live because we can ping it, but he can't get access.

I've never seen anyone work so intently. It would be admirable if I didn't know his concentration was rather artificial." But at that very moment, Levi jumped up from his chair. "We're in," he called out. "I've started the download."

"How long?" asked Fairfax. "Every second we're on increases the risk." Levi looked irritated. "Sorry, I'm stating the bleedin' obvious." It was clear to Harry that Fairfax was nervous and this, combined with his uncharacteristic candour, gave credence to the Colonel's concerns about his old comrade at arms. As if to confirm Harry's own observations, Fairfax remarked that now they could only wait. "It's like the period before a battle. You know engagement is inevitable, and now you just have to wait until the battle is joined. Neither side knows who will make first contact, but contact is certain and the waiting is the most fraught part of the whole process. You must have had the same experience, Harry?"

"Sure," said Harry. "We need something to occupy us while we wait." He turned to Levi. "Can you estimate?"

"Several hours, I would guess. The routing slows everything down but the rate it's coming so far..." he glanced at the screen before him, "...I'd say perhaps six hours, maybe a little more."

"Do you need to stay here?" Harry enquired. Levi shook his head. "Not really. Unless we lose the connection, this is just so much drying paint."

Fairfax stood, turning off his terminal. "In that case, let's get some rest. Hey you...Nick. Get your head out of that rack and come upstairs. You have a wife and kid who might be glad to see you, God knows why." Nick appeared from behind the equipment rack he was working on, his face a curious mixture of disappointment and relief. They left the hall, the humming machinery and blinking lights, securing the doors behind them as they went.

Chapter 22: Cold Fusion

Reuben jogged carefully through the woods, enjoying his restored health but watchful none the less. A full day had passed since his brother had started work on the data retrieval: the transfer had completed early this morning, but the unpacking and decryption would take some time. Levi was rebuilding the structure of the database, ready to import the data. Without it, the information was impossible to read, search, categorise or review systematically.

He pushed himself through the switch point and started to run fast, wind making his hair stream behind him. "To conserve battery power," Levi had explained, "you have to get a feel for the point where the muscle implants cut in, which is triggered by the level of lactic acid. Your eyesight and hearing are the same. The trigger must be different, but the effect is similar; when I strain to see something in the distance, it comes into focus. You'll get used to it."

For the first time, Reuben felt he was recovering something of himself that was lost. Muscle memory, Levi had called it. The thought of the other kind of memory made him shudder, even though he had experienced no subsequent resurgence of buried recollections, and for this he was glad. When he examined himself, he could make no emotional association with the acts he had committed, but the ambivalence made him feel guilty. It was as if some part of him believed he was deliberately suppressing his past, so as to avoid any responsibility for the terrible things he was told he had done. It seemed illogical to assume that he should feel guilt, to have a profound personal reaction to a story about someone else, for that was how it seemed.

He slowed to a halt, looking around him carefully. There was something wrong. He stared hard at the ground before him, at which his eyes refocused on small details not immediately apparent, revealing two sets of footprints barely described by flattened grass, already stunted by the winter frost, here and there a gleam of crushed ice or a toe stubbed against the hard ground. He listened intently, but heard nothing except the occasional call of winter birds, made shrill and loud by his concentration. He walked forward slowly, each foot placed silently on clear ground away from twigs or debris. The motion was easy, fluid, something his body was familiar with. If he didn't think about it, the stalking action seemed automatic, a matter of will alone requiring no conscious effort.

He was going the wrong way. Ahead of him, the footprints ended at the perimeter wall of the grounds, walking straight up to the brickwork where they disappeared. This was where the intruders had climbed out over the wall, Reuben realised, so he turned and retraced his steps, following the faint trail as it led back towards the house.

Levi was surprised his back was so sore. Sure, he'd been sitting at the console for eighteen hours straight, coaxing the data through various programs, but he was disappointed his enhanced musculature could not cope with as mundane a task as sitting down. He had not anticipated how fragile the net had become, although it should have been an obvious assumption to make when most of the routes he was using ran through European hubs. Only the Scandinavian routes seemed stable, but he didn't dare use any one country's system for too long. Consequently, most of the automated routing he was using had to be monitored and managed manually when routes were unavailable or discontinuous.

At five this morning, the data transfer was finally completed and the whole recompiled from the fragments he had sent all over the world. Since then he'd reconstructed the database structure, and now he felt a surge of adrenaline as the access screen came up, the word Parkfield in small, plain green letters centred alone on a black screen. He hit return, and the first screen of menu options filled the blank space. Almost instantly and without contemplation, he selected 'Medical History', overwhelmed with a sense of foreboding. More menus appeared, breaking down into different categories of medical speciality, and there were two additional options beside each medical selection. Subject R and subject L. He was about to click on the first appearance of Subject L but an additional item caught his eye. It was called 'Shared/Comparative data', which he assumed was medical information common to both of them, so he clicked on it. His hand was shaking sufficiently that it took three attempts to hit the link.

Across the hall, Nick emerged from behind a large cabinet, having fixed the last errant machine on his list. All the repairs had been fairly minor, and Nick thought this was just as well. The equipment was fascinating and highly advanced, and although he was a good engineer and still considered himself pretty bright, most of the systems he examined were way beyond his experience or understanding. Picking up the meagre set of tools he had collected from around the house, he turned to check on Levi, and sensed immediately that something was wrong. Levi was clearly distraught, his face contorted in horror. "What is it, Levi?" Nick asked cautiously, but the frozen man apparently didn't hear him and continued to stare at the screen, so he walked gingerly over to the console. Peering over the top of the screen, he was shocked to see the blood drained entirely from Levi's face, his complexion chalk white and deathly. "Levi," he almost whispered. "Are you OK?" the question seeming quite stupid even as he said it.

Levi raised his head, his eyes blank. His lips moved but no words formed. Then he turned to one side and retched violently, his body heaving over and over as his stomach rejected what little it contained in a small pool at his feet.

Tom listened to Fairfax, sitting across from him and his son in the study. "Do you think there's something he hasn't told us?" he asked his puzzled associate. Fairfax raised a weak grin. "Well, I think that about everybody. Even myself on occasion. I just don't know Tom."

Harry had been content to listen, but now his curiosity could not be constrained. "I thought the idea was to make it look as if the CIA were retrieving the data, isn't that right?"

"Sure, Harry," Fairfax agreed. "Thing is, he did it so very cleverly, so much so it seemed rather too convenient somehow. I don't care how bloody modified he is, nobody's code works first time. Yet he hardly paused – writing complex routing code one minute, running it the next. No debugging, no mistakes. I couldn't follow what he was doing without literally sitting beside him the whole time, but on the console I was using I could surreptitiously monitor his progress on some systems. There was some traffic I couldn't understand – inbound stuff early on before he had connected to Parkfield."

The Colonel resumed his pacing, the only release for the mounting tension that made his muscles ache and his stomach contract. *I really am getting too old for this. Never thought I'd admit that to myself, but it must come to all men eventually.* All of them were affected, even Jimi, who was uncharacteristically quiet during breakfast, sticking close to his mother and avoiding Reuben, which hadn't escaped anyone's attention – indeed, Reuben looked a little hurt and somewhat disappointed. A sense of foreboding hung over the house like a damp blanket, both at the imminent revelations that might be contained in the Parkfield data, and the sense that any moment now the doors could implode, tear gas and flash-bangs hurled through shattered windows, as a special ops team assaulted the house. *Expect the unexpected. And count on hackneyed aphorisms when in a tight spot.* In other circumstances Tom would have laughed at himself, but today such frivolous introspection was inappropriate. "We will ask him about that later, perhaps. Now, we've got to review our options because I don't know how much longer we can stay here."

While Harry considered this, Fairfax voiced his agreement. "Two things then – where could we go, and how can we travel without being noticed? There's twelve of us to think of, and we can hardly steal a coach, can we? Don't suppose you have one hidden around the grounds Tom, by any chance?"

"But what does this mean for Etheria, Dad?" Harry wondered aloud. "Will you stay here, take your chances? Do you think you can bluff your way out?" The Colonel shook his head. "No son, I don't. Nor can we fight them – only the three of us have combat training we can count on..." He left the implication about the twins hanging in mid air.

"So this facility will be lost then? And the house – do you think you'll be able to come back here after they find what's in the cellar?" said Harry, clearly frustrated. His father shrugged. "No idea, but all things change. It's a foolish general who looks to fight the same battles over and over."

Fairfax grunted. "Poor old Tom always had this problem..." he told Harry, "...never quite the model officer, you know. Too concerned with what happened after the battle for the general staff to give him that last promotion. Too much humanity, not enough interest in the politics, eh Tom?"

"You know I disagree, John. The battle is a fighting chapter, but the whole book is a war: its cause, and its end, are political. But it is necessary to understand both parts of the conflict, not just the interest that looks down the rifle sight. No lasting peace was ever achieved through such one-sided analysis."

Fairfax uttered a short laugh, a contemptuous bark at the heels of a fool. "No lasting peace has ever been achieved. Full stop. War is part of our genetic makeup – tribe against tribe."

"Except that there are no tribes any more. Just a melting pot of humanity pushed to the edge once more by our own hubris. But there is still a chance we might learn, finally, from the mistakes we have made continually throughout our own history. I know you don't agree, John, but I have to believe it."

"That's because you extend your strategies beyond the battlefield, beyond the end of the battle. I live in a more immediate space, and it's simpler, more direct. The next enemy, the next order of battle. And when it's over – win or lose – I can go home and nurse my wounds, assuming I survive."

"That's because you are addicted to that immediacy." He turned to his son. "You've experienced it, Harry, so you know what we're talking about." Harry knew exactly what his father meant. Only in battle, when your next breath might be your last, were you so alive, so *present*. After such an experience, nothing was quite as real, as immediate. He had recognised the allure for the trap it was, but he knew many for whom life was incomplete once they fulfilled their service or were invalided out. Some re-enlisted, others became mercenaries. The worst affected, subject to terrible depression and a lack of any meaningful purpose, became violent and ended up in jail, killed themselves, an irony that always left Harry feeling bewildered; to survive combat, only to die in such futile and needless circumstances later. He shook himself out of the melancholy engulfing him. "We need transport, even if we don't know where we are going yet. Fairfax and I can deal with that, but we'll need one more driver. Nick is the only one of the band I'd want to take with me – if that's OK with you, John." Using Fairfax's first name came hard to him.

"Good choice," said Fairfax. "We'll go tonight once we..."

The door burst open and Reuben bounded into the room. "They've found us! I found a camera in a tree overlooking the house, and tracks in the woods made by two men," he announced, looking from man to man as he spoke. But before anyone could react to the news, Nick ran in, stopped dead and blurted out his own message.

"Come quick – something's happened...to Levi..." he began, but tailed off; before he'd caught sufficient breath to explain, the seated men had risen as one and left the room, Reuben in the lead, leaving Nick staring at their backs.

The only sign of Levi was a pool of vomit. Fairfax, Nick and Harry made a perfunctory search of the remaining cellars to no avail. When they returned to the equipment hall, Reuben was seated in his brother's place, now looking as wan and disturbed as his brother before him. The Colonel looked grim. "Well, we know what upset him," he muttered as he laid a sympathetic hand on Reuben's shoulder. "Are you OK, son?"

Reuben nodded, then rose. "You'd better see this," he said to no-one in particular, then walked over to the wall and sat heavily on the floor, pulling his knees up to his chest. The others crowded round the monitor to read the green text it displayed:

The initial parameters of the experiment are to examine the effects of genetic manipulation combined with the control (suppression) and enhancement technologies necessary to modulate excess stimulus applied to biological systems which previous experiments had suffered, leading to the termination of the subjects before project completion in all cases. The principle distinguishing feature of the project in respect of previous work is that the experimental design calls for two subjects to be developed as an operational pair consisting of one combat unit and one strategic unit. The subject pairing will be matched biologically for comparative metrication purposes, but development will be parallel only in part, and each unit will also receive exclusive training in their respective specialisations.

While a 'normal' control subject would have been the ideal way to establish a baseline against which to measure improvements in the subject pair, this was considered impractical for reasons of procurement. It was therefore decided at the outset that two identical subjects would provide the most beneficial study in lieu of standard methodology. The use of twins acquired after conception was rejected on security grounds, so the decision was made to bring in a specialist team in the initial phase to clone two subjects from a single cell cluster after DNA substitutions had been made. A staff member with no knowledge of the project or goals has will be used as surrogate, after which she will be transferred. Since we must assume that cloned subjects will display physiological similarity as would occur in twins and that their DNA will be identical, for ID purposes in addition to permanent QR code and passive implant RFID tags (both of which could be removed), a fluorescing gene will be expressed exclusively in the haemoglobin of the combat unit so that exposure to a blood sample under UV light will determine identity irrespective of physical similarity.

Harry, near overwhelmed with rage and disgust, glanced over to where Reuben was sitting, rocking back and forth in a foetal position, arms wrapped tightly around his drawn-up legs. Pity and shame displaced his first reactions but he could think of nothing even remotely appropriate to say. He turned back to the screen:

Against the advice of those involved in the work, the supervisory body requires implants to be incorporated in three stages – birth, five and ten year increments – to facilitate additional tests and procedures. This added layer of complexity has given rise to concerns about skewed test data if results from genetic modification become difficult to distinguish from technologically enhanced performance. However, it is anticipated that as the experiment progresses our analytical methods will improve and the test data corrected for previous misattributed inputs or faulty weighting.

A further complication is the use of the re-engineered antidepressant in order to produce weight gain, specifically the creation of excess fats through injections to suppress adipose gene expression, in combination with saturated solutions of high-value calorific compounds to fuel the conversions to body fat. While the project scientists expressed concern about the effects of extra weight, particularly in respect to muscular-skeletal degradation and skewed performance data during tests of physical prowess, the supervisory body concluded in the security review phase that the power requirements for the implants are best maintained at low potentials in order to preserve a passive state in the subjects; for the purposes of field testing and later training phases, induction chargers can be used to bring implants to full power, but additional security will be required during those phases to suppress inappropriate behaviour in the subjects (see budget annex 31/2.a). However, in the general acquiescent (child) stages and for all normal routine purposes, the implants will convert the fat into usable energy in order to maintain low implant activity just sufficient to ward off the known detrimental side-effects induced when power cells are completely drained, permanent exhibition of which previous experiments have demonstrated will lead to premature termination of the subject.

We have been unable to address two issues in this development cycle. The first is that we cannot devise a cut off mechanism (switch) to entirely subdue the subjects. This is a predictable aspect of the genetic modifications, but concerns about implants were heightened when we considered that without a method of remotely controlling the implants as and when required, additional risk would be posed to project personnel and civilians who may come in contact with the subjects (an event the security assessment has evaluated as 'probable'). It has been agreed with the supervising body that the research into autonomic/remote cybernetic countermeasures will take priority at other establishments in parallel with this project. Since we must assume that other military organisations will undertake similar research, the ability to disable an opposing force by jamming or disabling implants, possibly by firing EM or similar pulsed directional signals, would therefore be invaluable, especially in the form of a hand weapon, and phase three research will, if such technology becomes available, enquire into shielding and other protective measures to protect friendly forces from disruption to their own systems while using the subjects for additional testing. (Please note: staffing levels and budgets do not encompass cybernetic countermeasure research, and both must be reviewed if the technology becomes available to facilitate this). Given the term of the project, we require some kind of controlling technology for the latter half of the project, at which time the subjects will present considerable security problems if psychological difficulties are encountered consistent with previous experiments, although far more emphasis on management of the subjects' mental states will be incorporated in this project from the outset rather than as previous, where in later stages attention was only paid to emergent dysfunction without regard to prevention through better indoctrination, persistent scheduled psychological testing regimes and timely intervention.

The second issue we have not addressed, but by choice and in full consultation with the supervising body, is the shortened life span of the subjects. (Written confirmation of the agreement/instruction is filed under AS2414 and a sealed copy lodged with an independent arbitrator in order to secure the future interests of project personnel). Previous studies have been unable to pinpoint the biological processes that induce premature termination, but unexplained increases in apoptosis (programmed cell death) and highly stimulated metabolic functions are suspected as causative agents. However, due to the further security implications posed by subjects reaching full maturity, it has been decided to postpone research into the cause, since the self-limiting nature of the current project is convenient and simultaneously addresses security concerns should the subjects attempt to leave the project prematurely. Project termination has therefore been set to coincide with the predicted subjects' termination date. We expect this to occur in the time frame consistent with previous experiments, between year 19 and 20. At subject termination, full autopsies will be performed, the remains cremated on site and the facility stripped after the full audit of all work and file closure pending documented project review and submission of conclusions.

For security reasons, we are making use of the subjects' projected obesity, describing the facility publicly as an 'obesity research project', which we believe will address occasional sightings of the subject that the security assessment also views as inevitable if realistic field tests are to be conducted.

NB: Early discussions considered cell line maintenance through a breeding program when the subjects reached puberty, but this was deemed highly controversial and created unmerited security concerns *of such scope it was decided that, as in previous projects, the subjects will be sterilised.*

Chapter 23: Dividing Lines

The band went looking for Levi, spreading out from the house in different directions, Jimi and his mother remaining inside to search the house with her husband close by her side. All were glad to be alone, so as to avoid the contagious disgust and revulsion at what they had learned. Vicky and Alina wept openly, Vicky clutching her frightened son and making his hair wet, while Alina looked as angry as anyone had ever seen her despite the copious tears that ran from homicidal eyes. Nobody spoke. Nobody asked where Reuben was. Nobody wanted to face him right now. They just accepted the Colonel's instructions and went about their searches, glad to be alone, glad to be occupied.

Tom turned to the cellar stairs but his son stopped him. "This doesn't change anything. We still have to get some transport," Harry insisted. His father straightened his back. "Good boy. Clear thinking, and quite right too. You should set out as soon as it gets dark. I've been thinking about how far you'll need to go, but once you have the first vehicle you can travel further afield, since you need to spread out the missing cars or it will draw too much interest too quickly. We need to stay off the radar until we get to..."

"Get where, Dad? What were you going to say?" But his father merely shook his head and began his descent.

Reuben was back at the console, Fairfax standing behind him. They could hear him talking roughly to the other even before they reached the bottom of the stairs, his voice the hard metal of military imperative. "...people will die unless you can put things out of your mind that you cannot use right now. Later, if you survive – and live long enough – you can consider what you have discovered. I can hardly pretend I do not sympathise, but right now I really cannot indulge you. We have to find Levi, and you are the only one with a real advantage, so snap to it you poor fucker. Get the fuck up and do your job!" He was shouting at the last while taking a prudent step back to assume a combat stance.

But Reuben rose slowly, a terrible world-weariness making him appear ancient. "I'm just tired," he told Fairfax, his voice without inflection, a despairing monotone. "I feel as if all the life just ran out of my body. All the feeling. I just feel numb. And tired." He turned and walked to the door. "Harry, come with me," he called out. With a quick glance at his father, Harry reluctantly followed Reuben out of the hall.

"Tom, go and get your computer and that petabyte drive you've never bothered to take out of its box," demanded Fairfax, thrashing wildly at a communications console. "I'm just trying to get in at home – on the firm's system – to alert them and pick up any intel, but we need to grab the data we can fit on your machine. We can't take all this with us, but the key information is the medical and personnel files. Then we need to wipe these machines." He looked steadily at the Colonel, waiting for the implication to sink in.

Tom understood at once, but was irritated enough at the patronising manner in which it had been explained to obfuscate instead of cooperating. "Can't your firm help us? Isn't there something they can do, for Christ's sake?"

Fairfax was taken aback. "Why Tom, I do believe the pressure is getting to you. Long time since I've seen you on edge like this."

The Colonel shrugged, his face bleak. "I'm losing my home. I've gone soft, I guess."

"No Tom," said Fairfax. "Not soft, but comfortable. You can't fight a war from your study and you're in one now. It came to you, but they do have a habit of turning up even when we don't go looking for them. Some men attract it, as if the threads that bind all the forces together converge on certain people, men and women who have no option but to collect all those threads together in an attempt to pull them at the right time, and with the right strength. You are one of those men, where I am not, because of the way you extend yourself past the battle into the culture that gave rise to it. I stay focused on what I can fight. I'm standing in a shadow at the edge of the world. You are the one casting that shadow."

The Colonel felt weary, but knew it was only sleep he was lacking. "Enough philosophy. You're trying to keep the Parkfield data from being retrieved, I assume?"

Fairfax nodded without looking up from the screen he was staring at. "Ah...good. I'm in," he finally declared. "Yes, I don't think we should let them recover the data," he continued, his tone vague and delivery abstract now his concentration was split. "Right now I don't think they have a copy. They couldn't afford the risk of keeping it in London, or at GCHQ. It isn't just about covering their arses, I think it's about the results. They want the results so they can pick up later where they left off."

"Sounds about right. But we don't need to copy anything," Tom conceded at last, "It's all been mirrored at the second site. With that, he left Fairfax to burrow with professional speed and familiarity into layer upon layer of the GCHQ database.

Reuben was moving quickly, but allowed Harry to keep pace. Neither spoke, each concentrating on scanning the surroundings. Reuben had picked up a track almost immediately, noticing that when running at enhanced speed, Levi's tracks were more deeply embedded; no visual effort was required to follow them. They halted when it became evident to both men where Levi had climbed over the wall near the gateway. They stood beneath the patchwork of rough bricks, unsure whether to take the risk of following him.

"Let's go back," said Harry finally. "We have no idea which way he went, and we're exposed enough as it is." He looked round at the trees behind him, but Reuben shook his head. "No cameras here, Harry." Then he fell silent, as if waiting for a cue indicating whether Harry wanted to broach the subject that no conversation between them could now avoid. Harry thought it was the least he could do, since Reuben clearly needed to discuss it, so he spoke up.

"Tell me then," he said, and his face assumed an expression so like his father in his stern military mode that it made Reuben smile. "What the hell...?" Harry muttered.

"Sorry, but you look so much like your father. The hawkish look. Didn't think I could smile, to be honest..." he gazed about him with an air of bewilderment. "I didn't think my life could get any more strange than it was when I first came here. I remember talking to Tom about it, right here actually, as we walked around. He drew it all out of me, the strangeness, the impotence, the uncertainty. *My boat is so small.* I envy you Harry. Not just for having a father, but having such a fine one." Harry allowed himself a small ironic smile, but said nothing.

"But now, after reading that stuff...I just don't know anything. I can't feel anything at all. About any of it – I'm a killer, apparently. I was born in a test tube – my broth..." He drew a breath. "My brother isn't my brother after all, but something I don't even know how to think about. We are made of exactly the same thing, are we? Can that be true? "

"It must be, if you are clones," said Harry.

"But what am I supposed to feel towards a clone rather than a brother? Anything? More, because we're even closer? Or nothing, because we are un-natural and there is no connection except through chemical engineering? It's like we're parts of a machine, we're a weapon system instead of human beings. What am I supposed to think about myself?" Reuben sighed loudly, his body visibly deflating.

"Do you feel that way when you're with Alina?"

Reuben had no answer, but the question gave him pause.

"Think about it this way," Harry continued, "just because you find a long-lost brother doesn't mean you are going to love him. That must come from knowing someone, growing up with them, and you don't remember that, or him. You didn't know you had a brother until two days ago, so losing him can't be a huge wrench. You've barely spent any time with him, so tell me this: were you filled with brotherly love when you met, or just curiosity and a sense of shared hardship?"

Reuben's face became a little brighter. "That makes sense. It's why I asked you to come with me. I think you must have been a fine squad leader...I'd certainly follow you."

Harry laughed, feeling better himself. "You follow me – are you kidding? The other way round, surely, given your abilities?" Then he sobered, remembering the most devastating part of the Parkfield report. Reuben's thoughts had turned in the same direction. "You wouldn't follow me for long, Harry. Not now I have no uncertainty. I know when I'm going to die. And do you know what the most terrible thing is? Some part of me is actually relieved."

"Hey, don't you guys ever answer the doorbell?" said a voice in a distinct American accent. They turned to watch a face appear over the top of the wall, followed quickly by its owner as he pulled himself up, swung his legs over and dropped neatly to the ground in front of them, regaining his feet in a fluid, athletic motion. "Been ringing the damn thing for ages – I was thinking of climbing over when I heard you two talking. You must be Reuben." He offered his outstretched hand, which Reuben shook politely. Harry was less formal. "Who the fuck are you?"

The visitor turned and offered his hand a second time. "Marty Morgenstern," he replied, his face as smooth as his demeanour. "Harry Bracey, I assume?" His hand remained assertively outstretched until Harry shook it reluctantly. "We don't have much time. Let's go to the house. I need to talk to the Colonel and my old friend John."

Harry and Reuben exchanged a glance but the newcomer forestalled them. "If you're looking for Levi, he'll join us soon. You Brits, so damn phlegmatic. What the hell kinda word is that, anyway? Makes me want to spit. C'mon boys, the clock is running." With that and a cheerful grin, he turned away and started jogging towards the house, leaving them little option but to follow the confident, forceful young American.

Brash though he might be, Morgenstern waited politely at the front door for Harry and Reuben to catch up and usher him in. Vicky and Jimi were standing at the top of the stairs, while Nick descended quickly, a look of alarm marring his features. Harry motioned their visitor into the lounge, where he sat at the piano and started to pick out a melody with one finger. "Wait here," said Harry. "It's OK, Nick – just keep an eye on him will you? Reuben, let's find my father." In the hall he stopped Vicky and the trailing Jimi. "Best stay out of there for a minute Vicky. Why don't you get Jimi something to eat?" Vicky accepted his suggestion with only a raised eyebrow and led the boy towards the back of the house. Jimi, instantly more interested in food than the visitor, willingly followed his mother after casting a quick but appreciative look in Harry's direction. He and his mother both studiously ignored Reuben.

In the equipment hall, they found Harry's father and Fairfax staring at various screens. "We're watching paint dry," said Fairfax as he looked up. "Hullo, what's up?"

"We've got a visitor. An American. Says he knows you, John," said Reuben.

"Does he have a name?" asked Fairfax, his face assuming his customary bland expression. Harry nodded. "He says it's Marty Morgenstern. Late twenties, college type but well built. Moves well."

"You know him, John?" asked the Colonel.

"Sure. Cousin – met him a few times in liaison meetings," Fairfax replied cautiously. "What the hell is he doing here? And did you find our missing link?"

"Levi?" said Harry. "No, but Morgenstern seems to know where he is. Said he'd be along shortly, or something to that effect."

"That's right," said an American-accented voice from the doorway, where Nick stood uncertainly, frightened stiff. From behind him, Morgenstern appeared, a pistol pointed at Nick's back. "Move into the room please," he instructed his hostage and as Nick complied, the American remained where he was, his attention focused on Fairfax. "Hello John, nice to see you again. Colonel Bracey? Sorry about this, don't have time for niceties. We think the assault team will be in place in about forty-five minutes, so we've got to hitch up the wagons and get out of Dodge...unless you're looking for a fire-fight, that is?" Morgenstern put away the gun and walked to the top of the steps to address Nick. "Sorry about that, man. Most impolite – never would have shot you in a million years. Just in a hurry, that's all." He briefly looked about him. "What is this – a museum?"

"Very droll, Marty. What on earth are you doing here?" demanded Fairfax.

"Saving your sorry British asses again, it seems. I've got transport, but we've no time for manners right now. Colonel – I am instructed to tell you that the CIA would like to offer you assistance. *Immediate* assistance."

Tom Bracey drew himself up, looking every inch the old soldier. "We'll need a bit more information than that, Mr. Morgenstern. What is your interest in this?"

"The boys of course," he replied, looking pointedly at Reuben, his voice and manner betraying his impatience. "Can't have them falling into the wrong hands, now can we?"

"Ah, right..." said Fairfax, "...handy acquisition for you chaps. We Brits do the work, you steal the results."

Unexpectedly, Morgenstern threw back his head and roared with laughter, which would have been offensive were it not for his patent amusement. "Jeez, you guys still think you're the fucking empire, don't you? Talk about old habits..." He constrained his mirth with some difficulty and turned to the Colonel. "You Brits crack me up. Your infrastructure is a shambles from one end to the other. You don't have a pot to piss in, let alone the capabilities to mount a project of this scale or cost. Your governments rise and fall faster than a tart's drawers and your military is so busy fighting itself it doesn't have time to defend what's left of our nice aircraft carrier." He turned back to Fairfax. "This was never a British project. It was ours, John, but nothing to do with the CIA. We've always been plagued by different factions in the intelligence community – 25 agencies at the last count – and one in particular seems to think it can do whatever the hell it wants. You know DARPA of course?" He didn't wait for a reply, his words coming rapid but sharp. "Research boys, madder than Republican senators and ten times as dangerous. They did a deal with MI5, who would provide the facilities, cover maintenance and so on, in return for which they'd get a share of the results. Backstabbing bastards to a man...and woman, I guess. We got wind of this because we've been keeping tabs on our mad scientists so they don't get us all in trouble, which they have a habit of doing."

He paused, looking speculatively at Reuben. "Sorry Reuben, I know this is hard for you." Then he turned back to Fairfax. "Thing is, your guys decided to steal the results and keep them for themselves. After the little problem on the moor..." he offered Reuben another apologetic look, "...after that, they knew the project couldn't keep running without blowing its cover, their complicity exposed. They approached the boys, suggesting more or less the same thing we did, except they would arrange for the them to be hidden away somewhere in the UK where they couldn't get into any more trouble – a small Scottish island was our best guess. Anyway, when we found out what they intended, we came up with some alternatives – the boys did a shrewd bit of bargaining actually, not that Reuben can remember it– and we organised a jail-break. We were all ready to assist, but all our plans came to nought because events overtook us, what with the fire an' all and Reuben here running off in his bathrobe. Is that your idea of preparation?...ah...sorry, you don't remember, of course."

"How did you find us?" Harry asked.

"Levi called us," said Morgenstern, and for the first time he appeared guarded. "Called in the cavalry. And here we are."

"Levi..." Reuben repeated wonderingly.

"Charge of the bloody Light Brigade," Harry retorted, slightly confusing his history. "Another example of the yanks doing the right thing, but only after they've tried everything else. Seen your thugs in action too many times. Hanging out in the rear, then sneaking off to do their dirty work, coming back at sunrise having enjoyed themselves immensely. Fucking wet teams; all a game to you types, isn't it? All night-vision, sniper rifles and drones."

"We're not all like that, buddy," said Morgenstern, taking no offence. "And better drones than clones. But hey, this is not the time to swap war stories. Y'all coming, or what?"

"So you've come to rescue the twins? What will you do with them – and with us – if we go with you?"

For the first time, Morgenstern showed what he was made of. "That's entirely my business," he retorted. "You can suit yourself, buddy. The bangers will be here shortly, and I don't intend to be here when they arrive. If I were you, I'd pull the plug on this lot – it does have a self-destruct for the data surely – even you Brits aren't that dumb. I'm leaving now. Either follow or fuck yourselves." He started to leave, then thought of something and turned back to address Nick. "Your son – nice kid – do you want him to be in the house when they arrive?" With that, he left.

"Time to go, Tom," said Fairfax quietly.

The Colonel nodded. "Seems like it."

"Do you know how to wipe the systems?"

Tom nodded, walked over to a small cabinet mounted on one wall and opened it to reveal a massive red handle with a safety lock, a plethora of warning signs, and another palm-print reader/scanner combination. He reached in and placed his palm on the glass. The eye scan cast an eerie green light over his face, making him appear to Harry like a corpse, which made him shiver and turn away. "We've got to find the others, quickly. Will you help me?" he asked Reuben, whose thoughts turned to Alina. "Let's go," Reuben replied, and followed Harry from the room, Nick close behind.

Fairfax studied the equipment then turned to the Colonel. "Pull the handle, Tom. Let's get out while we still can."

"Such a waste," Tom Bracey said, almost to himself. He pulled the handle sharply down. There was a high-pitched squeal which quickly died away, but a large green light marked 'SAFE' lit above the panel, blinking several times then glowed steadily.

"Is that it?" Fairfax asked as they moved towards the door.

"Yes," said the Colonel. "No bangs. Just a huge voltage discharged to EM-burst modules in every unit. Fried, the lot of them. Every single chip. You disappointed, John?"

"I suppose I am," said Fairfax grimly. Together they left the equipment hall for the last time, neither man looking back.

The others were quickly rounded up, most having stayed close to the house. They gathered in the hall with instruments and what little possessions they had brought with them or found around the house. Harry and his father had disappeared briefly into the study, only to appear a few minutes later with two rucksacks containing items the Colonel had hurriedly selected. As they reached the stairs, Morgenstern was talking into a mobile phone while Nick explained the stranger's identity and purpose.

"Good, all here then?" he stated, the question rhetorical. "We need to exit through the back. Stick together and stay close." The band followed him obediently, but only after Jake had cast a wary glance at the Colonel, whose only response was to nod his head by way of confirmation. As they trooped out in a silent gaggle, Harry and his father remained, staring about them. Fairfax paused at the kitchen door, waiting. Harry turned away first and squeezed past Fairfax, who called out to the stiff-backed Colonel. "Come on Tom; you know what they say. 'One door closes, another one slams in your face.'"

Tom Bracey took one last look at random things that came into view from where he stood, feeling as if he was about to abandon his memories in an act rather like betrayal. He lingered longest on the piano, part visible through the lounge door. Music was scattered over it, silent testament to the glory they transcribed. *Oh Marion, what has happened? So many hours I listened as you played. You bore me a son, loved me with a conviction I never understood and that frightened me because I could never equal it. You played piano like you lived your life – with grace, patience and a witty intelligence that made me love you the first time I heard you speak.* A series of images flashed through his mind: his wife in a bathing suit at the beach, languidly sipping a drink through a straw; in the bath, soap bubbles on her nose and shrieking with laughter; playing with the infant Harry in front of a most incongruous artillery piece, posing for a photograph he had lost during a patrol in Iran; Marion in uniform, skirt hiked up and blouse buttons disgracefully undone, exciting him with filthy talk and lewd gestures so unlike her, yet acted out with inexplicable fluency; his angry spouse throwing crockery at him with harmless dexterity – for her anger was as passionate as her love-making – her face a mask of fury as paradoxically attractive as he'd ever seen her, so that his admiring stare would stop her mid-throw and her fury would melt into something nicer; and finally, with a shock, Marion Bracey's chalk-white face, so terrible in its cold, timeless beauty as she lay in her casket, the shadow of a shadow. *I will never...I could never...forget you, or this place that you filled with love. Always there for me. Always. I'm not saying goodbye, Marion. I won't say it. I can't. You are my home, where my soul resides, not these bricks and mortar and empty windows. I cared for the garden just like I promised. The flowers must stay here, for I can't look after them any longer. Marion, I'm so sorry to have to break my promise but I think you will understand. In fact, I know it. But I make you a new one: like the music on your piano, I will be your transcription. The glory of you is written in me and I will carry that secret light as the sheet music carries the promise of its un-played melodies. Where I walk, you will walk beside me.*

Always. This I promise you Marion – and this promise, only death will break.

He reached up with his hand, surprised to find his eyes were dry. Summoning an effort of will, he assumed the impassive mask of command and turned to Fairfax. With only a curt nod, he left his house.

Harry was waiting for them, the others huddled in a group close by. Morgenstern was by now so impatient he was jogging on the spot. As the stragglers caught up, he led them at a quick pace through the woods, following a clear path that appeared well used. Harry caught up with him, his eyes scanning for movement almost without thinking about it. "They'll see us," he muttered to the American, who shook his head. "Funny thing about you Brits. All those years complaining we were too in love with our toys, and you were right. Best intelligence you can get is from people, and we learned our lesson. So what do you guys do – fall into exactly the same trap when the money gets short and cameras are cheaper than people. There's no watch on this place, only the cameras. We took care of them, so now the assault team are blind. What they are seeing is just yesterday's footage replayed back to them."

"Yesterday's footage?" said Harry. "How did you capture that if Levi's only just called you?" Morgenstern glanced sideways but kept up his pace. "He called us before he entered the house. We made a few enquiries and put some assets in place. I'm one of those assets."

"So Levi's been working with you all the time?"

"Both of them, but Reuben doesn't remember it," said Morgenstern. Harry detected a false note in the explanation but didn't have time to explore it, for they had come suddenly on a small clearing, just large enough for the small US military personnel carrier to park there, resplendent in all the markings of its service. As the others came into the clearing, Morgenstern ushered them towards the boarding ramp. Reuben ignored the ramp and walked up to the front. Inside, Levi was staring at a map while the driver stared blankly ahead. Reuben tapped on the window, which lowered. "You called them – the CIA?"

Levi stared at him, his eyes calculating. "Yes. Sometimes you have to make decisions, and after I read the files, I knew what I had to do. You read them?" Reuben nodded, impassive. "Then you know what they did to us. How long we have left. Do you want to spend it here, in this miserable fucking country with its shitty weather and terrible food. I don't trust these people..." he glanced at the driver, who showed no interest, "...but America sounds like a good place to die, doesn't it? They want us, and I expect they'll treat us well since our cooperation would be much more useful to them given the short amount of time available to study us. I know we'll be like lab rats, but well-fed. And Morgenstern told me they might be able to prevent...you know...not that I believe him." He tailed off and returned to the map, seemingly indifferent to any form of response, so Reuben turned away, walked to the rear of the vehicle and climbed in. Tom Bracey, Harry, Fairfax and Jake were discussing destinations. Having pulled up the ramp and closed the back door, Morgenstern appeared in the cab, turning to view them through the grill. "Where to?" Fairfax asked him. "You must have figured out somewhere safe we can go."

Morgenstern grinned. "The Colonel knows, don't you Sir?"

"What?" the Colonel exclaimed.

"The safest place, Colonel. The one you helped to create. The place where you sent the copy data from your little library project. The place in the mirror, you could say."

Harry was astounded. For the first time in his entire life, he saw his father at a complete loss, face stunned and immobile with shock, a stuttering wreck.

"You know about...about...?" was all the Colonel could manage by way of response.

"Sure we know. We know everything," said the American with complacent relish. "Just don't know what to do with it half the time." He swept a hand towards the windscreen, at which the driver started the engine and pulled away with a smooth motion.

"Know about what, Dad? It was what you nearly said earlier, wasn't it?" asked Harry, voicing the question which everyone wanted answered. But it was Morgenstern who replied, calling out to them from the cab over the growing noise of the engine as they picked up speed having reached the road.

"Etheria!"

3

A
Promise
Made
To
Abraham

Chapter 24: Walkabout

"This is Etheria?" said Billy, shaking his head in disbelief.

All looked equally uncomfortable, shivering in the cold wind that had driven the rain into their faces as they trudged across the mile-long Avonmouth bridge. As the grubby dawn broke the rain took a brief respite, but the damp chills were hard to shake off no matter how quickly they walked. The only exceptions were the soldiers – Tom and Harry – who either felt no discomfort or chose to ignore it, and the twins, whose resilience was by now both expected and accepted. Morgenstern looked far from happy.

King Offa got around quite a bit for an eighth century ruler, so it's possible he visited Hadrian's Wall and, returning to Mercia with the usual holiday sketches, booze, trinkets and fractious children in tow, came up with the notion that the best way to contain the marauders from the west was to emulate the Romans. Lacking the wherewithal to build a wall, but having plenty of shovels and the forced labour to wield them, he did the next best thing, ordering his minions to dig a trench from north to south and pile the spoils up on their side, from which elevation they could get a good view of the scenery and throw things at the Welshmen in the trench below. Those benighted souls, far from being aggrieved, saw the dyke as consistent with their desire to keep the English out and laughed in a musical way while catching the weapons, household implements, pots, hods, trowels and other useful materials the English aimed at them, finding this far less tiresome than making the stuff themselves (thus developing the skills that, on the rugby field in later times, would serve them so well).

So much for Offa's Dyke. The advent of Offa's Fence provided no such amusement. Like all emasculated governments, this one found a futile gesture more attractive than doing nothing at all. The English in Westminster, at a loss as to how they could contain so many refugees without simply shooting them outright (something considered at the highest level so

269

despicably 'Chinese' that further discussion was rarely engaged, if at all) decided to follow Offa's example. They had little choice, or so they convinced themselves: the Scots had devolved entirely from Disunited Kingdom hegemony, demonstrating several times at their border the kind of violent mass resistance to invasion that so terrified the Romans. Meanwhile the reunited Irish, clearly in no mood post-independence to take any more shit from the English, had finally dispensed with the iniquitous border imposed on them for several hundred years. The only place left with sufficient cultural identity to persecute meaningfully was Wales.

As it was also necessary to provide employment, two purposes could be served. Thousands were given shovels and barrows and the dyke was restored to its full depth and breadth, both as a useful way to keep the workers busy under a watchful eye and sniper-scope, and a handy reminder to everyone else of how insular and foolish the English could be when the worst was already behind them. New spoil was piled on old and when the height was judged sufficient, the fence set upon it.

Twenty-five feet high and topped with razor wire, the fence ran uninterrupted from the Severn estuary all the way up to Prestatyn, thus completing the project that Offa never fully realised. It was observed day and night from wooden towers – concrete being in very short supply – which routinely 'fell down', the wood mysteriously disappearing so that no trace of the construction could be found except for a few holes in the ground or the remnants of the uprights sawed off at ground level. That not a single guard was ever killed, nor a single report of any attack submitted, was rarely discussed and investigated even less, since the guards were usually rather hard to locate after the event. (Many were believed to have taken short-term partnerships in timber yards).

It was hard to say how many people now lived in mid- and north-Wales, the south being out of bounds and protected by Welsh and English regiments, both keen to preserve the industry and vital coal-mining operations that kept the Welsh economy going even as climate change tried to kill it. Estimates varied as to how many refugees had been sent, but the stories that emerged suggested that the survival rate for newcomers was as appalling as the infant mortality rate for those with the misfortune to be born there. Typhoid, measles, cholera and general diarrhoeas, acute respiratory infections, malnutrition and malaria – now a common problem anywhere south of Newcastle – took a terrible toll. The government were widely believed to be glad of it. Indeed, there was always talk of deliberate infection to stimulate the death rate; the rations sent in each week under guard were a staggering drain on depleted Westminster coffers. While the Welsh raised only passive complaint at the influx, and again at the erection of the fence, it was considered most unrealistic to ask them to pay for the rations without provoking yet more civil disorder.

The setting up of the camps was a fiasco from the very start. Resource centres were located at choke points like the end of the M4 motorway bridge across the Avon (use of the M42 motorway bridge further north was restricted to military and privileged commercial vehicles). Each cluster of ten adults and any children with them under the age of twelve – at which age they were now deemed adult enough to be treated as cursorily as everyone else – were grouped arbitrarily, irrespective of familial relationships or the lack of them. Each group was given materials said to be enough to make a shelter for the group (the supply actually calculated on the basis of that which could be carried by ten adults and six children), a ration pack per person allegedly sufficient to keep them alive until the shelter was constructed, and directions that led vaguely northwest. Instead of building shelters on sloping ground with natural drainage, refugees huddled together in what they perceived as the sheltered valley bottoms, so that water accumulated quickly around them and facilitated the deep mud and disease that became a more or less permanent feature. Where shelters should always have road access, they were built in areas where no access was possible except by foot or beast of burden. Registration – the only way to properly assess the support needed – was dropped in a matter of weeks. New arrivals in possession of their meagre belongings, issued the statutory rations, building materials, a hammer and a saw, were robbed as they left the resource centres, the goods exchanged at the back of the same centres for surgical alcohol or anti-depressants retained by canny warehouse staff.

Cooking was supposed to be done on portable gas stoves, but the gas cylinders were replaced at the depot by empty ones and refills were rare indeed, leading to rapidly denuded environs where anything flammable was burned in the increasingly desolate landscape. Taking their cue from the UNHCR, food was distributed under armed guard to women preferentially, since it was thought that more would actually go to the families as a result. In fact, it made it easier for the men to take the food and sell it for more alcohol, or repay gambling debts, another contributor to the high mortality rate. Health centres were so corrupt it was widely held that you stood more chance of dying in one than out, the result being that the ill shared their diseases equitably by remaining with the healthy. Communal latrines were rare; only when camps are created in advance can most services be provided with some logic, but when shelters were already built and occupied no such facilities could then be installed. The refugees were left to their own devices; in their despair, little was done communally except to form gangs whose plunder was shared locally with the favoured, thus asserting the only kind of consistent political or social function found throughout the camps. Schools were as rare as grace. Ignorance blossomed like an evil flower, fast-growing tendrils of hatred and fear expanding in every direction. Curiously, the dead were for the most part treated with reverence and buried with modest ceremony, usually before they smelled so bad no one would touch them.

In the course of the journey it had become clear why the Americans had supplied such a conspicuous vehicle: as each road block or checkpoint caught sight of the insignia they were waved through without delay, since US forces stationed in England were by now largely impervious to any form of authority. Tom Bracey and Morgenstern had resisted all entreaties to reveal their destination, the Colonel's face so angry and severe not even Harry had dared to press him. Morgenstern, protected by the wire mesh separating him from the passengers in the back, had simply ignored the questions. Levi too, sitting with the American up front, had shaken his head several times when addressed, but it wasn't clear if he didn't know, or didn't want to divulge the information. Harry thought it strange that Levi should be in front with Morgenstern, but avoided drawing any conclusions, in part because he didn't have enough information, but also because he was thoroughly sick of spooks and their constant dissimulation.

They had travelled in silence for the most part, each immersed in observing anything outside that might give some clue to their destination. Only when they joined the M5 and headed south was the alarm raised, Jake being the first to realise where they were heading. "Christ...not the camps? Not there, surely?" he sputtered at no-one in particular. Consternation spread quickly, but still the Colonel remained mute.

Harry felt a curious detachment. He'd heard the same rumours, the same horror stories, some hilariously gross yet swallowed whole by the credulous, including members of the band. He glanced at Phil, who caught his look and grinned. One sane man at least, Harry reflected. For all his japery, Phil was no stranger to the streets and, during drunken confrontations, had employed a skilful violence that Harry knew came only with practice. *Twelve adults and a child. Six adults who can be counted on when we have to defend ourselves. Not too bad in the circumstances.* It occurred to him that they were moving in a familiar direction; he felt the same stirrings of fear and excitement mixed, for he was going into battle once more. He glanced at his father, who appeared to have picked up the same feeling, reflected in the steely light of his eyes and an alertness only recently reacquired. Whatever had troubled his father had been put away in order to focus on the present, and Harry felt quite relieved at the soldier's welcome return. He glanced at Fairfax, who had been studying the Colonel for some time. "Are you coming with us?" Harry asked him. Fairfax adopted a rueful expression and shook his head. Harry turned to the front. "What about you, Marty? You coming in?"

Morgenstern looked round, his face creased in the knowing smile he used too often for it to be mistaken for the real thing. "Sure – got to protect our investment, Harry. Wouldn't dream of letting y'all wander around in there. Bad place by all accounts. Hell, no..."

Harry was relieved, having counted on Fairfax. *Still six then. And I don't discount the others – none of them are shy. I've seen all of them stand up for themselves. I'd give anything for some weapons though. We've just got to look out for Jimi; he's our biggest liability and also the choicest target.* He looked speculatively at Morgenstern, wondering if the smart-arsed American had a plan. Spooks like him rarely did anything without one.

The driver had pulled over a mile from the bridge. The lights of the checkpoint raised a bubble of luminosity directly ahead; in all other directions the night was thick and murky. Levi and Morgenstern jumped out and opened the back doors.

"This is as far as we can ride. Now we have to walk a while," said the American sourly as he pulled up his collar against the rain. The air was sharp with winter frost and faint salt from the estuary, the wind harsh and persistent. Tom shook hands with Fairfax, who in turn offered a hand to Jake. "I'm really sorry about the bus. I've arranged something I hope will make it up to you, Jake. When you cross the bridge..." He tailed off, the proffered hand ignored. Jake scowled and turned away.

"He'll get over it," Harry observed quietly, unable to suppress his sympathy for the nonplussed agent, to whom he offered his own hand. Fairfax shook it appreciatively. "What did you arrange?" asked Harry.

"A little gesture, that's all," Fairfax replied, then shrugged and turned away to climb into the cab. The vehicle pulled away and faded into darkness.

The approach to the bridge was an exchange of protective night for a nightmare false day, the ghastly light both strident and imperative, floodlights mounted low and pointed at them so that anyone approaching from darkness was partially blinded. Six lanes were reduced to one in either direction by metre-thick concrete barriers and mounds of earth, adding to the appearance of a war zone that Harry found regrettably reassuring. A war with no warriors: the approach and fortifications were deserted, not a single person to be seen. The pavement, lined with cameras that tracked them as they walked, was double-fenced on either side, funnelling those seeking to cross on foot towards a rusty but substantial gate on the side of a vast grey blockhouse. Beside them ran a series of concrete blocks set in the remaining open lane, through which vehicles had to zigzag repeatedly at low speed before reaching the inspection point and a wicked spiked barrier set into the road which, unless lowered, no tyres would ever survive. Pedestrians were herded to the side and into long wire-mesh cages, eight feet wide and perhaps fifty feet in length, with gates set at either end so that small groups could pass through the first, then be held under observation and questioned at random before release onto the bridge proper.

Levi and Morgenstern led the way, the others close behind. The first gate opened, its keeper unseen in the dirty concrete bunker whose armoured glass observation window was so thick that nothing could be seen of those inside. Cameras recorded every movement, while an ill-concealed gun traversed a slit above the window, keeping pace with them as they filed in. When they were all past the first gate, it slid shut behind them with a crash, its message loud and clear: they were going nowhere until the second gate allowed them to move on. Jimi, who had been holding his mother's hand with steely determination since they climbed out of the transport, looked around him nervously. Since leaving Clare House he had avoided Reuben' company. Now, he let go his mother's hand and approached to tug unseen on his sleeve. Reuben looked down, understood at once and lifted the boy up to straddle his broad shoulders. Jimi looked back at his parents apologetically. "I've got to look after him now," he stated, grasping Reuben round the neck in a grip that would render a lesser man unconscious. Reuben patted Jimi's leg, his quick glance at Nick and Vicky equally apologetic.

"Put your cases on the ground in the squares. Open them then step back. Three at a time." The voice was tinny and its tone brooked no discussion, echoing unpleasantly between the metal speakers set at various points along the fence. Harry looked up and saw three cameras mounted on the fence nearest the bunker, each pointing to a square marked out in yellow paint on the ground below. Cas, Billy and Jake placed their instruments in the square and opened them ruefully, resenting the instruments' exposure to the rain more than the indignity of the inspection. "Cleared. Remove the cases. Next three," demanded the voice. Nobody else had cases, only bags and backpacks. The musicians hurriedly reclaimed their possessions. No-one else moved. After several harrowing minutes, the second gate opened and without requiring further encouragement, they all trooped quickly out.

The pavement stretched out before them, flooded in the same harsh light. A single fence on either side was augmented by a wire-mesh roof: many making this passage in the early years, overcome with fear, had climbed over in order to end their journey, drowning themselves and their terror in the river below. The rain, nearly horizontal, lashed them furiously, carried by blasts of wind that forced them to lean forward against it like determined drunkards. Time stretched out along the endless wet pavement, gleaming water cascading across it so that each footstep raised a splash that soaked their legs and filled their shoes, all except Jimi, whose attention was focused high above them on a stark monochrome gull swooping and hovering in the bleak dawn, its occasional cry the echo of their despair.

At the far end of the bridge they endured a second inspection in an identical enclosure, except that the second gate opened directly into a long shed with tables running in rows the entire length. Several armed guards were positioned along the walls. All looked bored and paid them little attention. Two men wearing indeterminate black uniforms beckoned them towards a table flanked by two more guards . "Sieg Heil," muttered Cas. Phil placed his hand on Cas' shoulder and leaned towards him. "Can it mate," he advised, his voice an urgent whisper. "No time to be clever. If you want to keep hold of that guitar, be dumb, like me."

"Put your bags here then step away," said one of the men, pointing to a table before folding his arms as he waited for compliance. His companion lit a cigarette, taking little interest. Harry had seen all this before in the middle east. He knew that any attempt to confiscate the instruments would lead to trouble and that this was the most likely purpose of any inspection, especially with no-one else around to witness it. After glancing at Jake, who had obviously reached the same conclusion, he walked over to Morgenstern.

"Anything you can do here?" he asked quietly. The American shook his head. "No influence," Morgenstern muttered. "Up to you, buddy." He surveyed the group. "Do they know?"

Harry looked over to his father, who had remained at the back of the group. Tom raised a quizzical eyebrow, as if to say 'it's up to you'. His mind made up, Harry approached the man who had spoken. "Got a minute?" said Harry conspiratorially. "I'm on walkabout." The man looked surprised. "With this lot?" he said, making no effort to conceal his contempt. "What's the day code?"

"August," was Harry's contradictory reply. The man flicked his eyes lazily over Harry's bedraggled appearance and shrugged. "Come with me then." He glared at the sodden group. "Fucking spooks. All the same," he muttered with undisguised malevolence, adding; "You won't keep them long." He glanced meaningfully at the instrument cases, then turned and walked casually away, hands in pockets, towards a small office in the corner of the shed. Harry followed.

"What the fuck?" whispered Cas to Jake, who was experiencing something of an epiphany. So many times in the past he had seen Harry charm or disarm in situations like this, but never within earshot. In a flash, he understood why, and how. "Our Harry's secret life," he told the guitarist. "Guess there was a reason he was with us after all."

"Reason? What reason? Where's Harry going?" said Billy, who had joined them. But Jake made no reply, his face set hard, eyes boring into the back of the receding tour manager. Reuben, Vicky and Nick remained with the Colonel, Jimi now back on his feet beside them. Alina, her hair flat against her head, stood alone for a moment, then walked over to Reuben and looked up shyly.

"You OK?" It was the first time she had spoken to him since reading the medical records. Still shocked to the core, she couldn't decide if she felt betrayed by the certainty she would lose the man she loved, or vile and selfish for thinking of her own loss when she should have been more concerned for the lover she would certainly outlive. Reuben said nothing, but smiled gently and reached a hand out half-way between them. She closed the gap with her own, placing her hand in his, then stepped forward to lean against his chest, her eyes shut tight in a futile attempt to block out the understanding in his eyes that shamed her. Reuben placed his hand at the back of her head and stroked her wet hair, smoothing it down. "I'm so sorry," he said, his voice distant. Without knowing what sorrow he expressed, Alina silently wept for them both. "Go ahead and cry...it's OK." he said with the merest echo of amusement. He pressed her face tight against his chest. "I can't get any wetter."

Several nervous minutes passed before Harry and the customs agent – for this was the way the uniformed men styled themselves – emerged from the office. Harry looked relieved until he neared Jake, when his expression became sombre.

"Can we go?" said Jake, his voice colder than the rain. The customs agent signalled to the guards and pointed to the exit. "Good luck," he said, the words entirely at odds with his indifferent expression as he watched them file out into the gloomy morning light.

"This is Etheria?" said Billy, shaking his head in disbelief as they headed along the side of the motorway. Trucks had appeared at first light and were now emerging from the vast car-park beyond, queued ready for inspection,. Morgenstern picked up his pace, his expression eager as he studied the rows of parked vehicles, yet it was Jimi, back on Reuben's shoulders, who saw it first. "Look, look..." He was pointing into the car park. They all turned to follow his outstretched arm.

"Well fuck me," said Cas wonderingly, staring at their truck. "How on earth did that get here?"

Chapter 25: The First Church of Strange Attractors

Due to the enthusiasm with which the previous driver had thrust the keys into the exhaust pipe, it took half an hour to retrieve them. While Nick and Billy took turns trying to fish them out, the others stood huddled on the sheltered side of the truck, but still the wind howled under the chassis and around their legs. Harry stood a little way apart from the band, all of whom were eyeing him speculatively. Jake walked up to him, followed by Phil. "I've seen you pull that trick one time too often. Code words? Who are you Harry? What are you? And what are you doing here?"

Harry looked Jake in the eye. "I was recruited by MI5 after I lost my nerve during the invasion of Iran." His voice was flat, calmed by the imminent release from his distasteful burden, irrespective of what should come of its passing.

"So what?" Jake shouted. "That doesn't answer why you're spying on us. Isn't that what you've been doing all this time? You're just like that shit Fairfax. Like blowing things up do you, you fuck...?" Jake paused as another thought dawned on him. "Christ, are you two in this together?"

Harry shook his head. "No, certainly not. Look Jake, this is all really stupid, my 'undercover' role..." His tone became sarcastic. "...I was sent to spy on these dangerous subversives who, under the cover of being a band, were arming dissidents and supplying half the UK with drugs. That's what they thought, honestly."

"They really thought that?" said Jake, somewhat mollified by the perverse compliment, but not for long. "That doesn't excuse your behaviour, mate. How can we trust you now?"

Harry snorted dismissively. "Hold on a minute, Jake. When I joined up it was made clear to me that the past was only what we wanted to reveal about ourselves, and that questions were considered bad form. I accepted that. Now you're coming the high and mighty, but what about you? What about Alina and what happened back in Poland that made her so hard? Phil here – I don't know a single thing about what he did before he joined the band, and I've never asked. So what's the big deal, Jake. I never once betrayed you or the band. Not once."

Jake studied Harry intently. He considered himself a good judge of people, especially under pressure – performance always sorting hats from cattle – and he knew that unless Harry was a most accomplished liar, his sincerity could not be meaningfully questioned. Jake's outlook was non-judgemental; he rarely sought to focus on the bad in people because it seemed cynical always to look for the worst, a habit he'd seen in many a musician over the years. He knew Harry well enough to know he lacked the furtive skills of someone like Fairfax. He also acknowledged, at least privately, the debt of friendship that had built up over the years Harry had been part of the band. But he was not ready to forgive and forget – he needed time to consider how he now felt. He turned to Phil, who was looking rather pale. "You OK?" he asked? Phil shook his head, dismissing the question. "I'm OK, it's nothing. I'm just really thirsty. And hungry."

"We should eat," said the Colonel, overhearing the remark. "Vicky, you're the quartermaster. What can we have?" Vicky gave a grim smile of acknowledgement and opened the voluminous backpack she had placed on the ground in front of her. Holding part of the contents of the Clare House pantry, the remainder were carried in two more packs by Cas and her husband. She reached in and retrieved a hard-boiled egg, which she handed to her son. "Make it last, like I've taught you," she reminded him. Jimi nodded, his face serious, eyes already devouring the egg. Some flat bread spread with chicken fat was solemnly shared out amongst the rest, washed down with a small amount of water.

Cas watched the distribution with interest. "Have you noticed how, as food gets scarcer, eating it becomes more like a religious ceremony?" he observed, placing a hand over his small portion to keep it dry as more rain fell. Jake stared at the water bottle and gave a harsh laugh, lifting his head to the dour skies overhead. "I don't think we need to ration the water, Vicky. Not with it falling from the sky by the bucket."

Before Vicky had time to ask how they were supposed to collect the water and get it in the bottle without the aforementioned bucket, Phil pointed to the end of the car park.

"There's a stand-pipe, I can see it from here. We can drink all we want." He started towards the pipe, but Harry called after him. "No Phil, you can't drink it." He turned to the others. "From now on, all water we drink must be boiled first. The biggest threat to our health isn't hunger, it's dysentery."

The Colonel and Morgenstern agreed. "That's right," said Tom. "Different rules here. That applies to everything. Your best bet now is to assume nothing at all is safe and that you're way out of your depth. Harry knows what he's talking about. He's been here before – not literally – but he knows the rules of this jungle, so best listen to him. Harry...?" He motioned with his head to encompass Morgenstern and the three walked up to the front of the truck.

"Harry, you're going to have to lead. Forget the past. This is your new squad, so do what you can for them. As for you..." he turned to Morgenstern, "where do you stand in all this? Are you on our side, or your own? You're the only one with a weapon, or did you leave that behind?" The last remark was rather pointed, since Morgenstern had demanded they leave behind all the weapons stored in the cellar, insisting that being caught with one would be more trouble than it was worth.

Morgenstern eschewed his trademark grin, exchanging it for a cynical one. "I'm just an observer, keeping our investment safe."

"Really? Then why didn't you just take them to the nearest base and fly them out?" Tom demanded. Morgenstern was untroubled. "Because we must get the data. We can't help them without it and don't have enough time to find out through research what's killing them. We have to get access to the mirror site. You wouldn't deny them access to the information that could save their life, would you Colonel?" He looked over at the twins standing together, seemingly oblivious of the downpour, and grinned. Levi nodded in return.

"They hear everything," said Morgenstern, a warning in his voice. "And no, I haven't got a gun. Left it in the transport." He held his arms away from his body, smiling broadly. "You can search me if you want." To his evident surprise, Harry stepped forward and patted him down, finding nothing. The smile evaporated. "Wow, you guys are suspicious," he observed and walked off to join Levi and Reuben. Harry and his father continued to stare after him, until Nick at last called out from the rear that he had recovered the keys. Everyone crowded round the back, which puzzled both the Colonel and Morgenstern until it dawned on them that the band's immediate interest lay in discovering if their gear was intact. A wiser Harry smiled inwardly, retrieving an oft-recorded memory of Jake's voice: 'The show must go on!'

No bloody way of stopping it, thought Harry. *It's the show that never ends. Christ, I'm tired.*

The contents of the truck remained undisturbed. Several hands were turned to install webbing that would ensure the cases didn't crush those who were to travel in the back. Jake examined the arrangement, pulling on the various straps and hooks until he was satisfied. "Nick, you take Vicky and Jimi in the back. You too Alina. Safer there."

"No," said Harry. The girls and Jimi in the front. If there was a problem, it would be the people in the cab who would bear the brunt of it. That might leave the girls vulnerable if we couldn't hold our own. Reuben, Levi, Morgenstern and I will go in the back."

Tom nodded. "That way, we have experience in reserve. You can attack down both sides of the truck simultaneously if you need to. You should wait until the doors are opened; anybody stopping us will concentrate on the cab because that's where the people appear to be. A smaller contingent will come to the back to see what's inside. If it isn't us opening the doors, you know what to do." He turned to Nick. "Can the doors be opened from the inside?" Nick confirmed they could if they were left unlocked, so they took their respective places in the truck and set off.

Their palpable relief at being mobile and in possession of the instruments they had left behind lasted only a short while. Leaving the car park, they had no option but to follow the motorway to the outskirts of Newport, where huge signs directed them towards the refugee reception centre and its vast warehouses.

"Pull up close as you can to the door," Harry told Jake before they set off. "Keep the engine running. I'll go in with the boys in back. Best for them to see how many of us there are." Jake apparently didn't grasp his meaning. "Safety in numbers, Jake," he explained. "These people are used to dealing with weak, hungry, frightened people. The less we appear like victims, the less likely we are to be treated like them. Ignore the reception centre and get as close as you can to the distribution bays when you park."

Harry's words proved prophetic. In front of the distribution centre stood a feeble line of haunted souls shuffling forward inches at a time. Others emerged walking quick as they could in the opposite direction, blinking and suspicious, clutching their ration packs to their chests as if the little parcels were lost children, now found. Lounging near the line were half a dozen men, better clothed and fed, whose watchful eyes followed the truck as it approached. Several men picked up heavy sticks and stood, but when the back door opened and Harry's contingent emerged they slumped back, dropping the sticks as quickly as their interest. Jake, ignoring the letter of Harry's instruction, jumped down from the cab, Cas taking the wheel.

The distribution centre was another shed like the customs hall they had passed through earlier, but considerably bigger. It smelled of damp, urine and mould. Lined with row upon row of racks stretching out into the distance, mostly full, a counter ran from wall to wall, behind which several men sat playing cards. Only one attended the long line that ran outside. Harry, normally the most polite of people, pushed brusquely past the queue, ignored the single attendant and lead the group towards the counter nearest the card game. An armed guard sitting high above them leaned forward to watch.

"Hey – get off your arse, one of you. Don't waste my fucking time," he called out. The nearest man cast a shrewd eye over him. With an apologetic look at his companions, he rose with feigned lethargy and a pained expression, to the general amusement of the others.

"What?" he demanded, hands on hips behind the counter.

Harry leaned forward and spoke so quietly the attendant couldn't hear him, so he rested his elbows on the counter-top and leaned forward. "Say that again?"

"I said do you want to do business or fuck around?" said Harry, voice still low but the tone flinty. "I need twelve packs, full measure. I'll also sign for twelve building kits, but you don't need to actually give them to me, just send them straight down to the back door, all nice and trouble-free, and none of your mates needs to be cut in."

"I'll need twelve thumb-prints" said the attendant. "There's only five of you."

Harry stood abruptly. "I told you not to waste my time. I'll get the stuff elsewhere." He started to turn away but the attendant reached out and grabbed his arm. "Calm down, son," he said through a watery smile. "Calm down. We can do business, sure we can." He fetched some papers from a rack. "Fill these in, then I'll get your stuff."

"Nope," said Harry. "Other way round." He ignored the papers thrust in front of him. The attendant sighed, but walked over to a rack and started pulling ration packs down. "Open them," Harry instructed the others. "Keep four back and use them to replenish shortfalls." As the packs were placed before them, they opened each and checked the contents. All were missing some items, but three packs were sufficient to make up the shortfall. The attendant watched with a look of dismay.

"These are short – replace them," ordered Harry, indicating the remaining three. The attendant complied, keen to return to his card game nearly as much as he wanted to be rid of the aggressive strangers, who were rapidly becoming more trouble than the deal was worth. But Harry said nothing more, checking the replacements quickly and satisfying himself that there was nothing substantial missing. He distributed the forms to the others. "Fill them in, and mix up thumb and fingerprints." The forms were duly faked and handed back. Ignoring the attendant, Harry took up the replacement packs and walked towards the exit. The others collected the replenished ones and followed him out. As they reached the door, Jake caught up with Harry and, as they exited, looked nervously towards the thugs leaning against the building. Harry shook his head. "They won't do anything here. If it was going to happen at all, it would be down the road a bit, out of sight of the guards. They're probably in on it too but there are too many eyes here, too many different loyalties. People like this only like trouble when they're dishing it out. The mark of a thug is his cowardice. They know we're more trouble than they need. They like it easy: it's these poor bastards they prey on." He pointed to the queue, then turned away abruptly. "The weak shall disinherit the earth. Let's get in and get out, shall we?"

Jake stared out of the window at the wretched creatures that lined the roadside. Huddled in small groups, women and children attempted to smile at the passengers in the passing vehicle. Only a few had the energy to beckon. Many were in rags; all were emaciated, sunken eyes unable to hide the toll levied by the constant companionship of terror and despair. With wet hair flattened over slumped shoulders, some women and a few of the children – boys and girls equally – had rubbed ghastly colour over their cheeks using whatever substitute for makeup they could find. The effect was deathly, like the attempts of an inept mortician preparing a corpse for an open casket. A few women opened coats disinterestedly to reveal naked flesh beneath, as if what they were showing no longer belonged to them. When he could bear no more, Jake turned away to find Cas and Vicky staring past him through the window with expressions alternating between pity, sadness and disgust. "Is this what we've become?" Vicky asked, her voice breaking. "Is this our future?"

On either side of the road driving north from Newport, the ground was denuded as if a huge razor had excised every green living thing from the surface. Tom told them how the army had sprayed thousands of good acres, poisoning the land in order to deny the area to the refugees, to force them further north and away from the populated industrial areas. The strategy had evidently failed; scattered shelters lay dotted like wind-strewn litter between stretches of sour ground, mile after mile of them, the placement as chaotic as the lives of those attempting to survive in them. Villages and hamlets had been subsumed by the tidal wave, locals forced out, relocated elsewhere, burning out their farmhouses and cottages as they left to deny any use to those they blamed for their loss. Bricks and unburned timber had been removed and put to other purposes, so that the area resembled the aftermath of a fierce battle that left nothing untouched.

Before reaching Raglan they turned west towards Abergavenny. Now the shelters were more dense, clustered in tight groups with makeshift wires above the shelters running in every direction, lending an air of permanence. The stench of human effluent was overpowering. Jake was surprised to see several satellite dishes perched on tin roofs between dirty solar panels. Away from the road, stunted swatches of greenery contested here and there with the barren earth. A few buildings on either side of the road were in better repair, some still sporting unbroken windows. Listless people clustered round the houses; some were sitting or squatting in the mud, others standing or leaning against the wall; all were bored and sullen. Few expressions changed at the sight of the truck; fewer cared when it passed without stopping. Resigned to their fate, they expected nothing and were rarely disappointed.

As the density of the shelters increased the road gradually became thronged with slowly-moving people who moved out of the way with resentful lethargy. Some pushed hand-carts while occasional bicycles weaved between the shells of burnt-out cars, many of which were occupied. Children peered at them from the roadside, their dirty faces morose but vaguely watchful, showing only the barest interest in the passing truck before their stares became glazed, turned inward and away from an unbearable present and a stolen future.

There was a roadblock coming up, and for the first time Jake could see some evidence of organisation, albeit unwelcome. The barricade was manned by a group of men, each wearing an armband, all carrying clubs. One – the leader evidently – had a rifle, which he pointed at them as he stood in the middle of the road in front of the barrier. The others remained behind it, alert and prepared for violence. Jake glanced at Cas, who was at the wheel. "What do you think?"

Cas shook his head. "I can't just drive through them, or the barrier. We have to stop, don't we? What do you reckon,

Colonel?" From behind him, Tom eyed the barrier speculatively. "Lower the window only a fraction. Keep the doors locked." He turned to a small hatch in the rear. "Road block coming up. Militia, one rifle," he called out. "Twelve men, leader in front. No reserves."

Cas came to a halt before the militia leader, who stood directly in front of the truck in the middle of the road. As he began to walk round to the driver's window, Cas made him jump by suddenly letting the truck lurch forward another foot. The Colonel chuckled and patted his shoulder. "Nice touch."

The militia man, cautious now, approached the truck from the side, well clear of the bumper, rifle held at the ready. He tapped unnecessarily on the window, which Cas opened half an inch.

"Turn off the engine. Get out – inspection," the man demanded, trying the door handle with no success. Several others were now moving round both sides of the barrier. "Can't help you," said Cas evenly. "If there's a toll we'll pay it, but that's all." He stared hard at the men below him, and revved the engine to cover the sound of the back door being opened.

"Stop the engine," said the militia man, banging hard on the door with his rifle butt. When Cas ignored him, he reversed the rifle behind a vicious smile and pointed it straight at the window. Then, as sudden as a jump cut in a movie, he was lying on the ground, sucking in air as he clutched at his chest in pain. Levi stood above him, holding the rifle. He ejected the magazine, saw it was empty and threw both to the ground. The men behind the barricade were immobile, uncertain, watching the man on the ground as he scrabbled for the gun, wiped the mud off it, grimacing as he clambered to his feet. His breathing was ragged and rasping, his expression ugly. He backed away, calling out to the nearest men. "Get them!"

As the militia men moved to obey, Harry and Morgenstern appeared at the other side of the truck. Both were swinging microphone stands with heavy cast iron bases. The men rounding the barrier stopped, turning to their leader, who surveyed the situation nervously. "Jake, Cas – get out now to back them up," said the Colonel. "One either side, stay by the door. Let Harry handle it." Cas opened his door and Jake followed suit. As they dropped to the ground, Phil, Tom and Billy moved forward in the cab into clear view. Nick stayed pressed against the back of the cab with Vicky, Jimi held firmly in his mother's arms. Alina was leaning forward, fists clenched, staring at the militia with a predatory anticipation that Vicky found shocking in someone she thought she knew so well.

Levi and Reuben, whispering to each other, advanced fast on the militia leader, who shrank away until his back was against the barrier. Harry and Morgenstern moved to the right, while the twins moved to the left. Jake and Cas stood by the truck. The militia leader, standing alone in the middle, was cut off unless he chose to vault over the barrier. All the others had stepped back.

"Move away," ordered Harry in a loud voice. He whirled his microphone stand, smashing the heavy end into the metal sheeting of the barrier to make a crashing sound so loud everyone froze where they stood. All except Reuben, who walked calmly up to the barrier, laid his hands on it, and lifted it, unaided, to the side of the road. The militia watched in silent amazement: the barrier, comprised of sturdy wood and steel plates lashed together, required three of them to move it.

"Mount up," said Harry in a quiet voice. They backed away from the crowd without turning, Jake and Cas taking their places in the cab. When Cas heard the back door slam shut he pulled away, accelerating hard towards the channel of mud and filth that ran down the driver's side, splashing the contents over the militia men in range and forcing them back. Those on the other side beat ineffectually on the side of the passing truck with their clubs, creating deep booming sounds that drowned out their screams of rage and frustration, the abuse they hurled at the receding prize denied them.

"I enjoyed that. Can I have a mike stand next time?" asked Phil.

Jake turned in his seat and rolled his eyes. "Fuck that. You're the worst singer I've ever heard."

Everyone laughed, far too loudly.

Like all the towns of a decent size, the roads into Abergavenny were carefully controlled by the citizen militia.

Once a thriving town of fifteen thousand, only two thousand now remained, but those that did were determined to weather the storm and they had organised themselves well. As Cas drew up to the roadblock set across the main road, a cheerful young man with a shotgun slung across his shoulder approached the truck, water streaming off his face. Several other men manned observation posts and Jake admired the cheek of the metal rods meant to look like gun-barrels that swept the checkpoint. The young guard stood politely in front of the truck, peering up at them through the windscreen with a puzzled expression. When he walked round to the driver's window, Cas kept the truck in neutral.

"Hello there," said the guard cheerfully. "I...well...I don't suppose you're a band or anything, are you? You look like one, that's all..." He tailed off, faintly embarrassed.

Cas grinned down at the first friendly face he'd seen since their last gig, now a distant lifetime behind them. "As a matter of fact, that's exactly what we are. We are..."

"THE VIKINGS" came the shout from behind him, followed by a roar of genuine, heart-felt laughter, with which the young man could only join in. "Bloody hell boyo," he beamed. "Haven't seen any live music for five years. You'll be finding a welcome in these hillsides, that's for certain. Oh boy..." He glanced over to the nearest observation post and his expression assumed a dutiful sobriety. "Sorry, but how many of you are there? I have to ask, you know. My job, isn't it? And where you're going, why you're here..." He laughed in a musical way. "To hell with it. Tell you what, drive into town and go to the church. Talk to The Vicar. He'll be pleased to see you I'm sure..." He tailed off, something on his mind.

"What is it?" Jake called out. "Something we should know? We only want to stay out of trouble, and if we can play a gig we'd be delighted. It's what we do, y'know..."

The young guard shook his head, his expression suddenly sombre. "It's not a bad town, don't get me wrong, but there *are* a few bad people in it. That's all I'm saying." He looked penetratingly at Cas, then at Jake. "You know what's what by the look of you. Don't mind me. You'll be fine." He stepped back and waved with a cheery grin. "Move on now, and I'll see you at the gig. You can play a song for my girl." Cas pulled away as the road block was lifted aside. "Her name is..."

But her name was lost on the wind, drowned in the persistent rain. Cas hoped the young man and his girl would make it to a gig – assuming one could be arranged – grateful for his smile and his civility, the first exception they had encountered to the harsh rule of fear and distrust that infected every living thing in this primal wilderness.

The Abergavenny council, men and women of resolve, were widely credited for the invention of the 'Skirrid Defence', named after the mountain that stood impassively over the town. As the less resolute abandoned their homes, they were prevented from burning them down as the rural dwellers had done. Instead, as places became available in the centre, those on the periphery were moved closer to the town. Early refugees – for the town was one of the first affected – were encouraged to share the vacant dwellings in the suburbs. They were clothed and fed. Those willing to work were given tasks to occupy them, those that were not were left to their own devices and encouraged to move on. As more waves of desperate people approached the town, the newcomers on the outskirts took the brunt of the ragged assaults, much as the council anticipated. The towns-folk saw far less of the deprivations and violence since it rarely penetrated as far as the well-defended centre, while the newcomers, keen to hang on to their new homes and make some kind of new life for themselves and their children, fought well and with determination to protect what little they were given, winning hard-earned respect in the process.

Consequently, the charming town centre still looked at first glance much as it did before the floods and the uprooting of millions of people to the east. Most shops no longer traded, but they were all occupied. Some attempts had been made to keep the streets clean, and from the lack of smell it appeared the sewage system was still in operation. But the streets were full of apathetic people, standing around in the rain with no purpose and little direction.

"They don't look dangerous," said Jake, "they look..."

"Bored?" Cas suggested. "To me, they look bored out of their minds. Why don't they stay inside in weather like this? Why are they all standing around?"

"Harry told me it was so they could see each other," said Jake. "Kind of shared burden, rather than sit in some room on your own. When you can see others in the same plight, apparently it makes people feel better."

"A community of despair?"

"Maybe," Jake said cautiously, "but what a great audience."

Cas hauled the truck round a tight corner and into a street than ended in front of a big stone church. "Woah! What's that?" said Jake. The others leaned forwards.

"Hey, right up your street," Phil called out to Cas, who was staring open mouthed through the windscreen. The church was stolid, a gothic-revival facade with square towers either side little higher than the building they flanked. The entrance was wide, divided by two single-point arched doorways lodged between plain pillars. From the side, the effect was rather less imposing, as if a shoe-box had been tacked on to a frontage on which rather too much money had been spent. The church proper appeared impoverished; a simple, sturdy box, high plain windows set in high flat walls, over which presided a shallow tiled roof covered in solar panels, the whole kept in place by functional brick buttresses every twenty feet down the length of the building. As the architect had originally intended, the most notable aspect of his design would have been the thirty foot diameter rose-window, its panes arranged in a simple flower pattern, coloured glass set in petals bordered by local grey granite and sandstone insets. Now the focal point had moved; the towers were draped with two long vertical banners, each hanging down the front of a tower nearly to the ground. The banners were vermillion, shocking and stark against the dour stone and morbid sky, like giant streaks of blood pouring from the leaded windows set across the top of the towers. Half way down each banner was painted an obscure character, black against the red. The symbolism was impossible to mistake. "Fuck me," Cas muttered at last. "Gestapo headquarters ain't in it. Let's hope this isn't the church the kid was talking about."

But it was. As they drew nearer, they could see three men on either side of the entrance, standing straight as the pillars beside them. Each wore a hooded vermillion robe that reached to the ground, tied at the waste with a black cloth band. In their right hands they held tall staves, keeping them perfectly upright by their sides, left hands folded across their chests in deference to their duty. Immobile, they appeared oblivious to the rain or the cold, their robes billowing without constraint in the strong wind that capered irreverently around them like a playful imp.

"Brilliant," said Cas sardonically. "How well done is that?" Several of the band chuckled in appreciation: they knew good theatre when they saw it.

The church faced the apex of a right-angle bend in a main road which flanked the building on either side, as if it stood on an island. At the intersection with the main road opposite the church entrance stood a tall plinth, the bronze statue it once supported long melted down. A robed figure stood beside the plinth; throwing his hood back as they approached he held up his hand to them, palm out. Cas had to slow to negotiate the junction, allowing the man to approach Jake's window. The six figures outside the church were unmoving.

Jake lowered his window and leaned out. "Good afternoon. We're looking for The Vicar." The robed man looked up at him, his face solemn. "Good fortune to you. You have found what you seek..." he motioned to the church with his staff. "You may park to the left. Are any of you ill, or need help?"

Jake smiled experimentally. The man below remained impassive. "We're fine, just passing through, you know. We...we're a band..." He tailed off, uncertain if he'd been wise. The robed man nodded thoughtfully but his expression did not change. "So we understand. You are welcome here. Do the Lord's work." With that, he pulled up his hood and resumed his post beside the plinth.

"Oh yes," said Billy in a droll voice. "I sure feel welcome. Really I do."

"Good communications though," Tom remarked. "Knew who we were – expecting us, by the look of it." He really wanted to travel in the back with Harry, Morgenstern and the twins, but he had been consigned the task of looking after these damn children, and resented being little more than a nursemaid, all the while knowing it was the right assignment.

There was nobody watching the car park at the side of the church, which loomed over them as they clambered out. Harry, Tom and Morgenstern clustered together, Jake and Cas joining them. As Vicky doled out a little food, it was agreed that only Tom and Jake would go in, the others remaining with the truck, but Cas insisted he come along and would not easily be dissuaded, his demands born out of a lurid fascination for the church and its inhabitants that worried everyone else. In the end, Tom agreed and Jake went along, too cold and tired to argue.

"Harry, if we're not out in fifteen minutes, you bring in the twins – Morgenstern too if he's up for it," said the Colonel. "If not, bring Phil."

The drummer grinned. "Now can I have a mike stand?" The others shook their heads in exasperation and concentrated on their meagre rations.

As they entered the vestibule, a tall man in a crimson robe approached them, his hand held out to Jake, who was nearest. "Welcome, welcome," he said as they shook hands. "I'm known around here as 'The Vicar', but my name is Edgar." He led them up the aisle between desks and computer stations, their screens blank. All religious artefacts had been removed, all colour and texture. Only a factory functionality remained, so it seemed appropriate that when they climbed the steps to the nave, instead of an altar they found a large executive desk standing alone, from which the occupant could look out over the scarlet flock. Edgar rounded the desk and sat down, placed his elbows on the top and steepled his hands in a gesture of exaggerated piety. He smiled warmly as an acolyte appeared with mugs of tea on a tray. Cas reached out and took the nearest, sniffing the steam rising from it. "Earl Grey!" He looked up, surprised but caught a warning glance from Jake and placed the mug back on the desktop.

Edgar smiled reassuringly. "All clean water, nothing to fear." He took a deep swig of tea, then thanked the acolyte by way of dismissal, who turned away without a word. Tom reached out and took a sip, grateful for the heat and the flavour, unafraid because he knew that bad water favoured no man, no matter what robes he wore. The others followed suit and there followed a moment of grateful silence as they all drank deeply, allowing the heat to have its welcome, comforting effect.

Edgar broke the silence. "I hear you are a travelling band. Is that so?"

"It is," Jake confirmed. "We're called The Vikings. The lad we met at the checkpoint suggested we talk to you, that maybe we could play for you folk, cheer you up a bit."

"Well, that's a fine thought, I'm sure," said Edgar carefully. "But the young man you spoke to was perhaps not aware of the difficulties. To be honest, I don't believe such an arrangement could be made."

Jake was taken aback. It hadn't occurred to him that there might be any objections. Now he felt out-manoeuvred and strangely vulnerable. "We wouldn't want paying or anything," he added, ashamed at how desperate he sounded.

Edgar wasn't swayed. "It isn't about payment," he told them. He sighed and leaned back in his chair with the air of a man about to give a tiresome, over-familiar sermon. "This church is the hope of the town. We call it the First Church of Strange Attractors." He studied them for reaction. Cas raised his eyebrow, so Edgar addressed him. "We are the church of chaos, from which order must rise. We believe in science, not myth. Facts, not spin and corruption. We brethren call ourselves Deniers, a name that used to signify contempt but that we gladly adopt, because we are the ones with the courage to deny that man was guilty of such a terrible sin that nature, in God's blessed hands, would turn on us the way it has. We deny our guilt, and yours." Mistaking the fixity of attention for interest, Edgar gained enthusiasm. "Think about it – I insist – give yourself time to think clearly and not be taken in by the lies. Think about how unlikely it is that tiny amounts of a gas you can't even see could do this? That man, so arrogant and cock-sure, believes we have the power to alter the world so drastically, when science says that is impossible?

"I tell you this: some of us know the truth, have always known. From the very beginning, when the scare stories first started and the money-men started rubbing their hands with glee, there were brave scientists who spoke out. Like any dictatorship, they were quickly silenced, many of them executed at night where they worked, bullet in the back of the head." He bored an index finger into the palm of his open hand to illustrate the effect. "So much for free speech. Others had their funding cut off, and of course no newspapers or TV would give them space. The truth was ruthlessly suppressed by the solar and windmill companies, and the government controlled media working hand in glove with them."

Edgar paused, his voice ragged. He signalled to someone unseen, and a moment later the acolyte returned with a single glass of water which he placed carefully on the desk before retreating again. Jake was watching Cas apprehensively; the guitarist had been squirming in his seat for several minutes and Jake knew what was coming. He glanced at Tom, who raised one wry eyebrow but otherwise didn't seem much perturbed.

"If man didn't cause climate change, then what did?" said Cas in a neutral voice, his face blank. Edgar studied him. "I suspect you're one of the lost," he said, gently placing the empty glass on the desk. "I understand – we all do." He swept one hand in a regal arc. "Like most people, you have been wholly taken in by the propaganda without ever checking to see if it is true. You're not a scientist, so you have to trust what they tell you. But the scientists were in the pay of the government; they did what they were told, else their funding was withdrawn and they were put on trial for heresy. Those who wouldn't go along...well, I've already told you what happened to them – same fate as President Trump, shot dead by his own secret service detail for telling the truth." He was stabbing the palm of his hand again.

"But the world got hot, just like they said," Cas ventured. "The seas rose, parts of the world turned to desert and the glaciers melted. Food ran out. Millions died. And the reason was that we put so much CO_2 in the air it heated up the planet and released all the frozen methane, which made everything much hotter. Surely you don't dispute that?"

"You're not talking to a child," retorted Edgar, now with an edge to his voice. "Of course the world has heated up. And you are correct, in that scientists knew it would get hotter, since they were responsible for the warming."

295

"I'm not a child either," replied Cas evenly, a small smile starting to form as he warmed to his task, all the while refusing to heed the warning looks Jake kept sending in his direction. "How could scientists be responsible for warming the whole planet up? That's just ridiculous."

"Really?" challenged Edgar. "Yet you believe that a tiny amount of gas – less than a fraction of a percent of the atmosphere – could heat up the world so much the sea actually rises? How quaint. Too bad you never asked yourself how that could possibly make sense. Please, just think about it. Such a notion is hardly scientific, is it? Not when you think about it logically? And remember this; once you've swallowed their nonsense, you're trapped. Look how hard it is for you to admit you're wrong, now I've told you the truth. But you shouldn't be ashamed, any of you. We are at the beginning of the new age of enlightenment. Now the truth shall be known and science freed from the hands of those who would use it to control us. Don't feel bad - all of us used to think like you. There's no shame in admitting you've been duped. We all were, but now we can move forward together and use science for our own benefit, not that of the money men, the Jews and Freemasons and their secret police." He sat back, flushed and expectant.

"But it's also logical that if you put more of a gas in the atmosphere that traps heat, the planet would get hotter, isn't it?" Jake asked, trying to head Cas off before he did any real damage and blew whatever small chance they had left of organising a gig.

"Only if you accept that CO_2 does trap heat. There may be other explanations," Edgar retorted with an arch look.

"That's fucking ridiculous," said Cas, all restraint abandoned. "Of course it traps heat. It's in every bloody science textbook since the nineteenth century. Are you saying they're all wrong?"

Edgar stared at him with obvious pity. "And who do you think paid for those textbooks to be printed?" he said, clearly exercised by his audience's failure to recognise the self-evident validity of his argument. "*The same government, that's who!*" he revealed, slapping his hand on the desk with smug finality. "See how very devious they are? No wonder you've all been fooled. They controlled the information, just like they've always done, slowly and secretly building up to the world government they had planned for so long. To keep us as their slaves, in poverty while they grew richer and richer. Not any longer, I tell you. No longer!"

"Then why did the Earth heat up, and why did it happen so fucking fast?" demanded Cas, his voice rising, anger no longer hidden. "Where did all this heat come from?"

Edgar gave him a look of studious contempt. "Out of the mouth of babes. The speed was not natural. In that, you are – accidentally – correct. As to where the heat came from, let me ask you this: have you ever been down a mine?" Edgar paused to shake his head. "Of course you haven't; don't suppose you've done a day's work in your entire life. A *musician*, eh…yeah, right.

"My father worked in a mine, and I went underground with him a few times. I never liked it, because it was so hot. The deeper you go, the hotter it gets. Why, you should be asking yourself, does the temperature go up as we go down? The answer is simple; the Earth's core is a vast store of molten rock – and it's heating up. That's where the heat is coming from, right under our noses you might say.

"But the real question is, as you say, why is it happening so fast – and why now, come to that. The answer lies back with the scientists, because climate change only really started after certain experiments were performed, experiments that involved setting off huge nuclear weapons deep underground. I'm talking about the atomic bomb tests after the second world war. That's how scientists knew climate change was coming, because they knew their bombs had triggered some kind of chain-reaction heating effect deep in the Earth's mantle. And they had no idea at all how to stop it.

"Once the heat started coming out of the oceans and the atmosphere began to warm up, that's when the first theories of climate change appeared. *At exactly the same time.* Coincidence? Hardly. But that's how it all started – a massive cover-up supported by endless dodgy computer models that only ever gave the right answer after the event, never before it.

"I can see you don't believe me…" he looked from face to face, "…and of course I'm used to the truth being dismissed. It is so easy to be smug and dismissive towards people like me, but I tell you this; these scientists recognised no restraint. They were completely immoral, bought and paid for by the CIA of course. No-one could control them. You would not believe some of the perverse experiments they performed, worse than the Nazis...many of them on human beings..."

This remark, somewhat to Edgar's surprise, appeared to strike home. Cas was stunned into silence, while Tom and Jake exchanged wary looks. Edgar relaxed in his chair, pleased to see he was finally getting through.

Jake tried to change the subject once more. "Anyway, getting back to the gig issue," he started out, keeping his voice level and polite. "You didn't say why we couldn't play. Is that really up to you?" The last was a risky challenge, but Jake didn't know how much control Edgar really had over the town's affairs and wasn't prepared to take anything he claimed at face value. Edgar's expression hardened. "We *are* the town. Of course it's my decision. These people are under my protection and I will not see them harmed by outside influences, especially..." he glanced at Cas, "...especially by seditious anti-science propaganda whose only purpose is to make us all feel guilt and shame. Your application is denied." He stood up quickly to make clear the finality of his edict, Cas and Jake standing with him.

Tom remained seated and in a leisurely fashion finished the tea he had nursed throughout the meeting. He looked up at Edgar. "I saw a number of people who appeared to be putting up some kind of decorations," Tom said mildly. He leaned forward, put his cup on the desk and rose. "Would it not be nice to add some music to whatever it is you are celebrating?"

"Whatever it is we are celebrating?" echoed Edgar incredulously. "Well, whatever it is, we don't need any music. Take my word for it." His voice was mocking. Looking at each in turn, he relented somewhat. "You really don't know?" All three shook their heads.

"Tomorrow is Christmas day."

Chapter 26: The Band With No Name

With Jake dragging Cas by the scruff of his neck, they rounded the corner to find the truck surrounded by townsfolk. It didn't appear to be an altercation, but two of the robed figures were standing amongst the throng and there was a notable space around each. In the centre of the crowd they could see Harry, seemingly the focal point of whatever was going on, flanked by Phil and Morgenstern. Jake strode up followed by Tom and Cas, the three pushing through the crowd until they reached Harry. Everyone else was in the truck and the engine was running as far as they could tell.

Harry was glad to see them. "Jake, Tom – meet the town council. Some of them, anyway. You may be interested to hear what they have to say."

A stout man at the front of the crowd turned to Jake and, without introduction, carried on from the point he'd reached with Harry. "They said no, didn't they?" he began, glancing ominously at the two robed figures a few feet away. "I just told your friend here that's exactly what they'd say." He turned to Harry. "Didn't I say that?" Harry confirmed that he had indeed said just that, just now. Mollified, the stout little man turned back to Jake and fixed him with a beady eye. "Well, let me tell you mister, they have no right to speak for this town, or the council. This is still a democracy and the council represents the majority of the people, not *them*." Several people murmured their assent; the robed men ignored them, staring impassively at the speaker from beneath their hoods. The stout man was unabashed, his tone defiant.

"Are you the leader of the band?" he asked Jake, who nodded. "Then let me tell you – this town welcomes you, wants you to play. Christmas night with real music – how could we possibly turn that down? You can play in the town hall, *and* we'll pay you for your work. I swear it – we'll find food for you, and you can sleep in decent beds tonight, and tomorrow we'll find you some fuel. You'll be wanting fuel, for sure. How about it?" He scanned his companions who, with wary glances at the hooded men, smiled cautiously and made vague but promising gestures of support. Reassured, he turned back. "Well, what do you say?"

After so many years on the road, the undercurrents were not lost on Jake. He struggled to separate his desire to play from his sense of disquiet.

"Well, we need to have a look at the venue," interrupted Harry. "If it's OK and you have power, we can discuss it." He shot a look at the robed figures. "In private," he added, somewhat pointedly. The stout man took the hint and gave them directions to the town hall. The crowd dispersed and the robed men walked into the church without a backwards glance.

"Thanks for getting me out of that, Harry," Jake acknowledged gratefully.

Harry grinned. "I'm still tour manager then, by the look of it?"

"Well, I guess we can put up with you a bit longer, until we can find someone actually competent enough to do the job properly. Have to make do with whatever's available for now, I guess..." Jake tailed off, unsmiling.

They took their places and Phil backed them out. "I don't get it," he said to Cas as he drove towards the town hall. "There aren't that many people wearing robes. What's the big deal with this mob if there's so few of them?"

"Two things," said Cas. "First, there's fear running through this place like electricity, so we can assume there are substantial numbers of hoods: if it was just a handful, there wouldn't be this level of tension, would there?"

Phil had to agree. "Hoods on both sides?" he suggested.

"Sounds right," said Cas. He looked round. "Tom, any thoughts?"

"Only what I think you were about to say," the Colonel replied from the rear. "The other thing that's far more insidious. If they don't wear their robes, they look just like everyone else. Fascists always do. That way, you never know who's listening, who you're talking to, who will betray you. Isn't that right, Cas?"

"Sure is," Cas agreed. "They aren't going to walk around all day like fucking glow-sticks, are they? All lit up, flashing neon signs round their necks saying 'here I am, look how I'm spying on you.' They're going to blend in, listen, record, report...then turn up later that night – always at night – in the robes with the hoods up, with those big staves and baseball bats and chains and wearing masks. That's how this shit works. A nation of informers."

Alina leaned forward, her head between Cas and Phil in the front, her face a mask of granite. "You got that right, Cas. Exactly how it works," she muttered. "At night...in their masks..." She stopped, her words choked off, the rage in her voice barely suppressed. Everyone looked at her in surprise. Billy, sitting next to her, put an arm round her shoulder and pulled her back while saying nothing. Alina shrugged in irritation as if to throw off his arm, then fell back against him, suddenly deflated. "Bad memories?" Billy suggested softly in her ear. She nodded, unresisting: the two had an understanding, unspoken and rarely acknowledged. She laid her hand on Billy's enfolding arm and squeezed. "You're welcome," murmured Billy.

The town hall was easy to find, atop a hill and sporting a tower with a bright green roof that could be seen from pretty much anywhere. The front of the building was grim stone but handsome, lifted out of architectural penury by arched windows twenty feet across and as many high, like a series of pious ecclesiastic prayers offered up in penance for the clock tower's lack of modesty. Behind the facade were offices, but also a theatre – once called 'The Borough' – which now served as a meeting place, market, court or hospital, depending on the need. While Harry negotiated with various townspeople, Nick and Jake investigated the backstage facilities, most of which seemed intact and, miraculously, in working order. Lights, gantries, cabling, a serviceable PA; Jake was pleased because he intended to leave as much of their equipment on the truck as possible. Another bonus was the loading bay – a long enclosed area with lockable roller shutters, big enough to drive the truck right inside the building and secure it. To Jake, this was reassuring because guarding the truck had become a major obsession since leaving Newport. His obsession: losing the bus had affected him more than he cared to admit.

"Cheer up mate, might never happen. Or maybe it will, depending on what it is." Jake looked up from the loading bay. Above him on the concrete apron stood the genial young man who had greeted them at the roadblock. He was wearing industrial gloves, blue overalls and a dog collar. "Are you a vicar?" Jake asked.

"I am indeed, for my sins. Suppose I shouldn't make that joke..but I'm the apprentice really. I'm not The Vicar." he descended the steps to join Jake on the loading bay floor as Nick walked up to join them. He held out his hand to Jake. "I'm called Piper." He shook hands with Nick. "Need any help...?" he held up his gloved hands. "I need some exercise. Been standing around at the roadblock all day."

"What's a vicar doing on a roadblock?" Jake asked him. "Anyway, we don't need much gear so there's nothing to unload. Sorry about that."

Piper leaned against the truck. "Well, we all do our bit. All except the red menace. They have other ideas."

"Was that who you wanted to warn us about? You seemed reluctant, but in that case why tell us to go see them?" said Jake.

Piper frowned. "I said no such thing. I told you to see The Vicar – that's my da actually. I was going to tell you to stay away from the red menace, but it seemed uncharitable of me so I changed my mind."

"They look like a bunch of thugs to me," said Nick, checking the back doors were locked. "Thugs always love a uniform, seems like. Are they local?"

Piper sat down on a crate; the others joined him. "The acolytes are mostly from round here. Edgar though, well he turned up here two years ago, him and four others. The inner council, they call themselves, although one turned up dead a few months ago, stabbed in the back...I'm sorry..." Piper blushed. "...sorry if I sound a bit gleeful, it's probably because that's how I feel. It is very un-Christian of me and quite reprehensible. I do apologise." He looked down at the floor, contrite and pensive.

"It is hard not to dislike them, as much as I should feel more charitable. My da says the same, but I'm quite certain he hates them more than I do. He was a scientist; I think the way they bend science and the truth of it to fit their own purposes really

302

offends him, like the accusations about corruption. It's their stock answer to any science they don't like: it isn't true because those who produced it are corrupt. It used to be the Jews or Muslims, now it's scientists."

"How many of them are there?" asked Jake.

Piper rubbed his chin. "Very hard to tell. They appeal to many people because they provide a focus for blame. What people want more than anything now is to be able to blame someone for what's happened. It has taken this long for the magnitude of the problem to sink in. It will take longer before people realise that out of any collapse, something new emerges. Right now, nobody wants to hear that. They seem numb, insensible. But also irresponsible, or perhaps wanting absolution. We all had it good there for a while – at least, the west did – but the whole thing has fallen down and we did it to ourselves, whether we like it or not. But for those of us who cannot accept the blame, who will not face the consequences of their actions, or inactions come to that, this pseudo-religion offer exactly what these people want – a focus for their rage. Nominally, it targets science and scientists – they lynched one a year ago – but their aim is flexible. When Edgar feels the fear start to diminish, a new enemy is announced, a new witch-hunt begins. Jews, of course – they saw it coming and disappeared before any more harm could be done. But the doctors, the nurses, the teachers...?" Piper blanched, his young face creased with anxiety. "People do terrible things, don't they?" He sounded sad and sorely puzzled.

"But they're the minority, right?" Nick asked Piper, who shook his head. "Maybe not. The believers – those who have robes, pretty much – they are the elite, the hardcore element. Maybe thirty all told. But the mob, that can vary enormously. It's an excuse to be violent, part of a group that nobody can stand up to. They feel powerful when they roam the street at night in the name of the church, but what they are really doing is acting like religious police, beating up anyone they don't like the look of."

Jake understood. "We ran into a vigilante group a few miles back. Militia, they called themselves. But why would this lot want to stop us playing? That I don't understand."

"Because people flock to them when they feel bad, when they want someone to blame and to hurt. When the sun shines, there's less fighting. When the food convoys show up, there's less fighting. I don't think anyone's going to want to listen to their hatred and bigotry when they could be dancing, know what I mean? You playing here could be the best thing that's happened here in ages." For all his charming optimism, Piper sounded as uncertain of his claim as Jake felt of its provenance. "Let's join the others," he suggested and all three walked down the corridor to the front of house.

Morgenstern was the bearer of bad tidings. Discovering his mobile had a signal, he made several brief calls, the last of which evidently bothered him. Joining Tom, Harry and Levi in the foyer, he conveyed the news. "We're being followed. A team came through Newport a few hours after we did, and they're on their way here. They have different orders now, apparently. No prisoners."

"Who told you this?" Harry asked.

"Fairfax. I just spoke to him," Morgenstern replied. "He left a message for me. We've quite pissed them off, by the sound of it."

Harry looked to his father, who appeared deep in thought. Their eyes met, and Tom reached a decision. "Let's talk to Edgar before it gets dark," he said and, without waiting, pushed through the front door into the street. They walked over the crown of the hill and down the other side in the general direction of the church, keeping close together. A red-robed man with a stave tried to deliver a cunning ankle blow to Levi as they passed: a short cry: Levi had acquired a stave: the previous owner was sitting at the kerbside rubbing a swollen foot. The space around them grew a little.

The plinth across from the bloody church had no attendant this time. Harry read the plaque; a tribute to the 3rd Battalion Monmouthshire Regiment and the men who died in 1915 at the second battle of Ypres. He looked across the road at the hooded figures and the banners that framed them, and marched forward determinedly behind his father. As they reached the portico,

Edgar came out to stand on the steps above them. "What do you want?" he sneered.

Tom Bracey walked up the stairs and stopped directly in front of Edgar, his face imperious. "I am Colonel Thomas Bracey and I am imposing martial law on this town, effective at midnight. I have been sent by the government to clean out fascists like you and I'd do it even if they weren't paying me. You and your kind are scum..." Edgar stepped back, alarmed, because Tom was shouting now with a parade-ground authority acquired through years of command. "You have terrorised this town and its people, and your time is up. I will give you one hour to vacate this town. If you are not gone in that time, you will be subject to the full force of law. Do you understand?"

Edgar studied the Colonel for a moment, before starting to laugh. "And you're going to enforce this edict how, exactly?" he asked as he cast a contemptuous look over the four of them, pausing only when he noticed the staff Levi was carrying. Several of the acolytes around them were equally amused. Tom Bracey raised one arm to point at Edgar. "You will see, I tell you. In a matter of hours, we shall see for ourselves what gutless bastards you people are." He glared at the nearest acolytes. "*I made a call,*" he hissed malevolently. "Cowards, all of you. Hiding behind hoods, beating up defenceless people under the cover of darkness. And you, Sir..." he turned back to Edgar, who shrank back to escape the spittle flying from the old man's lips, "...you are nothing but a parasite, evil and stupid. These idiots have no loyalty to you, they wouldn't fight for your cause in a million years. In two hours, you'll be cowering in here in a pool of your own piss and fear, you and your gutless..."

Harry grabbed his father's arm as he raised it, seemingly to strike Edgar across the face. "C'mon Colonel, let's go...please...they'll be here soon...it doesn't take long from Newport..." He pulled his father away roughly, Levi standing between him and the acolytes on one side, Morgenstern on the other. Edgar wiped his face with the back of his hand, walked to the top of the steps and watched them thread their way back through the waiting crowd across the street. His face assumed a cunning look: far from displeased, he signalled the acolytes to follow as he walked back into the church, a plan already forming.

The townspeople had been busy fulfilling the first of a series of obligations negotiated by Harry. Trestle tables were laid out on the stage, each laden with a surprising amount of food, not all of it strictly edible but largely free of maggots and mould. A stove had been set up and water boiled cheerfully on it. The band were seated around the tables, making steady inroads into the provisions with little conversation interrupting their concentration. Reuben sat with Vicky, Jimi perched on his knee. Harry, Morgenstern, the Colonel and Levi were not to be seen; Jake asked where they were.

"Talking to The Vicar," said Billy. "Didn't smell too good to me – hence the urgent feast." As Billy spoke, Jake noticed that several bags were being carefully loaded under the table while people consumed whatever they could. Without further ado, he joined them.

The foyer door burst open and the absentees walked quickly down the aisle to the stage, where Tom issued urgent orders. "Pack whatever you think we can take and get to the truck. You have thirty minutes. Make sure you get as much boiled water as we can carry. Reuben, Levi – if you haven't done so already, find a power source and charge up."

"What's going on?" Jake demanded. Morgenstern studied him casually. "Seems my little rescue has irritated someone. Sounds to me like they've sent another team in after us, or maybe the same one. Be here fairly soon, we think." He gave Jake his lop-sided grin. Jake looked to Harry, who was also grinning. "You know Yojimbo?" Harry asked him. "The man with no name?"

Jake had no idea what he was talking about, but Cas did. "Wow. Are we the band with no name now? You went to the red devils?"

"It was my father's idea," said Harry. "But this is only a diversion. We have to move now, or we'll be trapped. Didn't you notice how the crowds suddenly thinned out half an hour ago? Call to arms." He picked up a sandwich and took a big bite. "I need to get a message to The Vicar. Any ideas?" Piper stood up, catching Harry's attention for the first time. "Who are you?"

Harry asked; he'd been in the back of the truck at their first encounter. After a brief introduction, he drew the young man aside and while the band prepared to depart, outlined his message for Piper's father.

They stopped at the top of a hill outside of the town to watch. In the darkness below they could see several fires. Sporadic gunfire broke out here and there, and when the smoke occasionally cleared an armoured personnel carrier could be seen crawling through the town centre, its pace hampered by the second carrier in tow – an IED had smashed its drive shaft during the ambush. The vehicles were flanked on either side by lines of wary soldiers, guns at the ready.

Tom was studying the carnage with a small scope. "Seems the Gestapo HQ is on fire. Looks to me like the townsfolk took advantage of our little diversion too."

"Smart of you to mention it to The Vicar," said Morgenstern. "You could have asked me, though." Tom straightened up, rubbing his back. "Did you know about the assault team because you picked up the intel from Fairfax, or because you were the one who called them, told them where we were?"

Morgenstern looked surprised. "Why Colonel, ain't you the suspicious one?" Without waiting for a retort, he climbed into the back of the truck and pulled the door shut behind him. Tom walked to the cab and climbed in. "Where to now?" Jake asked.

Tom stared out into the darkness ahead. "That way."

Chapter 27: Axis Mundi

I know that I hung on a windy tree
nine long nights,
wounded with a spear, dedicated to Odin,
myself to myself,
on that tree of which no man knows
from where its roots run
No bread did they give me nor a drink from a horn,
downwards I peered;
I took up the runes, screaming I took them,
then I fell back...

Ódin's Rune Song; Hávamál, The Poetic Edda

They sat in facing rows, like benches of government, Jake a caged animal pacing between them. On one side, the band – Cas, Alina, Billy, Phil and Nick, with Vicky and Jimi standing behind them. In opposition: Tom Bracey, Reuben, Levi, Harry and Morgenstern. They were parked at the edge of the Brecon Beacons, the truck hidden inside the ruined barn in which they had rested overnight. As dawn broke, so did Jake's patience. He woke them, crow angry, and demanded a meeting. He bullied them into unloading various cases and other items to sit on, insisted on the confrontational arrangement, and assigned each band member their seat, lines drawn clear: *them and us*. Now all eyes were on Jake as he strode up and down between rows, his hostile stare fixed on the opposition.

"First, happy fucking Christmas. Second, let me make this clear: we will not move another foot until you tell us where we are going, and how this is going to end. Until we get a satisfactory answer, we're staying put. I don't care if the fucking forces of darkness catch us up and melt every last one of us with alien plasma cannons. I don't care what happens to the twins, and I definitely don't care what happens to any spooks, freaks, clones, old soldiers, disgraced soldiers or any other stray motherfuckers we seem to have picked up along the way. I'm completely fed up with the whole fucking deal and the only thing I care about now is me and my band." (Vicky put her hands over Jimi's ears, but he squirmed away; nothing on Earth could make him miss all this bad language, and there was every chance of a fight!).

Jake didn't notice. "In thirty years I've looked after several generations of musicians. That's what I do. It's my responsibility and my pleasure and my duty, because this is *my band*. I'm the leader, and that's what leaders do. I've played every major venue in the country, probably played every decent size town there is, and my guess is that I've brought good quality music to maybe hundreds of thousands of people in that time. I've tried to live a decent life. I'm not very dutiful, nor am I patriotic: I don't like nationalism, never seen a damn thing come out of it worth having. I've just tried to be honest, to act with some awareness of others and some consideration for their feelings. I've never willingly hurt anyone in my entire life, emotionally or physically, not that I'm any kind of saint mind you – I've been as selfish and inconsiderate as the next bastard, but you know what I'm saying. I try at least to respect others, if they'll let me. If they don't – fuck 'em. But I'm not greedy. I don't steal or swindle. I've never wanted more than a place to sleep, some food, a beer and a joint, a chance to play some good music and to maintain my self-respect. Hardly the capitalists' rapacious dream, is it? Hard to say I've been gluttonous, wanted more than my share.

"So what I want to know is this: what the fuck am I doing hiding in some woods in the middle of nowhere, scared for my life and for Jimi's and for my band, *and for what*? Have we made any progress, because it doesn't seem like it? We're just running and running and getting absolutely nowhere. But those fuckers back there are getting closer – this is the first time we've actually seen them, and that's once too often. What are we doing, for fuck's sake? All I ever wanted was a modest existence. Nothing greedy, nothing obscene. How do I come to be mixed up in this shit – me and the rest of the band? How have we become victims? *How*?

"Simple: we've been betrayed. My betrayal, the betrayal of my generation, is the most brutal in all history. For the most part of history, ordinary people had no recourse, no hope, no justice and no understanding of what they were missing. Change occurred so slowly that it didn't really seem like change at all –

309

people died faster than change could be observed. From one generation to the next, nothing much seemed to happen. But our thirst for knowledge was self-fuelling, little by little. The church knew this and tried to prevent it, but Pandora's box was unlocked. Once the Pope was obliged to orbit the sun along with the rest of us, and Newton divorced the celestial mechanics from their pious mystery, man began to predict the essence of things, robbing religion of its purview, its exclusive doctrine of wilful mystery. The common man began to find out things that religion had claimed were unknowable. The first lies were exposed by evidence, by proofs and rationality. We didn't need God any more, except as a spiritual luxury or an indulgence like a security blanket to wrap us up warm against the chills of our ignorance and the fear that festered in it. But the light was slow in spreading. The workers in the field knew little more than their forefathers. Hope didn't spring eternal; if you weren't an aristocrat, it didn't spring at all. Knowledge may have been gained, but there was no way to communicate it to those outside of the elite, which of course were the ruling classes.

"This is what changed in the twentieth century; this is what sealed the fate of the robber-barons. Communication; we started to find out what was going on. We started to hear the recorded stories of old soldiers, of sailors and travellers, of adventurers and explorers. We began to discover the price of colonialism. We learned to read and write. We read about emancipation, about women who dared to act like men and demand the same rights, the same political status. As we tended our machines and our ledgers, we heard about people who formed unions, who stuck up for themselves. We heard that we had power, and we could exercise it. We heard we were no longer victims of every venal fucking bastard, that they needed us as much as we needed them. Most of all, we could hear a storm of change coming, through the telegraph wires and the squeaking of tank tracks, in staccato rattles of mechanised guns and the glissando shriek of bombs dropped by flying machines.

"At no time has mankind ever been closer to greatness than during my lifetime. At no time has mankind actually been more depraved in its actions. In all history, the humanist promise was never more gravid, more ripe and bursting with wondrous

310

potential. Huge numbers were lifted up out of penury and despair after fighting the most terrible wars of all time. The world was rebuilt by men who knew we could do better. They knew that poverty could be beaten and enough food could be grown that nobody need starve. *Nobody.* They recognised that healthcare could be a universal right, that education was not exclusive to a more deserving class. So much wealth could we create, it was impossible to imagine anyone, anywhere who would not share in it. Equality and merit might finally be awarded without prejudice. The fact of Empire was the past, it's disintegration the present, egalitarianism the future. We looked over the sea to the countries of those who stood by us in the trenches, those who defended our freedoms as we did theirs, and for the first time we saw how much we had in common. Despite their poverty, they fought for the same freedoms we did, died in their own shit and vomit as we did. Death knew no skin colour, no language or ideology. Now, finally, we were all equal. No longer could we turn away from the imbalance between the rich nations and poor. No longer could we pretend we didn't know how bad things were, and in any case TV wouldn't let us forget, for the story of other people's penury is the stuff of mass entertainment everywhere, from Circus Maximus to Big Brother.

"Armed with this new awareness, this social responsibility without borders, we would build something better, something worthy of the awful sacrifices of the twentieth century. It was a distant horizon but we could already see it, because science and technology reinforced the idea that we could create so much wealth, so many benefits, such a flood of good things as would pour out of factories, powered by virtually free nuclear energy, staffed by healthy, well-educated and upwardly mobile people made equal in law and opportunity by knowledge and communality and sharing of all this wealth. The end of baseless fear, the end of warfare, the end of 'the other' and the perpetual anxiety of the victim. The end of the divide between rich and poor, well and sick, educated and ignorant. We had men on the moon, computers, jet planes and DNA. Like I said, we didn't need God any more; we became our own singular deities, each person a religion of one. We had the welfare state and CND, free education, the National Health Service, free speech, unions, stocks and shares and pensions. We had the vote and the democracy it promised. And this democracy, this caring socialism without the madness of totalitarian communism, was spreading, along with the wealth and the ideas and the freedoms. We stood at the Axis Mundi, the axis of reality, the bridge from earth to heaven, ready to step into the brave new world on the other side. We really thought that. *We were so fucking dumb, we really did think that!*

"So we accepted the promissory note that consumerism held out, thinking it was the ticket that allowed us entrance, that got us through the pearly gates. Then we tried to redeem it and found out how worthless the promises were, how little value was placed on probity or legally binding obligation, on the word of the rich when given to the poor. The only obligation on us, it turned out, was for us to keep believing the liars and cheats and conmen and hucksters long after we had a media powerful enough to expose them daily, and corrupt enough not to bother.

Our duty wasn't to king and country, our duty was to remain credulous and easy to manipulate, no matter what we found out. It was no longer possible *not* to know how criminal and corrupt our leaders were. Our trust was betrayed over and over, in ever more public ways, while increasingly strident demands were made to maintain and even extend that trust. And if we were reluctant to play our sheepish part in the latest scam, if we questioned our status as perpetual victims, things blew up and people died and the police state eroded our freedoms little by little, all in the name of our protection, but the effect was to force our compliance. The old credulity of the field and the hayseed working it, replaced by the new credulity of a little knowledge, rampant cynicism dressed as wisdom, and a fatalism constantly oiled by the media with stories of how helpless we were in the face of so many things we could not comprehend: a world now so complex, driven by arcane science and technologies we barely understood, even as we filled our homes with the stuff, so that instead of our lives being enriched with quality and experience, we were flooded with anxiety and reproach, the sense that even as we appeared to gain so much, we were losing far more.

"What did we do to deserve being manipulated like puppets? I've lost my bus, my few possessions, pictures and trinkets and little bits of my past, my way of life, all the tiny things that were so valuable to me, that required very little to sustain them. What price it is I'm paying here? I'm no consumer. My lifestyle required no sacrifices by people a long way away, no inequalities, no colonial injustices and raw materials dug out of the ground by slaves, no lash of the whip, no poverty in my name, no sickness and disease to measure the gap between my wealth and everyone else's deprivation, no back room deals where countries are carved up and populations beaten into submission. No fucking corruption, no filthy dictators propped up in my name. No mercenaries lurking about with guns and night-sights, no prison camps and forced migrations, no pogroms or tribal wars, no religious zealots beating people with sticks, flogging women because they were improperly dressed, no sham democracies where every vote is rigged. No spies and satellites, guided bombs down chimneys dropped by invisible drones. No devious manipulation of everything and everyone – not in my name, anyway. But still it goes on and on; ordinary people just get fucked again and again. Just like we are now. I'm sick of it. I've been sick of it my whole life. I've tried to escape it, to not be a part of it, and perhaps I've run away from it, but now it seems I have no choice. Perhaps I never had one. If I did, I'd choose to have nothing to do with this fucked up way of life of yours.

"From the beginning of this century, the story has been one of relentless decline everywhere you look. Another fucking empire going down the toilet, flushed by its own hand. What the fuck happened to the Age of Aquarius? Peace and love? Drowned at birth, that's what happened to them. Trampled on by successive governments who were so busy getting their snouts in the trough they didn't see the end of the world coming at them, even when everyone on deck was shouting out 'ICEBERG' at the top of our lungs. Instead, they trampled on liberty and law and decency in their rush to fill their off-shore bank accounts. They didn't hear the warning shots, didn't heed the terrorism or the growing fear. Instead, they told us to go full speed ahead and don't spare the CO2. We steamed on into Iraq, then North Korea, then Iran, then Saudi Arabia, then what was left of Israel and the Venezuelan oilfields, until finally we had to stop for a while because the Americans were so caught up in killing each other they didn't have time to kick the crap out of anyone else.

"And all the time the sea was rising millimetre by millimetre. Big business did fuck all about it – taking their lead from all the governments that signed protocol after agreement after declaration, all totally ignored when they got home. Worthless. Lions led by donkeys ain't in it, not even close.

"So we watched all the ice melt and the climate go mad, and then looked really fucking amazed when a billion people tried to move elsewhere, as if they were going to stay in a place with no food, water or future. And what did we do, in our wealthy compassion? We built walls and fences to keep out the people, the ones we had condemned by our complacency and greed. We watched through the fence as they died of every vile disease and consequence of their abject poverty, shaking our heads and telling each other how terrible it all was while giving our credit card numbers to the latest TV charity show. But our charity only went so far, didn't it? If they got too close to the fence, we shot them. In case we didn't have enough bullets, we built new nukes, developed new poisons that could kill millions with just a few drops in the right reservoir, we brought back conscription until it took more soldiers than you were recruiting to round up those who refused to fight.

"For every failure of capitalism, more growth was advocated despite having no energy left to fuel it. When the lights went out, who did we blame? When the oil ran out and we had no petrol or heating, who did we blame? *We blamed everyone except ourselves.* We raided the pantry like it had infinite contents; when there was nothing left, we blamed other people even as we were wiping the last of the jam off our chins. The media cranked out lie after lie blaming the US, Russia, China, Jews, any Islamic country you care to name but especially Iran, Poles, Romanians, Turks, the Saudis, the Kurds, the EU, the Bilderbergers, Rothchilds, the Trilateral commission, the UN and the IPCC, even the scientists that had been warning us for years. Left or right, name any group and we'd pin the blame on them for something. We wallowed in blame, perpetual victims of our own complacency and laziness. A civilisation built on institutional lies and conspiracy theories, and we went along with it. For every iniquity exposed, new ones were designed, sold to us by straight faced demagogues as benefits, inevitably for our own good. Every truth was perverted and undermined by new lies, better lies, cleverer and more slippery lies, lies foisted on us by a whole new class of people, a profession whose job it was to work out the best architecture of lies, the best way to deliver lies, how to balance and package them, how much the truth could be stretched before it snapped, and how to obfuscate when it did, to cover their lying arses. In the end, people didn't trust any messengers at all, so no wonder we didn't hear the messages we should have listened to. The society that cried wolf. And the more we realised what a venal bunch of shits were running the country, the slicker the lies became, the better the packaging and the lures and the bribes and the appeals to self-interest and short-term gains.

"I've watched the progressive destruction of honesty, of probity, of manners and civility and care and honour and dignity and generosity. The demolition of society, of a welfare state that says we should look after each other, be subject to one another, that we are not equal in gifts or opportunities, but we *are* equal in importance, in human value. No man or woman is more valuable than another; all should be cherished and protected. But what was it we aspired to as our backs bent under feudal rule? What crippled visions did we dream in the mills and factories and offices? To become free of it, all men equal before god? *Did we fuck!* We peasants aspired to be become the new feudal overseers, the new aristocrats. Scratch any serf and you'll find a baron underneath. Our governments knew this, understood it. How could they not, since they were cut from the same coarse cloth? They knew how to simulate the illusion of plebeian power – just like democracy itself – maintain the chimera by expanding colonies, sailing our warships and marching our armies across the face of world so we could all be feudal chiefs, all us peasant imperialists lording it over the wogs and niggers, over some poor Bangladeshi or Thai or Indonesian, over Chinese men and Indian women and their children driven to drugs and prostitution, enjoying our superiority over Ethiopian wage slaves in refugee camps just like the ones we passed through. Feudalism at a remove, so we needn't be burdened with our guilt over the way we became rich, the way we chose to keep ourselves that way, the way we refused to share anything good, everything worthy and enriching, every real humanistic benefit, the knowledge and medicine and science and experience. Fairness was never on our agenda; only our profit, made by exploiting the weakness of others in our hidden fiefdoms, distance discounting the terrible price of our moral corruption. What we can't see, we can't be blamed for, can't feel guilty about, can't be made to recognise the way we have utterly failed to shoulder our responsibilities to one another.

"But despite all our protestations to the contrary, it has *everything* to do with us: we hoarded the wealth of our knowledge so we could reflect our cleverness compared to those we denied, pretending not to notice the terrible cost of our vanity paid by those we kept in the darkness. Rich and poor are sides of a single coin; for someone to be rich, someone else is obliged to be poor.

"I have personally been witness to the relentless erosion and ultimate collapse of everything mankind has worked for since the dark ages, all the science and technology and progress, the humanity and care, the notion of democracy and free speech, of art and egalitarianism, law and culture; the stuff of civilisation itself. Degraded and corrupt, all of it, traded for the technological equivalent of a few shiny beads, a hand mirror, a condom, some dirty postcards and a quart of rotgut whisky. Bought off like the fucking children we've been, fobbed off with a few toys and a porn film. Now it turns out that story wasn't a fairy tale, it was a nightmare – and we're living in it. You've seen them, the towns and villages of the new dark ages – we've just passed through them on our way here. Superstition and religious fundamentalism are back in a big way, like we've stepped back four hundred years. Rationality? Reason and logic? All thrown away, put to the torch by the howling mob. How many times have we done that since the Greeks codified the intellectual rigours? Thrown away the progress we'd made so we could return to the slums and shanty towns, the shit in the streets with no light and no illumination, violence the only rule of law, no education, no medicine, no justice, no order and no fucking future. And we threw all this away for what? *FOR WHAT?*"

Jake paused for the first time since launching his attack, staring at Morgenstern as if expecting an answer. The American responded by standing up, his grin as inane as his eyes were hostile, an air of violence about him. About to speak, he suddenly sat down again, the involuntary movement abetted by a sudden pained expression and the arm Reuben was holding. "Best to listen Marty," Reuben advised, and let go the arm. Morgenstern rubbed it resentfully but said nothing.

Jake turned to Tom. "You're a decent man, Colonel Tom. You sheltered us and I thank you for it. But you and Fairfax...and Harry..." he looked apologetically at Harry "and the twins and Mr. CIA here – you're what we threw our culture away for? People like you, and what you represent, your methods and propaganda and violence and means always justifying ends. And yet we've been following you all this time. I feel stupid, frankly. People like you got us into this fucking mess, and here I am trailing round the country at your behest. Don't have a fucking clue where we're going, but I can trust you, *right*? You'll look after us all, just like you always have, *right*?

"Well, no more. Here we stay until you explain what's going on here, and how we're going to get out of this mess. I can't see any way out at all, except at the hands of those bastards back there. But at least I can see them coming and spit in their eyes as they kill me. With you lot, I see only people keeping secrets. I can't tell if you're friends or enemies. All I see is the next minute of my life, the rest of it hidden in your hands, or so you'd like us all to think. Fuck that. No more secrets, Tom; Harry, no more deception. Yank, what's your plan?...no, don't bother – I'm sure I won't believe a single word you say. So I'm asking you Tom: where is Etheria? What is it, and what happens when we get there?"

Winded, Jake sat down, his anger unabated. Every member of the band burst into spontaneous applause. "Top speech, dude," said Phil admiringly. "Fuck, I'd vote for you anytime." Everyone grinned, with the exception of Morgenstern, preoccupied with rubbing an arm largely devoid of feeling.

Tom cleared his throat and scanned the row of eager faces looking to him expectantly. "Fair enough Jake," he said in a reasonable tone. "You – all of you – aren't used to this life. I understand this. I also understand how hard it is to follow people you don't know, to be involved in something this serious without really knowing how you got involved in the first place. Harry and I - and Marty here, Fairfax too – we all signed up for this. You didn't. But nor did the twins, so let's not forget that please." He cast a fleeting look at Levi and Reuben, both watching him impassively. "They are how we come to be here, all of us, and while you've lost your bus Jake, I've lost my family home. Perhaps I can go back to it, just like you might be able to return to your touring. Just not right now: we are all being called on to make sacrifices, but it is the twins who face the greatest sacrifice of all and I don't think we should allow that fact to escape our attention. It's also true that while we here..." he waved a hand towards those seated by him, "...signed up for a certain kind of life, an itinerant one, so did you – all of you. You're a band...a band of gypsies living a life free of responsibility towards anything except your own immediate future, the next gig, the next meal, the next joint. You didn't build the society you depended on, you merely entertained it. You haven't furthered the civilisation you want to live in, just played like kids in the car park while the adults held business meetings inside to try to figure out what to do. Your safety depended on people like me, who were prepared to deal with a world rather more complex, and considerably more dangerous, than the safe little environment you've occupied, a little bubble existence insulated from anything you don't like and free of any obligation to change it. Instead, when the going gets tough, you jump in the bus and drive off into the sunset, shouting 'your world is shit, but it's nothing to do with us' as if you had no part in any of it, no duty of care towards it. You justify your existence by claiming to bring music to the world, which is fair enough, but it's all you do, not all you are capable of doing.

"Now, that's been your choice and I respect that up to a point, the point when the real world has gate-crashed your little party, dragging me in with it. What I do not respect is you whining about it like spoiled brats. Indulgent, irresponsible, rootless. Hunter-gatherers. *Vikings*? How very romantic. All very well, of course, but only if you don't want light bulbs or antibiotics or computers. Travellers never designed an amplifier, never built a guitar factory, never made a truck, never discovered penicillin or DNA or electricity. You exist in some romantic illusion, seeing yourselves as outsiders, but only until you need guitar strings or diesel, paracetamol or a bag of grass..."

Cas cut across him, voice ice cold. "We never made nukes either. We never made Sarin or VX gas, drones or guided bombs or ICBMs. Stealth bombers or napalm..." Tom held up a peremptory hand. "Please do not interrupt. And please do not blame science for the way it is used. That argument is so vapid; it is the fault of the knife that a man chooses to stab someone with it instead of using it to cut up his dinner? This is more of the same vacuous irresponsibility, where a good idea takes the blame for our poor execution of it. And strangely enough, this brings me to the questions Jake asked, and the answers I am prepared to give you. If they are not satisfactory, then you can remain here while the twins, Morgenstern and I continue on our journey, on foot if we have to.

"Jake, I remind you of the reality of your position. We do not need you at all, for anything. We could have found alternative, and rather more discrete transport. We would be a smaller group, less conspicuous, travelling faster and lighter and further. Your band is a hindrance in nearly every way now. You make demands as if you are calling the shots. You are not, and while I understand your frustration, if you threaten me again I will simply walk off and forget about you. Then see how much spit you can muster when the specials catch you up. How brave you'll look kneeling in a puddle of your own piss as they turn off your lights for the last time."

"But wouldn't that be the best thing for us now – for you to bugger off and leave us alone?" retorted Jake, quite unabashed. "If you lot were to clear off, the hard-nuts would chase you, not us. We don't have the data. We don't have any proof of anything. We're just a bunch of drug-addled musos and we're no threat to anyone. The twins are what they want, along with the data you say is mirrored, I assume in the real Etheria. They have no interest in us. Your threat is empty, isn't it?"

Morgenstern interrupted with a grim, humourless laugh. "You have no idea son, do you? It's the economics of secrecy. They don't know what you know and what you don't. They don't know what risk you pose, what data you have or don't have. They don't know much about you, but they do know you've been in contact with secrets that are dangerous to certain people, dangerous if revealed, that is. They don't have time to make fine calculations, spend days interrogating each of you to see what you know and if you are a threat. It's all too complex; alive, you represent any number of potential threats. Dead, *you are nothing*. Erased from the equation, a redundant expression now eliminated, no longer a part of the calculation. It's the logical decision and it is the one they will make, have made already. If I were the commander of that squad we saw last night, I'd stuff you all in that truck, lock the doors and set light to it. Job done, we all go home. You don't know this, but I've been begging the twins here to dump you, begging Tom too. It was what we should have done – just left you in Tom's house. But Reuben wouldn't have it, and nor would Tom, for all his imperious military logic. It doesn't make sense, but I'm stuck with it. But do please shut the fuck up about how hard done by you are. We're keeping you alive, in case you hadn't noticed."

Alina stood and walked over to Reuben. She held out her hand and he took it. "Come and sit with me." Reuben stood and followed her. Levi was clearly annoyed. "You're choosing the wrong side again," he told Reuben, his voice a low hiss. Re-seated, Reuben inspected Alina's hand, pale and fragile in the vast expanse of his own. "Again? I didn't realise there were 'sides' to this until now. I don't know you, Levi. Whatever friends I have in this world are sitting beside me now. Harry, I think you should be over here too, if you don't mind me saying."

Harry shook his head and glanced at this father expectantly. Tom smiled at him. "It's the other half of our misunderstanding, Harry." He turned to the others. "My son has for a long time laboured under the impression that I'd gone soft, turned into a hippy. Not the image a soldier wants of his soldier father, is it? But the strange thing is that in some respects he was absolutely right. Fairfax said it; I look beyond conflict to what happens next. Etheria is a solution I helped create. It is virtual – the storage of knowledge – and it is also physical, a place, a community, a future. Son, your father helped to build a hippy commune – from a distance, admittedly – but don't that beat all? And this is where we are going. First time I'll have seen it after all these years."

"That's all very well Dad," said Harry, bemused but still focused. "But aren't we leading the bastards straight to it, to the data and the twins. We're riding round in the most indiscrete vehicle imaginable – a band truck for Christ's sake – so we're more or less impossible to miss on these deserted roads. What was Fairfax thinking when he set that up? Or maybe that's exactly what he was thinking, eh? Either way, you know they will catch up with us. Even if we make a stand, even if we *could* win a fire-fight, they'll just send more, then more after that. It won't stop. What's the point of going there, in other words? What are the mission objectives? Do we have any?"

"Mission objectives," muttered Cas, remembering the conversation he had instigated at Clare House. "Fuck me, after all this and we still don't have a clue what we're doing."

"Sure we do," said Reuben quietly. Everyone turned to stare. "It's obvious really. There is only one lever we have, one lever we can pull. It is the lever that exposes those behind this experiment."

"You're saying we should expose them? Would that stop them coming after us?" said Jake.

"No, I'm saying we have to get in a position to be able to *threaten* to do so. My safety, and that of Levi's, is more or less assured. We get out of here, and live what we have left of our time in the US somewhere. But your safety – the whole band's – depends on having a way of preventing them harming you. If you keep running, they will catch you and the results will likely be terminal. Morgenstern will not agree to take you all to America; I've asked him several times, and in any case I never assumed you might want to go." He looked at Alina, but she turned away. "We have to make a stand, and fight back, but with the weapons we understand. We have just one such weapon: the data. It's the only thing that will stop them; it is the thing they fear most."

"It's the names," said Cas. Everyone looked at him. "The names of the people behind this. The people who would be exposed. If we don't have the names, we have nothing at all. Without the names, it's just a load of weird science by some crazy

321

Americans. With names, it is a grenade ready to be thrown at MI5."

"You didn't find any names so far, I take it?" said Morgenstern to Levi, who stared at him curiously before shaking his head. "No Marty, we didn't have time. I told you that already."

"Very well," said Tom Bracey with abrupt finality, silencing the others, "We need the names, and we must think of a mechanism of exposure should they attempt anything foolish. We also need to work out how we're going to communicate this, and what Fairfax will make of it. I don't know if he wants to catch them, neutralise them or play them. Hard to tell with his firm. Frankly, I don't care, but he could be useful to us." He turned to Jake. "You called this meeting, Jake. Have your terms been met, and can we *please* get a move on? The clock is still running and it's perishing out here."

Chapter 28: Wimpedo

The road across the Brecon Beacons traversed a dun landscape; attractive if you were a well-fed tourist with reliable transport to carry you through it, but otherwise a barren, hostile environment where nobody but the most desperate would live, or make the attempt. There were no farmhouses, no hamlets here; just bare scree, broken moor and wind-wrapped bog, dominated in every direction by idle wind turbines. The unfortunate shelters still standing were rusted and derelict, yet occupied. Between them were scattered the remains of others that had collapsed or been abandoned. As far as the eye could see, the moorland and rock was littered with the flotsam and jetsam of the wretched. Small rivers were backed up, forming fetid pools of stagnant, poisoned water, flow blocked with plastic bags and strips of agricultural sheeting, shards of sodden plywood, nylon netting, tin cans and chicken wire. In a single mile, they saw seven corpses lying by the roadside, three of them children.

Past Builth Wells, with the Cambrian mountains looming, the road was forced to follow the valley through which the River Wye flowed. Here, the shelters grew less and the scenery more rugged, the grubby works of man progressively dwarfed by imperious nature. As the rain eased off, they passed the mouth of the Elan valley and turned off the main road, leaving the river valley for another that was wider, gentler. For the first time since they entered Wales, they saw cultivated fields – tilled and cleared ready for planting in the spring - and here and there livestock foraged, few in number but strangely reassuring.

"God, this place is lovely," said Jake. The mountains, still distant on his left, were pastel shades made soft in the winter afternoon. Streaks of sunlight shot through the peaks as they erupted out of pink-topped clouds, whose shadows crossed the slopes below at surprising speed as they tumbled before the wind. By way of contrast to the rugged distance, the immediate foreground was a land quilted out of natural shades, rising and falling in strange but pleasing rhythms towards constantly shifting horizons as the road wound sinuously between the skirts of undulating hills. By the time they reached the next town, the band were considerably cheered.

"We're here," Tom announced.

"Where?" Jake asked, surprised and mystified.

"This is the nearest town; you could call it the gateway to Etheria," he replied, pointing at the road-sign announcing the sleepy little market town of Llanidloes. "Where to, then?" asked Jake. Tom shook his head. "No idea, Jake. I have to find someone in this town, someone who I last met 20 years ago. I just hope he's still alive."

It was hard to tell if Llanidloes actually had a town centre. It seemed to wend its way round a series of streets, each of which boasted several ancient timber-framed buildings in fine condition and daily use. Between them were Georgian terraces with grand windows fronting small rooms, nondescript Edwardian semis and parades of small shops built between world wars, unimaginative but fairly inoffensive, now residential for the most part. Further out, the later chocolate box developments spurned the notion of straight roads in favour of meandering and mystifying eccentricity: no such indulgence in the centre, such as it was. The streets were generous and tree-lined; as they drove slowly around the bend in the River Wye that cradled the town, the atmosphere seemed purposeful but cheery. A number of people were mounted, others driving little carts pulled by ponies or donkeys. People were out walking under a silvery sky; here and there a few groups stood gossiping. In some windows, Christmas decorations peeked out from between curtains, lending a festive air to the proceedings the band found somewhat inappropriate after the desolation they had left behind. Sweet-smelling wood smoke rose from many chimneys, drifting tenuous and lacy in the bright light. To his amazement, Jake heard music wafting gently through the air. Then it was gone, tantalising but also, for Jake, quite uplifting. "Did you hear that?" he asked the others, but no-one had. It didn't matter; in a few seconds, Jake had been reminded that hope springs eternal, and for that he was profoundly grateful.

They turned a corner to be confronted by a long, timber-framed pub calling itself the Mount Inn. "There," said Tom. "Drop me off and wait for me. I'd let the others out to stretch their legs and be seen, but stay by the vehicle." He squeezed past Jake and out of the door, Jake following.

"No," said Tom, stopping short. "I have to do this alone."

Jake laughed, clapped him on the back and propelled him towards the pub entrance. "You don't know much about show biz, do you Colonel? They've been watching us from the window since we pulled up. We may as well have driven the truck into the bar, for all the difference it would make." He opened the door and ushered Tom Bracey through it. "Anyway, I fancy a drink and I suspect I might get a decent one here. Wonder what currency they accept."

The bar was low, dark and crowded. Unnervingly, the entire establishment went quiet as they crossed the threshold, and stayed that way. All eyes remained on them, neither hostile nor welcoming. The Colonel walked towards the bar; Jake grinned at the staring host and joined him. The silence persisted. Behind the bar, a portly man with an apron draped over his rotundity put down the glass he was polishing and walked over. "Help you?" No one moved nor made a sound.

Glancing nervously at the hushed audience, Tom leaned forward. "I...that is...I am a friend of Llani's father. I would like to meet him," he said in a low, solemn voice. To his utter surprise, everyone burst out laughing. "Oh, fair enough then," said the man behind the bar. "Let me get you a drink, lad. Haven't heard that in a long while." He was still chuckling when he returned with two pint mugs of something brown and frothy. Tom and Jake raised their glasses with caution, but even before they could taste it a ripe smell of hops and yeast had expressed its own invitation.

"Ah... dear God...that was good," said Jake, his admiration directed at the empty glass he placed reverentially on the bar. He looked around the room; nobody paid him the slightest attention; the hubbub of conversation had resumed. "What was so funny?" he asked the barman.

"It was the 'secret' phrase for people who were on their way somewhere. Used years ago, when it all went bad. It was supposed to be secret and all that jazz, but so many people knew it and so many people came in here during the day, desperate, blurting it out to whoever would listen, it became a bit of a joke."

"A secret code for what? On their way to...?" said Jake, regretting he hadn't taken more time over his drink; Tom was still supping his patiently.

"Ask the Colonel," said the barman pointedly, looking towards Tom, whose head snapped upright. The barman grinned. "Yes, we know who you are. Had some fun with those nut jobs in the red dresses, did you? We heard all about it, see..." He turned away to serve another customer. Jake cast one more regretful glance at his empty glass before returning to the matter in hand. "That didn't seem to get us far."

The Colonel shook his head. "No idea, Jake. Not the reaction I was expecting. I'll have to ask a few more questions, it seems."

"Who is it we came looking for? Who is Llani's father?"

"That would be me, I expect," said a voice behind them. Both men turned. "I'm Jaq. My father was Jack. You're Jake, I expect. This could get confusing." A middle-aged woman offered her hand, and Jake shook it. "And you're the Colonel," she said with a shy smile. "Never thought I'd get to meet you." They shook hands, Tom rather bemused. "You're his daughter? I never knew..."

Jaq smiled. "Why should you? We kept quiet about most things back then. Still do. Try to be discrete...that is, until a truck shows up full of mad bastards who just pissed off half the county with their antics. You're leading them to us, Colonel, you know that, right?"

The Colonel nodded, his face impassive. "I know it. There was no choice. Now we're in your hands."

Jaq grimaced. "Thanks a bunch. It's one way to devolve yourself from responsibility, I suppose. Well, let's get out of here and get you lot stowed away. Then we'll have a chat and see what's what." With that, she led them outside, unhitched a tidy chestnut mare from the rail and climbed easily into the saddle. "Follow me," she called out, and set off at a trot.

Limited to the pace set by the walking horse and its rider, everyone had climbed out of the truck to walk alongside. No-one was quite sure how Jimi had managed to ingratiate himself with the rider, but he was now seated in front of her, the reins held carefully in his small hands, trying to mimic the movements Jaq showed him from time to time that kept his hands in touch with the horse's soft mouth without nagging or losing authority.

The introductions had been cursory; Jaq wouldn't wait for the convoy, so conversations were few and far between. Morgenstern had bearded the Colonel at the first opportunity, clearly annoyed at his exclusion from the meeting in the pub, but Tom largely ignored him and kept walking. The others split into smaller groups; as Nick drove along behind the horse, Jake, Cas, Billy and Phil were sitting on the open tailgate of the truck, sharing the last, precious joint that Billy had produced from his bass case (although Jake did note in a casual and carefully non-confrontational aside that this was the fifth 'last joint' Billy had produced since leaving Thieves' Wood). Vicky walked beside the pretty horse, glancing up at the riders occasionally but with no apparent concern, while Tom, Reuben, Alina and Harry followed, each casting a rueful look at the horse's rump from time to time as if expecting a sudden discharge. Levi and Morgenstern trailed the rest, neither looking particularly pleased, a notable contrast since everyone else was enjoying the quiet forest road and their leisurely pace along it.

"Are these woods very old?" Vicky asked the woman on the horse. Jaq chuckled quietly. "Keep your hands still, just softly tension the reins so the horse knows you're still paying her the right amount of attention," she told Jimi, voice soft and encouraging. "Good, just like that..." She looked down. "Actually, it's entirely artificial. This is the Hafren Forest, and it was planted in the nineteen-thirties. Before that, there were remains of Bronze Age mines – copper and lead – we've re-worked some of them now, and a dozen or so farms . But the forest kept changing, first commercially, later as a nature reserve. It's nearly all fast growth timber, so it's farmed for fuel. Consequently, there's lots of good track and a few decent roads, and excellent water supplies all through it, just like this." She waved expansively at the vista that opened out before them as they left the forest boundary; a long, crooked lake, bounded steeply on all sides by rolling hills. Spruce and pine grew arrow straight along parts of the shore, brown grasses and greener moss decorating steeper inclines where the earth was too thin to support anything more. The water had the texture of silver cloth, a fine weave of chain-mail glinting randomly in the winter light. Long shadows stretched out towards the onlookers. A weak sun touched the furthest hilltop, beams of light like a fanfare through broken cloud constantly brushed away on irritated gasps of wind that chased their shadows over the vivid water.

"We must keep moving," urged Jaq, and spurred the mare into a trot, one arm protectively round the boy's waist, a fact that didn't escape Vicky's attention. The truck sped up, making the tailgate a volatile place to sit. In a few minutes, everyone was jogging to keep up with the chestnut mare, now several hundred yards down the road. But Jaq dropped the pace again after a short while, allowing Jimi to rein in the trot with coaxing motions of his hands.

They journeyed for another half an hour before coming to a large tarmac area with several small log huts on the perimeter, none occupied as far as they could tell. "This used to be a car park," said Jaq, dismounting after giving Jimi a hand down. She tied her horse to a post and beckoned to the group. "Come and have a look," she urged. "It's a view not to be missed, and it explains what a thousand words never quite manage."

Jaq led them down a short footpath through the trees, which stopped abruptly at a viewing point right on the edge of a small promontory, beneath which the ground fell five hundred abrupt feet to the swathe of landscape far below them, and then kept going for forty miles. It was a breathtaking panorama, unfolding in layer after glorious layer rising towards the sky in waves, verdant textures of greens and browns gradually superseded by towering red rock and the snow-blushed peaks of distant mountains, almost luminous in the fading light. Hills and dales ran into one another, swapping woodland for heath, grasses bounded by snaking hedgerows and meandering streams. The folding hills were gentle and lush with promise, even in mid-winter, tilled dark fields contrasting with earthy tracts under rotation. Cultivation and woodland merged gracefully from one to another, with a balance that appeared almost deliberate, textures and tones interposed; hill flanks tree-lined, soft canopy like hair; lustrous grassland drama-scarred with rusty heathers, dark green heath like a stain over amber rock and dusty earth. The geometric intentions of field boundaries were pleasingly compromised by the landscape, which would not allow such mundane division of the workable land, forcing the hedges through improbable convolutions. High above them, a bird hovered in the sky, it's keening hard and clear.

"That red kite is saying 'welcome to Etheria," said Jaq triumphantly, and cast her arm in a wide arc across the landscape with a proprietorial air.

It appeared there were many small fires down below, to judge by the plumes of smoke. Jake was puzzled and turned to their new companion. "What are they burning down there?"

Jaq smiled, addressing the group with the jaunty, familiar tone of a bored tour guide. "How many people do you think are down there?" she asked, her leading question rhetorical enough for nobody to bother answering. She looked strangely disappointed. "No guesses? Never mind. There are, as best we can reckon it, about two hundred thousand people living here now. And apart from a few farms and houses that were here before we came, you can't see any of them. But look, you can see their fires. Evening is drawing in, and people are getting ready to cook their suppers." Indeed, as they watched, plumes of white smoke seemed to be rising out of the ground as far as they could see, thousand on thousand of them. "Doesn't that cause pollution?" Cas asked, quite fascinated. Jaq shook her head. "No, the stoves we designed only smoke for a few minutes – there...you can see some are already dying down..."

Tom was stunned. "Two hundred thousand? I can't believe it. Where's the town – the city more like? Where's the centre, the administration?" He gazed out in wonder at the landscape, now growing hazy as the wood-smoke mingled with wispy ground mist lying close to the valleys and streams.

Jaq laughed. "Why Tom, that's the whole point. It's what you helped us build – a city of refuge that could not be destroyed. This is Etheria, our city of refuge. It cannot be destroyed because it doesn't entirely exist. It is the first non-localised civilisation.

And no longer the only one, thanks to the knowledge we have shared – the knowledge you provided, Tom." She looked around at the baffled faces. "There is no centre," she explained. "We thought we'd see what it was like not to have one place more important that another place. Found it didn't matter much, not the way we live, which is key of course. You'll see..."

Gradually the sky darkened; thousands of tiny pinpricks grew visible in every direction, spreading across the darkening landscape like migrating stars. Reuben and Alina, standing side by side, watched the shimmering procession. He turned, took her hand and smiled. "Do you know, I think this is the most beautiful thing I've ever seen. Except you." Alina said nothing, snuggled beneath his strong, protective arm. Leaning together in the frosty night air, they marvelled at the peace they drew from the breathless dusk landscape, its contours bound by so many flickering lights beckoning to the lost and lonely.

"The thing about Tolkien depends on how you come at it," said Jaq to Vicky, sitting next to her. They were watching Jimi and his father grooming the chestnut mare. "Some of us do roll their eyes a bit, but others – myself included – just wonder at how well he managed to crystallise the agrarian ideal – the Shire, the hobbit homes built into the hills, the cosiness and all the rest. Form follows function? Not here – it's more complex than that – a feedback loop where each element is constantly modulating the others, and being modulated in turn. Complex cause and effect, no simple explanations. Like most things really, don't you think?"

"Yes, I do," Vicky agreed. "But it is a simple metaphor that strikes you immediately. I couldn't help it, I'm afraid; first thing that came to mind last night as we arrived."

She looked round again at Jaq's house, or what little could be seen of it – a series of irregular arches set into the hillside, each framed by oak boughs leaning together, and whose shapes determined the irregular spans. Between expanses of turf roof and sloping grassy walls, windows peeked out over a curving veranda bordered by rough-hewn logs, each set vertically to support the turf-covered eves overhanging the rough plank door set in a thick, rendered straw wall. The whole facade merged seamlessly into the surrounding hillside so well that Vicky found it hard to imagine anything more natural, or more discrete.

"Oh sure," Jaq replied. "It's the usual reaction. People also think it's tiny, like a tent. We always have a good laugh when they walk inside."

" Like last night?" said Vicky. They had been met at some point on the road by a small group of people who seemed to be expecting them. Without discussion, the entourage were instructed to retrieve whatever they needed from the truck since they would be proceeding on foot from this point. It struck Vicky even then that there was some unstated plan in action, but it was dark, cold and she was too tired to contemplate anything more than sleep and some food for her son. But then a strange argument occurred. She wasn't sure who started it, but it was Harry voicing dissent as he closed the back of the truck.

"They'll be coming down this road at daybreak. We don't have time for a vacation," he insisted.

"Oh, what do you suggest then?" Jaq asked, mildly enough. Something about the way she asked the question appeared to amuse Tom Bracey.

"Council of war," said Levi emphatically, Morgenstern in agreement. Harry also concurred. "We've been ducking it ever since we started our journey, but sooner or later we have to make a stand." And Vicky remembered how Jaq laughed, clear, infectious, without malice or mockery, just generous amusement. "Man talk; *make a stand*. You go get a hard-on some other time, soldier boy. Tonight everyone gets some rest. Tomorrow, we talk. We have time; they need a new drive shaft for their broken APC. Unfortunately, there appears to have been some sort of error in the army dispatch system, and the parts have been sent to Newcastle by mistake. Tomorrow they are going to be sent to Brighton by mistake. After that, no more mistakes without giving the game away, but meanwhile, we have a day to plan, and a day to prepare. Let's make the most of it. Get some rest." She turned away, motioned to Vicky and was about to set off when Jake shouted out: "HEY, WHAT THE FUCK!..."

The truck engine had started, one of the men that greeted them in the driving seat. Jaq grabbed Jake by the shoulder and span him round with considerable force. "Hey, calm down, man. You think we're stealing your gear?" She smiled at him, her calm authority giving Jake pause. "Where's he going?" he asked in a more reasonable tone.

"To hide the truck, of course. It's the biggest giveaway right now; damn thing can be seen from any satellite still working, for all I know. Don't look at me like that: I've seen online maps showing my smalls hanging out on the washing line, for chrissakes."

With Jake reassured, and consistent with Vicky's notion of a plan in execution, they were split up into groups, each of the people waiting for them called out a string of names; once called they were led away, each in a different direction. Jaq called Vicky, Nick and Jimi, and also Morgenstern, who objected immediately. "You want our help?" Jaq stated. "Do one of two things: stay here and fend for yourself, or come with me. You're not in charge here."

"Then who is, honey?" Morgenstern demanded. He looked round the clearing but everyone else had disappeared.

"Search me, *babe*," said Jaq with emphasis, "but one thing's for sure, it won't be some patronising American cracker."

They walked for an hour along narrow paths, several times crossing a tarmac road but never following one. Jimi rode the chestnut mare, led by Jaq; Vicky and Nick followed in silence, walking hand in hand for the first time in many years and smiling at each other fondly as they enjoyed a nostalgic intimacy. Morgenstern, morose, brought up the rear. From time to time, small lighted windows would appear off the track to either side, some close while others were deep into the woods, but no buildings could be seen. Eventually they took a narrow track which led to a doorway into the hillside flanked by windows from which light spilled in a welcome yellow haze across a small cleared area with a stable on one side and, under a roofed shelter, a communal stone oven opposite. Vicky could see nothing through the windows, but noted they were set into a small artificial hillock covered in turf with a chimney atop the mound from which smoke drifted into the darkness. From the size of the mound, which reminded her of a big circular tent cut in half,

Vicky wondered how there could be enough room to accommodate them all.

Her question was answered after Jaq stabled the horse, led them to the door and ushered them inside. They halted on a landing at the top of a flight of wooden steps which lead down to a wide circular room, twenty feet below them. Radiating out from this central area were openings cut into the hill, some of which led to private rooms, others connecting with communal spaces like the one they entered. Small rechargeable solar lamps hung in niches and from low rafters, casting strange shadows across the crooked lattice of poles and trimmed branches that rose on all sides towards the centre of the domed roof. Along one side were a bank of computers, several people sitting at them. A quarter section of curving wall was lined with books. Several tables were built around wooden supports, others fitted to the walls; every item of the furniture had been built to conform with the irregular aspect of the structure, for there was not a straight line to be seen. Decorated with cloth hangings, paintings and plants, the effect was welcoming and, to Vicky's eye, remarkably natural. "It's like a cave," said Nick reverentially as they descended. He looked back at Morgenstern, who merely shrugged.

"You sure did look surprised. I always enjoy that when I show people round," said Jaq.

"I had no idea how big it was. All those tunnels...thing is though – don't you feel like you've taken a step backwards? Living underground like that, in caves. It seems..." Vicky sighed, uncertain.

She looked up at Nick, who had walked over. "Ideal?" he suggested, sitting beside her. "I think it's wonderful, unlike our American friend. Where is he, by the way?"

"Still asleep," said Jaq. "Someone will let us know if he's up and about."

"You know," Nick continued, "it's easy to be cynical. There's a reason this all seems idealised, and that's because it is. We have this notion of an uncomplicated life, an idyllic existence and this is the shape of it. Yes, it's like returning to the cave. Yes, it's underground, at least in part. But it's not disconnected from nature. Nor is it the victim of it. Everything I've seen here integrates itself with the land, with the wind and sky and rain and sun. It's a living place. I find it profoundly peaceful."

Vicky raised her eyebrows in mock astonishment. "My God, you've turned into a hippy overnight. I thought you'd hate a place like this."

"No you didn't," retorted her husband playfully. "You know me much better than that. It's you having the problem, so don't try to foist it on me."

"Nick's right about this being a living place," Jaq agreed. "When my father and others started setting this up – years ago we're talking – the people in Llani took the piss, called us hobbits and so on. We took no notice; they weren't malicious and we kept to ourselves. They got used to us after a while, and when they started visiting us, there was a gradual change. People started moving out of town and making their own homes here, because it was part of a greater movement and they were drawn to it."

"What movement?" Nick asked.

"We saw all this coming, the end of the industrial empire," said Jaq.

"The end of capitalism, you mean?" said Vicky. Jaq nodded. "Same thing really. So many things happening at once; there was no way to keep it all together. Fossil fuels become too dangerous to use, and a world built on the stuff, utterly dependant on it, grinds to a halt. They saw climate change coming, and did nothing. What they didn't appear to see was that a system predicated on material reward can't work if the rewards can't be granted. No point in working like a dog if you can't buy anything with the money, is there? People became more and more disillusioned; they lost faith in governments because in the rush to extract every penny of profit by globalising trade, banking, finance; countries lost control over their own economies. They were helpless unless they all worked together – especially over climate change – and this was the one thing they couldn't bring themselves to do. Not until they were forced into it, by which time it was too late.

"But people like my father knew where all this would lead, and looked for somewhere we could build an alternative, one that didn't depend on the outside world hardly at all. We were concerned that we might be going backwards – Millenarianism in other words – but there was no theology in our thinking, just practicality. We didn't want to see civilisation implode, but when it becomes inevitable, only a fool sits by and watches it happen. It was the end of an epoch, the logical conclusion to a system that required more and bigger from everything. Things got so big, nobody could control it, nor control the side-effects like global warming. We learned from that and opted for small, decentralised, and instead of seeking growth – economic growth – we sought a stability by accepting limits to what we could have, but not to what we could be. Those limits are what nature and sustainability allow. The growth is intellectual, spiritual, creative; internalised. It's a balance, and once you have it you find a tranquillity in which moral values can be reasserted because they don't conflict with ambition."

"So it's a socialist paradise then?" said Morgenstern, who had defeated Jaq's early warning system. He joined them, his unconvincing grin worn like the mask it was. "Wonderful. If only everyone could live in a hole in the ground. How very lefty."

"And that's exactly where the premise fails," said Jaq. "Left and right; capitalism and socialism. These are the polarities of materialism. These divisions are inevitable, because the system demands some people have more than others; you can't have rich people unless there are poor people to compare one's wealth to. One side wants to keep it that way, asserting a moral superiority in the ability to exploit the world for personal profit, but at the expense of other people; the other side asserts their superiority by forcibly redistributing wealth to level the playing field, denying individuality in the process because everybody *must* be treated the same. Neither side understand that it is the obsession with who owns what that promotes the conflict in the first place. When you don't care about material things, you don't have much to fight over."

"Yeah – the hippy ideal," scoffed Morgenstern. "Funny how the people advocating the rejection of wealth are always poor, ain't it? Easy to say you don't care about material benefits when you don't have any."

Jaq grinned. "Thing is – and to cut to the chase, as you yanks like to say – the system you defend is broken. It is inflexible, requires corruption to maintain it, and makes ever-increasing demands that, when met, ultimately sow the seeds of its own destruction. Communism went first, and everyone thought capitalism had won, but you can't have one without the other; no coin can exist in only one dimension. In fact it was a draw, but the winning army took longer to demobilise, to dissolve in the vat of its own expediencies, because it had more money with which to stave off the inevitable; and by appearing to win the war, became totally complacent and self-righteous. The debasement of socialism was taken as proof of capitalism's superiority, and its durability. Yet it's gone. So much pride, such a big fall."

"All systems have setbacks," Morgenstern replied. He ran his fingers through his hair. "Jeez, I need a shower."

At midday, Jaq led the group to a farmhouse where they met up with the others. All had tales to tell; of strange accommodation, of dwellings linked by tunnels and covered walkways that extended in every direction, communal workshops where all kinds of crafts and skills were practiced and passed on, school-rooms full of attentive children, of extended families who told them how sharing their burdens made them lighter and their joys more profound; and of the vast, paradoxical village heartbeat in a city that extended for miles around them.

"It's like a huge thing constructed out of loads of tiny pieces, all connected, all interdependent but quite individual," Cas told them excitedly. "This is completely brilliant. Even Phil likes it here."

The farmyard was bordered by several barns, in one of which the truck was parked. Another was a workshop from which industrious sounds were emerging; two more housed livestock. The farmhouse itself was in good repair, painted bright white and clean in the weak morning sunlight; rainbow highlights cascaded off the solar panels on the roof and south facing walls, making the house sparkle. Inside, the rooms were clean and tidy, with functional furniture and few fittings. "We build the new homes around an existing structure, which is used communally. It's a good setup – this house, the workshops and barns – serves around two hundred people. They work here, meet here, plan the agricultural year, store grain and so on."

They were standing in a farmhouse kitchen like most farmhouse kitchens, with its range and its scrubbed wooden table. Harry, with a potent sense of regret, missed the home he had only recently come to know he loved. He felt a hand on his shoulder and turned to find his father staring at him with an unreadable expression; the expression of a soldier. He turned to Jaq, who had been joined by two men and a woman, none of whom they had seen before. Harry could read nothing in Jaq's expression. "Should we be introduced?" he asked. Jaq shook her head. "It doesn't matter who they are. They have a right to be here, because this is where they live. You have no right to be here and you've brought trouble with you. I'd get on with it if I were you."

"There's a good case for discretion," said Morgenstern. His eyes flicked from Reuben to Levi to Tom Bracey, who remained impassive.

Jaq gave him a thin smile. "For secrecy, you mean," she stated flatly. "We don't do things like that around here. Everybody who's interested knows about you lot. They know why you're here. They know what's following you. There are no secrets in Etheria."

"How could they all know?" said Morgenstern, his tone contemptuous. "Have you put it on the net or what?" To his evident surprise, Jaq nodded. "That's exactly what we've done. Everything that affects us communally is posted. If people are interested, they can find out what's happening. You've been the subject of much discussion, I can tell you."

Morgenstern was furious and he made no attempt to conceal it. "Now listen to me," he demanded, his voice low. "I've had quite enough of this hippy shit. People's lives are at risk, possibly including your own." He glanced at the twins. "We need to neutralise the soldiers coming after us. Then we need directions to the Etheria system..." He paused, reconsidering the assumption he'd made. "Do you know what I'm talking about? Any of you?"

"Sure, you want the data on the boys, here," said Jaq. "Do you seriously think we wouldn't notice a vast amount of data being pumped in here, without notice, just like that, in a system that had been dormant for decades?"

"You've looked at it?" said Morgenstern. This possibility hadn't occurred to him; evidently he had no idea what to make of it.

"Of course," said the man standing behind Jaq. He turned to the twins, his expression sympathetic. "We're very sorry. Terrible thing: we will help you if we can." Levi raised his hand in acknowledgement; Reuben looked at Alina, found she was staring at him strangely.

Harry cleared his throat noisily. "One thing at a time, I think. Jaq, we have to do something about the people following us. There will be a fight, I'm afraid. Some of us know how to handle ourselves, and if we must we'll try to deal with this situation. Can you help us, or is this against your..."

"Our principles? Is that what you were going to say?" Jaq asked. She shook her head. "You can take this hippy stuff too far, you know. We didn't build Etheria with flower power, Zen meditation and a bag of dope. We've had to fight to keep what we have, to defend what we believe. What's your plan?"

Levi stepped forward. "We have to get them out of the vehicles. Inside, they are impossible to...to target. So the first step is to immobilise them. When they leave the vehicles – if they are forced out – then we can deal with them. Best to split up the carriers if we can, so one can't reinforce the other."

"What we need most is weapons," said Harry. "They are well armed; only four of us have combat training. Can you help us?"

Jaq rose and turned to her companions; both shook their heads. "The trouble with your plan is that someone will end up getting killed. We will not help you do that. It is clear to me that we are going to have to sort out your mess, and we will require you to help us. We've selected the best plan – posted last night on our web by a teenage girl as it happens – and you can help us. I think you might find it instructive."

"How's that?" asked Harry.

"Consider it a contrast in styles," said the man behind Jaq. "You know there are many forms of martial arts; ju-jitsu, karate, aikido and so on. They are split roughly into soft and hard forms. Soft martial arts are deflective, using an opponent's aggression against him. Hard martial arts seek to inflict great damage by striking with hardened hands and feet, all that painful stuff. Our strategy is like something between those two extremes. A wet art, you could call it."

Jaq agreed. "That's right. We're all wet pacifist pinko hippies according to James Bond here, so it should come as no surprise that we practice an appropriately pitiable form of defence, which we invented. Its great virtue is that nobody actually does any fighting, and nobody gets hurt. We call it Wimpedo."

Chapter 29: Friendly Fire

Alison Haynes was certain she was being punished. The cab of the leading APC was hot and smelly, as were the men she was jammed between. Her body armour – no longer optional after the ambush – was ill-fitting, rank with fear, sweat and diesel fumes. They were crawling along at a snail's pace behind foot patrols on either side of the road, a stable-door precaution after the roadside bomb in Abergavenny, but not one she was willing to forgo. She was, at least nominally, in charge of the patrol, but the squad leader clearly had orders of his own and was prepared to accommodate her only as far as his orders would allow.

It wasn't her fault, she told herself yet again. After the interview with Harry Bracey in London, she'd been certain of her support and her position, but it was only when it became evident that the data never reached the Okehampton telephone exchange that she started to suspect she had been given only part of the story; she was a single piece in a jigsaw whose design had been concealed from her. At about the same time, she noticed a temperature change in her relationship with her supervisor. Until then mentorship, even intimacy, had seemed inevitable: as quick as an April shower, the older man had suddenly become unavailable or, during a rare telephone call, chilly and distant. Eventually summoned to the fifth floor, she had to explain herself and the faulty intelligence she had collected during her first meeting with the dreaded committee. More like an interrogation, the stern men and women, six in all plus her supervisor, asked dry questions and made dryer observations. There was no overt blame, no hostility, but it became clear to her they knew far more about what was going on than she had realised – or been led to believe. There was something perfunctory about the questions, as if they were tidying up after the event.

It was only later, when she had time to replay the interview in her mind, that she realised her supervisor had betrayed her to the committee. They appeared to believe she was allied to, or at the behest of, the 'rotten core' (as one member of the committee put it) but it now seemed obvious her supervisor had been the one to expose her involvement in the operation, hoping that by doing so he would gain some measure of protection for himself. Made scapegoat for the loss of the data and the bungled raid on the house in Thieves' Wood, she was hustled out of the building before she had time to speak to anyone else, taken straight to the station and thrown on a train bound for Newport. Once there, she was to join an armed expedition going into the camps, her only instruction being to support a CIA operative already in place who would provide tracking signals that she should follow. It didn't take long after leaving the station for her to wonder if she would return from this mission alive; she had become a considerable liability to the conspirators, and she knew only too well how they dealt with uncertainties like her. She glanced at the soldier sitting beside her, rifle between his knees. He leered at her, but said nothing.

The secure phone on the dashboard rang, a light blinking in concert. The lieutenant picked it up, listened attentively, then passed it to her.

"Yes?"

"This is Jasper," said an American voice giving Morgenstern's code name. "Stay in the town. Do not follow on. It's a trap." The line went dead. She turned to the lieutenant. "You got that?" He nodded, wincing as the small wound on his neck rubbed against his body armour; a mere scratch compared to the injuries of the six injured men in the following vehicle. He touched the cut gingerly, finding it sore but dry, and wondered how many more of his men would be hurt or killed before this crazy mission was over.

"They stopped outside Llani, made a camp there," Jaq reported. The band members were busy unpacking the truck, which they had driven into a much larger barn several miles into the forest. At only the slightest suggestion, the band had agreed – with some alacrity – to play a 'thank you' gig after they had dealt with the soldiers. Now they were setting up the lights and sound system, practicing once more with reassuring familiarity the crafts of their trade.

Across the barn, Tom and Harry, Morgenstern and the twins listened in silence to the news. "What are they doing?" Harry asked. He felt curiously relieved; like his father, he had little faith in Jaq's plan, which consisted largely of luring the vehicles along a road in which two deep trenches had been dug, both normally covered with carbon-fibre sheets to allow passage, but that could be removed at will by people concealed in the bushes either side of the road. As explained to them, the plan was to remove in advance the further sheet, which would halt the lead vehicle at it approached. The first sheet dragged away once the second vehicle had passed over it, thus trapping both. The road was bordered by stone walls and ditches either side, so the patrol would be trapped with no option but to abandon their transport. It was not clear how the soldiers would be dispossessed of their weapons, which bothered Harry a great deal.

"Nothing," Jaq replied. "They're just sitting there, tending their wounded – six injured, no dead as far as we can see – waiting for something by the look of it."

"A signal, perhaps?" offered Tom, looking squarely at Morgenstern. But it was Levi who answered. "If they stay put, we should retrieve the data. That's the only thing keeping us here, isn't it?" He was looking at the American, who obviously agreed. "Sure, this is no time for a rock concert," Morgenstern quipped, to nobody's amusement.

"What do you think they're talking about?" said Billy. The other band members looked across the barn at the huddled figures with their secretive gestures and low voices. "Whatever it is, I don't like, y'know?" Alina declared. She was still rather pale, having picked up a bug of some sort that was making her nauseous and even more touchy than usual. Jake put his arm around her shoulder, looking down at her with a fond expression. "You know we'll understand if you want to go with him," he reassured her. She smiled weakly. "I know Jake. Thanks; you all good people. Even you Phil, you wank..." Phil looked up from his drum cases and grinned. "Not me, you tart. I'm a complete bastard and you know I hate Polacks more than anything. Anyway, don't drag me into this; I'm having enough trouble remembering how to set up my own bleeding drums. I'd give your right arm for a roadie right now."

"Anyway, I don't think he wants me to go. He hasn't asked," she confided to Jake, who walked her over to the side of the temporary stage they had built at one end of the barn.

"Do you want to go with him?" he asked. Alina shrugged, her hands fluttering with agitation. "He...Christ, Jake – you know. How long does he have?"

"Isn't that the best reason to go with him, to make the most of it?" Jake suggested. "Anyway, don't talk to me about it. Talk to him. You don't have time for the usual lover's quarrels, sweetheart. You know that, so does he. Stop fucking around. All this spy shit got us all confused. Remember who you are, what you want to be. I can't be taken up with this crap of theirs any longer."

"You blame him, Jake?"

"No. Really...it's just..." Jake was puzzled; he studied Reuben, standing silent across the barn. The same affable chap he'd been from the start. What did Reuben want, except more time than fate would allow? No hubris on his part – a more modest chap you couldn't think to meet. How did he deserve a fate like this? Or his twin, this nearly-brother? Jake couldn't bring himself to like Levi, but with so few opportunities to talk to him, and in circumstances so strange, he thought little of it. Reuben though – there was a man Jake could admire. He shook his head wearily, baffled by the strangeness of it all. He felt like a stranger in his own life, divorced from everything that gave him meaning and purpose. More disturbing was that this feeling was oppressing him at the very moment he was preparing to play, the act that for so long had been the reason for everything he did, the culmination of every plan, every movement. The great joy of his life, yet it seemed trivial now. Why did he feel so dispossessed, so removed from his music, the thing he loved more than any other?

"Is it possible to understand?" said Alina intuitively. "All so weird, Jake, so strange. I love him. I love band. Playing is most joyful thing, only thing ever keep me going back when...hey, you know what I talk about, right? Now I find some man, a good man. Man with no fucking future. Great then. So now, do I have no future too?"

Jake couldn't find an answer, so he put his arm back around her shoulders and they sat in comfortable silence watching Phil get really angry with some cymbal stands. "No talk since we left Tom's house, you know," she continued. "I don't know what to say to him. He don't know neither. We like two dumb people trying to make talk. He never say he loves me, but he does and I know this. Is OK, too – never trust man who says 'I love you' a lot, because they don't do anything about it. He loves me and I feel it in what he does, in his eyes and his touch. Words, cheap; love most expensive thing of all."

Jake was surprised. Alina never spoke so unguardedly, with such candour. "But he never say nothing to me since...and I don' say nothing to him. So strange, we can't even know what we want any more. I want him, to be with him, but I see him and feel terrible sadness. He looks at me like I feel 'bout him; happy heart, sad eyes. But I think, well – all people die. We don't have long, but we should be happy when we can, not like this. Sad and afraid. Running like this. If I know I will die for sure on some day, exact day, then I will make every day count. Make sure I love as much as I can, every minute. We are wasting this, Reuben. How many times people tell me 'you don't have time'. This is so true, Reuben. Please, it is so true..."

Jake, silent and still, looked across the barn and realised that Alina wasn't really talking to him at all. From forty feet away, Reuben was watching her intently; he could hear her perfectly well, and of course she was taking advantage of this. Jake's part in the conversation with Alina was a pretence merely cover. "You don't need me," he told her, looking all the while at Reuben, who smiled apologetically. Behind Reuben, Levi was also staring at Alina, but his expression was unreadable and made Jake feel cold. "I don't suppose you two could just discuss this among yourselves without needing me as a middle man?" he quipped before striding off to locate his sax, music the only constant he had left.

Acrimony divided the faction at the other end of the barn. Morgenstern insisted they retrieve the data immediately, but Jaq insisted the retrieval must be conditional on neutralising the threat from the special ops unit pursuing them. Morgenstern grew angry, demanding an explanation for the delay that Jaq refused to provide, and had stormed out into the surrounding woods. Jaq caught Tom's eye, and inclined her head towards the door, so he followed her out; she was sitting on a stone water trough, watching ripples expand from one fingertip as she dipped it gently. She looked up. "I'm sorry about earlier. I would have broken the news to you with a bit more...I just thought you knew he was dead. Never occurred to me you didn't."

Tom sat next to her on the stone lip of the trough. "It was just unexpected. It isn't like I knew your father that well...although I would have liked to. I kept expecting him to turn up sooner or later – I was looking forward to seeing him again after all this time. He seemed quite a character from what little I did know. And he worked something of a miracle here, by the look of it."

"You two would have got on well, I think," said Jaq. "He would have made a good soldier, I expect. He had what you've got – that quiet authority that comes from accepting you may be wrong, but you can live with your mistakes even when people die as a result. It's a burden, for sure. He carried it..."

"And so do you," said Tom. "Once you've been marked by making decisions in which people's lives are at stake, you can see it in others too. An exclusive club. You're in it – I saw that quite clearly when we met in the pub."

Jaq laughed. "I wouldn't want to belong to any club that would have me as a member. Who was it said that?" Tom didn't know. He was watching the door to the barn, saw something that caught his attention and tilted his head imperceptibly for Jaq's benefit. She glanced in the same direction, nodded and continued.

"Thing is, Tom – this is all rather tricky. We didn't know anyone wanted this information. We just read it, assumed it was backed up to us automatically, and when we realised what it was, well...truth is, we deleted it – as much out of revulsion as anything, I guess."

"*You deleted it?*" said Tom loudly. Jaq jammed an elbow into his ribs with considerable force, winding him. "Keep it down, for God's sake," she demanded rolling her eyes in exasperation. "My father trusted you, so I'm doing the same, but the least you can do is act your age. You're a Colonel, remember, not a bloody child."

Tom looked round, suddenly furtive. "By God, woman...hell's teeth! You scrubbed it? All of it?" Jaq nodded, contrite. "I'm afraid so. We didn't want it, didn't want to feel contaminated by having it. A bit moral, I know, and of course in retrospect it was foolish. Too late now, but I don't want the spook to find out. The only value the data had to us was as a bargaining chip, and it still is while he thinks we have it. Not just him, either. Lots of people want it. I haven't figured out how to turn this situation to our advantage, but I am quite aware of course that there is also some danger here. That data, the ghastly experiments...that information is radioactive; everyone who touched it may end up getting burned, even by association. That's what's happened to this lot – the band, I mean. Anyway, it's probably keeping the twins alive right now."

"What do you mean?" said Tom.

Jaq cast an uneasy glance towards the barn. "Haven't you wondered why the American is dragging the twins through the camps like this? If you had assets that valuable, wouldn't you get them out of the country as quick as you like? Why keep them here, in danger, protected by a single agent? Is that really the best the CIA can do? I bloody doubt it, Tom, I tell you."

The Colonel looked equally perturbed. "Well, he wants the data. That much is certain. But I agree, it is odd – bad strategy on the face of it. Why not just come after it on his own? Much less trouble, less suspicious. I would have brought him here in any case, if it saved the band, my son, and helped...well, helped stop the people behind this. But perhaps only the twins can access the data, or copy it."

"Well, we thought about it, and we spoke to a few people. You know one of them – called himself Seafour..." she spelt it for him, "...John Seafour. He was the one who had the spares re-routed to delay the soldiers – said I should mention his name to you, pass on his regards."

Tom Bracey laughed delightedly. "*Seafour*? That crazy bastard Fairfax – that's his real name, by the way – John Fairfax. C4 is the plastic explosive – his favourite kind, as it happens. Quite old fashioned but very reliable: bit like him, really. He does love things that go bang. How long has he been helping you?"

"Oh, quite recently," said Jaq. "First time he turned up here...about a month ago, maybe more. Said he knew you; that you'd told him about this place and he had been protecting us, although he wouldn't say what kind of protection he was providing. Since he knew about Etheria and you'd trusted him with that information, we felt we had to take him seriously. Also, the tips he gave us checked out, so we started working with him. He's another spy, I take it?"

"Yes, he is – and he knew about us long before I talked to him. But what did he tell you? About the twins?"

She glanced once more at the barn door, from which stray drum beats and spiky guitar notes were now emerging, shaky and uncertain, like stiff, ungainly creatures waking from hibernation, coughing and spluttering. She raised her voice slightly. "He suggested the twins were there only as backup, in the event the data could not be retrieved." She spoke with a sobering gravity. "It makes sense, in that world: get the data, the twins are not required, so dispense with the evidence. If the data can't be retrieved, at least he has the living experiment to cut his losses. Their losses." She shook her head. "I can't believe I'm saying these things. Listen to me; how callous can one be and still be human. They really do contaminate us, don't they?"

"You're saying that if Morgenstern had gotten the data, he would have disposed of the twins? Is that it?"

"Not for certain. But would you put such calculations past people like that? And as I said, I don't know why else he's keeping them here instead of evacuating them. Have you considered what he planned to do if we had been able to give him access? He doesn't have anything to store such a vast amount of data. What could he have done with it – transmit it somewhere else? Maybe that's why he needed the twins, or at least Levi. Otherwise, he could have taken them to the nearest US airbase and that would be that. Bye bye twins, have a nice –

if short – life." She shook her head sadly. "What a terrible thing to do, even to think about doing. And of course the real implication is more terrible still, not just for the military, but the human race."

"What do you mean?" asked the Colonel.

"The changes are genetic, Tom. We're not talking about implants – they were used mainly to control the twins. What happens when they perfect the design, get the obedient psycho killers they want? It's obvious isn't it? They'll breed them, of course. Don't you get it? How cheap a production line is that? Loyal women queuing up to do their duty and bear a child for the good of the nation. A surrogate army; a million mothers, one father – the state. A new species, Tom. Better than humans. The master race? We've been here before, haven't we? And this is why we have to stop them, Tom. Why we destroyed the data."

"But our plan's gone out of the window now," Tom complained. "Without the names, we can't use the data to protect ourselves, or to bring down the guilty. You've destroyed the only evidence we had – apart from the twins themselves."

Jaq gave him a sly grin. "*They don't know that, do they?* And there are other people who may know the names – like Mr. C-4." She looked towards the barn door, where a shadow flickered momentarily; looking back to the Colonel, she winked. "Walls have ears. Let's join the others."

Morgenstern walked only a short distance before coming across a small pool with a rustic seat beside it. His anger disappeared as quickly as it came; it was a tool rather than an emotional reality and he switched it off when it was of no further use. He was still sitting there when Levi found him. "You were right. There is no data."

Morgenstern studied him languidly. "What did you pick up?"

Levi could almost hear the gears and cogs working, and felt little inclination to be quite so candid as he had been in the past. He'd been foolish – he knew that now; so naive and trusting, so willing and so damn grateful. *I'm a teenager,* he reminded himself. It was a thought that had struck him with great force after reading the files, now he had little chance of reaching adulthood. Childhood stolen, future denied. Levi's blood began to boil. "They destroyed the data after they saw what it contained," he told the American, standing over him with fists clenched, after being obliged to explain the circumstances in which he had acquired the information. "One thing for sure, Marty. There's no reason to stay here any longer. Reuben and I can go with you right now; nearest US base, evac, no more of this horror show. Whatever your scientists can do to save us, they'll have to manage without the data, that's all."

Morgenstern stood, brushing himself off as Levi took a step backward. "Seems that way, son...seems that way. Tell you what; why don't you join the others – I'll come down there in a bit – I better make a call to find out which way we're headed. Better tell the Brits, too. They can come and pick us up." He took out his phone and started dialling, turning away from Levi, who eyed him speculatively before walking off. As he walked away, he could hear the conversation between Marty and the girl in the APC, which appeared, remarkably, to be about the weather. *The weather?* He looked back; Morgenstern was watching him. Levi smiled to himself and increased his pace.

Harry pulled up a flight case and sat heavily on it, joining Alina and Reuben who were leaning companionably against one wall.

"There's game afoot," said Reuben unexpectedly. Harry was taken aback, since this was what he'd come over to say. "How did you...?" Reuben grinned. "It's weird how people forget you can hear better than them. I don't mean to do it, you know that, right?" He was genuinely concerned; Alina, sitting next to him, gave Harry a curious look, at once both demanding and hostile.

"Christ, Reuben. You're the straightest guy I know," Harry admitted. "Don't worry about it; you have bigger fish. Anyway, you should know what's going on, in case there's any collateral damage. You too Alina." He had their attention. "I had the idea that the only way to get the spooks off our backs – specifically, out of Etheria, since I feel bad about bringing these killers into a city of refuge…anyway, the only way was to convince them the data wasn't here. We set your…Levi up with this notion, and he'll tell Marty of course. We think the special ops may rather lose interest."

"You think the spy talks to patrol?" said Alina. "He works with them?" Harry nodded. "Sure – they followed us accurately, probably homing on his phone. They stopped when we threw them some bait: the holes in the ground."

Alina did the math. "The trap – it was lie?"

"Sure," said Reuben. "We didn't trust the American, so we gave him something to chew on. I'm surprised, because it was a stupid plan, but he believed it because of his innate contempt for those who proposed it. Confirmation bias; he expects to see foolish hippy nonsense, and they obliged. "

"Levi seems to trust him, but you don't," Harry observed.

"I don't remember him. I don't know him. Same goes for you, it turns out. Why did you help me that night, Harry? Why take the trouble? Look where it's got you. Or was it because you were a spy?"

Harry's gaze was level. "The QR code. The search party. They were the reasons. It was secret wars all over again – far more than I ever realised, it turned out. I was a fake in the band, who I considered my friends. I was a failure as a spy. But most important, I was a forgery of myself. The secrets game was a ruse, a cover up for my cowardice. I didn't fail as a soldier, I failed as a leader, not because of what I did during combat, but what I did afterwards: the option I took to run away. That choice I made was to formalise my guilt, to codify it, package it up and bury it somewhere secret. What more attractive to a man seeking escape than a new, state-sanctioned purpose, a mission born of that failure, ennobled by that guilt. Now those deaths would not be in vain, because it had become a virtuous act to fail in the service of the state; there is little more virtuous than a body bag – brings out the piety in everyone who sees it. And I saw you lying there, and saw the QR code…the helicopter above me…the vehicles in the town and on the moor…all the apparatus of the state, ranged against some naked fat bloke with a fucking bar code on his foot? What kind of shit is that? I could not stand to be part of this. I could not help them anymore. I would not see you in a body bag, not with my hand on the zipper. I didn't understand the situation, but I discovered I had a moral obligation to be on your side against anyone who would put a fucking QR code on a human being. The QR code was the symbol of my failure and the catalyst for my rebellion. Worked out all right, as it happens." Harry looked at his father, who was sat dozing against a bale of hay, and smiled to himself.

"Sure Harry," said Alina, who was also smiling. "Big discussion on moor with rat boy. You talking philosophy in bushes, right? *My arse!* You men, later you invent big reasons, but I know you Harry. You trust gut, act like you mean it. You feel strong, Harry; honest and real. Do what you feel, be in present. This is lesson any musician could teach you, but I think you also know this. Soldiers, fighters..." she drifted away momentarily, then snapped back, "...you live in the moment, right now. At the point of a knife, the edge of razor, speed of bullet. For me in music, I stand on cliff edge all the time, with the sea of all music, all possibilities, for me to dive into if I am not afraid. Huge sea, so many notes. Wow – scary when you supposed to be doing rock and roll medley. Freak out. But both of us make decisions on instinct. No time for analysis. You find Reuben, and in one tiny second you make decision; that's that! *Rescue.*" She leaned back, triumphant, her logic plainly unassailable. The men grinned at each other, earning Reuben a punch in the arm that obviously hurt him, followed by an apologetic kiss that clearly did not. Then she turned to Harry.

"Do you trust him, Harry?"

"Who, Morgenstern...?" Alina nodded. "No, not at all."

"Alina thinks he has no intention of taking us to America," Reuben confided. Harry could not but agree. "If he did, you'd be lab rats. They wouldn't have time to let you sit on a beach somewhere..." Harry tailed off, saddened by the inevitability of his observation.

"Not much kind of life, I agree. That's why I'm not going," said Reuben, causing Alina and Harry to sit bolt upright.

"When you decide this?" Alina demanded. Reuben stared at her. "Every time I look at you," he replied simply, which stopped Alina in her tracks. He turned back to Harry. "Don't look so shocked. You came over to test me, didn't you?" Alina was puzzled, and said as much.

"By telling me about the planted story, the way they used Levi, Harry was putting me on the spot, making me choose sides. Either I tell Levi – and therefore Morgenstern – that the data still exists, or I keep a secret from them, which aligns me with Harry, Jaq and the Colonel. Damned either way, ain't that right, Harry?

"You know your bible. Remember the promise made to Abraham? God promised Abraham that through his offspring, all nations will be blessed at some unspecified time in the future. That was the gift of the brothers, Isaac and Ishmael. When do they fulfil their promise, Harry? How much time do they need to stop slaughtering each other, killing themselves? Thousands of years and they still haven't got it together, something that works and sustains virtue and honour? When will all nations be blessed? So forgive me if I sound a bit cynical, but it's always the way with religions; tomorrow never comes and the package never arrives, even though you're constantly assured it's been dispatched.

"And remember, this is the same God that, for a laugh, thought he'd see just how faithful Abraham was – test his faith by asking him to kill Isaac, cut his son's throat, make a sacrifice of him. An act of barbarity. Then, at the last minute, an angel taps Abraham on the shoulder and tips him off that the whole thing is a reality TV show with an audience of one. But here's the thing; Isaac nearly got his throat cut for a laugh. What do you think he might think of his father's religion after that?

"So I ask you this, Harry. Would you believe any of this shit given the broken promises, capricious gods and a long history of enmity and warfare between those descendants of Abraham who, apparently, bring the embodiment of God's promise to us, albeit on the leading edge of a sword. To me, Morgenstern is a follower of another kind of fucked up religion – a cult of death, more like – and I'm not planning to join up any time soon. I don't believe anything I've been promised – no blessings for me except the one thing I'm not allowed to have. I'm being asked to sacrifice Alina, but I will not do it. I'm sticking with the band, my girl and this wonderful countryside. I believe what I can see, what my senses tell me. The rest...it's just so much faith required for so little reward. I could be happy here, for what time I have left. That's my decision. I will spend my time here."

"Have you told Levi or Morgenstern?" Harry demanded. His mind was whirring as his stomach was churning. There were dangerous currents here. He looked at Reuben. "Well, have you?"

"No, not yet," said Reuben. "You think there's a problem?"

"I don't know," said Harry carefully. "But I recognise the ingredients when I see a barn stuffed full of them. This place is one big blue touch-paper."

"I agree," said Reuben. "Has it occurred to you, Harry, that there is another solution? Rather more in keeping with God's test of faith."

"What do you mean?" Harry asked. Alina was watching Reuben like an anxious hawk, for she suspected her lover had imagined the same terrible finale that she had. "If Levi and I were not alive any more. Wouldn't that solve everyone's problems? We *are* the evidence, after all. We could also be the sacrifice."

Harry stood up, angry. "Fuck you, Reuben. Too much trouble you've been, for you to give up now. I don't care for where this conversation is heading, but I've never trusted martyrs and I cannot abide a man who runs from a fight...starting with me, obviously. But I didn't pull you off the moor for you to top yourself, so fuck off, all right...just fuck off. That's all." Reuben looked quite abashed, and stared at his feet. Alina stood up, walked up to Harry and kissed his cheek tenderly. "Now you fuck off," she whispered, and turned back to her lover.

Alison Haynes was on the phone, sitting alone in the cab of the lead APC. The squad were exercising in the street outside the pub, where an exchange of valuables had encouraged a steady flow of food and drink. "Why do I have to do it?" the CIA agent was complaining. "Christ, you've got a whole squad – most of one, anyway – at your disposal. These guys are tough bastards. I might get one, but two...I dunno..."

"I have my orders, Jasper," explained Haynes. We're here to assist, but no extra-judicial...termination. Like you say, I've got a whole squad – and they would all make excellent witnesses, know what I mean? Are you sure about the data?"

"The boy overheard the woman 'Jaq' talking to Colonel Bracey. No reason to suspect she would lie to the Colonel, especially as she had no idea anyone could hear her. You have to watch your step around those boys – they pick up stuff like hunting dogs. Anyway, you can go ahead and clear the site now – that's part of your orders, isn't it?"

"That's none of your concern," she told him. "My job is simply to destroy the data if you do not. Dealing with the twins is your problem. Are you capable of completing your mission or not?...well?...Jasper, are you there..."

There was no reply, although the phone remained live; she could hear a strange scraping sound as if the phone were being dragged along a wall. Then the call was terminated. Haynes rang back several times, but the phone was no longer in service. Without further delay, she pulled a whistle out of her pocket, leaned out the window and blew it three sharp times. The assault team mounted up obediently and the lieutenant climbed into the cab. "What's up?" he asked as the driver started the engine.

"We're going in," said Alison Haynes. "I'm sick of waiting for other people to get their act together. Let's take care of the data centre, OK?" Since the lieutenant had been advocating this very course of action for at least the last day, his reaction was entirely favourable. The location of the data centre was already stored in the map display; he dialled it up and radioed the second vehicle with the coordinates as the convoy pulled laboriously up the hill towards the forest.

Reuben looked down at the body, the strange crookedness of it, and a jolt passed through him like high voltage electricity. He had seen this terrible shape before, in woods like this, in the dark like this, his enhanced eyes straining to capture the detail of the broken neck, the dislocated arm, the twisted angles, staring eyes. But last time there were several bodies, all broken and twisted in the same way. All dead, all killed just like Morgenstern: with bare hands and gleeful relish. How did he know this?

A pain like a blade cleaved his skull in two. And then: there it was. His memory returned, not light in the darkness, but dark enveloping day, smothering it, the violence of the restoration commensurate with the murderous deed at his feet. The compulsive nightmare from which there was no more escape; Reuben's memories relentlessly advancing down the shadowy corridor of his entire life as it stretched away from him, from this narrow focal point crouched on his haunches in the cold beside one more body, travelling away from him in time, wider and wider, all the way back to the breadth of possibilities that was his infancy. He saw actual corridors, dank and oppressive, the tunnels in which he grew his furtive life. He saw his brother, the same yet different, love and hate mixed like coloured clays into a globular mass of grey ambiguity. The classrooms, the endless drills; strict, no laughing or punishment by deprivation. Regimen and relentless purpose. Duty; born to serve. Loneliness night after night, a lifetime of nights and never a sunrise; sly fears so deep-rooted and primeval they could not be recognised, let alone named. Strangers forever a friend and never meaning it. Deceit and betrayal. Purpose and work, trial and tests. Duty and obsession. Computer games; murder on line, any scenario: any time and place and victim, so long as it required skilful planning and efficient execution. The drugs, the constant injections, painful examinations that became experiments. The fat; humiliation and helplessness, a profound feeling of ugliness. Unwanted, repulsive; nothing but the pain, the combat training, the testing, the scores and measurements, the fat. Constant beatings, haranguing, disparagement. Doctors. White coats. Harsh lights. The distrust, the obfuscation, the professional smirk bereft of humour and full of malicious indifference. Therapists and endless questions. No answers. Never answers. The manipulation. Fake faces, empty smiles, glass eyes. Always watching. Security cameras. Grinning guards. Loveless dead eyes, swivelling as they tracked. Reuben looked down into more dead eyes and he remembered.

Everything.

Loveless eyes.

Levi.

He closed the staring eyes with gentle fingers, stood and strode off purposefully towards the music playing in the distance.

The entrance was almost invisible from the road, the track was so overgrown. They drove through the undergrowth until they reached an oval concrete space two hundred yards across, bordered by several portable cabins, all decrepit and disused, the entire space surrounded by mature pine trees. The lieutenant cast a professional eye round the perimeter before opening his door and stepping down. "What is this place," he asked. Haynes was occupied by a nondescript estate car parked in the trees to one side of the clearing. "It was originally a Hazres test site – hazardous research - for BAE, the defence group. God only knows what they got up to here, but they certainly managed to put the fear of Christ into the locals: the papers of the time were full of UFO reports." She chuckled mirthlessly. "After that it was made to look abandoned, but the whole underground structure was expanded to house a command and control centre, part of a network. The entrance to it is over by that car." She pointed to the estate car. "Alpha with me, Bravo to fan out above ground and cover the area from the perimeter." Chambering a round in her pistol, Alison Haynes walked cautiously towards the car.

The barn door burst open and Levi entered, slamming it shut behind him. Walking quickly over to where Alina sat, he stared down at her with a frightening intensity. "Where's Reuben?" he demanded. The room was hushed.

"He went to look for you," said Alina, her voice level, her expression one of curiosity. "There's been accident, Levi – you don't know this?"

Levi appeared not to hear her, or perhaps understand what she was saying. He seemed confused. "I must find him. We have to go. It's urgent. Tell me where he is"

Alina stood up, alert and poised. "He's not coming with you, Levi. He told me. He stays here with me. You go to America if you want. Reuben don't want to go." She stared at the big man defiantly. Levi smiled in a way that chilled her to the bone. From

356

one pocket he pulled out Morgenstern's pistol and pointed it at her. "So, he wants to stay, does he? And you're the reason. How sweet. Unfortunate too, since you're in the way. I'd tell you I'm sorry, but actually I'm completely indifferent." He swung round, ranging the gun through an arc in front of the band members, most of whom were resting against the walls, and now frozen in place. "You all stay where you are. You know what I can do."

On the makeshift stage Harry and Phil, unseen by Levi, had crouched behind a stack of speakers when the gun was produced. Phil was about to whisper something when Harry put his hand over the drummer's mouth, shaking his head vigorously. He removed his hand and pointed to his ears, then to Levi. Phil understood; he pointed to his massive drum case, which was parked behind the speakers, then crawled over to it, beckoning Harry to follow. Raising the lid carefully, he gave Harry an apologetic look, then reached into the case and triggered a concealed latch that released a panel in the floor of the case. Phil raised the panel so Harry could see the rack of weapons in the hidden compartment.

Harry was thunderstruck. *All this time, right under my nose. They were right all along, and I never saw it. Fuck me, just how useless spy am I?* With a rueful glance at Phil, he reached in, selected a short Russian automatic rifle and examined it carefully. Phil held out a magazine with six round in it, which Harry inserted gingerly after assuring himself the rifle was serviceable. He mouthed the words 'stay here' several times to the worried drummer until he was certain Phil understood, then turned on his heels and began to edge his way round the blind side of the speaker stack.

Ten feet behind the car, steps descended to the sunken entrance to the control centre. The rusty metal door stood open, revealing only darkness beyond. Alison Haynes motioned to the lead pair, who took point after turning on their barrel-mounted torches. Preceded by the darting beams, they made their way down a sloping corridor whose walls and floor were damp and slimy. The air was sharp, metallic. At the head of the stairs, Haynes peered over the parapet and was surprised to see light a long way below. Motioning to the others, they descended as quietly as they could.

At the bottom, as they congregated in the well the lieutenant peered cautiously through the open door. Beyond them was a partially lit corridor. At the far end a pair of huge blast doors stood wide open. Beyond them was a large room. Somebody was whistling softly, distracted.

With half the team behind her, Haynes crept down one side of the corridor, the lieutenant and a second file edging down the opposite wall. She reached the doorway and looked carefully round the edge of the frame. The room was large, and full of equipment. She could see no-one, but the whistling continued. As she turned to motion the squad forward, the whistling stopped. "Is that you, Ms. Haynes? Do come in, I've been expecting you."

In the centre of the room stood a tired, middle-aged man in a shabby coat. He was holding some wires and a grey block like a brick. Keeping her pistol on him, Haynes walked in as the two files of soldiers fanned out behind her. "Secure," called one file, echoed seconds later by the other. The stranger was the only man in here. He walked up and offered his hand. "Hello Alison – hope you don't mind me calling you that. My name is Fairfax. How do you do?"

She shook the outstretched hand, one eye on the brick he was holding. "Er...isn't that...?"

"C-4? Absolutely. I've been getting things ready. Come and have a look." He turned to the lieutenant, shook his hand, then led them round the room, pointing out the explosive charges laid in crucial places, each designed to undermine some structural aspect of the underground chamber. "What's the detonation method?" the lieutenant enquired. Fairfax reached into his pocket and pulled out a remote detonator. He flicked back the safety cover to reveal the red button, which lit up. "Time to go, I believe."

"You wouldn't..." said Alison Haynes in surprise. "Surely not..."

Fairfax looked at her with contempt. "Of course not. What on earth do you think I'm doing here? This isn't a fucking suicide mission, woman. Get a grip.

We have the same job, I'm just saving you the trouble. And making sure it gets done properly. Now, can we please go? This button makes me nervous." He closed the safety cover and the button stopped blinking. Haynes looked at him thoughtfully, then at the lieutenant, who shrugged. "This isn't something...if it doesn't blow, we'll come back and do it ourselves." He turned to Fairfax. "Seems like you saved us the trouble. Are you the same firm as Ms. Haynes?" Fairfax placed the last brick of explosive in position and inserted the detonator. "No, I'm SIS. But we're all on the same side, aren't we?"

His tone was sincere, but as Fairfax walked off down the corridor his laugher echoed behind him for too long a time.

Levi raised the pistol to point at Alina's forehead, standing only feet away, her eyes bright with defiance. She glanced behind him and her eyes lit up. Levi started to turn but a stone the size of a man's fist struck him with tremendous force between the shoulder blades, throwing him off balance. As he toppled sideways, Reuben swept across the room at astonishing speed, grabbed Alina round the waist and literally threw her across the barn into a bale of hay. Without stopping he continued to turn from the throwing movement, pivoting as he bent down to grab Levi by the collar and haul him to his feet. Levi, still holding the gun, started to raise it. Reuben struck him, a straight-armed blow with the heel of his hand to the point of Levi's nose. Blood gushed out and Levi fell back, training the gun on Reuben as he recovered his balance once more.

"Turn on the lights," Reuben called out to Nick, who was sitting at the console, afraid to move. He looked entirely baffled by the request. "TURN ON THE FUCKING LIGHTS" Reuben screamed at him, glancing up at the stage lights above his head. Levi stared up, equally puzzled. Able to flick the main switch with barely a movement, Nick did so without drawing attention. The stage burst into bright colours. On the 'dance floor' in front of the stage, the black light above their heads cast its strange ultra-violet glow on everyone, making skin glow faintly blue and white cloth gleam. Levi was holding one hand to his nose, a bloodstained hand. The blood was glowing with an unearthly green fluorescence.

"*A fluorescing gene will be expressed exclusively in the haemoglobin of the combat unit*" Reuben quoted from memory. It's you, Levi. I had to be sure. You always did bleed like a stuck pig when I hit you on the nose."

Levi's eyes widened in momentary shock. "You've remembered?" he whispered. Reuben nodded. "Everything. Came back to me when I saw your handiwork in the woods. You do love breaking their necks don't you?"

Now Levi stood up straight, wiping his nose disdainfully with the back of his hand. "That's right, you chicken shit. I love the snap, the limp body. Job done. You always were such a pussy. That's why I always beat the crap out of you. Fucking useless, wet little boy. Still wetting the bed then?" He glanced over at Alina, watching them with horrid fascination. "Did you wake up wet some mornings then?" he sneered. "Your boyfriend pisses himself when he gets frightened." He looked meaningfully at Reuben's groin, pointing the gun in the same direction. "So, you want to stay here, do you?" he said, waving the gun carelessly at Alina to indicate how he had found out. "You've been against me from the start. Delay, delay and more delay. Let's not be rash, Levi. Let's be careful, Levi. Let's think this through, Levi..." His voice was childish, taunting, and rising in volume. He started to circle Reuben, who turned on the spot to keep Levi in sight. "Chicken shit, that's all. No guts. You should have died on that moor. How the fuck did you survive?"

"You killed all those men. You forced me into it. I didn't want to break out like that, murder those people, no matter what they did to us. You planned the whole thing with Morgenstern, didn't you? The fire, the code room...?"

"That's right," Levi agreed. He stopped, keeping the gun level. "It would have worked out fine if you hadn't got out of the freezer. I thought I'd locked you in, that you'd be finished when the fire started. How'd you do it? How did you get out?"

"That doesn't matter," said Reuben, his voice quiet. "How does this end, Levi? You've killed Morgenstern, the only way out. Where will you go now? What can you do on your own? The path you have taken leads only to one place – surely you can see that, can't you?"

"Maybe, maybe not," snarled Levi. "Look Reuben. I've tried to explain to you a million times that actions speak louder, making words unnecessary. Here's a demonstration." He whipped the gun in a swift arc, delivering a crushing blow to Reuben's head that knocked him to the ground. He raised the gun and pointed at him. "Violence is not a means to an end. It is the end made manifest. One way or another, this is the one time when there is a clear winner and a clear loser, for one is dead and the other can celebrate or weep, up to them. I won't weep for you, Reuben. You are weak and contemptible. I could never have trusted you in the field, because you judge me from some moral standpoint because you feel superior. I'm the one who has to do the dirty work. You sit back with your maps and computers and surveillance toys. Your hands are clean, aren't they? Well, my job is to kill people, and I'm not ashamed, and nothing you can say will make me feel any different. And one thing's for sure. I'm going to finish the job I started. Your time is up. Say goodbye to your girlfriend, *brother*."

At the entrance to the control centre, the squad clustered round Haynes and Fairfax, who was holding the remote detonator. "All ready, then?" he asked her. Haynes looked at the lieutenant, who nodded. "Go ahead." Fairfax flipped back the safety cover and stared at the glowing button. This was the moment he loved; with relish, he pressed the button firmly and waited. Seconds passed by, then the earth began to grumble, softly at first, but growing in ferocity into a deep roar that shook the ground beneath their feet. Wave after wave rumbled deep in the earth, the growling overtaken by a rush of wind that tore through the doorway and past them into the night air carrying a plume of dust and smoke that all but obscured the sky, and the soldiers from each other.

Harry had never been in an earthquake, but as he peered round the speakers he assumed that the terrible, tortured sound emerging from the bowels of the earth was his first. To his alarm, the stack of speakers began to sway and he stepped out of cover, raising his rifle to his shoulder as he did. Levi, catching a glimpse of the movement, turned fractionally toward Harry; as he moved, Reuben propelled himself forward at tremendous speed, grasping Levi round the thighs in a tackle that sent them both sprawling. Locked together, they struggled to their feet despite Reuben's fierce grip, both hands wrapped around the gun and the hand holding it, and Levi's attempts to force it down towards Reuben. Like quivering statues on the brink of mobility, they swayed and strained in the centre of the barn, faces mere inches apart. Reuben shot a look at Harry, who still had the rifle raised and pointed at them.

"What are you doing?" said Levi. The gun was moving, the barrel turning towards Reuben's chest: Reuben was no longer resisting. Levi tried to turn the gun away, but Reuben wouldn't let him. "What are you playing at?" Levi hissed.

"It was always going to come to this, wasn't it? From the moment our DNA was injected into the cells, we were destined to struggle like this one day. And here we are, fighting for our lives. One of us must die, is that it? The only acceptable outcome? I won't do it, you know that. So can you do it, Levi? Can you be that cold, that soul-less, that you could shoot me here, looking into my eyes like this. You are the only person in the world that understands me. I must also be that to you – that must be true, Levi. How could it not? We are more than brothers. Can you kill me now, out of spite and anger and hate? Are you that murderous bastard on the moor, or was that the exception? Was that the result of Pavlovian training, or pathological psychosis?" Reuben was forcing the gun to his heart, pulling hard on Levi's arm to jam the barrel against his ribs. Sorely confused, Levi was now trying to turn the gun away.

"How does this end, Levi? They will keep coming after us, you know that. They'll find you and they will find me. They will hold us responsible for what happened. If we evade them, stay free, they'll come after Alina, and Jake, and Vicky and Billy. Jimi too. If I stay here, they'll come for me. And Jaq, who did nothing but help us survive. No matter where we go, they will come for us. What little time we have left, do you really want to spend it on the run? There are no cities of refuge for us, Levi. What kind of life are we going to have? What kind? And what must we live with in order to have it? How many more body bags? I won't fight you any more, Levi. I can't let you go, either, because I know what you'll do. Today, Morgenstern and me. Then what? I can't let that happen. But I know what to do: just two more body bags, and that's the end of it. You hear me Harry?" Reuben smiled at Alina but his eyes were full of terrible longing and regret. The gun fired. The report was muffled and thin, but the bullet found its mark and Reuben fell dead, shot through the heart.

"NO...." screamed Levi, as much to deny his complicity as his loss. He stared down at the body on the floor with an angry, puzzled expression, then at Alina, and finally at Harry and the rifle pointed at him. "It was him. He framed me. Fuck me, the bastard. He set me up. *I didn't do it, Harry. I didn't do it.*" His expression quickly hardened; Harry wasn't moved. "Well, soldier boy. Do you have the guts for it? I fucking doubt it." He spat out some blood, then raised the pistol at his side.

Harry watched the rising hand, the gun coming up in the slow motion of combat time. He looked beyond Levi, meeting Alina's eyes, the message stark and ruthless, as he knew it would be. His father was staring at him with profound, professional compassion; father and soldier inseparable. Harry returned his attention to Levi, looked into the eyes filled with hate. The eyes of the enemy.

'...*in one tiny second you make decision; that's that!*'

He pulled the trigger, holding it down until the clip had emptied. As each round went home, Levi's body was propelled back and back and back, until the hammer dropped on an empty chamber for the seventh time and Levi too was dead.

Chapter 30: Cities of Refuge

Five days on, everything seemed peaceful. The soldiers had gone; the destruction of the data centre and a thorough questioning of the band by Alison Haynes seeming to satisfy the authorities, such as they were. As Jake observed, they had the bodies, the data was destroyed, and it was clear the band could have no copy of it. As astonishing as their tale was, they had not a single shred of evidence for it, so they became just another bunch of web nutters with a conspiracy theory to sell. There was a palpable sense, as the two armoured carriers moved off, that it was over. The band had made it back to reality, albeit at a terrible cost.

Alina had been inconsolable. For two days she had disappeared; it was known she was in the company of Vicky and Jaq, so the others didn't seek her out. Jimi had discovered the pleasures of school, and being in one place long enough to make friends, so he circulated around an orbit of homes and classes that were mixed up so it was hard to tell when the lessons stopped and the fun began. He seemed to be getting taller by the second, and it had not gone unobserved by his watchful father that girls had suddenly become interesting to the growing boy.

The Colonel had been distraught at the discovery the data centre had been destroyed. When Fairfax breezed in with Haynes and her patrol, Tom was unusually curt, and remained that way for days. Only after Haynes and her soldiers had left did an amused Fairfax urge Jaq to take Tom and Harry aside.

"Calm down Tom," Jaq told him, her voice soothing as if talking to a child. "We've still got everything; nothing's been lost, not a thing. The horrible stuff on those poor boys, all the science and technology, the art and music and history and wonder – all safe, Tom. Quite safe. It's like I said; Wimpedo – the art of being somewhere else when the shit hits the fan. Anyway, you should know that all warfare is based on deception."

Tom was baffled. He had walked with Harry to the command centre and they had taken a look, but it was clear that

Fairfax had done his usual efficient work. Nothing survived. "But all the computers, the storage – it's all gone...isn't it?" He looked around him, half expecting to be told it was all smoke and mirrors. "Empty cases – computers elsewhere?" he added hopefully.

Jaq grinned. "Something rather better, actually. You remember that I told you this was a non-localised city? Some call it a cloud city. You know how cloud computing works, right?"

"Sure," Harry replied. "Stuff turns up on your screen when you ask for it, but you have no idea where the data comes from. It's like the route your phone call takes through wires and satellites and fibre and microwave – so many alternatives, but who cares so long as you end up talking to the person you called."

"That's about the size of it. We cut all the data we had up into millions of tiny bits. We used something a bit like the old torrent file sharing system to seed the data out all over the world, duplicated over and over, all little chunks that are unnoticeable, and on their own, quite meaningless. Our entire computing system is a cloud, and it is remarkably secure. And it's resilient in a way this old data centre could never have been. We think it is virtually impossible to destroy the data now – any of it – because in totality it cannot be located. Once this data is sliced up and sent round the world, it's going to be floating around in those pipes forever. Spooky, really.

"Anyway, it's all safe, because it's invisible. We're used to living in a world where things get big, easy to spot but also easy to destroy. This society has been built by thinking outside of that box. Industrialisation forced everything to centralise. Now we're undoing that paradigm because industrial society has come to an end at the scale it reached in the twentieth century. That scale, that vast apparatus – that machine was only possible because we had energy so cheap it was essentially free for a long time. Fossil fuels were like a rocket booster; ignite the blue touch paper and retire. Or turn the tap, like the cars that used to have a bottle of nitrous oxide under the dash, which would give them a huge burst of power for a few seconds – before it blew up the engine.

We fired that booster rocket and for a while there, some of us travelled at tremendous speed, making astonishing progress in science and technology but not, alas, in maturity. Others were not allowed to come with us, not allowed to enjoy this fairground ride of speed, novelty and satiation. Denied, they would bide their time; they could not build, but they could certainly destroy.

Now the booster's burned out and we're slowing down. Whatever we've done, that's it for the fast track, and the engine that carried us along it. Now we have to calm down – I think civilisation got far too excited at the sheer size of the train set – and build a modest, sustainable and dignified society that's fair and equal and so on – you know what I mean.

"And it doesn't need big, unmanageable structures. It needs small, distributed, human-sized architectures, natural social constructs whose scale is appropriate and whose geometry is natural, soothing, kind, nurturing. The world got so complex and power so unevenly distributed, we became incapable of running it and only greed was good. We need to be a bit more modest about what humans can manage. We may be able to invent the biggest vehicle in the world, but if we can't drive it, what's the point?

"So we make small things, but link them all together to form larger things. Like chaos theory; millions of simple, self-replicating pieces that form something far greater together than the mere sum of parts. And the best thing is that our strength is hidden, so we appear to be no threat to anyone. Two-hundred thousand people here, but where are they? Where are the huge buildings, the agglomeration of power, the swagger and the threat and the intimidation of ancient Rome, of Berlin, of the city of London, of New York or Bejing? Where are the skyscrapers that every day tower over us, reminding us of how poor and powerless we are. We have none of that; we are unseen, our strength needing no advertising to make us feel more important, or more secure. This is how we ensure our safety, even though in truth we are the most subversive movement on the planet – but only to the people supporting the status quo, because it's business as usual that we subvert."

Jaq stood, smiled at the Colonel and placed a finger gently on the lips of Harry, who had thought of half a dozen arguments but couldn't decide which one to deploy. "You're thinking too much, soldier boy. You need to come with me and have your mind blown." She took his hand, pulled Harry to his feet and led him away, her arm round his waist. She dropped one hand to his buttock and looked up at him with a wicked smile. "Nice." Harry couldn't think of a single thing to say. He was grinning inanely, couldn't prevent himself from doing so, and to his surprise he found he didn't care that much, for his happiness was no longer tinged with dark things that made him anxious and ashamed. "Where are we going?" he asked, the issue academic.

"My place," said Jaq as she squeezed her wandering hand. Harry, like the good soldier he was, knew that when faced with an overwhelmingly superior force, a sensible commander surrenders, so he offered no resistance.

Jake knocked on the door of the dwelling which Vicky's family were using, and where Alina had been sheltering under Vicky's care. He hadn't seen his keyboard player since the day of the remembrance service, a reading of poems by the various band members and a few locals, and some beautiful music played on an acoustic guitar by Cas, whose face was stained with tears even as he played. Alina had appeared at the start, hands clenched into fists and eyes so hard they might shatter if she blinked. She was the only person who shed not a single tear.

But four days had elapsed, and the band was coming back to life. Without the fear and the constant pressure it created, thoughts turned back to playing, and a modest jam had taken place the previous afternoon, with all the band except Alina taking part; reluctant at first, hesitant and apologetic, they quickly became more enthusiastic as people started to wander in from different parts of the forest. Within two hours, several hundred people were scattered about across the floor of the barn, dancing, chatting and listening.

Afterwards, Jake gathered the players together, along with Nick who had been working the sound system to notably good effect. "It was nice to see Piper yesterday," he started, and everyone agreed. They had been delighted to see the sweet-natured young man turn up, and his report of the rout of Edgar and his red-robed thugs pleased them even more. "And he was right – we do owe them a gig. We took all the grub and that was the deal, so that's one booking we have now. Then there's all the stuff on the other side of the fence – most of the gigs we cancelled could probably be reinstated. But now we have a new base – this is what I'm proposing, I guess – that we work mainly here in Etheria. Two hundred thousand people – that's a lot of folk needing entertainment, and we can provide it. While we're doing that, we can see what we can salvage from outside. That's my idea."

"What about Alina," asked Phil.

"I'll talk to her," said Jake. "We need her for the gig tomorrow night, but in the longer term we may need a replacement. That's up to her. But you have to promise me that you will stop the gun-running. I've made this clear to you, Phil – it's not on and you know it. You were very discrete, so I'm not going ballistic, but that's the end of it, or the end of you. Make up your mind by tomorrow morning."

Jake was about to knock again when the door opened. Vicky ushered him in. "Nick told me what your plans are," she said, leading him down the steps to the circular living area. "Sounds good to me." Jake was relieved. "What about the girl, though. How is she...where is she, come to that."

As if in answer to his question, the sound of someone retching reached them, although the origin was unclear. "Still got that bug?" said Jake. Vicky shook her head. "Ask her yourself."

Jake turned, and there she was, pale and straight-backed. But she had a strange look to her that Jake noticed immediately. She was glowing like marble, and there was a healthy aura about her as if she'd just returned from a jog, not vomiting crouched over a bucket.

"How are you?" he said, somewhat lamely. Alina smiled wistfully. "I'm fine, Jake. Sad, but life goes on." She glanced at Vicky, who smiled consolingly. "You want to ask about gig, yes? I play tomorrow, for him. OK. After that, well...things are bit uncertain, Jake. I need to go to Devon, see Guido."

Jake understood at once, but his heart sank at the implication. "I don't...I mean...whose is it? It's Reuben's, right...but he...I mean...didn't they say, y'know, in the report...?"

Alina grinned, even as she was brushing tears from her eyes. "Doctors – fuck, what do they know? Nothing wrong with that boy's equipment. I know Jake – you want some details maybe?"

"Fuck off Alina. What about Guido – you can't mean..."

Alina looked shocked, suddenly realising the impression she had given Jake. "Oh no, Jake. No. Nothing like that. I trust him to look after me, when I need it. How can I tell some strange doctor what to expect? Guido knows already, he saw Reuben, understands what happened."

"We should bring Guido here," Vicky suggested. "He'd like it, and I'm sure they would like him – and his food. Is that possible, Jake?"

"I think that's a really good idea," he replied, before turning back to Alina. "But it's you I'm worried about right now. You were so scared last time, so terrified..."

Alina offered a kindly smile. "I'm not afraid any more, Jake. There is love here, not like other times. This is reward for love." All three stood, silent, contemplating the strange paths their lives followed. Jake stirred, wondering. "What about the genetic thing? Isn't that going to...well, shit; I don't know. What's going to happen? Do you know?"

Alina shook her head. "No idea. But hey, this kid's going to be different, for sure. So I get to found new religion; give birth to new baby Jesus, be mother of new human race, and I get one over on Virgin Mary too."

"How's that?" said Vicky.

"I also got laid," said Alina cheerfully, and they all laughed.

The End

www.ingramcontent.com/pod-product-compliance
Lightning Source LLC
Chambersburg PA
CBHW060154260626

47160CB00001B/260